Acclaim for
Lost in Manhattan

"*Lost in Manhattan* reminds me of a Susan Elizabeth Phillips romance combined with the intrigue of a good romantic suspense. This fairy tale romance has all the tropes you love in a good romance. *Lost (in Manhattan)* pulls on your heartstrings, and you root for the hero and heroine through the whole story. The villains are truly villainous, and the author does a wonderful job of creating plot twists and subplots that all connect to the central story. Very romantic! A great bubble bath read!" — *Wall Street Journal* bestselling author Larissa Reinhart

Every romantic wants a knight in shining armor, and *Lost in Manhattan* delivers. Gold-digging relatives, fraud, blackmail, attempted murder, and an unfolding IRA plot, this book has it all. So much fun to read." —Award-winning suspense author Donnell Ann Bell

"Well written and interesting novel, moving constantly. Action and romance in balance. Awesome suspense ending. Not a melodramatic story but very well set facts. Loved the story! I have already read it twice." — Amazon reviewer

Angel lowered her head onto her hands and took deep breaths, fighting to control the panic rising inside her. She had escaped with the clothes on her back and enough money for one less-than-decent meal after she paid the cab fare. Maybe. As the taxi sped away from the airport, she began to question the wisdom of her impulsive decision.

Books by Lois Winston

Anastasia Pollack Crafting Mystery series
Assault with a Deadly Glue Gun
Death by Killer Mop Doll
Revenge of the Crafty Corpse
Decoupage Can Be Deadly
A Stitch to Die For
Scrapbook of Murder
Drop Dead Ornaments
Handmade Ho-Ho Homicide
A Sew Deadly Cruise
Stitch, Bake, Die!
Guilty as Framed
A Crafty Collage of Crime
Sorry, Knot Sorry

Anastasia Pollack Crafting Mini-Mysteries
Crewel Intentions
Mosaic Mayhem
Patchwork Peril
Crafty Crimes (all 3 novellas in one volume)

Empty Nest Mystery Series
Definitely Dead
Literally Dead

Romantic Suspense
Love, Lies and a Double Shot of Deception
Lost in Manhattan
Someone to Watch Over Me

Romance and Chick Lit
Talk Gertie to Me
Four Uncles and a Wedding
Hooking Mr. Right
Finding Hope (Writing as Emma Carlyle)

Novellas and Novelettes
Elementary, My Dear Gertie
Moms in Black, A Mom Squad Caper
Once Upon a Romance
Finding Mr. Right

Children's Chapter Book
The Magic Paintbrush

Nonfiction
Top Ten Reasons Your Novel is Rejected
House Unauthorized
Bake, Love, Write
We'd Rather Be Writing

Lost in Manhattan

LOIS WINSTON
Writing as Emma Carlyle

Cover design by L. Winston

ISBN-13: 978-1-940795-19-5

"The best protection any woman can have...is courage."
– Elizabeth Cady Stanton

DEDICATION

To those who have stood by me, encouraged me, and given me hope in dark and difficult times. You know who you are.

ONE

"What made you suspect?"

Abel Montgomery puffed at the cigar that was as much a part of him as his ten fingers. He raised his head from the papers which had held his attention, exhaled a large puff of gray smoke, and looked across the desk at his longtime friend and attorney, John Ferguson. "He couldn't look me in the eye. Never trust a man who can't look you eye-to-eye, John."

"That's all?"

"That's enough. Enough to raise my suspicions, anyway." Abel tapped one of the papers with his index finger. "And now you've confirmed them."

"Which explains your reason behind this." John handed him a sheaf of documents and a pen. "All changed, just as you spelled out."

Abel quickly perused the pages before dating and signing his name to them.

"How do you want to handle the situation?"

Abel pushed his chair back, rose, and turned to stare out the window of his corner office. Thirty-seven floors below people scurried along Lexington Avenue, most probably anxious to end the work week and begin the Labor Day weekend.

Abel, too, had been looking forward to the short holiday. The pressures of the past few weeks showed. The pains in his chest had increased, and no amount of Zantac or Maalox helped. He knew he should see a doctor, but there never seemed to be enough hours in the day. All he really needed was a relaxing three-day weekend alone with Whitney. She was the best medicine for his aches and pains. She could wipe years from his life in a matter of minutes.

"Abel?"

"Hmm?"

"I asked how you want to handle this. Are you feeling all right?"

"Never better. I'll take care of things. Let's keep this under wraps for now. I don't want anyone else to know yet. Okay?"

"You're the boss, but if you want some friendly advice, you should quit that vile habit." John gestured toward the cigar. "It's going to kill you someday."

"I'm an old man. If they haven't killed me yet, they're not going to."

"As your attorney, I feel obligated also to remind you that you're in violation of a city ordinance against smoking in public buildings."

"You going to turn me in?" Abel chuckled. When John didn't answer, he took several puffs before continuing. "I didn't think so. Now, get out of here. Enjoy the weekend."

John reached for the papers spread across Abel's desk.

"Leave those. I'd like to study them further."

"No problem. Try to relax this weekend. You look tired. I'll see you Tuesday."

Alone in his office Abel poured himself another cup of coffee from the pot his secretary kept filled on the credenza. Settling back into his desk chair, he studied the printouts yet again. Anger built within him.

Damn greedy, fucking son-of-a-bitch! He'd treated the man like a son, like the son he'd lost, groomed him to take over the company someday. And this was his thanks. Stabbed in the back by a common thief. If it weren't for Sarah, he'd have the bastard hauled off to jail.

Sarah. God, she'd be devastated by this.

One of the brighter young members of Abel's staff, Roger Caine caught Abel's eye early. Roger's polished charm and take-charge attitude paved his way up the corporate ladder with breakneck speed until he sat perched on one of the highest rungs.

When Cameron and Hollis died so suddenly, Roger had stepped in and kept the company running while the family dealt with its grief. Now, too late, Abel realized that Roger was an opportunist who'd taken advantage of a tragic situation. But had this always been his agenda, or had he seized the opportunity when fate dropped it in his lap?

All the caring, all the concern. Was it a carefully staged act? Even his feelings for Sarah? Roger had been especially attentive to her after the tragedy. The accidental death of her parents had left her with deep emotional scars, her liveliness and independent nature becoming additional casualties of the explosion that had taken her parents.

Roger had helped Sarah through those dark days, and Sarah responded by falling in love with him. Aware of the powerful healing nature of love, Abel and his wife had encouraged the relationship.

But Sarah's pale blue eyes, which once danced with laughter, now often reflected hurt and unshed tears. Abel suspected the marriage was in trouble and blamed himself for his granddaughter's unhappiness. He'd encouraged the union between his brightest executive and his sole surviving heir. And Sarah, God love her, would do anything to please him.

What had he done to his granddaughter?

Abel opened the bottom drawer of his desk, removed a large bottle of Maalox, and chug-a-lugged the antacid. Then he spun his chair around and stared out at the darkening late afternoon sky. Dense thunderclouds, an ominous precursor to a weekend washout, had skulked in from across the river. He watched them build in mass, casting a thick black blanket over the city. And blackening his mood even further.

He wished Sarah would confide in him, but he knew her too well. She wouldn't say anything, even if asked, not wanting to worry him. Ever since she was a child, she'd insisted on battling her own dragons, whether real or imaginary. Sarah never asked for anyone's help. So, why wasn't she fighting the dragon now? What had caused her shoulders to slump in defeat when she thought he wasn't looking?

Able knew that if Sarah suspected Roger of embezzlement, she wouldn't think twice about coming to her grandfather. Likewise, if Roger were cheating on her. And her career was thriving. So what was left?

He toyed with the idea of enlisting Whitney's help. After all, there were some things a young woman couldn't talk to her grandfather about, no matter how strong their relationship, and at thirty-seven his second wife was much closer in age to his twenty-eight-year-old granddaughter. With both her mother and grandmother gone, Sarah was sorely lacking in female confidantes.

But Abel had a bigger problem to contend with at the moment. Sarah's husband had stolen seven million dollars from Montgomery Aeronautics. The proof, in black and white, lay spread out across his desk.

He'd been a damn fool. He'd recover from the monetary loss. Seven million dollars was petty cash for a company the size of Montgomery Aeronautics. But could Sarah recover from her husband's betrayal?

Abel shifted his stogy to the side of his mouth, picked up the phone, and pushed the button for the lobby security desk.

"Yes, Mr. Montgomery?"

"Anyone left upstairs, Bill?"

"Just you and Mr. Caine, sir."

Abel placed the receiver back in its cradle and gathered the papers into a file folder. The evidence tucked under his arm, he strode down the hall to confront his grandson-in-law.

Roger stood at the bar in the corner of his office. Unseen, Abel watched from the doorway as Roger grabbed an ice cube with a pair of silver tongs and dropped it into a Baccarat tumbler. With a flourish he added a hefty splash of twelve-year-old Scotch.

"Celebrating?"

Roger spun around. "Abel! You started me. I thought you'd gone hours ago."

"And I thought you'd be home having dinner with my granddaughter."

"Soon. I had some work I wanted to finish up before the weekend."

"Anything to do with this?" Abel thrust the folder at Roger.

"What is it?"

"Why don't you tell me?"

Roger took a step back as Abel forced the file on him.

"Go on. Take it. Read it carefully. I'd like to hear your thoughts on the subject."

Roger sat down at his desk and opened the file.

Even in the dimly lit office, Abel could see the man turn gray, sweat breaking out across his brow. Roger's hand shook as he raised the glass to his mouth and polished off the Scotch in one gulp. "Surely, you don't believe this!" He laughed nervously. "Someone's gone to a lot of trouble to make it look like I've been stealing from the company. It's probably that practical joker Danbury in accounting. Never could stand the guy. This time he's gone too far."

"This isn't one of Danbury's jokes."

"Christ, Abel! Why would I steal from my own company?"

"*Your* company?"

"You know what I mean."

"Do I? Perhaps you should explain it to me. Starting with why you stole seven million dollars from *my* company. Why, Roger? How could you do this to me? To Sarah?"

"Yes, Roger, explain it to him."

TWO

Whitney's voice sounded from the doorway. "And while you're at it, explain to me how you could be so careless as to let him find out."

Abel spun around and stared at his young wife. She was pointing a small handgun directly at him. With the clarity of hindsight, he realized he'd been played for the foolish old man he was. All her love. All her devotion. All lies.

Sarah! Blinding pain ripped up his arm and stabbed at his chest. *What have I done?* He squeezed his eyes shut. *Forgive me!* Abel staggered back against the desk and collapsed onto the floor.

Roger jumped up and ran over to the body. He frantically searched for a pulse. "My God! I think he's dead."

"Well, that certainly makes things easy," said Whitney as she slipped the handgun back into her purse.

"Easy? What's so easy about being responsible for a man's

death? What should we do?"

"Drag him back into his office. The cleaning staff will find him later tonight."

"Yes, of course." Roger grabbed Abel's legs and slowly dragged him across the carpet.

"Roger!"

He looked up.

"The papers. Don't leave them on your desk."

Dropping Abel's legs, Roger hurried back to retrieve the file.

"Does anyone else know about this?" she asked, jutting her chin toward the folder.

"I don't know."

"You'd better hope not! How could you be so careless?"

Roger handed her the file, picked up Abel's legs, and continued dragging him down the corridor. "Did Bill see you come in?" he asked between labored breaths.

"Of course."

"How will we explain leaving without Abel?"

"We'll tell him he's going to be working for the next few hours and doesn't want to be disturbed. Just try not to look guilty, will you? If we act naturally, we won't raise suspicion."

"You have all the answers, don't you?"

"Seven million of them," she said as they entered Abel's office. She pointed to the far side of the room. "Leave him over there by the credenza."

Roger dragged Abel's body across the room, dropped it where Whitney had indicated, then collapsed onto the couch to catch his breath.

"Out of shape?"

"Don't push me. I had everything under control until you

pulled that damn gun."

"Under control? You were about to blow it! If I hadn't walked in when I did, you would've confessed to everything, bringing me down with you." Her lips curled into a wicked grin. "Instead, I'm now a grieving widow. A very *wealthy* grieving widow."

"I could have convinced him it was a setup. There are plenty of people in this company jealous of me. He trusted me. It wouldn't have taken much to sway him."

"You looked guilty as hell, Roger. Abel's no fool." A soft moan stopped her. "Damn! He's not dead."

"We have to call an ambulance."

"You idiot! Do you know what will happen to us if he survives?"

"But—"

"Oh, shut up, Roger! We wouldn't be in this fucking mess if you hadn't screwed up."

"We can destroy the papers. Tell him it was all a nightmare if he remembers anything. He was hallucinating from the pain. He'll believe us. We can make him believe us!"

Whitney reached for the heavy marble ashtray that sat on the corner of Abel's desk and dumped the contents into the waste basket. "And what if there are others who know? Abel may have suspected something fishy, but he probably had someone else in the company confirm his suspicions. Shall we suggest they've all been hallucinating?"

When he didn't answer her, she continued. "No, this is the only way. It will look like he struck his head on the corner of the desk when he collapsed."

Roger cringed. "You're going to hit him with that?"

"Don't be stupid." She thrust the ashtray toward him. "You

are."

"I can't!"

"Do it! And make sure you do it right."

Whitney dropped the hard, cold marble into his hand. Roger hesitated.

"Now!"

He kneeled beside the body and raised his arm high over his head. With a swift, decisive blow he smashed the sharp corner of the marble into Abel's skull. The skin split on contact. Roger stared at a growing puddle of blood. His body shook.

Haughty laughter ripped through the silence. "Powerful feeling, isn't it?"

"How can you be so cold? We've just killed a man."

"No, darling, *you* just killed a man. Maybe it will teach you not to be so careless next time."

"You're in this just as deep as I am."

"Then you'd better do as I say and not make any more mistakes." She smeared some of the blood from the ashtray onto the corner of the desk, then wrapped the bloody marble in a hand towel she found in Abel's washroom and slipped the murder weapon into her purse.

"He trusted me," Roger mumbled.

"That was *his* mistake. Ironic, isn't it? Abel always prided himself on being such a good judge of character, yet he was wrong about both of us." She glanced down at her husband's lifeless body. "Dead wrong."

Whitney took hold of Roger's arm and led him toward the elevator. "Don't take it too hard, darling. Everyone always told Abel smoking would kill him."

* * *

Sarah stared at the myriad of tubes snaking from frightening looking machines down into her grandfather's body. Lights blinked. Motors hummed. Abel's chest rose up and down in a steady cadence. She glanced out through the glass enclosure of the private ICU room to where her husband stood huddled in conversation with her step-grandmother.

Please don't leave me, Granddad. You're all I have left.

Could fate be so cruel? In the past five years she'd lost both her parents, then her grandmother. Abel was her only surviving blood relative. A tear trickled down her cheek. She brushed it away, wishing she could banish her loneliness as easily.

Somewhere along the way, she'd also lost herself. Gone was the spunk and independence that once defined her. Gone was the self-assurance, the courage, the confidence, the resourcefulness. She, who'd trekked across the Sahara and through the jungles of the Amazon, had found it impossible to work up enough courage to tell her grandfather the mistake she'd made.

Hell, it had taken her months to admit to herself that her marriage wasn't working, hadn't worked for some time. This weekend she'd planned to break the news to her grandfather. But how could she leave Roger now without breaking her grandfather's already fragile heart? He thought the world of her husband. Roger Caine was the Montgomery savior.

She never should have married him. She had been too raw, too needy. Grief had clouded her judgment. Roger had zeroed in on her vulnerability and used it to his advantage. And never having been in love before, she'd mistaken gratitude for love. How could she have been so stupid, so damned naive?

She watched Abel's chest rise and fall. *Live, damn it!* He had suffered too much over the past several years, first with the death

11

of his only child, her father, then less than a year later, the loss of his wife. Granddad's grief was finally behind him. He adored Whitney. At least Roger had that to his credit.

Roger had introduced Abel and Whitney. So what if Whitney was young enough to be her older sister? She was making her grandfather happy, and for that Sarah was grateful. No, even if it meant suffering herself, she would not hurt her grandfather. She would bury her loneliness deep inside her for whatever time he had left on this earth. She'd put up with her sham of a marriage this long; she could act the happy wife a bit longer for Granddad's sake.

"You should go home and get some rest, dear. He won't be waking up for some time. We'll call if there's any change."

Sarah's head jerked up, startled by the nurse who stood across the room jotting notes on Abel's chart. "I'd rather stay," she said.

The nurse shrugged and left the room.

Roger and Whitney continued to whisper in the corridor. Roger fidgeted nervously; Whitney looked extremely angry. Odd. Totally out of character for both of them. Roger, the consummate actor, skilled at manipulating people and situations to his advantage, actually seemed to cower in front of Whitney, who looked anything but her usual cool, calm, and collected self.

They're just anxious about Abel, she reasoned. Sarah knew that when confronted with the sudden illness of a loved one, people often responded in ways contrary to their nature. She'd even seen nervous laughter used to mask the frightening reality of impending death. Some people laughed, some cried, some lashed out in anger. Some made the mistake of falling in love. Grief could assume a myriad of disguises.

She felt guilty sitting by her grandfather's bedside, ruminating about her own problems. Selfish. But it did keep her from dwelling on the fact that the doctors had not given them a very encouraging prognosis. Only a fifty percent chance that Abel would recover. If only he hadn't hit his head when he collapsed....

Sarah studied Roger with the detached professionalism she used when setting up a camera shot. She noted the beads of perspiration glistening across his brow, the way he kept shifting his weight from one foot to the other, the steady beat he tapped out against the wall with his left fist as his right kept time on his thigh.

* * *

Roger yanked at the knot of his tie, loosening the suffocating noose. "What if he regains consciousness? We're dead."

"Damn it, Roger! Don't fall apart on me. You're turning into a sniveling wimp. What's gotten into you?"

"I've never tried to kill a man before. That's what's gotten into me!"

"Oh, yes. I see. Roger likes his crimes tied up in neat little packages, so he doesn't have to sully his hands. Roger only commits white collar crimes. No fuss. No muss. No ugly red stains left behind as evidence. Only this time, lover, you left a damn sloppy paper trail."

"I had it under control. You should have stayed out of it. He never would have suspected you. The fool had you on a pedestal. You're in this as deep as I am. Don't you have any conscience at all?"

"None. I'm the consummate sociopath. Charming, intelligent, and devoid of conscience. A trait you'd do well to cultivate if you want to survive. And yes, darling, I'm well-aware of our little predicament, but unlike you, I haven't panicked. Here." She slipped him a disposable syringe and small vial.

Roger stared at the items in his hand. "What's this?"

"Put them in your pocket. Don't let anyone see you with them."

"What is it?"

"Our insurance policy. Morphine. I palmed it off the medicine cart earlier while you were flirting with the charge nurse."

"What am I supposed to do with it?"

Whitney gave him a withering look. "You're going to slip back into Abel's room tonight and inject it into his IV. Bye-bye, Abel. No fuss. No muss. Mission accomplished. With the stock we'll control, the board will have no choice but to name you CEO to replace Abel, and no one's the wiser."

"You're still forgetting two small problems. The evidence and Sarah."

Whitney smiled sweetly. "Both will be handled in due time. The evidence will be easy to destroy. We'll plant some of our own to frame someone else. Who was it you said you wanted to get rid of? Danbury? A simple task for a man with your computer talents, my love. I've seen you do it countless times."

"And what about Sarah? She'll be the one controlling the stock, not me."

"Yes, but she's too wrapped up in her own career to care about Montgomery Aeronautics. The only interest she has in planes is for transporting her from one photo shoot to the next. She's not going to want to put down her camera to become a business executive. Persuading her to turn her voting rights over to you will be a piece of cake. After all, you've already charmed her into marrying you."

"It may not be that easy."

Whitney's glare could have melted steel. Her whispered words took on a deadly tone. "What do you mean? I thought you had her wrapped around your finger. Don't tell me you've fucked that up, too."

"Sarah isn't the pushover she first appeared to be. She's become increasingly defiant."

"Then handle her! There's too much at stake here. I don't care if you have to cover her bed with roses and croon under her balcony seven nights a week. Do whatever it takes."

Roger turned slightly and looked over Whitney's shoulder and across the nurses' station to where Sarah sat by Abel's bedside. "And if that doesn't work?"

Whitney sighed. "It really is a pity how tragedy has stalked the Montgomery clan. Such unfortunate accidents over the past few years. One has to wonder if there might not be a curse upon them."

"What are you implying?"

"You'll just have to find a way to get rid of her. Murder is like everything else, Roger. The more you practice, the easier it becomes. Especially when you have no conscience."

"Speaking from personal experience?"

Before answering, Whitney turned and glanced across the nurses' station into Abel's room and caught Sarah's eye. She leaned against Roger's body and flicked her tongue seductively against his ear. From Sarah's vantage point it would appear that she had collapsed in tears on his shoulder. "Observation, lover," she whispered. "Now, let's all go back to the apartment. You have a busy night ahead of you."

"She'll want to stay."

"She can't stay. We've got to get her out of here." Whitney pulled herself away from him and turned slightly so Sarah could see her dabbing at her eyes.

Roger allowed himself the luxury of Whitney's little drama. Playing the consoling relative, he wrapped his arm around her shoulder and drew her back into him. As his left hand patted Whitney sympathetically across her back for Sarah's benefit, his right hand made its way between the buttons of her silk blouse, pushing aside the cup of her flimsy lace bra. Whitney moaned with pleasure as Roger found, then squeezed her nipple between his fingers.

"I'm going to expect an ample reward for my overtime this evening," he said.

"You know where to find me, lover. Business first. Then pleasure."

THREE

Sarah hung back in the hallway of Abel's Central Park West apartment while Roger unlocked the door with his own key. She was upset with herself for giving in to Whitney's well-intentioned pleas to leave the hospital for a few hours of rest. She belonged at her grandfather's bedside. They all did.

Once inside, Roger headed straight for the bar without saying a word to either her or Whitney. Sarah had grown used to him ignoring her. She found it easier to handle than the forced conversations and phony displays of tenderness they both affected for Abel's benefit. Mumbling a goodnight to Whitney, she headed for the room she used when staying in town.

After undressing and slipping into a pair of silk pajamas she sat at the Victorian dressing table and numbly brushed out her waist-length hair. A gentle rap at the door broke through her morose thoughts. "Come in."

Whitney entered, carrying two steaming mugs. She offered one to Sarah. "Here. Drink this."

"What is it?"

"Warm milk with a splash of brandy." Whitney took a small sip from her own mug. "It will help you sleep."

Sarah climbed onto the mahogany sleigh bed that had once belonged to her great-grandmother. Leaning against the headboard, she drank some of the beverage. "Thanks. I don't know what I'd do without you, Whitney. You've been like a big sister to me. I'm so grateful for your friendship. And for how happy you've made Granddad."

Whitney chuckled as she settled on the bed next to Sarah. "Thought I was a gold-digger at first, didn't you? Only after the old coot's money?"

"At first, I suppose. But not for long. Granddad told me he practically has to force you to spend his money. And I can tell you really love him."

"What can I say? He's a lovable old coot." Whitney's eyes misted over with tears as she took another sip from her cup. "I just hope he stays my lovable old coot. I don't know what I'd do if I lost him. I love him so much."

Fighting back her own tears, Sarah set her mug on the nightstand and leaned forward to embrace her step-grandmother. "I do, too."

After a long moment Whitney pulled gently from Sarah's arms. "Drink up," she said, handing Sarah's mug back to her.

As Sarah sipped at the warm milk, her eyelids grew heavy. She fought to stifle a yawn. Whitney removed the cup from her hand. Within minutes Sarah was sound asleep.

"What did you lace it with?" asked Roger, walking into the

bedroom.

"Just something to ensure she doesn't wake up until morning." Whitney lowered Sarah down onto the bed and drew the quilt over her. "You have a long night ahead of you, and I don't want your wife sticking her nose where it doesn't belong."

Roger sauntered up alongside Whitney and pulled her into his arms. "Speaking of long nights—"

She wrenched out of his grasp. "Damn it, Roger, I could kill you! You weren't content to wait until Abel died. You had to start skimming. Well, I've spent too many years spreading my legs for that old goat to have you fuck things up now. Your greed caused this mess. Now clean it up."

Everything's under control, darling. You always see to that."

"And you're damn lucky I do!"

* * *

Roger stood in a shadowy alcove of the dimly lit ICU. At several hours past midnight there was no activity on the floor. The lone nurse at the station was lost in a mountain of paperwork. Of the six rooms surrounding the station only half were occupied, two with heavily sedated patients.

Abel was still unconscious. The private duty nurse they'd hired to stay in his room sat curled up in a chair in the corner, her head slumped on her chest. Her soft snores mingled with the sounds of the machines keeping Abel alive.

Roger withdrew farther into the shadows before removing the syringe and vial from his jacket pocket. With shaking hands, he tore open the protective wrapper encasing the hypodermic needle. Whitney hadn't taken any chances. The syringe she'd pilfered would probably hold enough morphine to kill a horse. He inserted the needle through the vial's rubber stopper and sucked the liquid up into the barrel of the syringe. His perspiring palms hampered his efforts, causing him to tighten his grip on both the plastic needle and the glass bottle to keep them from slipping out of his grasp.

Roger began to hyperventilate. *Damn!* He was scared shitless. He leaned back against the wall, closed his eyes, and took several deep breaths. Whitney should be doing this, not him. The callous bitch. She'd shove the needle into Abel's IV and never look back. Hell, knowing Whitney, she'd probably take pleasure in jabbing it directly into the old man's heart.

His talents lay in other directions. His stage was the corporate world. His instrument of destruction, a computer terminal. He had no conscience when it came to embezzlement or forgery. They were clean crimes. Easy to walk away from without a shred of guilt. Not murder. Murder was something else entirely.

Damn Whitney! That bitch had manipulated him into this. He stared down at the syringe, realizing he no longer had any choice. Whitney was right. He'd screwed up. He hadn't counted on Abel being more clever than he was. But it was her fault as well. She should have been doing what she did best, spreading her legs. She should have been driving the bastard to distraction.

Roger took one last deep breath before stepping from the shadows. He glanced over at the charge nurse. Her back was to him. Keeping close to the wall, he started down the corridor only to stop after several steps when a figure in green surgical scrubs and cap stepped from the shadows at the opposite end of the hall and entered Abel's room. Roger froze. His heart pounding in his ears, he ducked into another alcove. Within seconds the figure exited the room and headed for the nearest stairwell. Roger stepped forward, but this time he was stopped short by the shrill peal of an alarm.

The private duty nurse sprang awake and rushed to Abel's bedside. The charge nurse pushed a button on a panel in front of her and yelled, "ICU. Code Blue. STAT!" Within seconds the floor was alive with activity. From his hiding spot Roger watched unseen as a team of doctors and nurses worked frantically over Abel's body.

When it was over, he tossed the unused syringe in a nearby trash can and slipped down the stairs to the underground parking garage. He sat for several minutes behind the wheel of his Porsche, offering up a silent prayer to whichever saint or devil had been watching over him. He wouldn't have to live with the weight of Abel's death on his conscience, and Whitney would never know the difference.

* * *

Whitney had expected the call. She picked the phone up before the second ring, her grieving widow persona already in place. By the time she hung up, her mind was racing. Roger would return soon. He had more work to do before the night was over. Business before pleasure.

A few minutes later Roger entered the apartment. Damn if he didn't look like the Cheshire Cat, his grin running from ear to ear. He reached for her.

She sidestepped him. "We don't have time."

"What are you talking about?"

"It will be morning in a few hours. You have to plant that evidence against Danbury."

"We have plenty of time. It's a holiday weekend, remember? No one will be in the office until Tuesday."

"You can't be certain of that, and we can't afford any more

screw ups."

"Chill. I have everything planned out."

"Don't get smug, Roger. You have no idea who else is privy to that evidence."

"I have a pretty good idea." He made his way toward Abel's study. "And I know just how to handle it."

Whitney followed behind him. "Who? Tell me what you're going to do."

Roger settled himself in front of the computer and accessed the Montgomery systems. The monitor bathed the darkened room in an eerie glow while he played with the data on the screen. As he worked, Whitney paced. After a while, she leaned her elbows on top of the flat screen monitor and stifled a yawn. "How much longer?"

"Not long."

"What you're doing?"

He glanced up at her. The glow from the computer screen reflected in her jade eyes and bounced off her platinum hair. She reminded him of a Siamese cat. Whitney drummed her long scarlet nails on top of the monitor. A hellcat with vicious claws.

"As far as I know, the only person Abel met with yesterday was Ferguson."

"His attorney?"

"Hmm. Did you know Ferguson's married to Miles Osbourne's sister?"

"Who's Miles Osbourne?"

"Only the best computer investigator in the business."

"And you think Abel had Ferguson hire his brother-in-law to snoop around?"

"I'm sure of it. Osbourne's the only person I know who's good enough to have found me out."

"Terrific. So now what?"

"Now I discredit Osbourne's findings."

"And just how do you do that?"

"A crook always has to be smarter than an honest man, my dear. Osbourne stopped looking when he found me. Had he continued, he would have found that I was being set up by the real embezzler: Hugh Danbury." He stopped typing and shot her a devious smile. "In a few hours I'm going to call John Ferguson and tell him his inept brother-in-law is responsible for Abel's death. Then I'm going to give him the evidence that clears my name and hangs Danbury."

Whitney leaned across the monitor and ran her tongue along the rim of Roger's ear. "I like the way your mind works, lover boy."

FOUR

Across town Devon removed a thick scrapbook from a locked steamer trunk hidden in a storage closet and leafed through the pages of yellowed newspaper clippings. Mounted at the back of the album was a series of snapshots, three of which had thick red X's drawn through them. Uncapping a thick felt marker, Devon drew two diagonal slashes through a fourth photo, closed the book, and returned it to its hiding place.

FIVE

Sarah woke to a thin shaft of early morning light that sneaked around the edge of the drawn Damask drapes and settled across her face. Her head throbbed. Her muscles were stiff and sore from the stress of the previous night. Aspirin. Shower. Coffee. Then she'd be able to face a long day in the ICU.

Fifteen minutes later, neither the aspirin nor the shower had helped. Her mind focused only on her need for caffeine, Sarah stood in front of the fog-covered bathroom mirror and blindly sectioned her thick mass of hair into three equal parts before weaving the French braid that was as much a part of her as her two arms and legs.

Her fifth appendage, Granddad called it. *Linus has his blanket, and Sarah has her braid.* Then he'd give her hair a gentle tug. Her heart flip-flopped at the memory. Would Granddad survive to tug again? *Please*, she prayed as she headed toward the aroma of freshly brewed coffee. But once in the kitchen, all thoughts of a much-needed caffeine fix disappeared. One look at Roger and Whitney told Sarah everything she didn't want to know.

* * *

"Hugh Danbury's here to see you, sir."

Roger sat gazing out the window at the ominous skyline. He'd always been covetous of the view from Abel's window. Now it was his. It was all his. The office. The view. The secretary. The power. And thanks to Abel's wife, he'd soon control all of Abel's vast wealth.

Another late summer thunderstorm was about to descend on Manhattan. Sheets of rain had pelted the city on and off throughout the weekend and into the start of the work week, but Roger didn't mind. He loved to watch from this thirty-seven-story perch. It made him feel as though he were a part of the terrifying force of nature that captured the city and for a short time held it in a powerful grip. Reluctantly, he swiveled his chair back around to his desk.

"Send him in." He turned his attention to the computer screen on his desk as Hugh Danbury entered the office.

"You wanted to see me, sir?"

Roger never took his eyes from the screen. With his left hand he continued to work the keyboard. His right hand pushed an envelope to the edge of his desk and motioned Danbury to take it. "We're letting you go, Hugh. You'll find six month's severance and a letter of recommendation in the envelope. I want you packed and out of here in ten minutes."

"But...but why? I've always been a conscientious employee. Abel never had any complaints. My reviews are consistently excellent."

Roger turned from the screen and sneered at the Dockers and Nike-clad man who stood before him. He picked up the gold Mont Blanc pen sitting on his desk and scrawled a notation on a legal pad. *Institute dress code. Immediately.* He then underlined *Immediately* three times and added an exclamation mark to the end of the word before speaking. "Certain financial discrepancies have recently come to light."

"Discrepancies? What kind of discrepancies? I don't understand."

"There are large sums of money unaccounted for. I'm not making any accusations, mind you, but the evidence I've uncovered leads me to believe these accounting *errors*, shall we say, will cease once you are no longer in our employ."

"You're crazy, Caine! I haven't stolen any money from the company, and you damn well know it!"

"Do I?"

Danbury's hands clenched into fists. His face turned red. "I'll sue! This is libel. You're trying to destroy me. I'll sue this company for everything it's got, and I'll see you in the poor house, you son-of-a-bitch!"

Roger glared at him but kept his voice even, his tone not much above a whisper. "No, you won't, Hugh. Because I'm not accusing you of anything. We're simply making a few housekeeping changes now that Abel's gone and I'm in charge. I've given you a more than generous severance package and a letter of recommendation instead of notifying the District Attorney. Do the smart thing. Clear out your desk and leave quietly."

Danbury glared down at Roger who smiled as he held the envelope up and again offered it to the accountant. "Don't forget this, Hugh."

Danbury grabbed the envelope and stormed out of the office. In his wake the room reverberated from the sound of the slammed door, echoing the thunder rumbling in the distance.

Roger picked up the phone and buzzed his secretary. "Helen, hold all my calls." He sauntered over to the credenza, poured himself three fingers of Scotch, and settled in to enjoy the storm.

* * *

Felicia Sutton burst into Trent Caldwell's office without knocking. "Fairfield opened at one twenty this morning and gained another two already," she said. She sank into one of the two leather wing back chairs opposite his desk and crossed her legs, allowing more than a little thigh to show above her short hemline.

Trent glanced up from the report he was reading. "Having a good day, Felicia?"

"There's nothing like a successful takeover to start the day right."

Trent returned to his reading. At thirty-five Felicia was both a brilliant financial analyst and a royal thorn in his side. Hiring her as Vice-President for Acquisitions at Trentwell International had either been a resounding business coup or a tremendous personal error, depending on the day of the week and his mood.

He glanced up to see her smiling at him. Body, brains, and looks. Except for her annoying Long Island accent, which knocked her down from a perfect ten to a nine-point-nine, Felicia Sutton had it all. All, that is, except the one thing she wanted, and the lady was nothing if not persistent. If he could only get her to understand he wasn't interested. Not in her. Not in anyone. Never again.

"Everyone likes to run with a winner," said Trent. "Stop gloating."

"You're not even going to let me say 'I told you so'?"

"God, I hate it when you're right. What are you planning for an encore?"

"How would you like to add an airplane company to your collection?"

"I may be wealthy, Felicia, but not wealthy enough to buy Boeing."

"I was thinking a little less grandiose, actually. A manufacturer that specializes in small corporate and charter jets."

"Depends. Which one?"

"Montgomery Aeronautics. The stock's been taking a beating ever since old man Montgomery cashed in his chips last week."

Trent pondered her words. "Could have potential. I've been hearing rumors. Seems the stockholders don't have much confidence in Abel Montgomery's handpicked successor."

"Hmm. Roger Caine. Do you know him?"

"Not really. We've been introduced. Nothing more. His wife is Sarah Montgomery, the photographer."

"And you know her?"

"Never met the woman. Caitlin liked her work. We own several pieces."

He noticed the way Felicia tensed at the mention of Caitlin's name. He knew it annoyed her when he spoke of his late wife. Maybe that's why he did it so often in her presence. The woman was turning him into a perverse son-of-a-bitch.

"The stock dropped another three points already today," she said, changing the subject back to the business of acquisitions and corporate takeovers. "Do you want me to start buying?"

"No. Hold off. Wait until the will goes to probate. I have a feeling it's going to take a nosedive. Get everything in place to act as soon as it does." He stood and slipped on his suit jacket.

"A bit early for lunch, isn't it?"

He knew she was fishing for an invitation. Let her fish. This trout wasn't biting. "I have a meeting downtown with the boys from Unicor. I'm running late."

Without another word, Trent raced out of the office, down the hall, and into the elevator which led directly to the private side entrance of Trentwell Towers, headquarters of Trentwell International and home of the exclusive Trentwell Arms Hotel. He thought about his conversation with Felicia and clenched his teeth.

She had burrowed under his skin like some damn chigger, causing an annoying irritation. Every time he turned around, she was in his face with an open invitation. The woman was drop-dead gorgeous and incredibly bright, so why couldn't she take a hint and set her sights on someone who would appreciate her? If she weren't such a financial wizard, he would have sacked her long ago.

Unfortunately, in a moment of weakness and too much alcohol, he'd sacked her in an altogether different way. For Trent the episode had been a huge mistake, nothing more than a release of pent-up sexual tension and frustration. Felicia, on the other hand, had taken the evening as a hopeful sign, one she clung to with ferocious tenacity.

Then there was the bombshell she dropped upstairs. Montgomery Aeronautics would be a juicy acquisition, but it also had the potential for stirring up a shitload of trouble. There were things about the company Felicia was unaware of. Personal things Trent had every intention of keeping hidden from her.

When the elevator doors opened, he jumped out, signaling his chauffeur who sat chatting with a security guard.

"Let's go, O'Hara. I'm in a hurry."

The man gaped wide-eyed at his boss. "Go, sir?"

Trent stopped short, looked at the bewildered expression on his driver's face, then at the empty parking space. "Shit!" The Unicor meeting came up suddenly. Not expecting to need the limo today, yesterday he'd given O'Hara permission to get the vehicle serviced.

"I can call the livery and have a car sent around, sir. It would only take ten, fifteen minutes tops."

Trent glanced down at his Rolex. "Never mind. I'll hop a cab. Buzz the doorman. Have him hold one for me."

Trent raced through the main lobby of the hotel and into the back seat of a waiting taxi. "I need to be at twenty-fourth and Madison in ten minutes. Do it, and you've got yourself an extra twenty."

The cab driver turned around and gave him a wide, gap-toothed grin. "No problem, sir."

SIX

"As you all know," began John Ferguson, "Abel was very paternal about his company. He gave birth to it, nurtured it, and took tremendous pride in what he'd created. Above all else, he wanted the company to remain controlled by a Montgomery." His gaze fell on Sarah, and he smiled.

"What exactly are you getting at?" asked Roger.

Speaking directly to Sarah, John ignored both Roger and his question. "Ever since your parents died, you have allowed Abel to vote your shares of stock. Abel has named you sole beneficiary of his holdings in Montgomery Aeronautics. You now own a controlling interest in the company; however, there are several provisos."

He shot a quick sideways glance at Roger. "The will stipulates that you take an active role in the running of the company. You cannot turn over your voting rights to anyone."

Sarah followed John's gaze. Within a split second she watched her husband's expression turn from smug to indignant to enraged. A large blue vein began to pulse in his neck. Roger had just confirmed all her suspicions.

"Are you out of your mind?" Roger sputtered. "She doesn't know the first thing about running a company. She's a goddamn photographer for Christ sake!"

"In addition," John continued, ignoring Roger's outburst, "you must agree never to sell any of your shares. Abel has also requested that a will be drawn up for you stating that your shares be divided equally among your children—and only your children—upon your death."

"There are no goddamn children!" Roger practically spat the words.

John finally turned his attention to Roger. "I believe I was speaking to Sarah."

"You've had it in for me for some time, haven't you, Ferguson? I wouldn't be surprised to find you tampered with Abel's will. It's about the missing money, isn't it?"

"What missing money?" asked Sarah.

"Abel's good friend here tried to convince your grandfather that I'd embezzled a small amount of money from the company. He's responsible for Abel's heart attack, Sarah. The pain of thinking I'd stab him in the back was too much for the old man to handle."

Sarah grabbed for her braid, worrying the tail around her fingers. She looked across the room at Whitney. Draped in black from head to toe, including a black cloche with matching veil, Abel's widow sat staring blankly out the window, apparently too wrapped up in her grief to notice the accusations hurling around the room. Sarah turned back to John and Roger. *If looks could kill…*

"Seven million dollars is hardly what I would call a small sum of money," said John.

Roger snorted. "It's pocket change to a company this size. Besides, I found the true thief, didn't I?"

"Did you?" asked John. "Why wasn't the evidence turned over to the District Attorney? Why let him walk? If indeed, he was the real embezzler."

Sarah couldn't believe her ears. "You did what?"

"Stay out of this, Sarah. It doesn't concern you."

"Like hell it doesn't," said John. "It's her company."

Sarah turned to her husband. His skin flushed from scarlet to purple; the vein doubled in both size and tempo. Always needing to be in charge, Roger detested being challenged. He was furious over Abel's decision concerning the company, and now Abel's lawyer was accusing him of embezzlement. With tremendous difficulty Sarah managed to keep her voice even and calm. "I'm sure you had a logical reason for what you did, Roger. I'd like to hear it, please."

He smiled benevolently at her, but she saw the hatred behind his eyes, hatred now directed toward her.

"Seven million dollars is petty cash to Montgomery Aeronautics," he said. "If word leaked that the company was the victim of embezzlement, the papers would have a heyday. The stock would plummet, and in the long run, that and the cost of litigation would be far greater than the initial loss. I was acting in the best interests of the company and the stockholders." He tossed a quick sneer in John's direction. "No matter what some people might think."

"I understand," said Sarah. She nodded toward the attorney.

"Perhaps you should continue with the reading."

John cleared his throat. "Everything else is pretty standard," he said. "With the exception of what Abel left to Whitney and several charitable bequests, the estate goes entirely to you, Sarah."

At the mention of her name Whitney rose from her seat by the window and took the remaining chair opposite John's desk.

"And just what has Abel left his widow?" asked Roger. "Or have you managed to have her thrown out in the street?"

John directed his answer to Whitney. "In addition to leaving you the West Side apartment, Abel has set up a trust that will give you a generous yearly income, more than enough to live quite comfortably."

"By whose standards?" asked Roger.

Once again John ignored Roger and continued speaking to Whitney. "The principal is not available to you at any time. Also, if and when you should choose to remarry, the trust will be revoked with the principal reverting to Sarah."

"Son-of-a-bitch," muttered Roger.

"Did you have something to say, Roger?" asked John.

"Yes, as a matter of fact, I do, Ferguson." He jumped to his feet and leaned across the desk, his face inches from the lawyer's. "This will is outrageous, and it's going to be contested. By all three of us!"

John rose and gathered the documents spread across his desk. "If that's the way you feel, this meeting is adjourned." He turned to the two women still seated in front of him. "Good day, ladies."

Whitney rose from her chair and regally walked to the door of John's office, still not saying a single word. Roger began to follow her out, then turned back to Sarah. "Let's go, Sarah. We're getting out of here."

Sarah didn't bother to turn to face him as she spoke. "I'm not leaving, Roger. I have some things I need to discuss with John. In private."

Roger stalked back to her chair. She turned to face him. The blue throbbing vein had turned a deep purple and now covered the length of his head, from neck to temple, where it disappeared into a forest of thick jet-black hair.

He grabbed her arm, roughly yanking her to her feet. "I said we're leaving."

"Take your hands off me." He didn't love her. He had never loved her. She had been a pawn in his bid for power. Somehow Granddad had discovered the truth.

Roger's expression betrayed his contempt of her. He released her arm and stormed out of the office without looking back. Once he and Whitney were gone, Sarah collapsed into the chair. She sat for several minutes nervously toying with her wedding band, studying the row of flawless diamonds that caught the light from the window behind John's desk.

John walked over to a wall of built-in cabinets, poured Sarah a glass of sherry, then perched himself on the corner of his desk directly in front of her.

"Is it true about the money?" she asked. "Did Roger really steal it?"

"I'm sorry, Sarah. Abel was beginning to have his suspicions about Roger, and he asked me to look into the matter. I had the finest computer detective in the country at my disposal, and he found a trail leading from the missing money directly back to Roger."

"But what about this other person Roger spoke of?"

"My theory is he was either part of the scam and agreed to take the fall since he knew Roger wouldn't press charges. Or as I'm beginning to believe is the more likely scenario, he was an innocent victim. Someone Roger chose to take the heat off himself."

Sarah yanked the wedding ring from her finger and placed it on the desk next to John's thigh. "I have no intention of contesting the will."

"I'm glad to hear that."

"As a matter of fact, I'd like you to draw up some additional papers for me."

"What kind of papers?"

"Divorce papers. I've had enough. I want that man out of my life. I can't live like this anymore. Do whatever it takes. No matter what the cost." She rose to leave. "I'll be in touch. I don't want to go back to the house right now. I think I'll check into the St. Regis for a few days. I need some time to think."

She was reaching for the doorknob when John called to her. She turned to find him holding her wedding band in his outstretched hand.

Sarah took the ring, but instead of placing it back on her finger, she slipped it into her purse.

Her thoughts focused inward, Sarah walked aimlessly along Lexington Avenue ignoring the beckoning storefronts. With her parents and grandparents gone, divorcing Roger would leave her completely alone for the first time in her life. The idea both terrified and excited her.

She could travel more, explore the world, searching out and documenting its endless beauty. The jungles of South America. The African veldt. The islands of the South Pacific. Where to first? Charged with excitement and anxious to start mapping out an itinerary, Sarah picked up her pace.

Then just as suddenly, she stopped short. Accountable to no one? Hardly. Granddad had saddled her with an enormous responsibility, one she wasn't sure she wanted but knew she had to shoulder—the company. Her hand automatically reached for her braid, holding onto the thick rope of hair like a security blanket.

Roger was right. What did she know about running an aeronautics company? Or any company for that matter? She was a photographer. She'd gone to art school, not business school. She'd earned an MFA, not an MBA. Hell, she'd never even taken a course in economics.

Yet would Abel have entrusted her with his life's work if he hadn't thought her capable of doing a good job? No, not good. Good wouldn't be enough. Her grandfather had never settled for anything less than excellent.

Lord, what a mess, she thought, darting through the crowds of strolling shoppers and sightseeing tourists. And she still had an ugly confrontation with Roger ahead of her. Not only did she plan to divorce him, she intended to fire the crown prince. If her husband thought he was having a rotten day today...

Lost in thought Sarah didn't see the light change. She stepped off the curb just as the cab sped around the corner.

SEVEN

Sifting through the trash Dumpster, the small, wiry woman paid little attention to the sound of shrieking brakes halfway down the block. Only by chance did she happen to glance up in time to see the taxi slam into the hapless pedestrian. The impact sent the girl flying into the air. Her body bounced against the windshield of the yellow cab, then the hood, before landing face down inches from the taxi's front wheels.

The bag lady placed a few empty cans into her plastic sack and moved on to the next Dumpster. As she made her way down the sidewalk toward the crowd gathering around the taxi, her heart sped up with excitement. Treasure beckoned, trapped between the curb and a parked truck.

Her eyes darted around the chaotic scene. The crowd around the victim kept growing. No one noticed her. No one saw what she saw. Scurrying across the street, she reached down, scooped up the woman's purse, and dropped it into her black plastic bag.

After ducking into an alley, she squatted behind an empty construction trailer and dumped the contents of the handbag into her lap. A Mercedes car key. A parking garage ticket. A wallet bulging with bills and credit cards.

"Thank you, Jesus!" Who needed trash? She tossed her stash of empty aluminum cans under the trailer, dumped her lapful of treasure back in the handbag, and headed toward the address on the parking garage ticket. "Miami, here I come!"

EIGHT

The sight of the helpless woman, wrapped in miles of gauze and lost in a sea of tubes, brought unwelcome memories flooding through Trent. *It's my fault. Just like last time.* He shook his head in an attempt to rid himself of the thought, but even with his eyes open, he continued to see her crumpled body lying face down on the pavement in front of the taxi. When he closed his eyes the vision worsened, transforming into a similar scene nearly three years earlier where one victim had lost her life and the other his soul.

Trent hovered in a corner of the private hospital room. Half a dozen doctors and nurses swarmed around the patient, giving orders, taking notes, adjusting machines. After hours of surgery, they'd done all they could. The rest was up to a higher power. One by one they completed their tasks and departed until Trent was left alone with the head surgeon. And the comatose woman.

"Will she live?"

The physician nodded. "She's not as bad as she looks, Mr. Caldwell."

Trent stared at the woman. Bandages covered most of her head and face. Her left arm below the elbow and entire right leg were encased in plaster casts. "But she's unconscious."

"And will be for a while. She sustained an intracranial hematoma. We had to operate to relieve swelling to her brain. Luckily, her arm broke her fall, lessening the impact and the severity of the head injury. Her face took the brunt of the impact. Massive abrasions, fractures to her cheekbones and nose. Some of the bone is pulverized. Beyond repair. She'll need grafts to reconstruct a few areas, but we have to wait until the swelling recedes before we can proceed—in about a week, maybe two."

The doctor scowled as he scratched at his short dark brown beard.

"There's something more?" asked Trent.

"I just wish we could contact a relative. As you can imagine, the hospital hates situations like this. There's always the possibility of a lawsuit. Hell, we run the risk of a lawsuit for cutting her hair without permission, let alone operating on her."

Although well-dressed, the woman had carried no identification. No wallet. No house keys. Not even a Metro card. The evening news was set to broadcast a piece on the accident. Hopefully, within the next few hours someone would report her missing. Until then, all any of them could do was wait.

Trent glanced at the patient. Thin wisps of strawberry blonde hair peeked out from under layers of gauze, but he had no recollection of how she'd worn her hair. His concern had been for her survival, not her coiffeur. "You cut her hair?"

"Not me. An overly zealous intern in emergency got scissors happy. In the confusion of cutting away her clothes, he managed to lop off her waist-length braid. You know how women are. They can get pretty irrational about their hair. Our Jane Doe here might wake up spitting nails."

Trent considered himself a good judge of character, and as irrational as it sounded, he sensed she was not a shallow person. "She doesn't look like the nail-spitting type."

"I hope her relatives aren't, either."

But no relatives came forward that evening after the account of the accident aired on both the major and local networks. No reports of missing persons fitting her description were filed with the New York City police or any of the suburban precincts throughout the metropolitan area. No one was searching for the Jane Doe lying comatose in a private room on the fifteen floor of Lenox Hill Hospital.

Throughout the long night, as a parade of personnel streamed in and out of the room, Trent kept a silent vigil. On more than one occasion he sensed her watching him, but on closer scrutiny found her condition unchanged. Guilt and fatigue were joining forces to play mind games with him.

* * *

Images darted through her head as if her brain were in the control of an impatient channel surfer. Only one vision, repeating sporadically, lasted long enough for her to focus on it—a man staring at her from the corner of a dark room. But then he'd disappear and other shapes, other colors, other sounds took his place. A cloak of haze encircled pictures of extreme clarity. She tried to reach out and grab hold of an image, a thought, but each time her attempts proved futile and the effort exhausting. None of it made any sense to her. Was she dreaming? And if so, why couldn't she wake up?

The dreams repeated throughout the night or for days. She wasn't sure how long she was trapped inside them, but slowly the darkness lifted. The bombardment of sights and sounds receded, and the image of the man grew sharper until all else faded, and he became her only reality.

In the growing light she could see he was a handsome man, tall and angular with a thick head of disheveled dark brown hair sprinkled with a touch of gray at the temples. He wore his tie loose around his neck, his collar unbuttoned, his shirt sleeves rolled up to his elbows. A thick growth of stubble covered his face. But what held her attention most were his eyes. They were disturbing in their lifelessness, as though he'd lost his soul.

When he saw her studying him, he took a deep breath. As the air slowly released from his lungs, relief spread across his face. "Thank God," he said.

Then he was gone.

* * *

Overcome by exhaustion, Trent let himself into his apartment on the top floor of Trentwell Towers. He was immediately ambushed by a thick Irish brogue.

"Saints be praised, Mr. Trent!" His housekeeper shuffled out from the kitchen, wiping her hands on her apron as she confronted him in the foyer. "Where the devil have you been all night? The bloody phone hasn't stopped ringin'. Half the free world's lookin' for you. Why weren't you answerin' that little pocket phone o' yours?"

"I switched it off." Brushing her aside, Trent headed for his bedroom. "I'm going to bed, Mrs. K. If you value your life, you won't wake me for any*one* or any*thing*."

"Even Ms. Sutton?" she asked, following after him.

"Especially Ms. Sutton. Take the phone off the hook if you have to." He entered the master suite, slammed the door behind him, and collapsed onto his bed.

* * *

Several hours and a long scalding shower later, Trent sat at the kitchen table nursing a dull headache and his third cup of black coffee as Mrs. Kearn bustled around the kitchen.

"So?" she asked, placing a platter of fried eggs and hash browns in front of him. "I don't suppose you'd like to explain your vanishin' act an' strange behavior."

"Not particularly, but I know I won't have any peace until I do."

She settled into the chair opposite him and waited. Trent studied the older woman who had become more mother than housekeeper to him over the years.

Her hair, which he remembered as bright red from his youth, had faded to a dull sienna streaked with an overabundance of gray. Her skin was crisscrossed with a road map of fine lines that deepened when she scowled or smiled. At present her leprechaun-green eyes reflected her concern. He was acting out of character, and he knew that worried her.

Moira Kearn had been a part of his life since coming to work for his parents over thirty-five years ago. Her son Brendan had been like a brother to him. But that was in the past. Now all he and Mrs. Kearn had were each other. And the bitterness and emptiness that haunted them both.

He had no idea how old she was, but he guessed somewhere in her late sixties, maybe older. She rarely spoke of herself. Never of her past. Neither had her son. Trent remembered once, shortly after Mrs. Kearn and Brendan arrived, the boy began to speak of his home in Ireland. Unfortunately, his mother overheard him and yanked the child away before he could say anything further. Brendan stood at the kitchen table to eat his lunch that day, his bottom too sore to sit. The subject was never again mentioned.

As he grew into his teens and learned more of the violence devastating Northern Ireland, Trent's curiosity about Mrs. Kearn and Brendan's background increased. He scoured the newspapers for articles about the political upheaval in Ireland but soon sickened of the brutal savagery committed in the name of freedom and religion by men like Quinn and Curry and Timmons. He couldn't associate the two people he'd grown to love with the ongoing nightmare consuming that distant island. Burying his inquisitiveness, he never questioned either of them about their past.

Between mouthfuls of egg and a fourth cup of coffee, Trent told Mrs. Kearn about the accident. He didn't have to mention the memories the incident brought back. He could see she understood.

She reached across the table and took his hands in her pudgy ones. "Will the woman survive?"

Trent nodded. "The surgery to reduce the brain swelling was successful. The rest of her injuries aren't life-threatening. I left the hospital as soon as she regained consciousness, but I have to go back. If nothing else, I owe her an apology."

Mrs. Kearn began to speak but was interrupted by the ringing of the doorbell. "That could only be *her*," she muttered.

Trent raised an eyebrow.

"Ms. Sutton," she said over her shoulder as she made her way to the front hall. "She kept callin' all night. Every fifteen minutes or so. Said 'twas very important, crucial, in fact, that she speak to you."

"Is he back yet?" demanded Felicia when the housekeeper opened the door. "I told you to call me the moment he got in! Why haven't you been answering the phone?"

Trent could hear Felicia down the length of the long hallway. Her shrill voice, heavy with that annoying Long Island accent, ricocheted off the terra cotta tiles and stabbed at his already throbbing head. Why couldn't the woman have a voice that matched her looks? As the sound of her heels clicking against the floor grew closer, he rubbed his temples and winced. Felicia Sutton was the last person he wanted to see this morning.

"Trent? Where are you?"

"He's in the kitchen," said Mrs. Kearn, her sturdy Rockports thumping behind Felicia.

"Well, there you are!"

She stood in the doorway, hands on hips, staring at him. Or glaring. Trent wasn't sure. Her expression held a combination of surprise, relief, and anger. Not necessarily in that order. He raised his coffee cup in greeting and motioned for her to take a seat at the table. "Good morning, Felicia."

"Good morning?" She glanced over at the wall clock. "Try afternoon. Where have you been for the past day and a half? All hell is breaking loose. Why didn't you show for your meeting at Unicor yesterday? I've been frantic with worry."

"I was involved in an accident on the way to Unicor."

She reached across the table and grabbed his hand. "My God, Trent! Are you all right?"

"I'm fine." He pulled his hand out from under hers. "But the young woman my cab struck was severely injured. I stayed at the hospital until I knew she'd recover."

"Why? The accident wasn't your fault. Besides, you could have at least let me know where you were. With this latest development at Montgomery Aeronautics, we have to move fast, or we'll miss our window of opportunity."

Trent glanced across the room to the sink where Mrs. Kearn was scouring the frying pan. At the mention of the aeronautics company her posture tensed. "What new development?"

"Damn it, Trent! Haven't you even read a paper or listened to the news since yesterday?"

His gaze roamed to the morning papers, stacked neatly on the counter. He shook his head.

"Sarah Montgomery's dead. She rammed her car into the back of a disabled tanker truck on the New Jersey Turnpike yesterday. The body was so badly burned they could only identify her by the handbag that was found a few feet from the wreckage. The police figure it was flung from the car in the initial impact."

The skillet dropped from Mrs. Kearn's hands. Sudsy water splashed over the sink and onto both her and the floor, but she ignored the mess. Spinning around, she stared at Trent. "Evil begets them that do evil," she said.

"No," said Trent. "She had nothing to do with it. You know that."

"Nothing to do with what?" asked Felicia. "What are you two babbling about?"

"Nothing that concerns you." Trent glared at Mrs. Kearn, daring her into silence.

Muttering in Gaelic, Mrs. Kearn wiped the counter with the hem of her apron, then left the room. Trent stared after her. He recognized some of the epithets she directed towards the dead woman and her family. Her superstitious belief in divine retribution had always bothered him.

"Trent! Are you listening to me? We need to act *now!* Otherwise, you can forget it."

"Yes," he agreed, his eyes still focused on the doorway. "Go ahead."

* * *

"I'm buying Montgomery Aeronautics," he said to Mrs. Kearn after Felicia left.

"No! Please, lad! They killed Brendan!"

"We've been over this countless times, Mrs. K. You know that's not true. The FAA ruled pilot error caused the crash, not mechanical failure."

She shook her head, her conviction unshakable. "That man paid the government to lie. God is punishin' them. Him and his entire family."

Trent thought back over the last several years. It certainly seemed that way. Shortly after the plane crash that killed Brendan Kearn, his wife, and young daughter, members of the Montgomery family began dying in tragic accidents. All except Abel who had succumbed to a bad heart. With Sarah gone, only her husband Roger and Abel's second wife remained.

"Nothin' good will come o' this," said Mrs. Kearn. "Mark my words."

"It's over, Moira. They're dead. It's time to move on."

"Like you have?"

The barb hit right where she knew it would. In his heart.

"No," she said, sniffing back her grief. "My boy and his family cannot rest in peace. Not yet."

Trent studied the hard set of her jaw, the burning determination in her eyes. *Hate will consume us both*, he thought. *Hers for the Montgomery family and mine for myself. Eventually, there will be nothing left of either of us except a black hole of negative emotions.*

"I'm going back to the hospital," he said. "If anyone's looking for me, I'm unavailable." He regarded the unasked question on her face. "Especially Ms. Sutton," he added.

"She put you up to this deal, didn't she?"

He scowled at the superstitious beliefs that kept her from saying the company's name, as if its mere mention would taint them both. "It's good business, Mrs. K. Nothing more. Let it go."

On his way out the door Trent heard the unmistakable mumbling of more Irish epithets, only this time they were directed towards his Vice-President for Acquisitions.

NINE

Devon drew a thick red "X" across another of the photos at the back of the scrapbook. *Vengeance is mine, sayeth the Lord.* And He had taken it. Devon capped the marker, wrapped a woolen scarf around the leather-bound album, and returned it to its hiding place before heading outside.

* * *

Nestled between a unisex styling salon and a tattoo parlor on Christopher Street off Waverly, *The Emerald Isle* was not a typical Greenwich Village shop. Carrying mostly handmade, pricey Irish imports, it catered to a select clientele. Seamus Hurley, the sixty-year-old proprietor was on a first name basis with most of his customers.

The delicate silver bell above the front door tinkled. Seamus looked up from the crate he was unpacking and smiled at the customer entering his shop. "Devon! You must be clairvoyant! I was just thinkin' o' you."

He motioned to the wooden shipping container on top of the glass display case. Spreading aside a clump of white excelsior, he withdrew a delicate porcelain box decorated with tiny, hand-painted shamrocks and held it up. "They just arrived. I was goin' to set one aside for you."

Devon gently lifted the lid. The clear tones of a familiar tune filled the room.

Seamus sang along for a few bars, his rich baritone echoing off the crystal and china that dotted the shelves of the small room. "Lovely, 'tisn't it?"

"'Tis indeed. I'll take it. And the other items you were expectin', Seamus? Have they also arrived?"

Hurley handed Devon a key and motioned towards a door at the back of the shop. "In the usual spot."

After Devon left the room Seamus hung an *Out to Lunch* sign on the front door and drew the shades. A few minutes later he joined his friend in the hidden cellar room that served as a meeting place for the loyal sons and daughters of Hibernia.

"They act like it's over," he said, settling in behind the bar and pouring two pints of Guinness. "McGuinness and that bitch queen all lovey-dovey and meeting in Belfast like there was never more'n a dust up between lads."

"Tain't over," said Devon. "No matter what they say. No matter the handshakes. Thems that talk of bygones bein' bygones and all that political rot seem to forget the bastards occupied our land for too many decades."

"Don't see as how they can forget all them dead Irish fathers and brothers and sons and husbands," said Seamus. "I certainly can't."

"Nor I. Traitors the lot of 'em." With one hand Devon reached for the glass Seamus extended; the other hand idly stroked the barrel of an AK-47.

"An eye for an eye, Seamus. 'Twill be no peace until an equal number of *them* have fallen. We've a long way yet to go, many more comrades to avenge, and no politicians nor turncoats are goin' to stand in our way."

"I hear ya."

Devon took a long draught, then continued, "Too many fell to the bloody Limey scum and Protestants. It's up to us to continue the fight for what's right. 'Tis God's will."

Hurley clicked his glass against Devon's nearly empty one. "To our fallen comrades across the ocean!"

"Death to the bloody Protestant and English vermin!"

"Amen!"

They drained their stout, slamming the empty glasses onto the wormhole-scarred oak bar. Seamus poured refills while Devon set about dismantling the cache of weapons. Later that night other Irish patriots would repack the shipment, hiding the gun parts inside computer equipment headed across the ocean to the parish school of St. Brigid of Kildare.

TEN

"To fate! And the financial rewards it brings us." The Baccarat flutes clicked together. Whitney watched the bubbles rising to the surface and smiled before taking a sip of the Dom Perignon. Vintage 1961.

"Yes, it was quite considerate of my wife to get herself killed, wasn't it?" Roger downed the contents of his glass in one long draught. He reached across Whitney for the magnum and refilled the glass, pouring so quickly that the champagne spilled over the rim and dribbled onto his pant leg.

"Good thing you weren't that clumsy when you took care of Abel," she said, patting the stain with a napkin.

Roger gulped downed the second glass of champagne with a shaky hand that managed to add an additional damp spot to the front of his shirt. Whitney was eyeing him in that suspicious, calculating way of hers. He avoided her gaze.

"Why so jumpy, Roger?"

He bound to his feet and headed for the bar to pour himself a double Scotch. He couldn't understand why he felt guilty over keeping the truth of that night from her, but he did. He had to get it off his chest. What did it matter now, anyway? Abel was dead. Sarah was dead. The company belonged to him and Whitney. He gulped down the fortification, keeping his back to her as he spoke. "There's something I've been meaning to tell you about the night Abel died."

"You did inject the morphine into his IV, didn't you?" She sidled up to him and drew a long deep red nail across the edge of his ear. Her breath tickled his neck.

"Actually, I think someone might have beaten me to it." Roger proceeded to divulge what he'd observed from his hiding place in the shadows of the hospital corridor. "I don't think it was coincidence that Abel died shortly after the doctor left his room."

"What are you implying?"

Roger could think of only one explanation for what had happened that night. "Abel was the victim of a mercy killer—someone bent on reducing the number of critically ill patients in the hospital. When the alarms sounded, the guy ducked down a stairwell instead of rushing back. That's damned odd behavior for someone sworn to uphold the Hippocratic Oath."

"An angel of death as your guardian angel, Roger? How positively delightful!"

* * *

Panic seized her, squeezing the air from her lungs and hammering at her heart. Emptiness overwhelmed her. Try as she might, she could dredge up no memories other than the sound of a violent explosion, consuming fire, and a tall, handsome man with lifeless eyes.

With great effort she raised her head and studied her body—the casts on one arm and a leg, the tubes running from her uninjured arm to an IV pole holding a bag of fluids. A sharp pain surged up her neck and into her head. Dizziness overcame her, and she lowered herself back onto the pillow.

She felt a tightness in her face and a constant throbbing in her skull. Raising hesitant fingers to her jaw line, she gingerly examined the bandages that swathed her head, following their gauzy trail across her cheeks, the bridge of her nose, and up over her scalp. The slightest pressure caused extreme discomfort but not the kind she'd expect from burns. Her entire face felt more like one giant bruise.

Light streamed into the room from a window to her left. Turning her head, she peered out across a landscape of skyscrapers. *Manhattan!* At least she recognized that much. She was in a hospital in New York and had apparently been in some horrible accident. Something that involved an explosion and a fire.

But who was she?

"Good morning."

The husky bass startled her. She swung her head around. Too fast. She gasped, squeezing her eyes shut, the shot of pain nearly causing her to black out.

"Easy," said the voice. "No sudden moves."

Slowly the stabbing subsided to a dull throb. She opened her eyes to a blurry image a few feet from the side of the bed. As her vision cleared, the blur sharpened into distinct figures. Two men and a woman, all middle-aged and wearing white lab coats, stood beside her.

"I'm Doctor Gallagher," continued the larger of the two men, "and this is Doctor Pierce and Doctor Cataldi." He nodded in the direction of first the woman, then the other man. "How are you feeling?"

She stared at the three physicians. "I'm not sure."

"That's quite understandable," said Doctor Cataldi, "considering the extent of your injuries, but as bad as it looks, you're one very lucky young woman. In a few weeks you'll be as good as new."

"Do you remember anything of the accident?" asked Doctor Pierce.

She shook her head, this time slowly, but the effort still sent another surge of pain rocketing up her neck and throughout her skull. She winced. "Just an explosion. And fire. Everything was burning."

A perplexed look crossed the faces of each of the physicians. "There was no explosion or fire," said Doctor Gallagher. "You were hit by a taxi."

No! How could her only memories not exist? She felt the walls closing in around her. She closed her eyes again. *This is all a dream. When I open my eyes, I'll know who I am.*

In the background she heard the doctors conferring. Or speaking to her. She wasn't sure. She couldn't focus on their voices. Her fear held too tight a grip on her. "I...I remember a man," she said, wondering if he, too, was a figment of her imagination. "He was here. In the room."

"Mr. Caldwell?"

Mr. Caldwell. The name didn't help her recall anything, but at least one of her three memories was real. She forced her eyes open. Nothing had changed. "Please," she said, "who am I?"

* * *

Trent listened in confused silence as Doctor Gallagher explained the unexpected complication. "She remembers nothing at all?"

"It's not that unusual after head trauma for a patient to suffer retrograde amnesia," he said, "but our patient has lost both short-term and long-term memory. That's a bit more unusual; however, it should only last a few hours."

"Should?"

"In rare instances the memory loss is permanent. As you can imagine, the patient is quite distraught right now. She needs a supportive, secure environment among family and friends. This alone often leads to spontaneous recovery of missing memories. Unfortunately, as you know, no one has come forward to claim our Jane Doe."

Trent was as perplexed by this as were the police and the hospital staff. The woman certainly hadn't appeared to be a street person or runaway. Surely, someone must miss her.

"There's one other problem," said Doctor Gallagher. He shuffled his feet and avoided eye contact with Trent. He clicked his pen open and closed several times and shifted the clipboard from one arm to the other.

Trent cleared his throat.

"It's the matter of insurance," said the doctor, still not meeting Trent's gaze.

Of course. It always boils down to money. Trent regarded the physician with a look that he hoped conveyed his disgust. "Bill me for her care," he said. "We'll straighten everything out once she regains her memory." Without another word he strode down the hall to the woman's room.

When he entered the room, he found her sleeping. He stood over the bed and gazed down at her, a shattered body lost within a sea of white. White sheets. White casts. White bandages. Only the blue-black flesh that rimmed her eyes and a few short wisps of golden strawberry blonde hair peeking out from under the gauze broke the starkness.

Trent watched the steady rhythm of her chest rising and falling as she breathed. His eyes followed the path of a plastic tube that snaked its way from under the sheet and up the IV pole to a clear plastic bag. Every few seconds, like clockwork, a bead of fluid escaped the confines of the pouch and journeyed down the conduit toward her.

He had caused this. His blind ambition, his only escape from the pain of his past, had wreaked this devastation on an innocent human being. There were no words to express his remorse, no apology that could make up for the broken bones, the torn flesh. No magic to give her back her identity.

I wish I could trade places with you. What I wouldn't give to rid myself of the horror of my memories! But even as he silently spoke the words, he knew they weren't true. His memories were both his salvation and his damnation. They were all he had left of a life and a love that once was.

Not knowing what he would say to her should she awaken, he slipped out of the room.

* * *

She opened her eyes in time to see the door close behind him.

ELEVEN

Over the course of the next two weeks, she slowly regained her strength but not her memory. As her wounds healed, her physical pain receded, but her psychic pain increased steadily. Like the hospital staff and the police, she couldn't understand why no one missed her. The idea of being totally alone in an unfamiliar world terrified her. What would she do? Where would she go if the amnesia persisted?

The visions of an explosion and fire continued to plague her during the day. Frightening nightmares disrupted her sleep. Doctor Pierce took her through sessions of therapy where she employed various memory retrieval techniques, but whether the psychiatrist tried hypnosis or drug-facilitated interviews, the attempts proved futile. The emotional pain the images wrought created a barrier too steep to scale.

She agonized over the surgery that had recently repaired her face. Although various staff had assured her Dr. Cataldi was the best reconstructive surgeon in the city, he couldn't possibly know exactly what she had looked like before the accident.

She gingerly touched her healing face, remembering their conversation as he explained the procedure. "Grafts?" The word had terrified her.

"Some of your facial bones were shattered beyond repair," he had said. "I have to reconstruct areas of your cheeks and nose with a piece of bone I'll remove from your skull."

"I won't look the same. No one will recognize me."

"I won't kid you. Without photos to work from I can't possibly reconstruct your face exactly, but I can come damn close. The X-rays we took when you were first admitted will give me clues to work from, but you have to prepare yourself for some subtle differences in facial proportions and relationships."

Subtle differences. She hadn't liked the sound of that. "Subtle is a very ambiguous word," she said.

"I promise any changes will make you even prettier. "Eight, ten weeks from now, when you're completely healed, you'll be praising these gifted hands." He had wiggled his fingers in front of her face and chuckled.

She hadn't seen the humor in his words.

And then there was the subject of her hair, shoulder-length except for the large, shaved patch from the surgery. Several times a day one well-meaning nurse or another offered her a haircut, but she stubbornly declined. She had no idea why. She looked like a freak.

Balancing awkwardly on one crutch, she stared at her reflection in the mirror over the bathroom sink, studying the healing skin, wondering how different her new face looked from her old one. Were her cheekbones always this high? Her nose so pert? *Mirror, mirror on the wall*....Her lips, still slightly swollen, pursed in frustration. How could she remember the words of a fairy tale but not people or events? Not her distant or near past? Not herself?

She grabbed a handful of hair and twirled it around her fingers. For some reason the act brought her comfort. She watched herself run her fingers through the thick strands and realized how ridiculous she looked—like some refugee of a punk rock concert. *Oh, hell!*

An hour later when Mrs. Thompson came to take her vitals, she asked the nurse to even out her hair.

* * *

Trent deliberately avoided confronting her. His guilt overpowered and crippled him. However, something stronger tugged at him, and he occasionally found himself drawn to her hospital room in the middle of the night. He sat for hours watching her sleep, always slipping out before she woke.

Each day he consulted with the doctors, keeping himself apprised of her progress. When she had healed enough to be released, he was confronted with a new dilemma.

"She'll have the casts on for another few weeks," explained Dr. Gallagher, "but we can't justify keeping her here any longer. We need the bed space."

"Where will she go?"

"We can place her in a rehab center, but personally I think she'd do better in a less confined setting. Doctor Pierce feels she needs stimulation to trigger those lost memories."

As far as Trent was concerned, the woman was his responsibility, at least for the near future. He couldn't let her vegetate in a convalescent home with elderly stroke victims as her only companions. No. There was only one solution.

"Unacceptable," he said. "She'll stay with me. My housekeeper will care for her."

There was a long pause at the other end of the phone line. "What if she doesn't agree?" asked the doctor. "After all, Mr. Caldwell, she doesn't know you, and she's frightened enough as it is."

Trent was unused to having his decisions questioned. "She has no alternative. Your job is to make her see that." He ended the call before the doctor could argue.

* * *

She couldn't believe what she was hearing. "You want me to move in with a man I don't know?"

"That was Mr. Caldwell's proposal," said Dr. Gallagher. "I suggested a rehab facility. At least until we remove your casts."

"Then what?"

"Hopefully, by then you'll have regained your memory."

"And if I don't?"

He averted his eyes, his silence an answer in itself.

I'm a problem he wants to get rid of. She considered the alternatives. Neither sat well with her, but she didn't see that she had much choice. "Who is this Mr. Caldwell? I know you told me he was a passenger in the cab that struck me, but I don't understand why he feels responsible for my care."

"Mr. Caldwell is a man used to giving orders and not having to explain himself to anyone. I can't tell you why he feels you're his responsibility, just that he does."

She pondered on this for a moment. "I would be safe with him?"

"He's a very well-respected member of the community and quite famous. If not for the amnesia, you'd recognize his name. This is New York City, and in the Big Apple Trent Caldwell owns everything Donald Trump doesn't own."

The other name meant as little to her as Trent Caldwell's had. But if the man were wealthy enough to own a good chunk of Manhattan, maybe he feared a lawsuit from her. Was that why he was being so nice? Because he thought she'd sue him? *He* wasn't driving the cab that struck her. *She* certainly didn't blame him for her injuries. Still, she had to stay somewhere, and she wasn't very excited about the prospect of another hospital-type environment.

Uncertainty plagued her. She had no past experiences to call upon for assistance. For hours at a time, she searched her blank mind trying to find some hidden threads of the past to help her come to a decision. What would the *other she*, as she began to refer to her hidden self, do?

Female members of the hospital staff were unanimous in their opinion. Mrs. Thompson summed the consensus up best. "Angel," she said, "if Trent Caldwell asked me to move in with him, I'd think I'd died and gone to Heaven!"

"Why?"

"Damn, girl! He's just the most bodacious hunk of eligible bachelor this side of yesterday."

Her fingers automatically reached for a nonexistent hank of hair. A pang of regret surged through her. Her hand fluttered indecisively in midair, then dropped to her lap. "And what if I'm already married?"

"Angel, baby, if you're married, that husband of yours better have one damned fine reason for not looking for you, or I'll tan his hide but good when he finally does show up!"

And so, with a great deal of trepidation, she agreed to move into Trent Caldwell's penthouse apartment.

* * *

"You should be fetchin' her, not me," said Mrs. Kearn. She slammed a platter of eggs on the table in front of Trent.

He scowled at his breakfast, then shoved the plate aside. Accepting responsibility for the woman's care was one thing, facing her was quite another. He stared up at his housekeeper. Standing feet apart, arms crossed over her ample bosom, she challenged him. He wasn't in the mood to battle with her. "Will you at least come with me?"

"Of course," she said, pushing his breakfast back in front of him.

* * *

She sat in a chair by the window, her plaster-encased leg stretched out before her. Mrs. Thompson and the other nurses had chipped in to buy her a going-away present—a pair of loose-fitting cotton lounging pajamas with an elastic waist and front buttoned top in a pale pink, lavender and white windowpane check pattern.

When she'd hesitated to accept the gift, Mrs. Thompson had tossed her hands onto her hips and said, "Well, you certainly don't expect us to release you to Trent Caldwell in nothing more than a backside-exposing hospital gown, now do you?"

"What about the clothes I was wearing the day of the accident?"

Mrs. Thompson had rolled her eyes. "That bloody mess? Cut into shreds in the emergency room. Besides, even if we'd been able to salvage them, no way they'd fit over those casts."

Glancing up at the wall-mounted clock, she heaved a sigh. Part of her chafed at the slow progression of time. Another part of her hoped ten o'clock would never come.

Once again, she forgot and reached for a lock of hair, regretting her decision to allow Mrs. Thompson to cut her hair so short. She had an uncontrollable urge to wrap herself up in it. A security blanket of hair. How ridiculous! Her shoulder-length tresses hadn't been nearly long enough to accomplish such a feat. And now they were gone, replaced by a helmet of diminutive springy curls.

"Lordy, angel!" cried Mrs. Thompson handing her a mirror after the haircut. "If you aren't a curly headed beauty!"

"I look so different!" What had she done? Her fingertips patted the bouncy curls, her hand pausing over the stubbly shaved patch.

"That'll grow in soon enough," the nurse had assured her.

But it was the overall transformation that forced a shudder to run up her spine, not the bald spot. How could a haircut create such a total change in her appearance? Would anyone recognize her? Not that anyone seemed to care.

Nearly three weeks had passed without a single inquiry over the disappearance of anyone remotely fitting her description. As the days spilled into one another, she lost all hope, finally accepting that her memory was gone forever. She was adrift in a world without connection to any other living being.

At the sound of the door opening, her melancholy shifted to anxiety. Mrs. Thompson, pushing an empty wheelchair in front of her, bustled into the room. "Time to go, angel," said the nurse. "The prince himself is here to escort you back to his castle."

She cringed at the sight of the man entering the room in time to catch Mrs. Thompson's remark. A look of extreme irritation crossed his face. He cleared his throat.

"Mr. Caldwell! I...I didn't mean...I mean, I'm—"

"Leave us."

With words of apology continuing to trip over themselves, Mrs. Thompson scurried from the room.

"I'm sorry," he muttered after the door whooshed closed behind the nurse.

She studied him for the first time in the light of day. Trent Caldwell could have stepped out of the pages of a fashion magazine, the kind that always featured brooding male models. Bad boy type-A personalities.

He wore a navy suit that fit him so perfectly, she thought it must have been stitched directly onto his body. His shirt was as white and crisp as the hospital linens on her bed, his tie a conservative solid several shades lighter than his suit. A matching silk handkerchief formed an exact triangular peak above his breast pocket.

When her gaze reached his face, an unsettling flutter invaded her body. Although the muscles of his jaw were pulled tight and his mouth formed a taut line across his face, in his eyes, which she remembered having thought soulless, she saw remorse and uncertainty.

From her conversations with some of the more gossipy nurses, she had formed an impression of a man both controlled and controlling. At this moment, though, Trent Caldwell appeared to be neither. Beyond the multicolored flecks of gold, green, and brown that colored his eyes, she saw a man as unsure of himself as she was of herself.

"Mrs. Kearn will be taking care of you," he said.

Before she had a chance to ask who Mrs. Kearn was, he exited the room.

* * *

The ride to Mr. Caldwell's apartment was blessedly brief. He sat in front with the chauffeur, allowing her to stretch out across the back seat. Mrs. Kearn, whom she learned was his housekeeper, occupied a jump seat diagonally opposite her. Mrs. Kearn was as pleasant as her employer was enigmatic. She reminded her of Santa's missus, round and jovial, only instead of wearing red velvet trimmed with white fur, Mrs. Kearn wore a calico shirtwaist trimmed with lace at the collar. And instead of snowy white hair, Mrs. Kearn's hair was a combination of faded ginger and several shades of gray.

Throughout the short drive, Mrs. Kearn maintained a friendly chatter, her Irish brogue causing her words to sing. Several times she admonished her employer for his stony silence.

"You talk enough for both of us," he muttered.

"Humph! I suppose 'tis my own fault," she said, shaking her head. "I failed to teach you proper manners when you were a lad. Now 'tis too late. You're far too big to take a switch to and too pigheaded to learn on your own!"

He twisted around. She braced herself for the harsh words she expected him to hurl at the woman, but his eyes held only acceptance and love. He planted an affectionate kiss on the top of the housekeeper's head.

"You had your chance," he said.

She was intrigued by the dynamics between the two of them. Glancing up into the rearview mirror, she glimpsed the chauffeur attempting to stifle a chuckle. Apparently, she was not the only one who found the relationship curious.

"So is it to be Angel?"

Mrs. Kearn was staring at her.

"I'm sorry?"

"Your name, dear. We need to be callin' you somethin', now, don't we?"

"I suppose."

"I heard one of the nurses call you Angel."

"Mrs. Thompson. She calls everyone angel. At least everyone she likes."

"And what might she be callin' them she doesn't like?"

She felt a flush of heat wash over her face and neck. Mrs. Thompson's style was to call 'em like she saw 'em, and no one—from the chief of surgery on down to the guy who mopped the floors—seemed immune to her behind-the-back barbs. Opting for a diplomatic way out, she answered, "Depended on her mood and the person in question."

The housekeeper chuckled, reached across, and patted her hand. "Never mind, lass. Can't be too many angels. Don't you agree, Mr. Trent?"

"Whatever you say, Mrs. K."

Deep in thought, Trent was only half-listening to Mrs. Kearn's nonstop patter. The closer the limousine came to his Park Avenue address, the more he second-guessed his decision to provide shelter for the woman—Angel. He'd have to start referring to her as such.

Once Moira Kearn set her mind to something, a nuclear explosion couldn't sway her off course. She'd better not expect them to be one big happy family taking their evening meal together. No. He'd have to set some ground rules. Fast.

Given the opportunity, Mrs. K. would orchestrate his life. Not that she didn't do that to some extent already. But that was as much his fault as anyone's. Besides, they had developed a rather unique symbiotic relationship over the past few years, feeding on each other's pain and misery. Or was it more a parasitic relationship? Sometimes, he wasn't quite sure.

The woman—Angel—would take her meals in one of the spare bedrooms. Once her casts were removed, if her memory still hadn't returned, he'd have Mrs. K. escort her around the city, flooding her with sights and sounds. Until then he'd provide her with an endless supply of books and DVDs. Given that amount of stimuli, something was bound to unlock her mind. Then she could go back to her life and he to his. Such as it was.

TWELVE

Once again, the nightmare woke her. Angel lay in the darkened room waiting for her heart to cease pounding. She inhaled deep calming breaths, releasing each lungful of air to a measured count of ten. She should be used to the nightly onslaught by now. The pattern never altered. The nightmare remained the same—the explosion, the ensuing fire, the helplessness and terror that consumed her.

But there was no explosion. No fire. According to everyone involved in her care, her injuries were the result of being hit by a speeding cab. So what caused these nightly forays into hell? The nightmares had to have some connection to her past, to who she was, or why else would they plague her?

Her hand reached for a nonexistent mane of hair, faltering midway. In frustration she twisted a short curl around her index finger. Emptiness consumed her.

Who am I?

Slowly her eyes adjusted to the dim light cast by a harvest moon, its amber glow filtering through delicate ivory colored Irish lace curtains. Juxtaposed against the conflicts churning within her, the setting seemed more mocking than peaceful, like the opening frames of a period piece that would quickly morph into a horror flick. *Room With A View* meets *Texas Chainsaw Massacre.*

She wondered how she could remember movie titles but not anything about herself or someone as famous as Trent Caldwell or the other New York tycoon the doctor had mentioned. Was she the kind of person who watched historical dramas or the kind who got her kicks watching blood and gorefests? Squeezing her eyes shut, she tried to remember the plots of both movies but drew a blank. Maybe she'd never seen either. If so, how in the world did she remember their titles?

Each night since arriving at Trent Caldwell's apartment she'd fallen asleep by the lights of a city that never slept and the few stars visible in a sky that was never completely dark. She didn't want the nightscape shuttered from view by the room darkening shades housed behind the flimsy curtains. The city was one of her few familiar images. And if that were the case, she must live somewhere out there in one of those buildings. So why in hell wasn't anyone looking for her? Surely, she had friends, neighbors, coworkers, if not family. Everyone had someone. Except her, it seemed.

Her daily therapy sessions with Dr. Pierce were proving futile. She refused to believe the psychiatrist's latest hypothesis—that due to some previous trauma, Angel was deliberately repressing her memory. According to Dr. Pierce's theory, she didn't remember her past because subconsciously she didn't want to remember it. The doctor cited several scenarios which might have triggered such a reaction. They covered a wide spectrum—from the sudden death of a loved one to witnessing or being the victim of a violent crime.

The supposition had merit when analyzed in a logical fashion, especially when Dr. Pierce reminded her that she was found without any identification on her. But every fiber within her rejected the psychiatrist's theories. She may not know who she was, but she was certain she wasn't the kind of person who ran away from her problems.

At least she hoped she wasn't.

As she had on the three previous nights since arriving, Angel turned her attention to the furnishings of the guest room. Someone had taken great pains to create a warm, inviting environment. A decidedly feminine one. The walls were papered in a delicate floral print of peach, lemon, and mint against an eggshell white background. The carpet repeated the cool green but several shades deeper. The furniture was a honey-colored country French style with white accents. A grouping of landscape photographs and dried floral wreaths covered one wall. She wondered who had decorated the room and who normally occupied it.

Her gaze drifted back to the framed photos. In the dim moonlight-washed room they were no more than a collection of freeform light and dark shapes trapped within rectangular confines. Yet there was something familiar about them. Drawn to the images since arriving, she found herself spending hours at a time pondering the tranquil country settings. She found them at once both settling and unsettling.

Studying the scenes filled her with a sense of peace but at the same time triggered a barrage of questions. She knew with growing certainty that she'd seen those photographs at another time. In another place. But when? Where? If she could unlock the mystery surrounding the photographs, maybe she could unlock her memories.

On schedule the notes filtered into the room, breaking into her morose musings. Plaintive sounds, coaxed from a saxophone, drifted through the air. Like the autumn leaves outside her window, they clung in desperation before their inevitable descent. Always the same melody. Sad sounds that caused her throat to constrict and tears to trickle from the corners of her eyes.

Was she the kind of person who cried over sentimental Hallmark greeting cards and made-for-TV Lifetime chick flicks? Her reaction to the music seemed to suggest so. Or maybe she was just feeling sorry for herself, and the music offered an appropriate soundtrack to her state of mind.

She glanced over at the clock on the nightstand. Two in the morning. Somewhere nearby someone else couldn't sleep. Someone whose music spoke of crushed hopes and shattered dreams.

The melancholy strains of the saxophone and Dr. Pierce's words waltzed together in her mind—first one leading, then the other. Was the psychiatrist correct? Had her mind found a way to escape a pain too great to confront?

And if so, what then? What if she never regained her memory? That thought kept her awake for the remainder of the night, which was both a blessing and a curse. When morning came, she was dog-tired, but at least she hadn't suffered through yet another fiery nightmare.

* * *

The days drifted into a week, during which Angel saw Trent

Caldwell only occasionally and always briefly. He appeared uncomfortable in her presence, standing in the doorway, reluctant to enter her room. The conversation never varied. "How are you feeling today, Angel?"

"Somewhat stronger. The pain is lessening."

"Good. And your memory? Any progress there?"

She shook her head. "Nothing. Sorry."

He grimaced and muttered something under his breath she couldn't make out. Then he left.

Day after day, the pattern never varied.

She kept to her assigned room. Since her broken arm precluded the proper use of crutches, balance became a difficult feat to master. Walking even a short distance proved laborious. Besides, she hadn't actually been invited to wander through the rest of the apartment.

Occasionally Mrs. Kearn helped her to the kitchen table where she kept the housekeeper company as she prepared a meal. The kitchen was Mrs. Kearn's kingdom, and what a kingdom she controlled—state of the art stainless steel appliances including two dishwashers, a recessed refrigerator large enough to hold food to feed a regiment, and a six-burner stove that would set a Cordon Blue chef drooling. Black granite countertops covered white bead board cabinets. Copper pots hung in a rack above a large matching island. At the far end of the island and near the refrigerator, a honeyed wood rustic table with four matching ladder-back chairs sat in front of a bank of windows that overlooked Park Avenue.

Most of the time, though, Mrs. Kearn joined her in the floral bedroom, talking a blue streak about everything from pop culture to current events—everything and anything that might jar Angel's memory.

"The mind 'tis like a poorly stitched seam," said Mrs. Kearn. "All we need do is find that one loose thread and give it a good tug."

"Either you've been talking to Dr. Pierce or that's an old Irish proverb," said Angel.

The housekeeper's eyes twinkled, her smile deepening the roadwork of wrinkles that crisscrossed her face, but she said nothing.

Normally Mrs. Kearn kept the door to Angel's room open, but occasionally she would close it without a word of explanation. Each time Angel could hear that Trent Caldwell had returned to the apartment and brought someone with him. Always the same woman. Although she couldn't make out their words, the two were often engaged in heated dialogue.

She wondered if this was the woman responsible for the decor in her room. Who was she? A lover? She couldn't be his wife. She remembered Mrs. Thompson mentioning Trent was a bachelor. But maybe the nurse had been mistaken. Perhaps she was an estranged wife, one for whom he still had feelings. Was this why her host acted so distant? Was it *his* sorrowful music she heard at night?

Later that afternoon the scene once again repeated itself. From the other side of the door Angel heard the muffled voices. Trent. And the woman. Their words grew angrier. Loud enough this time for Angel to make them out. Then she heard Mrs. Kearn joining in.

The woman shrieked at Trent's housekeeper, the words spewing forth high-pitched and shrill. Her nasal accent reminded Angel of fingernails scraping across a blackboard. "How dare you speak to me in that tone! Trent, do something!"

Angel couldn't hear Trent's reply, but apparently, he had no intention of yielding to the woman's demands—whatever they were.

"You're so busy living in the past, you don't even realize you're being conned! For God's sake, Trent! She's not your responsibility! She's using you!"

Trent's muted reply was followed by the slamming of a door. Angel heard him and Mrs. Kearn speaking in subdued tones for several minutes before she heard another door slam. A short time later the housekeeper opened her door.

"They were fighting about me, weren't they?"

Mrs. Kearn shook her head. Anger filled her eyes, replacing the friendly sparkle that usually greeted Angel. "'Tis an ongoin' battle between them two, Angel. They're oil and water. Never will mix. Someday he'll realize he doesn't need her, brains or no brains. Don't pay it no mind."

But Angel did mind. A lot.

THIRTEEN

They hadn't factored Trent Caldwell into their plans. How the hell could they have known? Roger pounded his fist on the bar, rattling the Baccarat. *Damn the man!* Leave it to the greedy bastard to sneak in while their guard was down and steal nearly half the company. As if he didn't already own a sizable chunk of the free world!

He gulped down a full tumbler of Scotch, then poured another. His fourth in less than an hour. The last thing he and Whitney had anticipated was Trent Caldwell as a partner, albeit a junior one. If the man started snooping, Roger could find himself up shit's creek. Without a paddle and drowning in rapids. No fucking way he was doing time over anything that had gone down. Not now or ever.

The only solution, however distasteful, was to suck up to the bastard. Become bosom buddies. Not give him any reason to suspect a fucking thing. Once again, his fist made contact with the highly polished marble.

"Enough, Roger!" Whitney rose from the sofa and crossed the room. She lifted the tumbler from his hand and drained it. "At least he can't execute a hostile takeover. No matter what he does, we still own fifty-one percent of the company."

Roger gave her a withering look. Fucking was Whitney's strong suit, not business. A thought crossed his mind, but he dismissed it as quickly as it had come. He didn't think even Whitney was a great enough thespian to trap the likes of Trent Caldwell.

Besides, he'd heard too many rumors about the man. Carried his wife's ghost around in his breast pocket, they said. Abel had been easy for Whitney to snare—a lonely old man unable to live without the love of a woman. Not Caldwell. Not from the rumors Roger had heard.

"He can make life a living hell for us," he said. "Until we get down on hands and knees, begging him to buy us out. The man's too cunning. Too devious. Ruthless. When he wants something, he stops at nothing until he owns it. Lock, stock, and goddamn fucking barrel."

"So we have to be more cunning. More devious. More ruthless."

"Exactly."

"And just how do we outfox the fox, Roger?"

He stared at her sexy body, her luscious pouting lips and wished it were that simple this time. "Damned if I know."

* * *

The memory of Trent's fight with the mysterious woman gnawed at Angel. She tossed and turned for hours that night, not an easy task given the two cumbersome chunks of plaster encasing her arm and leg. Damn, she couldn't wait to be rid of the hot, heavy casts. She'd give anything—if she had anything to give—to soak in a steamy tub. Shave her itchy legs and underarms. Dress herself.

She stared out the window and thought a great deal about fate, realizing that in some ways she had been quite lucky, broken bones and amnesia notwithstanding. She shouldn't complain. If not for some cosmic quirk of the universe and how she landed, she might be staring at life in a wheelchair. Or worse.

Except for the part of her brain that controlled her memories, her mind was still fully functional. She could think and reason and communicate. Once the casts were removed, she'd have her mobility back. Yes, it could have been a hell of a lot worse. Vegetable-like worse. A rutabaga in a bed, rotting away for decades and decades. And with no next of kin to step up and pull the plug for her.

She chuckled. *Whoever you really are, Angel, you have one hell of a sense of humor.* But facts were facts. Where would she be today had someone other than Trent Caldwell been in that cab?

Whether the mystery woman was girlfriend or estranged wife, she couldn't repay his kindness by causing an even deeper rift between them. It didn't matter whether their love affair was on the skids or their marriage dissolving—no matter what Mrs. Kearn thought of the relationship.

Angel stared at the luminous numbers on the bedside clock radio. Ten past midnight. She'd heard Mrs. Kearn retire earlier. She imagined Trent had done the same. Within the apartment all she heard were the eerie sounds of night—the spooky creak of a floorboard, the ghostly rattle of a pipe.

She reached over and flicked on the table lamp. With considerable difficulty she managed to first shrug into the robe that lay at the foot of her bed, then retrieve her crutch. Anchoring the support under her good arm and keeping her weight off her broken leg, she hobbled slowly and cautiously down the hall toward the kitchen.

Her next task proved even more challenging. While balancing on her good leg, she propped the crutch against the kitchen counter and reached into the overhead cabinet for a mug. Then she opened the refrigerator and withdrew a carton of milk.

So far so good. *And now for my next trick*....But with success came overconfidence. Or maybe she was just tired. Either way, the carton slipped from her hand and hit the edge of the granite countertop. The lid popped off. Milk splashed across the counter and onto the floor. As Angel lurched for the sponge near the sink, she knocked over first the mug, then her crutch. Both landed on the floor—the crutch with a loud thud, the mug with an even louder crash. Shards of porcelain flew across the terra cotta tiles.

Shit! Angel hopped over to the kitchen table and sank into a chair. She stared at the milk that continued its steady drip-drip-drip off the countertop, splashing into the spreading white puddle on the floor. Damn it! If she couldn't manage warming a mug of milk in the microwave, how would she ever clean up this mess?

"You should have asked Mrs. Kearn to do that for you. That's what the portable intercom is for."

She jumped at the sound of his voice. He stood in the doorway. Dressed in tight fitting, worn black jeans and a white T-shirt. A shock of hair had fallen across his forehead. Dark stubble covered his cheeks and chin and upper lip. She'd never seen him so casual. And so incredibly sexy looking.

The thought nearly smacked the air from her lungs. She had no right to think such things. Not about him.

Flustered, she tried to wrap her mind around what he'd just said. Something about the intercom. A baby monitor sat on her nightstand. She'd thought it odd that a bachelor would have such a device, but he'd probably instructed Mrs. Kearn to purchase one prior to Angel moving from the hospital to his apartment.

She tripped over her words. "I. ..I'm sorry. It's late. Mrs. Kearn has already gone to bed. I didn't want to disturb her."

"Mrs. Kearn is paid quite well to be disturbed."

Angel sensed the annoyance behind his measured words. She didn't want to see it in his face, as well, so she concentrated on the puddle at her feet. Rivulets of milk branched out along the grout channels. "I didn't think I'd have a problem. If you hand me a sponge and help me to the floor, I'll clean the mess up."

"You'll stay right where you are. One damn fool stunt tonight is more than enough."

She winced at his words and fought back tears as she watched him first soak up the milk with a dish towel, then sweep the broken mug into a dustpan.

He pulled open the cabinet beneath the sink and dumping the remains of the mug into the waste basket. "Did you have another nightmare?"

Angel gasped. "Who told you about my nightmares?" What ever happened to doctor/patient confidentiality? Or didn't her sessions with Dr. Pierce apply, given that Trent Caldwell was footing her bills? Was he receiving weekly updates from the shrink?

"You had them in the hospital."

Someone watching her, staring at her from the shadows. She'd attributed the disturbing sensations to her medication and disorientation from the trauma. But there had been someone in the hospital. Someone watching her. "You were there, weren't you? At night?"

"Sometimes. I was concerned."

"I'm sorry I'm causing you so much trouble."

* * *

Angel's words caught him off guard. Turning his back on her, Trent stowed the dustpan and brush in the utility closet, buying himself a moment to gather his thoughts. Damn. She'd sure as hell thrown him for a loop. What the fuck was she apologizing for? *He* was responsible for *her* injuries. None of what had happened was her fault. Only his. All his.

"You have nothing to apologize for." He stood and leaned back against the counter, crossing his ankles and his arms. She refused to look at him. Apparently, her clasped hands, half buried in the folds of the pink chenille robe covering her lap, held more appeal.

Then it hit him. Like an anvil dropped onto his thick skull. *She's scared to death of me.*

The realization heaped another huge dose of guilt onto him. He stared at her as she avoided making eye contact with him. She reminded him of the wounded, frightened outcasts Caitlin had felt compelled to help. Battered women who blamed themselves instead of the bastards who'd beaten half the life and all the hope out of them. Was that her story? Was she escaping an abusive husband or lover when their lives literally collided?

"I'm causing problems for you," she said.

"Like hell! Where'd you get such a ridiculous idea?"

"I've heard you arguing about me. With your...wife?"

"My what?!"

"I didn't mean to eavesdrop. Mrs. Kearn always closes the door, but you were all so loud today. I couldn't help but overhear. I'm not faking. I really can't remember who I am. I'd give anything to know. You have to believe me! Please! I can't repay your kindness by causing more of a rift between the two of you."

She finally raised her head and looked at him. "I think maybe it would be best for all of us if I went to that rehab facility."

Trent wasn't often at a loss for words, but he sure as hell was at the moment. He pulled out the chair next to her and sat down. Damn. Where'd she get the idea that Felicia was his wife? He placed his palm on her upper arm. Big mistake. She flinched and shrank even farther into her chair, her gaze focused back on her lap. Trent withdrew his hand. "Angel, look at me."

Her good hand reached for a curl of hair and twisted it around her finger. Like some sort of security blanket. He'd seen the nervous habit countless times over the last few weeks. Maybe he should add that particular quirk to the news bulletin circulating about her. If her face was so changed by the accident and subsequent surgery that no one recognized her, maybe the hair twisting would cause someone to claim her.

"Please, Angel."

She raised her head, but instead of looking at him, her eyes focused on something over his right shoulder.

"The woman you heard is *not* my wife. She's an employee. A very opinionated and often difficult employee. One I don't even like very much."

Angel stopped fidgeting with her hair and finally looked at him. "Why would you employ someone you don't like?"

"Because Felicia Sutton has the most brilliant financial mind of anyone I've ever met. I put up with her and pay her very well to keep my competitors from luring her away."

"She thinks I'm some sort of con artist."

"I don't care what Felicia thinks, and I certainly don't want you worrying over what she thinks. I believe you, and so does Mrs. Kearn. That's all that matters. That and getting your memory back."

Angel exhaled a deep sigh. "I'm trying. It's just so damn frustrating. Nothing seems to help."

She explained Dr. Pierce's newest theory to him.

"Do you think that's possible?"

"I don't know what to believe any more. She's the doctor. I suppose her theory makes sense."

"But you think she's wrong."

"At first. Now I'm having my doubts. I don't want to find out I've been abused or committed some awful crime, but maybe the truth is so god-awful that my mind is deliberately keeping me from remembering."

"You just need more time to heal." Trent rose from his seat and extended his hand toward her. "And rest. I'll help you back to your room. It's late."

Instead of guiding her down the hall, he surprised both of them by lifting her into his arms. Big mistake. What the hell was he doing? He marched toward her room, avoiding eye contact with her, but the damage was done. He quickly reined in the adulterous sensations seizing control of him. He would not, could not succumb to such lunacy. In his heart he was still married to Caitlin. Always. Forever.

He entered Angel's room and lowered her onto the bed. Without another word he headed for the door. He needed to get the hell out of there. Douse himself with cold water. But he stopped short at the doorway. He was behaving like an ass. Again. "Please, no further talk of leaving. Not until you're well."

"I only thought it would be best for both of us."

He turned to face her. "For neither of us. You shouldn't be locked away with the sick and elderly."

"And you?"

"Mrs. Kearn would have my head on a platter if I let you leave before you've recovered completely."

Angel smiled. "She's very nice. I like her."

"She feels the same about you." He took several steps back toward the bed. "You're good therapy for her. She needs a project like you to take her mind off her grief."

"Her grief?"

Trent hesitated. He should leave. Instead, he sank into the chair near her bed. He stared out the window at the darkened city and spoke to the moon. "Mrs. Kearn lost her family in a plane crash a few years ago. She's had a hard time dealing with it."

"I didn't know."

"No. It's not something she would have told you." He rose to leave.

"Mr. Caldwell?"

"Hmm?"

Angel pointed in the directions of the photographs. "Do you know where those photos were taken?"

He didn't want to look. He knew the photos. Knew each flower, each blade of grass. Even if he hadn't glanced at them in nearly three years. He didn't want to see them now. Didn't want to be reminded of that place. That time. Those memories. Because when he looked at those photographs, he saw not what was there but what was missing. Caitlin.

"Saint Marie. It's a tiny village in Provence."

"France?"

He nodded. His back to the wall of pictures, he watched as she focused her attention on the photos. "Angel?"

She chewed on her bottom lip. "I don't know. Something about them keeps nipping at the edges of my mind. I think I know that place."

Trent reached behind his back and rubbed at the knot growing between his shoulder blades, the one that always appeared when he thought of the past. He could feel the scowl lines deepening along his jaw and the ridge forming between his brows. "Perhaps they remind you of another place, or you saw the photos when they were first published several years ago. Saint Marie is no more than a mote of dust on the French landscape. It's highly unlikely you were ever there."

"Did you take them?"

"No. They're the work of a well-known photographer. Sarah Montgomery."

"She's very talented."

"Yes, she was."

"Was?"

"She died in a car crash recently. Ironically, the same day as your accident."

Angel visibly shuddered. She looked so helpless, so defeated. In one hasty command to a cabby he'd shattered her life in much the same way he'd once devastated his own. "What is it?"

"So many accidents. Mine. Mrs. Kearn's family. Sarah Montgomery. So much tragedy."

More than you know, thought Trent. Unable to control his mutinous body, his gaze strayed to the wall of photos. The bitterness welled up inside him.

* * *

Her encounter with Trent Caldwell left Angel more confused than ever. She needed to focus on regaining her memory. A blindsided attack by wayward hormones only complicated an already difficult situation. Yet she found it impossible to deny her body's response to his touch. And harder still to forget the look in his eyes before he deliberately looked away. Whatever had passed between them in that brief moment, Angel was convinced that he'd felt it, too—and found it equally unnerving.

Moonlight filtered in through the lace curtains and danced across the French landscapes. Angel had sensed a growing level of discomfort in him when she questioned him about those photos. His refusal to look at them hadn't escaped her notice. Neither had the catch in his voice or his near-reluctance to speak about them.

A mote of dust on the landscape of France. He spoke as though he knew the place intimately. Perhaps with the photographer? If Sarah Montgomery and Trent Caldwell shared a history, had once been lovers, it would certainly explain his reaction.

So what? You're losing sight of the real problem, Angel. Trent Caldwell's past was none of her concern. *Forget the hormones! Forget the man!* She needed to concentrate on discovering her own past, not clogging her brain with useless speculation over someone else's life.

Pulling the quilt up to her chin, she forced all other thoughts from her mind and focused her attention on the framed scenes. Why had these particular photos triggered a glimmer of memory within her? They *had* to be a clue—the only tangible one she sensed so far, other than a nightmarish recurring dream that might or might not be real. Perhaps, if she stared at the photos long enough....

* * *

Several hours later rocketing flames and deafening explosions again jarred Angel out of a deep sleep. Her limbs quivering, her body bathed in sweat, she opened her eyes and searched for the photos in the darkened room, needing the serene settings to quell the fear that had seized her.

The nightmare had changed. Had grown far more sinister. Now she heard screams forcing their way beyond the blistering inferno and earsplitting blasts. Cries for help. And they were calling for her. Yet not her because the name never reached her ears, never offered a clue to her identity.

In the distance melancholy saxophone chords fought to drown out the memory of the nightmare. Angel drew air into her lungs and sank back against the pillows. She didn't need to glance at the clock. She knew the time. And now she was certain she also knew the musician's identity.

FOURTEEN

After her encounter with Trent Caldwell, Angel's connection to the Saint Marie photos grew more intense.

"The moment I saw them, they seemed familiar," she told Dr. Pierce at her therapy session the next day. "And the feeling only grows stronger each time I view them, but it's such a remote, out-of-the-way place that it hardly seems possible." She shrugged her shoulders and sighed. "Mr. Caldwell suggested I may have seen the photos when they were published in a magazine several years ago. Maybe he's right."

"You don't sound convinced," said the doctor.

Angel shook her head. "I felt something inside." She pressed her fingertips into her chest. "Here. Like an emotional tug. I haven't felt that way about anything else other than the nightmares. It *has* to mean something."

The psychiatrist nodded. "Then, perhaps, it does. You need to give yourself permission to explore these emotions, Angel. See where they lead you."

Angel's gaze shifted from Dr. Pierce to the tall double windows behind her desk. Twisting a lock of hair around her forefinger, she focused on the canopy of foliage masking Central Park several stories below. The trees were donning autumn attire, lush green limbs slipping into dresses of flaming golds and reds. Soon the landscape would be ablaze in fiery colors. Like her nightmare.

Angel squeezed her eyes shut. She knew where the emotions were leading. They were adding a more frightening dimension to her recurring nightmare. She shuddered, fighting away the memory of the screams in the night.

"Angel?"

The concern in Dr. Pierce's voice brought her back to the here-and-now. The doctor was offering her a tissue. Angel stared at the flimsy white square, puzzled for a moment until she realized her cheeks were wet with tears.

"I'm sorry," she said, accepting the tissue.

"Can you tell me why you were crying?"

Angel dabbed at her face, then blew her nose. Part of her feared giving voice to this new chapter in her nightly terror. Speaking of it would give it substance, allowing it to escape from the confines of her mind into the real world.

But Angel was certain the screams were another clue to her identity. With so little to go on, she knew she had to confront her fears. After taking several deep breaths she forced herself to speak. "The nightmare has changed," she said.

* * *

Listening was a skill Trent had honed well over the years. He listened to his employees, and he listened to his competitors.

Often, he listened not to the words that were spoken but for the ones which weren't. And he watched, becoming a keen interpreter of the nuances of body language.

With Felicia's words serving as background, he observed the group assembled around the inlaid rosewood conference table. There was no need to concentrate on Felicia's report. He had already approved the strategy she was presenting to Montgomery Aeronautics' new CEO and his Board of Directors. He was more interested in their silent reactions. To a man—and woman—they were as Trent had predicted.

With occasional nods to each other the sixteen men who comprised the Board embraced his reorganization plan. No surprise there. Their disapproval of Roger Caine had rattled Wall Street enough to downgrade the stock twice since Abel's death.

Nor was Trent surprised by the actions of the two most interesting cast members of the drama playing out before him. Both Roger Caine and Whitney Montgomery did little to mask their anger. Roger's face was nearly the color of Whitney's crimson lipstick, and Whitney's palms were clenched so tightly that even across the long conference table Trent could see her wrist veins throbbing.

The glances they exchanged lent credence to the rumors circulating about the *merry widow* and equally *merry widower*. If only a fraction of the stories were true, Trent would relish destroying them both. He had respected Abel Montgomery and admired his granddaughter's talent. As far as Trent was concerned, there were way too few Abels and Sarahs in the world and way too many Rogers and Whitneys.

Felicia concluded her presentation. Before she could take her seat, Roger jumped to his feet.

"No!" He pounded both fists on the table hard enough to rattle the water pitchers and glasses. "This is *my* company, Caldwell. You're a minority shareholder. How dare you waltz in here and tell me how to run it!"

With a voice as calm as Roger's was hysterical, Trent answered. "According to my projections, if you continue on your present course of action, Montgomery Aeronautics will be in receivership by the end of the year. As a stockholder, I refuse to allow you the latitude to jeopardize my considerable investment in this company." He turned to the Board members. "And I believe I have the backing of your directors."

All sixteen heads nodded in agreement.

"So you see, Roger, like it or not, I'm the only hope for the survival of this company. *And* your continued wealth." For the first time since entering the room Trent removed the invisible mask he wore to conceal his emotions. He smiled slightly in Roger's direction, but it was a smile filled with hidden meanings and devoid of mirth. "I suppose that makes me your savior."

Roger sputtered, his face turning several shades closer to purple. Whitney seethed. The directors all began to speak at once.

Trent held up his hand, silencing everyone. "If the rest of you have no objections, I'd like to speak with Mr. Caine privately."

Felicia and the directors rose, exiting the room quickly and silently. Whitney refused to budge.

After jotting a few notes to himself Trent placed his pen on the table, leaned his elbows on the arms of his chair, and steepled his fingers in front of him. The calm of his voice did little to disguise the underlying menace of his words. "Mrs. Montgomery, you have ten seconds to leave this room on your own volition before I do it for you."

Whitney's eyes narrowed into two jade slits. Her words spat out between clenched teeth. "You can't speak to me like that!" Turning to Roger, she hissed, "Don't just sit there like an ass! Do something!"

For the briefest of moments Trent almost felt sorry for the man. Roger Caine was trapped. Beads of sweat peppered his brow. Panic, anger, hatred, and fear all vied for position on his face. Veins bulged from his neck and along his temple. His eyes darted between Whitney and Trent—the lady or the tiger. But this was a no-win scenario. Trent was certain that this lady was a tiger in disguise.

Roger cleared his throat. He glared across the room at Trent, but his words were directed to Whitney. "Do as he requests."

Whitney opened her mouth to object, but before she could say anything, Roger added, "For now."

This appeared to pacify her. She smiled over at Trent. Briefly. Maliciously. Then, rising like a queen, she threw her shoulders back, raised her chin, and headed for the door. When she reached the head of the table, she stopped. Before Trent realized what was happening, she swung her arm back and delivered a stinging blow across his face.

"No one makes a fool of me and gets away with it, Mr. Caldwell."

Whitney then pivoted on her heels and with a queen-like air of superiority and entitlement, exited the room, slamming the conference room door behind her.

"Charming woman," said Trent. He rubbed his jaw. At the other end of the table Roger was sneering in satisfaction. "So you're the brains and she's the brawn, Caine?"

"What's your game, Caldwell? You've already chopped my

balls off."

Trent rose and walked the length of the room to where Roger sat at the foot of the table. Leaning his fists into the table, Trent lowered his head until he was right in his opponent's face. "Then we no longer have a problem because it was your balls that were creating the public relations disaster that nearly destroyed this company."

Roger jumped to his feet. "Why you—"

Trent placed a hand on Roger's shoulder and shoved him back into his chair. "Sit down, and shut up if you know what's good for you *and* your bank account."

Roger glared at him but remained seated.

"That's better." Trent lowered himself into the chair at a right angle to Roger's. "Your sole job from here on is to mend fences. There's far too much negative gossip about you and the Black Widow. I don't like it, and our investors don't like it. I don't care what you and Cat Woman do behind closed doors, but in public you keep her on a short, tight leash, and you keep your pants zipped. Understood?"

"You have no right—"

"I have *every* right! Those two graves haven't had time to grow crabgrass, for God's sake! I don't care if you had the world's worst marriage. I don't care if your wife was a frigid emasculating bitch or if Abel couldn't get it up. From now on the two of you behave in a manner that reflects well on this company."

When Roger didn't respond, Trent continued. "You'll start by having a memorial retrospective of your wife's work. All proceeds will go to charity, with you and Whitney each matching from your own personal funds whatever is raised."

"You can't force us to do that!"

"Oh, yes I can, you greedy little bastard. And you'll do it graciously."

FIFTEEN

Talk about pulling a rabbit out of my ass! The idea for a charity fundraiser took Trent almost as much by surprise as it had Roger. However, Trent's poker face certainly trumped Roger's stroke-in-the-making deep purple features. Trent half expected to see puffs of black smoke spewing from the guy's ears and nostrils a la Yosemite Sam or Wile E. Coyote.

He could thank Angel for the brainstorm. He hadn't been able to shake her and those damn photos out of his mind ever since their late-night conversation.

The longer he'd studied Roger and Whitney during the meeting, the more convinced he'd become of their blatant avarice.

Abel had been a man known as much for his philanthropy as his financial empire. From all accounts his granddaughter had inherited his compassion and generosity. Although she'd preferred to keep a low profile, it was common knowledge that

Sarah Montgomery donated all proceeds from her photography to charity. How the two of them got mixed up with the likes of Roger and Whitney boggled Trent's mind.

Sarah's name and reputation would ensure that her memorial retrospective was a gala society event. Her remaining works could fetch conservatively half a million dollars—more if any were signed. The guest list would be comprised of people willing to pay top dollar for her photographs, especially now that there would never be any more.

Trent relished the irony of the situation he'd imposed on the gold digger and the gigolo. They wouldn't see a penny from the sale of Sarah's work, and forcing them to contribute matching funds was justice on a Biblical level. Sheer genius, thought Trent.

He'd stayed away from as many social functions as he could for nearly three years. Attending events without Caitlin was like a kick to his gut. However, he planned to enjoy this particular event. Thoroughly. If for no other reason than to watch Roger and Whitney squirm more and more as the night's gross receipts climbed higher and higher. If necessary, Trent would outbid every attendee on each photo just to make certain Roger and Whitney were forced to write exceedingly large checks.

* * *

Trent sat in the backseat of his car, unable to shake thoughts of Angel and last night from his head. He'd kept his distance, literally and figuratively, for reasons that had nothing to do with her. And in so doing, he'd acted more like her jailer than her host. Now he wondered if maybe his sullen disposition might be a contributing factor to her lack of progress in regaining her memory. He scared her. That much was evident in the way she reacted to him when he stumbled upon her in the kitchen. Damn! He'd wanted to help her, not make matters worse.

Angel was like some timorous sparrow. Tossed from the nest, unable to fly, she cowered at his approach. *She acts like I'm the goddamn Big Bad Wolf!* And rightly so, given the way he'd behaved toward her. Brusque. Cold. Distant. Trent knew he needed an attitude adjustment. He just wasn't sure he had the emotional reserves to effect one. Angel reminded him too much of all he'd lost.

Throwing his head back against the leather upholstery of the car, he sucked in a lungful of air, exhaling forcefully. He didn't much care for the man he'd become. His guilt had created a misanthropic bastard. Caitlin would be horrified by the transformation. That alone should be reason enough for him to change. But at this stage in his life, he just didn't know if he was capable of being anything other than the lifeless shadow he'd become.

Felicia's nasal soprano interrupted his introspection and self-flagellation. "Well? Are you going to tell me what you said to Roger Caine that had him leaving with his balls on a platter?"

Trent stared out the window. As usual, they were caught in midtown gridlock. "I demoted him to janitor," he mumbled, eyeing a storefront halfway down the block.

"You what?"

In no mood to offer Felicia even an abbreviated version of his encounter with Roger, Trent opened the limo door and hopped out. "I have something to do. Go back to the office without me."

Hoping she wouldn't run after him to question his erratic behavior, he hurried toward the entrance of the store.

* * *

Several hours later Trent let himself into his apartment. The distinct aroma of corned beef and cabbage wafted through the air in both greeting and admonishment. Since Angel's arrival, he'd taken his meals downstairs in one of the hotel dining rooms. The sudden assault on his senses reminded him how much he detested nouvelle cuisine and how much he missed Moira's down-to-earth Irish cooking. Feeling a bit like the prodigal son, he strode down the hall to the kitchen.

Standing at the stove, his housekeeper greeted him with a raised eyebrow. Trent responded by handing her the bouquet of russet and gold chrysanthemums he'd purchased in the hotel lobby. Then he pecked her on the cheek.

"Whatever 'tis you're apologizin' for, you're forgiven," she said, playfully swatting him with the flowers. "Does His Highness plan on gracin' us with his company for dinner?"

Trent chuckled at her impertinence. "How can I say no to your corned beef and cabbage?" He spied the pie cooling on the counter and bent down to sniff it. "Apple?"

"With raisins. Just the way you like it." With her chin Mrs. Kearn gestured toward the kitchen table where Angel sat, her attention riveted on something beyond the window. "Angel made it. With one hand."

Trent turned his attention to his reluctant houseguest. *She can't even look at me,* he thought, noticing the tension and worry in her face. What had he done?

Pulling out the chair next to her, he joined her at the table. "Thank you, Angel. The pie smells delicious."

* * *

Angel dragged her attention from the graying sky to Trent. He was very close, and he was smiling at her. The aloof coldness which normally colored his hazel eyes was missing. In its place she saw uncertainty. And kindness. She offered him a slight smile. "You're welcome, but I really only helped. It's Mrs. Kearn's recipe."

Trent withdrew a small package from under his arm and placed it on the table in front of her. "I thought this might help you," he said.

She stared at the navy words printed across the tan plastic bag. *Secondhand Prose. Rare and out-of-print books and magazines.* "What is it?"

"Something I thought might help you. Open it."

Angel slipped her good hand inside the bag and withdrew a five-year-old copy of *National Geographic*. She read the title of the cover story out loud, *"Remote Villages of Provence, a Photo Essay by Sarah Montgomery."*

Across the room, an empty pot clattered against the counter. Angel jumped from the sudden noise. She turned toward Mrs. Kearn. The housekeeper held a large stock pot with both hands. The color and tightness of her face made Angel wonder if she'd deliberately slammed the pot against the counter rather than accidentally dropping it. The woman looked downright angry. But why?

Angel glanced at Trent. A scowl settled across his brow, but he said nothing to his housekeeper. After what seemed like an eternity to Angel, Mrs. Kearn relaxed her grip on the pot, set it gently into the sink, and turned her attention back to the potatoes simmering on the stove.

Trent exhaled forcefully, then pointed to the magazine. "You seemed so certain about the pictures in your room," he said. "I thought if you saw more, it might help you remember something."

Touched by his thoughtfulness, Angel quickly dismissed the strange scene she'd just observed and flipped to the beginning of the article. She took her time, carefully scrutinizing each photograph. "I *have* been here," she said. Excitement rose in her voice. "I *know* I have. I feel it inside me."

"Can you recall anything else?" he asked.

Squeezing her eyes shut, she forced herself to remember. Something. Anything. But after several minutes she shook her head and sighed. "Nothing."

"In time." said Trent. He patted her hand.

Emptiness bubbled inside her. Angel choked back a sob. "I'm all alone. How can *anyone* be totally alone in the world? It's like I dropped from the sky in front of that cab. Like I didn't exist until that moment in time."

"Some help you are," muttered Mrs. Kearn, turning from the stove. She tossed her wooden spoon into the sink and headed for Angel. With one hand she cradled Angel's head against her ample bosom and stroked her cheek. The other pointed an accusing finger at the open magazine. "Those bloody pictures only upset the poor lass."

"I thought they'd help."

"She'll remember when God's ready for her to remember. Leave her be." She scowled at Trent. As she shuffled out of the kitchen, she muttered, "I should tan your fool hide. Lord knows, you need some sense beat into you."

Angel stared after Mrs. Kearn until the woman was out of sight. She noticed that Trent did the same, only where she was curious about the housekeeper's outburst, he seemed angered yet resigned.

"Thank you," she finally said after a minute or two had passed. "For the magazine. It gives me a connection to something. Even if I can't figure out what that something is or why."

"Maybe she's right," said Trent. "Maybe we're all pressuring you too much. Maybe the stress of trying to remember is having the opposite effect."

"You mean trying to remember might actually be keeping me from remembering?"

"Something like that." He shrugged. "Hell, I'm no shrink. What do I know?"

"It's as good a theory as any. Sometimes when I'm with Dr. Pierce, I feel like I'm a lab rat. She certainly doesn't have any answers."

"Psychiatry is far from an exact science. It's not like she can look up Memory Loss in the PDF and write a prescription for you."

"Yeah, that would be too easy." Angel pulled at one of her curls and twisted it around her finger. Her words tumbled out in a rush of frustration and emotion. "I just don't understand. No one is totally alone in the world. Maybe I don't have friends or relatives, but what about coworkers? Neighbors? Wouldn't I have had a job? Or maybe I was enrolled at one of the local colleges. I have no idea how old I am, so maybe I'm a student somewhere. *Someone* should have noticed my disappearance and reported it. I don't understand why no one is looking for me."

She shifted her torso to face him fully. "Why doesn't anyone care?"

* * *

Tears swam in her eyes. Trent was at a loss for words. An uncontrollable urge to scoop her up in his arms again swept through him. An urge to hold her against his chest, run his fingers through her curls, comfort her in any way he could. An urge he fought hard to shake, as once again, he began to feel stirrings in a part of his anatomy he thought long dead.

Angel rubbed at her eyes, then smacked her hand on the magazine, shocking him back to the here and now. "Nothing makes sense!" she cried. "Nothing!"

Trent had voiced similar frustration countless times over the past few weeks. With all the sophisticated equipment at their disposal—the police, the FBI, the private investigators he'd hired—all had come up empty-handed. It really did seem as though Angel had dropped from the sky.

She turned her attention back to the *National Geographic* and flipped a page. "I'll bet people miss her," she said. "What was she like?"

"Who?"

"Sarah Montgomery."

"I don't know. Why do you ask?"

"Last night, the way you spoke about her—I guess I assumed she was a friend of yours."

He shook his head. "No. We never met."

* * *

As she lay in bed that night, Angel thought about her conversation with Trent Caldwell. Every time she thought she'd figured out the reason behind the man's morose disposition, he threw her another curve ball. Felicia Sutton wasn't his estranged wife. Sarah Montgomery wasn't a former lover. After the events of last night and today's thoughtful gesture, she no longer believed she was the cause of his sullenness.

Especially after the way she caught him looking at her today. She may have convinced herself she was imagining certain things last night, but she sure as hell hadn't imagined that look. Or the sudden bulge in his pants she'd noticed as he sat beside her in the kitchen. Trent Caldwell had the hots for her. And that scared the crap out of her because against her better judgment, she was developing similar stirrings in her own anatomy. Luckily, hers weren't as obvious.

So if she wasn't responsible for the man's keep-your-distance attitude, what had placed that giant chip on his shoulder? The one thing Angel knew with absolute certainty was that all his wealth sure wasn't buying the guy much in the way of happiness.

SIXTEEN

Trent knew he'd been an ass where Angel was concerned. He wouldn't blame Mrs. Kearn for wanting to tan his hide, not that she really would, no matter how much he deserved a good smack. The woman was all bluster and bark on the outside, but underneath she was kinder than anyone he'd ever met—except for his Caitlin.

For nearly three years he'd buried his guilt and pain in his work, spending nearly all his waking hours at the office or traveling between his vast holdings. Losing himself in profit and loss statements numbed his mind and kept him from thinking about the past, about what he'd done. The end of the workday usually evoked as much enthusiasm in Trent as the prospect of a root canal. Without benefit of Novocain.

Not lately, though. As he rode the elevator to the top floor, he realized he was looking forward to a quiet evening spent in Angel's company.

"Two nights in a row?" asked Mrs. Kearn, raising both eyebrows when he walked through the door. "To what do we owe such an honor?"

"Leftover corned beef and cabbage," said Trent.

"Hmmph!" She eyed him up and down, then glanced over to where Angel sat at the kitchen table. "Believe what you want, lad. You won't be pullin' the wool over these old eyes any time soon."

He pecked her cheek. "I never could, Moira."

Trent turned to Angel. "Good evening, Angel. How was your day?"

"About the same as every other one, Mr. Caldwell. At least the few recent ones I remember."

"Trent," he said.

"Excuse me?"

"You're living in my home, Angel. I think we can drop the formality, don't you? My name is Trent."

Angel glanced at Mrs. Kearn who smiled and nodded, then turned back to him. "Sure. Whatever you'd like. Trent."

Trent had fences to mend. He surprised his houseguest and his housekeeper even further when he joined them after dinner as they watched television in the den.

"Saints be praised," mumbled Mrs. Kearn as he took a seat on the opposite end of the couch from Angel. "And to what do we owe this miracle?"

"Would you prefer that I didn't join you?"

"I'm just wondering if it's really you or some alien replacement Trent."

Angel laughed. For the first time as far as Trent knew. And for the first time in a long time, he craved the uplifting sound of laughter. He had no right to laughter, though, not after what he'd done.

"She's good medicine for you," said Mrs. Kearn later that evening after Angel had gone to bed. "Don't fight it. Time you started living again, lad."

"I have no right to live. You know that."

"T'wasn't your fault. What's done is done. Let it go. 'Tis time to move on."

"For both of us," said Trent. Besides O'Hara, Trent's driver, and a handful of other Irish cronies, he was all she had left in the world. And she was all he had left. What a pair they made. Two miserable souls. "But can we, Moira? Can *you* bury the past?"

She shook her head. "Not yet."

* * *

"Steady, now." Mrs. Kearn reached for Angel's arm.

Slipping from her grasp, Angel threw her head back and pirouetted across the living room.

"Angel!" Mrs. Kearn clasped her hands to her bosom. "Sweet Jesus! You'll be givin' me a heart attack, lass."

Angel flopped onto a wing back chair that flanked the fireplace and giggled. "I'm sorry. I just feel so free!" She jumped to her feet and broke into an awkward soft-shoe routine, the sound muffled by the large antique Sarouk Indian rug that covered most of the living room's hardwood floor.

"Lord, have mercy! You'll be wantin' O'Hara to take you cloggin' down at the pub next!"

"I wouldn't steal your beau, Mrs. Kearn." She tossed the housekeeper a sheepish grin. "But I'd love to go with the two of you sometime."

"My beau? Where'd you ever get that fool notion?"

Angel shrugged. "I don't think it's so foolish. You two make a perfect couple."

"Hmmph!" She grabbed Angel by the shoulders and forced her to sit on the wing back chair's matching ottoman. "My cloggin' days ended a long time ago, lassie, and the doctor told *you* not to overdue things."

After nearly eight weeks Angel was finally free of the heavy plaster casts. When the enormous weights were lifted from her body, her spirits soared. No longer dependent on Mrs. Kearn for the simplest of tasks, Angel was ready to seize control of her destiny and find the person hiding inside her—even if it meant pounding the pavement from Battery Park up to the Bronx.

Unable to sit still, she bounced off the ottoman and waltzed around the spacious room to the sounds of an imaginary orchestra. With her oversized sweatshirt hanging several inches beyond her fingertips and a pair of sweatpants threatening to fall off her hips at any moment, she felt like a child who had stumbled across a trunk of old clothing and decided to play dress-up.

Except she wasn't in some musty attic. She was in the living room of one of the most expensive pieces of real estate in all of Manhattan. Trent's living room, like all the other rooms in his apartment, was furnished with only the best. In the case of the living room, antiques from the far corners of the globe. But instead of a stuffy don't-touch look to it, the room gave off an aura of old money comfort. Sort of a shabby chic meets Neo-classicism. Chippendale with all the chips. And the nicks and scuffs and wear and tear of generation upon generation of use.

Mrs. Kearn laughed at her. "I think 'tis time we put some of that energy to better use." She reached into her apron pocket, removed a platinum AmEx card, and waved it in front of Angel.

"Now that you're out of those casts, 'tis high time we got you some decent clothes. Let's go spend some of Mr. Trent's millions."

Angel froze. She stared at the American Express card in Mrs. Kearn's hand, then at the woman holding it. Their eyes met. "I can't do that," she said. "He's done far too much for me already."

"Hmmph. I told him you'd say that. The two of you were poured from the same keg. Both stubborn as the day's long."

"And what did he say?"

"That you'd better suck up your pride because you can't go around wearing his old sweats anymore. And he's right. 'Twas fine while you were cooped up in the apartment. Nothing else fit over them casts, anyway, but 'tis high time you stopped lookin' like some potato famine refugee." Mrs. Kearn folded her arms across her chest and sized Angel up. "For once I agree with him."

Mimicking Mrs. Kearn's stance, Angel folded her arms across her own chest and held her ground. "Pride has nothing to do with it. I can't keep taking from him. It's not right. I have no idea who I am. What if I can't pay him back for all he's already done?"

Mrs. Kearn softened her stance. Uncrossing her arms, she placed a hand on either side of Angel's face. "Foolish lass, he doesn't want your money."

"Well, maybe for once it's not about what Trent Caldwell wants. What about what I want?"

"And what might that be?"

Angel turned and slumped onto the couch, lowering her head into her hands. "I don't want him thinking I'm anything like what that Felicia woman claims."

Trent's employee hadn't given up trying to convince him that Angel was a grifter out to scam him. Not a week went by that she didn't find some excuse to come to the apartment and start in on him about her. Angel heard nearly every word because even with her bedroom door closed, the woman's shrill voice carried to the far corners of the spacious apartment. Angel suspected Felicia was deliberately raising her voice so that no matter where Angel was, she'd hear her.

Mrs. Kearn grunted. "Huh! I should buy me a lottery ticket today. Told him you'd say that, too."

"Then you see why I can't accept anything more from him, don't you?"

"He's told you to ignore her."

Angel snorted. "Can you?"

"No one can ignore that woman."

"Exactly."

"Och, it doesn't matter, lass. Mr. Trent said he didn't care what I had to do. You'd best be havin' a suitable wardrobe by the end of the day."

"Or?"

Mrs. Kearn sighed. "Do an old woman a favor, Angel. Let me take you shopping. If you won't come with me, I'll just have to shop for you on my own, and I don't know your tastes."

Angel threw her arms up in defeat and laughed a hollow laugh. "Well, that makes two of us, doesn't it? How am I supposed to know what I like when I don't know who I am?"

"I suppose we'll just have to go with what looks best on you." Mrs. Kearn eyed her for a long moment. "Though I find it hard to imagine anything not lookin' good on the likes of you." She chuckled.

"What's so funny?"

"Just thinking about how someone's goin' to have the shock of his life when he sees what's been hidin' under those baggy sweats."

The thought might have pleased Mrs. Kearn, but it worried Angel no end. Ever since the night she'd spilled the milk and Trent carried her to her bed, she'd fought off renegade hormones whenever he was near. She was convinced Trent was engaged in the same battle. She saw it in his eyes, the way he sometimes looked at her before he caught himself and his expression hardened. Living together was taking a toll on both of them.

Angel hoped Mrs. Kearn wasn't bent on playing matchmaker. That was a complication neither she nor Trent could afford, not while Angel still had no clue as to her true identity.

* * *

Several hours later Angel and Mrs. Kearn, their arms laden with shopping bags, arrived back at the apartment. As Mrs. Kearn emptied the sacks and spread the garments over the living room sofas and chairs, Angel stood to the side shaking her head.

She groaned. "It's too much." Piles of lingerie, slacks, sweaters, blouses, and dresses covered every available surface. "I don't need all of this."

She lifted a pair of black silk Jimmy Choo heels from their box. Angel suspected the shoes cost more than the gross national budget of many a third world nation, but Mrs. Kearn had insisted she try them on, then insisted on purchasing them. "I'll never wear these, you realize. It's just a huge waste of money."

"You can't be wearin' tennies with this," said Mrs. Kearn, removing a low-cut black silk cocktail dress from its plastic garment bag.

"Yes, and just when will I wear that?" asked Angel. "I really don't think this is what Trent had in mind when he told you to buy me some new clothes."

"We'll see." Mrs. Kearn slipped the gown off its padded hanger and held it up in front of Angel. "You can never go wrong with basic black, lass." She winked. "Or so I'm told."

Angel was about to respond when she heard Trent enter the apartment. Throwing an uneasy glance at the tissue paper lined stacks of clothing, she took a deep breath and waited.

Trent hardly noticed her, though, let alone the new wardrobe. Holding a cell phone to one ear, he listened intently to the person speaking on the other end, passing on information to a woman who followed behind him on a second cell phone.

"Wait here, Felicia," he said, ending the call. He strode down the hall toward the master suite.

Felicia! The woman who accused her of being a con artist out to fleece Trent. Always before, Angel had been sequestered in her room. She had heard the woman's stinging words, the biting accusations, but had never come face-to-face with the woman hurling them. Until now.

Angel turned to Mrs. Kearn, but the housekeeper, her jaw set tight, was glowering at Felicia in a way that reminded Angel of a mother bear protecting her cubs. Angel took a step closer to the housekeeper and held her breath. The shit was about to hit the fan, and Angel stood directly in the line of fire.

From the sound of her voice and the little Trent had told her, Angel had expected a middle-aged woman who gave little thought to her looks. A dowdy nerd. A tight-assed accountant type woman with thick glasses, sensible shoes, manly dark suits, and oxford style shirts buttoned to the neck.

The reality of Felicia Sutton was quite the contrary. Dressed in a formfitting navy pinstripe power suit with a white silk camisole peeking suggestively beneath it, Trent's vice-president could just as easily have been posing for *Vanity Fair* as juggling stock quotes.

She wore her ebony hair pulled back into a tight chignon. The severe style, with not a hair out of place, accentuated her high cheekbones and sultry lips. Every inch of her suggested a woman who knew exactly what she wanted and would stop at nothing to get it.

Felicia continued her phone conversation, tossing out facts and figures at an impressive rate, occasionally pausing to listen, then supplying additional information. During the entire conversation, her nearly jet-black eyes never left Angel. They raked over her, as if mentally adding up the cost of the Donna Karan ivory silk blouse and Versace brown herringbone pleated pants she wore. Even the complimentary makeover she'd received at the Bobbie Brown counter didn't go unnoticed or unscrutinized.

Angel became acutely uncomfortable. She wanted to flee to the safety of her room, but she fought off the urge and held her ground, staring right back. As much as she quaked on the inside, she wasn't going to let the bitch intimidate her. She might not know who she was, but she sure as hell knew what she was, and she wasn't a scam artist. She'd had enough of Felicia Sutton's behind-the-back character assassination.

"Moira!" Trent shouted from his bedroom. "Where's my overnighter?"

Darting Angel a quick look of apology, Mrs. Kearn shuffled down the hall, leaving her alone with Felicia. Angel prayed she'd return before Felicia finished her call, but like all her recent supplications to the Almighty, this one, too, remained unanswered. No sooner had Mrs. Kearn left the room than Felicia ended her call and slipped the iPhone into the black leather case hooked at her Scarlett O'Hara sized waist.

Felicia's gaze swept from one empty shopping bag to the next before she sauntered over to the sofa and picked up a pair of black lace panties. "Looks like you bought out Bergdorf's." She waved the lingerie under Angel's nose and lowered her voice to a whisper. An extremely sinister whisper. "These won't work. He's on to you."

"I don't know what you mean. I haven't done anything wrong."

Felicia tossed the panties aside. They landed on the carpet at Angel's feet. "Really? Then why are you still here?"

Felicia's words were like a smack to her face. Angel felt the heat rising to her cheeks, but it wasn't the heat of anger; it was the heat of embarrassment. Angel had wanted to stand up to Felicia, defend herself against the woman's false accusations. But how could she? In her heart she knew she wasn't the kind of person Felicia claimed. At least she didn't think so. But what proof did she have other than a gut feeling? In reality, she could be anything from a high-priced hooker to a bank robber, let alone a con artist.

Maybe that's why she couldn't remember anything. Maybe she so regretted her past life choices that this was her mind's way of giving her a fresh start. And if that were the case, Felicia was right. She was taking advantage of Trent.

So much for telling Felicia Sutton off. Angel fisted her hands to keep them from shaking and clenched her teeth to prevent the quiver building up in her jaw. The sting of impending tears gathered behind her eyes, but she refused to let the bitch see her cry. Turning on her heels, she gave in to her initial urge, but instead of fleeing the room, she stalked off, her head held high.

Once out of Felicia's sight, though, she gave in to the emotion building inside her and quickened her pace until she was nearly running by the time she entered her room. She flung herself onto the bed, tears spilled from her eyes, but she clamped her hand over her mouth and nose to keep from sobbing out loud.

* * *

Trent and Mrs. Kearn reentered the living room in time to see Angel running down the opposite hall. He turned on Felicia. "What did you say to her?"

"Really, Trent! I told you she was a con artist." She bent to pick up the panties and dangled them from her index finger. "Do you need any more proof than this?"

Their eyes met. Hers gleamed with victory, and for the first time Trent wondered if she was worth the aggravation she caused him. He set his overnight case at his feet and reached for the scrap of lace. "Wait for me downstairs in the limo, Felicia."

"Certainly but don't be too long. We have a plane to catch." As she strolled past Mrs. Kearn toward the front door, she offered the housekeeper a triumphant smile. Moira responded with a Gaelic muttering and an evil-eyed glare.

Felicia laughed as she clicked the door closed behind her.

"You said to splurge."

"I know what I said, Mrs. K. You don't have to remind me." He fingered the delicate lace and grimaced. "Are these for her or me?"

"Of all the—" Mrs. Kearn grabbed the panties from his hand and stuffed them into one of the shopping bags.

"Do you think I don't know what's going on in that devious head of yours?"

She crossed her arms over her chest, jutted out her chin, and stared him down. "Wouldn't hurt, you know."

"Don't." He raised a finger in warning. "Mend your own heart.

Leave mine alone." He grabbed his overnighter and headed for the door. "I'll be back in a few days."

"So you're just going to walk out of here? Without even talkin' to the lass?"

He reached for the doorknob. "You deal with it."

"I never thought I'd live to see the day you turned into a coward, Trent Caldwell."

He froze. He *was* acting like a coward. Again. Running from anyone and anything that made him remember what life used to be like—before he destroyed all that was precious to him. Dropping the suitcase at his feet, he spun around. Their eyes met. Hers were filled with disappointment. His shoulders slumped. "You win. She's in her room?"

"That's where she was headed."

He felt her gaze follow him down the long hallway to Angel's room.

SEVENTEEN

Trent found Angel standing in front of the wall of Sarah's photographs, her posture stiff, tears silently streaming down her cheeks. She had shed her new outfit for his navy sweatshirt and pants—the ones with the fading World Series logo commemorating the 2000 Yankees/Mets subway series. The sleeves drooped over her hands; the legs bagged at her ankles. Her new blouse and slacks lay discarded on the bed.

"I never wanted the clothes," she said without turning to him. "I'll return them in the morning." She motioned towards the bed. "Except for those. They're worn. I...I'll send you a check for them when I get a job."

"And how will you do that?" he asked. "You have no identification. No Social Security number."

He could tell she hadn't considered that problem. She tugged at a curl, biting her trembling lower lip.

"I don't know," she said. "I'll find a way."

A lump lodged in his throat, and once again he had a sudden urge to take her in his arms and protect her from the bleak uncertainty that dogged her. Instead, he stood in the doorway, clutching the knob to keep from acting on his urges and making a fool of himself. "I want you to have the clothes, Angel. Whatever Felicia said to get you so upset, it's not true. I told you to ignore her, didn't I?"

She lowered her head and clasped her arms around her body, as if attempting to shelter herself. Or maybe just offer herself a comforting hug. That thought and the gesture were Trent's undoing. He'd deliberately shut himself off from the world, caused his own fate, imposed his own exile from life. Hers was forced upon her. By him. Because he was in such a damn hurry that day, she no longer had a past. And if she couldn't regain her memory, what kind of future lay ahead for her? Unable to stop himself, he crossed the room and gently stroked her upper arm. "Look at me. Please?"

Angel raised her head but once again focused on the photos, not him. "How do you know she's not right? How do *I* know she's not right? I may be all she accuses me of and more."

Trent stepped between her and the wall of photos. Placing his hands on either side of her face, he raised her chin until their eyes met. "Do you really think I'd want you in my home if I believed that?" His fingers brushed at the tears on her cheeks. "We may not know who you are, but I've come to know what you are."

"You can't be sure." Her eyes filled with fresh tears. "How can you when I don't know?"

When Trent wasn't consumed with anger or blame over his own loss, he wallowed in self-pity. He allowed no other emotions to break through the wall he'd constructed around his heart. Until Angel entered his life. She might be filled with self-doubts, but he had no such skepticism concerning her character. Even though the facts of her life lay trapped inside her, her true nature shined through. And it touched him in ways he never expected. Angel was the personification of all that was good. "Trust me," he said. "I'm sure."

He led her over to the bed and sat down beside her. Lifting the cast-off blouse and slacks from the bedspread, he held them out to her. "I'm sorry I didn't get the chance to tell you how pretty you looked in these."

"You were busy." She took the garments from him and placed them in her lap. Her eyes fixed on the clothing, she added, "Besides, I wasn't expecting a compliment."

"No, you were worried that you'd spent too much of my money, weren't you?"

"I did!"

"Have I complained?"

"Not yet but you haven't seen the credit card receipts."

"I don't care what the clothes cost."

"You should. She's right. I'm taking advantage of you. I should leave."

No, I'm taking advantage of you. Suddenly he realized the truth that had been lurking all around him lately. A part of him didn't want Angel to regain her memory because he didn't want to lose her. She was the only good thing that had happened to him in too long. Did he feel guilty about that? Hell yes! He had no damn right to feel happy about anything anymore. But the feelings were there, and no amount of self-flagellation had managed to rid him of them.

He placed his hands over hers. "I have to leave for a few days. There's a crisis brewing in Chicago that needs my attention. Promise me you'll still be here when I return."

"Why?"

Because you're the only glimmer of joy I've known in nearly three years. "I want to take you somewhere Saturday night. It may help trigger some memories." He rose and walked to the door. "Promise?"

Angel nodded.

His nerves felt like they'd passed through Mrs. Kearn's sausage grinder. His gut following right behind. Part of him was glad that three nonstop days of intense business meetings lay ahead. But those meetings involved Felicia. Three nonstop days of Felicia. At that thought he had to force himself to leave the apartment. He had no choice, though.

Trent headed for the front door where Mrs. Kearn waited. "Don't let her out of your sight," he said.

He picked up his overnighter, opened the door, and made his way to the elevator.

* * *

Hell hath no fury like a woman whose pocketbook is threatened, thought Roger. It took a full week before Whitney calmed down enough for him to reason with her about Sarah's memorial retrospective show.

"He has no goddamn right!" she raged, grabbing a Limoges cigarette box from an end table. Roger rescued the expensive knickknack before she hurled it against the wall. Piles of smashed crystal and china lay in her wake as Whitney grabbed and smashed her way from room to room.

"Enough!" He placed the case on an upper bookshelf out of her reach. "Do you want him to win?"

"Don't be stupid. Of course not."

"Then we have to make this work to our advantage. Otherwise, he'll destroying us."

"*Destroy us?* You said you buried the evidence so deep no one would ever uncover what happened to that money. *Under layers of maze-like cyber twists and turns*, remember Roger? Remember how you bragged to me about your cleverness? Your skills? You said— and I quote— 'No one can uncover a Roger Caine coverup.'"

"I don't want him digging. Period. Yes, I'm good, but Caldwell has too many resources at his fingertips, and we're already dealing with an antagonistic Board of Directors. Trust me. It's better to suck up to the bastard now and get even later."

"This is all your fault, Roger!"

"Fine! It's all my fault! There I've admitted it. Are you happy now?"

"I won't be happy until you dig us out of this mess."

He grabbed her by the shoulders. "So let me handle things, damn it!"

"Handle things or screw them up more?"

He pushed her aside. "Just remember, lover, I did what I did for us, and if I take a fall, you tumble with me. All the way. So stop acting like a spoiled bitch, and help me get us out of this fucking mess."

Getting Whitney to go along with his plan took a hell of a lot of convincing on Roger's part, and the hellcat went out of her way to show her displeasure with him in private. In public, though, she stepped into the role of charity organizer with both Manolo clad feet. All graceful and reserved. In no time she had the press and everyone else eating out of her talons. Overnight Whitney

Montgomery, the Black Widow, went from pariah to saint in every goddamn fucking society column. Just the way Roger had planned.

* * *

Logic told Angel the most sensible place to begin her search was the scene of the accident. So, with Mrs. Kearn trudging alongside her, she headed down Lexington Avenue to Seventy-ninth Street. From there she planned to fan out, hoping that something she passed might trigger a memory. Somewhere along those streets was the place she'd come from or the site she was heading to before the cab struck her.

"If I can recognize one of those locations," she told Mrs. Kearn, "everything else might fall into place."

"Best not to pin all your hope on trudgin' miles and miles around the city," said Mrs. Kearn. "O'Hara's already driven you up and down all these streets dozens of times over."

"I was walking that day," said Angel. "Maybe walking again will give me a different perspective."

Mrs. Kearn huffed and puffed beside her. "If you say so, lass."

Angel stopped and turned to the housekeeper. "You don't have to come with me. I'm perfectly capable of doing this on my own."

Mrs. Kern grunted. "'Tis good exercise."

Angel eyed her. With a portly build and far from young, Mrs. Kearn was ill-equipped for such strenuous exercise. Angel suspected the housekeeper was under orders from Trent, proving he didn't trust her. She had given her word not to leave before he returned. That should have been enough. "Somehow I think Trent Caldwell is behind your sudden health kick."

Mrs. Kearn sidestepped Angel and continued shuffling down

the sidewalk. "Heaven might know what you're babbling about, lass, but I sure'n don't."

"Right."

Each day Angel walked and searched, spending hours in every shop, bank, and gallery along her route, studying faces, furniture, merchandise. She entered office buildings and carefully read the names of the businesses in the lobby directories. At doctors' offices she approached the receptionists and asked if she looked familiar to them.

By mid-afternoon each day her injured leg began to throb, and still she pushed herself block after block. The ache grew into a stabbing pain that caused a limp, but Angel refused to quit until Mrs. Kearn insisted.

"Damn fool's errand," she muttered, shoving Angel into a cab she flagged down. "You'll be killin' yourself over this."

Depression was a constant companion, threatening to suffocate her at the end of each fruitless day. She kept the despair at bay by spending hours each night pouring over a New York City street map, planning the next morning's itinerary.

Mrs. Kearn fretted over her. "You're wearin' yourself out, lass. 'Tis no good."

Angel set down the yellow highlighter she was using to trace tomorrow's route and looked across the table at the older woman.

"I can't just sit here hoping I'll someday remember who I am. I have to do *something*."

"Aye, but surely not everythin' all at one."

At the end of the week, she was no closer to discovering her identity. All she had to show for her efforts were a sore right leg and a blister on her left heel.

"We'd best be doin' somethin' about that foot," said Mrs.

Kearn, filling a basin with warm water. "Or you'll never get into those fancy pumps tomorrow night."

"The black heels?" Angel removed her sneaker, wincing as the shoe scraped the back of her foot. "You know where he's taking me?"

"Hmm." Not looking at all pleased, Mrs. Kearn sprinkled some baking soda into the water and placed the pan on the floor. "Soak your foot," she ordered.

Angel removed her sock and placed her foot in the basin of water. "Tell me."

"You're goin' to a showin' o' that woman's photos."

"Sarah Montgomery?"

"Hmm."

"You don't sound like you approve."

"Not my place to approve or disapprove," said the housekeeper, peppering her statement with a loud harrumph. "Just a total waste of time, if you ask me, and bound to get you upset. Like when he brought home that magazine."

"No," said Angel, "you're wrong. The photos in my room are the only things I've felt a connection to. Seeing more of her work might help. I'm sure that's what Trent has in mind."

She paused for a moment, then voiced a thought that had danced around inside her head ever since Trent gave her the *National Geographic*. "What if *I* knew Sarah Montgomery? If that's the reason her photos are familiar. Maybe someone at the show will recognize me."

Mrs. Kearn puttered around the kitchen counter, keeping her back to Angel. "I can't imagine a sweet lass like you mixed up with the likes o' them," she muttered.

Uncertain she had heard correctly, Angel asked, "What did

you say?"

"Keep your foot in that bath for twenty minutes," said Mrs. Kearn.

"You didn't answer me."

"Never you mind." With that Mrs. Kearn stomped out of the room.

* * *

A Nor'easter backing up air traffic along the East coast delayed Trent's return flight to New York Friday night by nearly four hours. He arrived back at his apartment well after midnight. Darkened rooms and silence greeted him. The stillness intensified the brooding mood which had accompanied him to Chicago and never left his side the entire trip.

Having Felicia in tow hadn't helped. She was beginning to annoy the hell out of him, from her deprecating treatment of Mrs. Kearn to her insinuations and condemnation of Angel—not to mention her ongoing one-woman campaign to become the next Mrs. Trent Caldwell. But that uncanny financial genius of hers made it hard for him to do without her. And she knew it.

Mrs. Kearn could take care of herself. So could he, but Trent railed over Felicia's treatment of Angel. "Damn her!" he muttered, tossing his suitcase on a chair in the corner of his bedroom. He kicked off his shoes, loosened his tie, and threw himself across his bed.

When he closed his eyes, he saw Angel, standing forlornly in her room, lost in a pair of oversized navy sweats. Her face reflected the fear and self-doubt Felicia had fed with her harsh words, and it pained him that Felicia could act so maliciously. Especially toward someone as sweet as Angel.

It was then that Trent realized how much he had changed

since the accident. Felicia's behavior had never bothered him before. He'd accepted it as part of her barracuda personality, just another of her killer instincts that served him so well. Had he gravitated toward her because she was the complete opposite of his caring, sensitive Caitlin? Were his eyes now opened by someone so much like the love he had destroyed?

Although exhausted, sleep eluded him. Too many unsettling thoughts raced through his mind. Comparing Angel to Caitlin sent the present colliding with the past. Aspects of then and now merged into an unsettling reality he tried to deny, but the act of denial only reinforced the truth. And that released another huge jolt of the guilt that continually festered inside him.

He rose from the bed and headed for his private study.

* * *

"No!" Angel screamed at the wall of flames. Through the blaze she could hear them, their desperate cries searing into her head. Pleas for help. Shrieks of pain. "Please!" she cried, her soot-stained face streaked with tears. "Do something!" But the figures on either side of her only shook their faceless heads and held her back.

* * *

With her heart threatening to break through her chest, Angel bolted upright in bed. Her eyes sprang opened; her lungs panted for oxygen. *It's not real, damn it!* Or was it? Her body shaking from the aftermath of the nightmare, she raised her knees to her chest, lowered her head, and quietly sobbed.

As her body slowly calmed, she became aware of the distant music. The faint, sorrowful melody, nudged its way into her consciousness. Calling to her for the first time in several days. The notes, as they had in the past, echoed the emptiness inside her. The music understood her pain. Swiping at her damp cheeks, she rose from the bed, slipped on her robe, and silently padded down the dimly lit hall.

The sprawling apartment branched out from two corridors at either end of a central foyer that opened onto the main living area. One hallway led to the kitchen, laundry, and several bedrooms, including hers and Mrs. Kearn's. The other led to Trent's master suite. She hesitated at the entry to the second hall, unsure whether to proceed. She had never entered any of those rooms, but the saxophone notes tugged at her like an invisible hand yanking at her robe sash. She had no choice but to follow.

The door stood partially open. A small brass table lamp with a parchment shade sat on an end table and bathed the room in a subtle glow. Its soft warmth spread across the Berber carpeted hardwood floor and onto the tiled corridor, settling at Angel's bare feet. A navy suede sofa wrapped around two sides of the bookcase filled room. At the far end, a large desk sat in front of a wall of floor-to-ceiling windows.

Trent leaned against one of the window casings, a saxophone to his lips. Staring out into the darkness, he coaxed and stroked one heartrending note after another, forming a bleak melody of loss and desolation.

Angel stood in the shadows, feeling like a voyeur, yet unable to move. This was a side of Trent he kept well-hidden, at least from her. She knew she should leave before he saw her. But her feet refused the command her brain sent it. She wasn't sure which pulled at her more, the haunting sadness of the music or the sight of the man playing it.

* * *

Trent felt her presence before he saw her. Turning from the window, he lowered the sax after the last note and stared into the shadows beyond the doorway. He'd picked up his sax in an attempt to drive Angel from his thoughts. Instead, the music had beckoned her to him.

"Angel?"

"I...I'm sorry." She took a step into the light. Her arms were shoved up into the opposite sleeves of her nubby pink robe, giving her the appearance of a geisha in a kimono. A geisha with strawberry blond curls. And instead of bowing like a geisha, Angel hugged her torso. "I didn't mean to disturb you. I heard the music."

"Did I wake you?"

"No." She shook her head. A haphazard mass of short springy curls bounced in emphasis of the word.

"Another nightmare?"

She nodded. "I should have stayed in my room. It's just that the music you were playing...I couldn't help myself. It's so sad."

It was then that Trent noticed she'd been crying. Her eyes were red-rimmed and puffy. Remnants of moisture remained on her cheeks. The sight of her wrenched his heart. Her sorrow and loneliness were his doing.

"What's the piece called?" she asked.

He glance over at the photograph in the antique silver frame on his desk. He remembered the day he and Caitlin bought the frame at an antiques fair up in the Berkshires. A crisp autumn day. He could still see the bright hue of the sky, the puffy cumulus clouds drifting across mountains dressed in golds and reds and purples. The smells of roasting chestnuts and hot chocolate and hay. The sounds of families strolling the outdoor marketplace. The laughter. The chatter. He remembered everything. Whether he wanted to or not.

Part of him envied Angel. She didn't know how lucky she was not to have memories of her past. Damn! That thought brought on a fresh onslaught of guilt. He was one selfish son-of-a-bitch if that's what he really wanted. But he knew the truth, and the truth was that the only thing that kept him going were his memories, no matter how painful.

He should send Angel back to her room. Keep the past and the present separate. But Trent knew it was already too late for that. Angel had pricked the bubble of emotional detachment he'd wrapped around himself. She'd invaded the sacred space where he kept the remnants of the person he used to be—the man he thought he had destroyed.

But that man was now fighting his way up to the surface, and although the person he'd become couldn't offer assistance, inwardly Trent hoped he would succeed. He despised the ruthless bastard that had taken his place. Caitlin would despise him. Angel suffered because of him. He couldn't dismiss her without explanation. His gaze still on the photograph in the frame, he said, "*Rhapsody for Caitlin.*"

Angel stepped toward the desk and followed his gaze. "Is that Caitlin?"

Trent's shoulders sagged. He nodded.

Angel lifted the frame off the desk. Without having to look Trent knew what she'd see. The woman inside the frame was smiling, her eyes sparkling with the joy of life, her face radiant with love. His Caitlin with her windswept auburn hair and azure eyes. The last photograph he'd ever taken of her.

Angel's gaze shifted to him. "She's very pretty. Who is she?"

"My wife."

Confusion clouded Angel's eyes. Her hand shook slightly as

139

she set the frame back on the corner of the desk. She scanned the room as if expecting to see Caitlin hiding in the shadows. If only....

"I don't understand," she said. "Where is she?"

Trent sucked in his breath. It was too late to turn back. In a voice that seemed not his own, he uttered the words that made everything too real to endure. "She's dead."

One hand flew to Angel's mouth; the other reached out for the arm of the sofa as she backed into it. In the dimly lit room, the shadow she cast against the opposite wall trembled, as did her words when she spoke. "I...I'm sorry. I didn't know."

"You couldn't."

"No one ever said anything."

"No one would." He never spoke of Caitlin's death, and Mrs. Kearn knew better than to bring up the subject to anyone.

Angel's reaction surprised him, though. Most people would want details. How? When? Not Angel. She turned to leave, whispering an apology as she headed for the hall. "I shouldn't have intruded. Forgive me."

Forgive her? She hadn't done anything that begged forgiveness. What had happened was his doing. And his undoing. "Angel."

She stopped and turned back toward him. "Yes?"

"I killed her."

EIGHTEEN

To say that Trent's words caught her off-guard was the understatement of all understatements. Angel felt as though Trent had smashed her with a wrecking ball. Her legs could no longer hold her weight. Her chest tightened. Taking several wobbly steps, she made her way back to the sofa and collapsed. The soft cushions swallowed her up. She pulled herself into a ball and squeezed her eyes shut, attempting to will away the emptiness that filled her. Him. The room.

She didn't know what she'd expected to hear, but certainly not what Trent had blurted out so bluntly. So matter-of-factly. So darkly. *I killed her.*

She opened her eyes. He stood at the windows, staring out into the bleak darkness that blanketed the city. No stars. No moon.

No hope.

Not for me.

Not for him.

"I don't believe you," she said.

"Believe it," he muttered.

No. Trent was not the kind of person who could kill anyone, least of all someone he loved. There had to be another explanation. Yet, if he were somehow responsible for his wife's death, it would certainly explain the enigma that was Trent Caldwell. And perhaps, why he felt compelled to open his home to her. Trent Caldwell was doing penance.

Angel pounded her fists into the sofa and screamed. "No! No! No!"

* * *

Trent wasn't sure what to do. Her outburst was so out of character, so un-Angel like. He crossed the room and sank to his knees in front of her. She continued to pound her fists into the cushions. Tears spilled down her cheeks and bounced into her lap. Her cries grew more hysterical. He reached for her hands to still them.

Angel lashed out at him. "No more, please! Make it stop! Let me wake up! This isn't real! None of this is real!" Her wracking sobs soon drowned out her words.

Trent pulled her into his arms and held her tightly against his chest to stop the thrashing. "Oh God, Angel! I'm so sorry for what I've done to you!" His fingers wove through her hair. With his lips pressed up against her temple, he whispered alternating words of comfort and apology, not certain whether she heard him through her hysteria.

Between sobs she uttered desperate pleas for an identity that eluded her and an end to the nightmare that plagued her. "Fire," she cried. "So much fire. They won't let go of me! Help them, please! I can't save them!"

What was she saying? Trent pulled her away from his damp shoulder and held her at arm's length. This had to be a clue to who she was. Shaking her gently, he forced her to focus on him. "Who, Angel? Who couldn't you save?"

She shuddered, then stared at him as though seeing him for the first time. Or maybe she wasn't seeing him at all. Her tear-filled eyes reflected a fear and loss that Trent knew all too well. A shroud of remorse settled over her features. He now knew why Angel remained in her cocoon of amnesia. It was the only way she could live with what she'd done. Or failed to do.

"Who?" he repeated, hoping to force the truth from her.

"I don't know." The words ushered forth a fresh stream of sobs. Collapsing back into his arms, she cried, "Oh, God! I don't know! I don't know!"

Trent lost track of time. He continued to hold Angel in his arms as she sobbed and hiccupped. His words and fingers never wavered in their soothing ministrations. Eventually, exhausted, she fell into an uneasy sleep. And still he clasped her to him, reluctant to break the spell that bound them together.

When he finally carried her back to her bed, he found himself unable to leave the room. Sitting on the edge of the mattress, he brushed aside the halo of golden curls falling across her face and watched as she slept. Occasionally, her body tensed. Her breathing grew shallow and rapid. Soft moans and whimpers escaped through her lips, and Trent knew her dreams had once again grown dark.

Without giving his actions a second thought, he stroked her back and whispered words of comfort until her body relaxed and he was certain the blackness had passed.

The first rays of dawn were fighting their way through the night sky by the time he tore himself from her side and headed back to his room. Scrutinizing his reflection in the mirror above his bathroom sink, he shuddered at the stranger confronting him. The man staring back wore a desolate expression, his cheeks stained with dried tears. Trent swiped at his stubbled face. Only one other woman had ever made him cry. When she left him. Forever.

* * *

Early morning sunlight filtered through the Irish lace curtains, teasing Angel from deep sleep into the surreal world suspended between dream and reality. In both places she found Trent. She remembered him in his study last night. Remembered the saxophone. The music. *Rhapsody for Caitlin* he'd called it. Caitlin. His wife. A shiver passed through her. *Trent said he killed his wife!*

Then she woke up in the bed in the floral bedroom. *Trent said he killed his wife!* She shook the thought from her mind. No, she must have dreamt that—along with the other shadowy visions that lurked on the edge of wakefulness this morning. Tears and caresses that mingled together. His fingers running through her hair, stroking her cheek. His warm lips against her temple. Feeling safe within his arms. Protected. Loved. None of it could have been real. Her mind was playing tricks on her. Again.

Or was it? Angel looked down and saw that she was wearing her robe. In bed. She glanced around the room as if expecting the furniture to have the answers she sought. How much of last night had actually occurred? How much had been dream? And what really happened to Caitlin? Angel knew of only one way to find out.

After a quick trip to the bathroom, she headed down the hall to the kitchen.

Mrs. Kearn took one look at her and scrunched up her nose. "Sweet Mother o' God, lass! Didn't you sleep any?"

"I'm not sure," she said, slipping into a chair at the table. She hadn't bothered to look in the mirror as she brushed her teeth. Pushing a stray curl from her face, she asked, "Do I look that bad?"

"Nothin' a little trip downstairs won't correct," said the housekeeper, placing a glass of orange juice in front of her. "How many slices o' French toast?"

"Two, please." Angel lifted the glass to her lips. "Downstairs?"

"At that fancy spa in the hotel. Mr. Trent had me make an appointment for you today." She speared a piece of egg-soaked bread from a bowl on the counter and dropped it into the frying pan. It sizzled and sputtered, sending up clouds of steam. Turning from the stove, she studied Angel with a discerning eye. "Hmm. A day o' pamperin' 'tis just what you need. Take your mind off your troubles." She fished another slice of bread from the bowl and added it to the frying pan. "Two, you said?"

"Two," murmured Angel, taking a sip of juice and wondering when Trent had suggested the spa visit. After their encounter last night?

"Trent isn't up yet?" she asked, trying to mask the uneasiness growing inside her.

"Haven't seen him. He came home after I went to bed. Must've taken a late flight."

Angel relaxed against the ladder-back chair, unsure why she felt such relief but feeling it just the same.

"Bacon?" Mrs. Kearn lifted two golden brown slices of French toast from the frying pan and slipped them onto a plate. She added several strips of bacon without waiting for an answer, then set the platter of food in front of Angel. Filling two coffee cups, she joined her at the table.

"You've already eaten?" asked Angel between mouthfuls of food.

"Hours ago."

They sat together in companionable silence for several minutes—Angel eating her breakfast, Mrs. Kearn sipping her coffee—before Angel found the courage to speak. "How did Caitlin die?"

Mrs. Kearn set her coffee cup on the table and stared out the window. "Told you about her, did he?" she asked.

Angel nodded.

"When?"

"Last night."

Raising the cup to her lips, Mrs. Kearn took a long sip before speaking again. "What did he say?"

Hesitating, Angel lowered her eyes. She automatically reached for a curl and twisted it around her index finger. Maybe she shouldn't have brought the subject up. He couldn't have said what she thought she heard, could he?

"He told you he was responsible for her death, didn't he?" asked Mrs. Kearn, as if reading her mind.

Angel's head shot up.

The housekeeper's emerald green eyes focused on her, one eyebrow raised in question. "Well?"

Angel fought to force words around the lump that had lodged in her throat. "He said...he said he...tell me he didn't...he wouldn't..." Her voice trailed off, the idea too hideous to bring to life with words.

Mrs. Kearn sighed. She reached across the table and patted

Angel's hand. "No, he's not a murderer, if that's what you're thinkin'. As much as he's got it in that fool head of his that he is."

Another wave of relief flooded through Angel. She didn't want to think of Trent that way. Couldn't. Now she didn't have to. But why would he tell her such an awful thing if it weren't true? How could he believe it himself? "I don't understand."

Mrs. Kearn twirled her coffee mug around in her hands, staring into the empty cup as if in search of answers. "Mind you, I'm not in the habit of talkin' about the lad behind his back. The Caldwells have been very good to me."

"You've worked for him a long time?" The question was more a statement. Angel knew Mrs. Kearn had been with Trent for years. She just didn't know how many years.

"First for his parents. I arrived from Ireland with my young son and little more than the clothes on our backs. The Caldwells took us into their home. Treated me like family, not hired help. Treated my son like one of their own. Trent's folks were good people."

She rose to refill her coffee cup and puttered around the kitchen for a minute before she took her seat and continued. "I know he told you about my family."

Angel nodded.

"That was five years ago. I had no one left. Trent and Caitlin convinced me to move in with them. We Irish are a proud lot. As much as I loved the two of them, I wasn't about to accept charity from anyone. I insisted on taking over the responsibilities of the house in exchange for my keep."

She paused for a moment, either to collect her thoughts or reign in her emotions. Angel wasn't sure which, but she could tell the tale was taking its toll on Mrs. Kearn.

"Caitlin died almost three years ago," she finally said. "We're all each other have left now."

"How did she die?"

* * *

Moira studied Angel. The lass had the most sincere eyes. The sweetest disposition. Trent could do far worse. She'd have to make him see that, drag him kicking and screaming back to life if she had to. The Lord worked in mysterious ways. Maybe Angel getting hit by that cab was all in His master plan to help Trent return to the living.

Lord knew she wasn't getting any younger, and where would Trent be once she was gone? Fair game for every conniving woman who wanted to trap him into marriage, that's where. Like that harlot Felicia Sutton.

No. Angel was here for a purpose. The lass was the answer to her prayers. And Trent's, too. Only he didn't know it yet. Moira felt no guilt in telling Angel about Caitlin. 'Twas for the lad's own good.

"Caitlin Hennessey was the love of Trent Caldwell's life," she began. "The night she died, a part of him died with her. He hasn't been the same since."

She took a deep breath and rose from the table. She couldn't look at Angel, not for this last part. She turned toward the sink, picked up a rag and began wiping down the already spotless countertop as she recounted the events surrounding Caitlin's death.

"They had a weekend home in the Berkshires. Mr. Trent was drivin'. 'Twas winter. Dusk. A young boy lost control o' his sled and skidded out into the street. When Mr. Trent swerved to avoid hittin' the lad, his car skidded on a patch o' ice. The car spun out o' control and into an oncomin' pickup. Mr. Trent walked away without a scratch."

She stopped wiping but still kept her back to Angel. This time she shuddered as she inhaled another deep breath. For her the last part of this gruesome tale was always the most difficult to accept and one she had trouble even thinking about. She never spoke about it. Tried not to think about it. "They'd tried for years to have a child. Caitlin was six months pregnant when she died."

There were times during that first year when she thought she'd lose Trent as well. His pain had overwhelmed him. She knew at times it still did. She understood the emptiness, the motions of going through life but not really living it. It's what bound the two of them together. He and Caitlin had given themselves without reserve to pulling her through her loss, and she could do no less for Trent.

Moira finally turned back around to face Angel. Tears streamed down the lass's cheeks. She brushed away the moisture that had collected at the corners of her own eyes. "Go get dressed, lass. You're due downstairs in a few minutes."

Angel rose and silently left the room.

* * *

Nine hours later Angel stood in front of the full-length mirror mounted on the back of her closet door and gaped in awe at her reflection. With her hair streaked with pale blonde highlights, the unruly curls styled into sophisticated waves, she hardly recognized herself. Stepping back, she twisted her body slightly and studied her profile. Dramatic makeup, professionally and artfully applied, highlighted her flawless complexion and large, crystal blue eyes. She lowered her gaze to the cocktail dress. The silky black fabric slid like a waterfall over her figure, accentuating every feminine curve and creating a look that was at once both elegant and sensual. Angel giggled. Once again, she felt like a little girl playing dress up, but this time with a princess's wardrobe.

Picking up the black beaded evening bag Mrs. Kearn had insisted they purchase during their shopping spree, she headed for the living room. Nervous anticipation over the reception and gallery show awakened a host of sensations in the pit of her stomach.

The more she dwelled on it, the more convinced she became of a connection between herself and Sarah Montgomery. She had no idea what that connection might be, only that a tug of familiarity grabbed her whenever she studied Sarah's photographs. Sarah or her photos must hold some key piece to the puzzle of Angel's missing life.

Unfortunately, whatever Sarah might know, died with her. Angel's only hope now was that someone close to Sarah might recognize her tonight.

* * *

Trent took one look at Angel as she entered the living room and lost his tongue. Breathtaking. Striking. Radiant. The words paled in comparison to the sight standing before him. He'd received a brief hint of what lay hidden beneath Angel's baggy sweats and bulky robe on the day he left for Chicago, but nothing could have prepared him for the vision standing in the middle of his living room.

"You look lovely," he finally managed to say.

Angel blushed at the compliment. "I hardly recognize myself." She swept a hand in front of her body. "Thank you. For the dress. And the day at the spa. For everything you've done. I feel like a princess."

"Princesses don't walk around half naked," said Mrs. Kearn,

shuffling in from the kitchen. "Or at least they shouldn't."

Looking aghast, Angel clasped her hands over her exposed cleavage. She felt her neck and face flush to the color of ripe cherries. "But you picked out the dress, Mrs. Kearn. You said it was perfect when I tried it on!"

The housekeeper pursed her lips and shook her head. "The dress is fine, lass. Don't go gettin' all upset."

Bewildered, Angel asked, "Then what's wrong?"

Ignoring her, Mrs. Kearn turned to Trent. "Them sapphires would be perfect. Bring out the blue o' her eyes, don't you think?"

Trent stared first at Angel, then glared at Mrs. Kearn. "You're pushing, Moira."

She flung her hands onto her hips, stamped her foot, and growled at him. "Why keep them if you're goin' to hide them away? 'Tain't doin' anyone any good buried beneath your jockey shorts."

She had a point. Damn her. "No...no they're not," he finally agreed.

"Well?"

He glanced at Angel and felt the ever-present emotional tug-of-war she stirred inside him. Whenever she was near, she lifted his spirits and filled him with guilt at the same time. He focused on her bare neck and pictured the sapphires draped across her porcelain skin.

He'd always intended to return the necklace, the one he planned to give to Caitlin the day she gave birth, but he could never bring himself to part with it. Angel was a woman meant for precious jewels, but could he survive an entire evening looking at stones originally meant for another neck? A neck that had never had the chance to wear them?

Out of the corner of his eye he saw Mrs. Kearn tapping her foot in annoyance. Trent turned and headed for the bedroom, figuring that if he didn't retrieve the sapphires, she would. He had no energy to fight with her, and either way, he knew he'd wind up losing.

Angel gasped when he returned and opened the dark blue velvet box. She took a step back, shaking her head. "I...I can't wear that."

Trent understood her hesitation. It didn't take a rocket scientist to figure out from his exchange with Mrs. Kearn that the series of deep blue round stones, each surrounded by a ring of sparkling white diamonds, had been intended for Caitlin.

"Of course, you can," said Mrs. Kearn, removing the jewels. "Hold still." She moved behind her. Looping the necklace across Angel's throat, she fastened the clasp at the base of her neck.

Angel placed a hand over the sapphires and looked questioningly at him, but all he said was, "We need to leave." Placing his hand on her upper arm, he guided her toward the front door.

* * *

Trent spoke little during the short drive to the SoHo gallery where the invitation-only cocktail party and preview showing was to take place. Questions about last night swarmed inside Angel's head, but she was wary of broaching the subject with him. Somehow, she got the impression Trent would rather she forget what had taken place in his study and later in her bedroom. And maybe that was for the best.

At least she could take comfort in knowing he hadn't killed his wife. Mrs. Kearn's revelation had gone a long way in explaining the enigma that was Trent Caldwell, but it had also filled her with an overwhelming sorrow. She now understood his loneliness and pain.

She glanced to her side and found him watching her, but once again his features gave no hint to his thoughts. She quickly averted her eyes.

"Nervous?" he asked, placing his hand over both of hers to still them.

Still them? How long had she been fidgeting with the beadwork on her purse? She nodded, offering him a shy smile. "I hope I'm not expecting too much. I realize this is a stab in the dark, but I've had no tangible clues, only vague feelings, and they all center around Sarah Montgomery's photographs."

"And a recurring nightmare," he reminded her.

A vision exploded behind her eyes. The cries rang in her ears. Angel felt the blackness closing in on her, the hope draining away. She blinked her eyes in a vain attempt to shake them off. No longer satisfied with tormenting her sleep, the sights and sounds now invaded her days as well. "They're trying to drive me mad."

"Who?"

Snapping her head around, she stared wide-eyed at Trent. She hadn't meant to voice her fear out loud. The words came out on their own.

He didn't wait for her to respond. "The voices? The ones that cry for help?"

How did he know?

As if reading her mind, he answered her silent question with two words. "Last night."

Last night. Was all of last night real? None of it a dream? Angel stared blankly out the window. She touched her cheek with the tip of her fingers, remembering the heat of his caress. How safe she had felt in his arms. And loved. She turned from the window and searched his face. In his eyes she found a perplexing mix of emotions that left her more confused than ever.

Trent reached up and withdrew her hand from her cheek. "It's all right, Angel," he said. "Everything will be all right."

Before she could ask him what he meant, the car pulled up to the curb in front of the gallery. O'Hara cut the engine.

"Don't bother getting out," Trent told him, opening the door for himself. He stepped from the back seat, then held his hand out to her.

With his palm at the small of her back, Trent escorted Angel towards the already crowded gallery. Twice he stopped along the way, allowing the photographers hovering on the sidewalk and clogging the street in front of the entrance to snap their picture. When she attempted to shield herself from the bright flashes, Trent wrapped his arm around her waist and held her close to him. "Smile," he whispered into her ear. "If we wind up in *People*, someone might recognize you."

Unlikely, she thought. Her picture had already been plastered across newspapers and television screens without results. Besides, as far as she could tell, the woman in the mirror this evening bore little resemblance to the one in the hospital—the one with shoulder-length hair, a swollen face, and pulverized nose and cheek bones.

For that matter, contrary to the surgeon's opinion of his reconstructive skills, her new face might bear little resemblance to her old one. She had no way of knowing. It wasn't like he'd had photos of her to work from. So what was the point?

But she smiled anyway. Weakly. Not because Trent was right. Not because someone *still* might recognize her. All thoughts of *that* had flown from her mind the instant he pulled her against him.

Her body took on a mind of its own. The rebellion began with a touch of hands in the car. It kicked into overdrive moments ago when he rested his palm against the bare skin of her back. And now, snugly tucked under his arm, she felt herself tumbling. Liquid heat flooded her limbs. Bells and whistles and sirens exploded in her ears, but were they heralding an awakening of desire or sounding a warning? Probably both.

Angel paused at the entrance to the gallery. Before stepping across the threshold of the open door, she took a deep breath, hoping to gulp in a dose of common sense along with the air. *This is insane. You can't have these feelings. Not for him. You don't even know who you are, for God's sake.* And besides, her life was complicated enough. The last thing she needed was to compete with a ghost.

Trent moved his arm up to her shoulders and gave her a reassuring squeeze. "I'll be right beside you," he said.

She nodded, more than slightly unsettled by both his touch and her thoughts. Unfortunately, his nearness was a major part of her problem at the moment. She let the air slowly escape from her lungs, bit down on her lower lip, and stepped into the noisy crowd.

NINETEEN

Devon retrieved a small box from inside a boot at the back of the closet, then withdrew a case from a carton on the top shelf. Skilled fingers cautiously removed the contents of both, lining up each item on the polished wooden table. When all the necessary components were assembled, Devon collected a third package from a bureau drawer. Inside, nestled within a bed of pale yellow tissue paper, lay the delicate shamrock-adorned white porcelain music box. Overcome by emotion, unsteady hands cautiously lifted the hinged lid. Devon listened as crystal clear notes filled the room, and in a voice choking with emotion, sang along:

> *O Danny Boy, the pipes, the pipes are callin'*
> *From glen to glen and down the mountain side*
> *The summer's gone and all the flowers are dyin'*
> *'tis you, 'tis you must go and I must bide...*

"In the name o' the Lord, Thy will be done!" Devon lifted a fist up to the heavens, then closed the music box lid, and with the skill of a Swiss watchmaker, set to work.

TWENTY

"Impressive turnout," said Trent.

Angel scanned the interior of the packed room. Scores of men in tuxedos and women in a multitude of designer glitz and glam crowded together inside the white walled gallery.

"Kind of small for so many people," said Angel. Her heart sank. She wondered how anyone would have a chance to see her with such a packed mass of humanity. Somewhere in this room someone might recognize her—*if* that person had a chance to spot her. With so many people hip-to-hip and elbow-to-elbow, what were the chances of that? "Why such a small gallery for such a huge event?" she asked.

"This was the gallery that always exhibited Sarah's work," said Trent. "They have a contract."

The mass of people left little room to maneuver, let alone view the dozens of photographs hanging throughout the gallery's two rooms. As a passing waiter gingerly negotiated in front of them, Trent lifted two glasses of champagne from the waiter's tray and handed one to Angel.

She took a small sip of the sparkling wine, hoping it might steady her nerves and keep her voice from sounding as shaky as her limbs felt. "You sounded surprised by the crowd a moment ago."

"Hmm, but pleasantly so." He nodded a greeting to a group of people off to his left. They seemed to be vying for his attention, but Trent didn't stop to chat with them. Instead, he continued to maneuver her through the crowd.

When the group in front of them drifted to the right, creating an opening on the floor, Trent raised his glass in the direction of an elegant looking woman dressed in flowing jade crepe who stood at the opposite end of the room.

The woman stared at Trent for no more than a millisecond, ignoring his gesture of greeting, before she zeroed in on Angel. With a calculating gaze, her lips set in a taut line, she scanned Angel from head to toe before another group drifted between them, effectively cutting off their view of each other.

Angel thought she noticed a glimmer of recognition in the woman's eyes. Her heart began to beat faster in her chest. She needed to speak with that woman. "Trent, that woman in green across the room. The one you raised your glass to? I think she recognized me."

Trent appeared not to hear her. Between the noise from the crowd and the string quartet playing off to one corner, Angel barely heard herself. However, he continued to maneuver them toward the part of the gallery where she'd seen the woman. Acting like Moses parting the waters, Trent sliced through the room, groups stepping aside to enable him to pass.

As they made their way toward the start of the exhibit, Angel sensed the gaze of dozens of people following them. Voices began to lower to hushed whispers as she and Trent passed. She wished he'd stop to let her speak with some of these people, but Trent seemed to be on a mission and other than a curt nod here and there, he pressed on, moving her along with him.

"Are all of these people friends of yours?" she nearly shouted.

"They'd like to think so."

* * *

Trent nodded and sometimes offered a stiff smile to the various faces but kept a firm hand on Angel's elbow as he guided her toward the start of the exhibit.

He was all too aware of what he was doing but completely helpless to stop himself. Ever since he held her in his arms last night, he hadn't wanted to let go of her. When he touched Angel, he felt alive in ways he thought long dead.

He maneuvered them around yet another group. He had no patience for small talk this evening and even less desire to share Angel with any of the circling buzzards.

As much as Angel might cling to the hope that someone in this room might recognize her, Trent knew there wasn't a chance in hell of that happening. These people traveled in the same circles he did.

Although Angel had carried no identification at the time of the accident, her clothing labels suggested she shopped on Madison Avenue and Fifth, not some outlet mall on Staten Island or in Secaucus. For that reason, in addition to scouring the designer boutiques of the Upper East side, SoHo, and TriBeCa, his private investigators had questioned Trent's crowd at length. What had at first seemed a logical beginning quickly proved to be no more than one dead end after another.

However, according to the investigators, several people had made similar comments upon viewing photographs of Angel. The irony of the situation left Trent grappling with what to tell her. In the end he'd decided not to say anything. The shock of discovering it for herself might be the catalyst she needed to crack open her locked mind. That was why he'd brought her here this evening.

And that was why Angel now stood face-to-face with herself. But not herself. The azure blue eyes of the woman 'in the photograph sparkled with just the slightest hint of mischief. Seated on the trunk of a massive fallen redwood, she cradled a camera perched on her khaki-clad knees. The fingers of her other hand threaded through a long thick strawberry blonde braid that draped over her left shoulder.

Trent felt Angel's arm trembling beneath his hand. He watched for signs of recognition but saw only confusion in her face. She stepped closer to the wall, pulling him along with her.

* * *

In a shaky whisper Angel read aloud the printed card mounted next to the framed eleven by fourteen color portrait. "Sarah Montgomery. Self-portrait, 2011."

Was this why she felt such a strong connection to the photos in the floral bedroom? Because she and Sarah Montgomery looked enough alike to be sisters? Was that all? Anger and hurt roiled inside her. She felt her control slipping away, and with it the last vestiges of hope.

She spun around and confronted Trent. "Why didn't you tell me?"

He made little excuse for the deliberate, cruel trick that so pained her. "I hoped the shock of discovery might jar your memory."

Angel yanked her arm away from him. Although stricken by his deception, she kept her words controlled, not wanting to create a scene. The last thing she needed was to break down in front of a roomful of strangers. "All these weeks! How could you, Trent?"

"No, Angel. I haven't known very long. You have to believe me. I'd never do anything to hurt you." He tried to explain, but his words fell on deaf ears.

"Believe you?" Her voice crept up several octaves. Angel quickly glanced around the room, fighting to control the hysteria building inside her. "How could you not know? You own some of the woman's work, don't you?"

"I told you we never met."

"Surely her picture was on the news and in the papers the day she died, Trent! You must have seen a photo of her at some point."

His mouth set into a tight line. His eyes narrowed. His voice grew cold and hard. "The day she died I had other things on my mind—in case you've forgotten."

No, she hadn't forgotten. She might not remember anything before that day or the day itself, but she was well-aware of how it had shattered her life. Whatever that life may have been. Angel turned away from him and stared once more at her near-double. "I'd like to leave now," she said.

"No."

Tears built up behind her eyes, dissolving Sarah's smiling face into a blur. Angel squeezed her eyelids shut. When she opened them, she saw Trent reflected in the glass. Why was he doing this to her? "Please, I don't want to be here."

He stepped closer, drawing her back against his chest. She

stiffened but didn't pull away. Lowering his head, he spoke into her ear, his voice a strange mix of forcefulness and sorrow that nearly broke her heart. "I am truly sorry if I've hurt you. That was never my intention. You're here for one reason. If we leave now, you may miss an opportunity to learn something."

"I don't think so." She forced the words around a baseball-sized lump in her throat. "There are no answers for me here. Or anywhere." She twisted her neck to look up at him. "Why pretend any longer? I think it's obvious what happened."

"Not to me."

She shook her head. "Subconsciously, I must have remembered that Sarah and I looked very much alike. When I saw her photos in your apartment, my mind grabbed onto them and in desperation blew everything out of proportion. There is no other connection. There never was."

"You can't give up."

Her body sagged like a deflated balloon. Her voice echoed the despair inside her. "I can't go on fooling myself, either, can I?"

Trent reached up and stroked her cheek with the tips of his fingers. "Searching for the truth often leads down blind alleys, Angel, but it's never a fool's journey."

He was right, of course. With all he'd done for her so far, how could she think he'd deliberately hurt her?

How could she think at all?

His touch was short-circuiting her brain. Reason and comprehension deserted her, leaving in their wake nothing but a raw confusing need that both frightened and excited her.

He lifted her chin, trapping her gaze. "Stay?"

To her ears the word sounded part plea, part command. But it didn't matter. Wild horses couldn't drag her from him. Angel nodded. "I'm sorry. I overreacted."

They were interrupted before Trent could say anything further.

"Well, isn't this a quaint picture. The corporate takeover king and his latest acquisition." Bloodshot eyes skewered Angel with a piercing stare, then, as the man drew closer, opened wide in disbelief. He took two steps backwards, his entire body off-balance, his words sputtering. "What the hell? Is this your idea of some sick joke, Caldwell?"

Something in the man's sneering accusation sent a prickle of uncomfortable familiarity up Angel's spine. She tried to grab hold of it, but as quickly as it appeared, the fleeting image dissolved. Whether it was the tone of his voice or the words themselves which had triggered the unpleasant fragment, the man was evoking equally strong emotions in Trent.

Every muscle in Trent's body tensed. Angel could feel it in the way he tightened his grip around her and pulled her closer to him. Trent, who was often so hard to read, did nothing to hide the contempt and loathing he held for this stranger.

She glanced over at the man who elicited such an intense reaction from Trent. He appeared to be quite drunk. His black bow tie hung untied from his neck. The top button of his pleated tuxedo shirt was unfastened, as were his jacket buttons. His hand tremors caused the contents of his tumbler to swish precariously close to the rim of the glass and threatened at any moment to deposit a large stain across his shirt and down his pants.

"Angel, this is Roger Caine, Sarah's widower," said Trent, his voice tight and clipped.

"Angel, huh?" He moved a step closer, his expression a mix of astonishment and distrust. "Perfect," he muttered.

Angel gripped her champagne flute with both hands, nodding her head slightly. "My condolences on your loss, Mr. Caine."

"Yes. To Sarah!" he said in a voice loud enough to carry over the din of the room. Several people nearby turned and stared at them. Roger raised his glass to his lips. As he polished off the drink, his eyes darted between Angel and his late wife's portrait.

"I'm as startled as you," said Angel. "I had no idea I bore such a striking resemblance to your late wife. Seeing me here must be unsettling. I'm sorry."

"Yeah. Fucking unsettling." Roger glared at her, then dropped his gaze to the jewels surrounding her neck and scowled. He turned to Trent. "Satisfied?" he asked, waving his arm to encompass the entire room.

"Only after you complete the second part of our agreement," answered Trent.

"Ah, yes, the second part. You always do enjoy twisting the dagger a bit deeper, don't you, Caldwell?" He turned his attention back to Angel. "Tell me, does good ol' Trent here fuck you as well as he does his enemies?" He reached out and fingered one of the sapphires. "He obviously rewards you well enough."

Angel gasped. Pushing his hand away from her, she sank farther into Trent's chest. She felt violated by the man's touch, and her skin crawled from the feel of his alcohol-soaked breath. Over his left shoulder she saw Sarah's smiling portrait and wondered what a woman capable of creating such beauty could have in common with this vile man.

"That's quite enough, Caine!" Trent practically growled his words.

"This isn't over yet, Caldwell. Not by a long shot."

"It is for this evening, Roger." The woman in the jade crepe appeared from behind Trent and Angel. She removed the empty glass from Roger's hand and whispered something into his ear. Like a child being sent to his room, he threw Trent one last malevolent look before storming off.

"You'll have to forgive Roger," she said. "That was the alcohol speaking." She sighed. "I'm afraid he's taking Sarah's death extremely hard."

Trent smirked. "Nice performance, Mrs. Montgomery, but we both know damn well what Roger's taking hard."

She skewered him with a hostile glare before regarding Angel. This time Angel was certain she noticed something in the woman's cat-like eyes. Shock? But aside from that brief glimpse her icy composure never wavered.

When she spoke, her words sounded calculating and acerbic. "You must be the young woman Trent ran over." Extending her hand, she introduced herself. "I'm Whitney Montgomery. Dear Sarah's grandmother."

Angel was certain her ears were playing tricks on her. "Grandmother?" She stared at the woman's face, ignoring her outstretched hand. Either Whitney Montgomery had discovered the Fountain of Youth or she had the best damn plastic surgeon in the world on retainer. The woman didn't look a day over thirty-five.

Whitney's laugh mocked her confusion. "Step-grandmother, actually." Raising her hand, she clasped Angel's jaw between her fingers and twisted her head, first to the right and then to the left. "Amazing."

After scrutinizing each feature, she shifted her attention to Trent, speaking to him as if Angel were nothing more than a lab experiment. "It seems the rumors are true, Trent. Your stray kitten bears a striking resemblance to our dear departed Sarah. If I didn't know better, at first glance I might think she *was* Sarah. But, of course, we both know that's impossible, don't we?"

"Quite. And for the record, Mrs. Montgomery—"

Whitney arched one perfect eyebrow and pouted her deep crimson lips. "My, my. You're always so formal with me, aren't you, Trent."

He ignored the interruption and continued. "For the record, Angel was hit by a taxi in which I was a passenger."

With a toss of her head, she flipped her platinum blonde hair off her shoulder and smirked. "Mere semantics. Why so touchy this evening, darling?"

Trent glowered.

"Oh, forgive me," she continued, her voice a sing-song taunt. "I forgot how sensitive you are about automobile accidents."

The cruel barb stabbed at Angel's heart, but if it affected Trent in any way, he never gave Whitney Montgomery the satisfaction of seeing it. Instead, he smiled politely and said, "If you'll excuse us, Mrs. Montgomery, we were just leaving." Then he turned his back on the vicious woman and steered Angel towards the exit.

* * *

Angel sat in the back seat of the car, her hands clenched tightly in her lap. She glanced to her left and found Trent wearing a brooding mask. "I don't blame you for what happened to me," she said. "I never have."

Without looking at her, he reached across the seat and placed his hand over hers. "I know, Angel."

Instinctively, she withdrew one of her hands and clasped it over his. The past hour had been traumatic for both of them. Trent claimed he never met Sarah Montgomery, but he apparently had a less-than-pleasant history with her husband and step-grandmother. Angel had no idea what caused the animosity between them, but whatever it was, Trent was hurting. And she hurt for him.

"This wasn't the evening I had planned for you," he said, breaking into her thoughts.

The corners of her mouth strained upward, feigning cheerfulness. "No?" She forced a soft chuckle. "Actually, I figured that one out on my own."

He grimaced. "Didn't anyone ever tell you sarcasm is unbecoming?"

Angel shrugged. "Possibly, but how would I know?"

Trent flung his head back against the seat and cupped the back of his neck with both hands. "How, indeed." His voice echoed her own hopelessness.

"Sarah's relatives aren't very fond of you," she said, fishing for some clue as to the nature of the hostility between the parties.

Trent turned his head towards her and raised his eyebrows. "More sarcasm, Angel?"

"Just observation. Why were they so nasty?"

He took a deep breath, holding it for several seconds before releasing it with a swift rush. "I thwarted their attempt to rape and plunder the company they inherited when Sarah died."

"Is that what you do? Play Superman to the big bad wolves of corporate America?"

"Sometimes."

"Does it help?"

He looked thoughtful for a moment. "I think so. The stockholders whose money I protect think so."

Angel shook her head. "That's not what I mean. Does it help

you?"

Trent stared at her. His hazel eyes glazed over, telling her without words that he understood the meaning behind her question. "No." He turned his head away and gazed out the window. "No, it doesn't."

* * *

That night Angel appeared once more at the entrance of Trent's study. Without a word she curled up on the sofa. He continued to coax melancholy notes from his saxophone. Within minutes she'd fallen into a deep, tranquil sleep.

Only when Mrs. Kearn entered the room did he lower the instrument from his lips. He glanced at the clock on the fireplace mantle, then the apple-cheeked woman who wore a heavy deep burgundy wool coat and an apologetic grin. "Just getting in?" he asked, laying aside the woodwind.

Her emerald eyes twinkling, she shrugged her shoulders as she removed her felt hat and shrugged out of the coat. "Good friends. Good music. Too much stout. Next thing you know, 'tis mornin'." She glanced over at Angel, not seeming surprised to find her asleep on the sofa. "How'd it go this evenin'?"

Trent shook his head. "Not well."

Mrs. Kearn sighed, pushing back a few rusty and gray strands of hair that had come loose from the bun secured atop her head. "Can't say as I'm surprised."

Trent weighed his next words carefully. A disturbing thought had begun to gnaw at him hours earlier, and he needed to give it voice. "Do you remember me telling you that some people have commented on Angel's resemblance to Sarah Montgomery?"

She grunted.

Trent pressed on. "I didn't think much of it at the time. Sarah's dead. It's just coincidence. But Angel keeps insisting she has some connection to those photos in her bedroom, and when I saw her standing in front of a photograph of Sarah this evening and the way both Whitney and Roger reacted to her..." He hesitated, uncertain how she would respond to his next words.

She crossed her arms over the starched ivory blouse that strained across her bosom and raised her chin in challenge. "Get it off your chest, lad. I won't turn into a monster from you sayin' it."

"No one knows what Angel looked like before the accident," he continued. "Maybe there was some kind of mixup. Maybe Sarah's not dead. Maybe Angel *is* Sarah Montgomery."

Mrs. Kearn stared at him, saying nothing, her face giving no hint of her thoughts. In the background Trent heard the mantle clock ticking away the long seconds. He held his breath, waiting for her to say something. Anything.

She walked over to the sofa and stared down at Angel. Finally she spoke. "I noticed the similarity the moment I laid eyes on her."

"You never said anything."

She turned to him and shrugged. "What was the point? 'Tis said we all have a double somewhere on God's green earth. 'Tisn't the sweet child's fault who the good Lord chose for hers. Angel's a gift from God. I feel it inside me. Here." She made a fist and knocked it against her breastbone, emphasizing her words.

Then she took a deep breath before continuing, "The Montgomerys are blood suckin' murderers. She's not one o' them. The good Lord would never be so cruel as to do that to you and me, Trent Caldwell. I'd stake my own life and yours on it."

She turned her gaze back to Angel. "Lookin' like one o' them doesn't make her one. Shame on you for thinkin' such horrid thoughts. She had nothin' to do with what they did to my

Brendan."

And neither did Sarah, thought Trent, but he kept the thought to himself. They'd beaten that dead horse into its grave countless times over the past five years. No need to do it yet again. Besides, he wasn't in the mood for one of her sins-of-the-father lectures or any other Biblical quotes with a twist of decidedly Irish retribution added to them.

"You want me to wake her?" she asked.

Trent watched the motherly way she adjusted the crocheted afghan he'd tossed over Angel, gently tucking the throw back where it had slipped off her shoulder. "No," he said. "Let her sleep. I'll carry her back to bed."

At least he could take comfort in knowing that no matter how fiery her Irish temper, Moira Kearn had too large a heart to ever act on her hatred toward the people she felt were responsible for her son's death. Not that there were any left at this point other than Roger and Whitney, and they both married into the family after the plane crash that robbed Moira of the only family she had.

* * *

"Welcome to *Catch Twenty-two*, my dear." Roger surveyed the near empty gallery. All the guests had departed. Only the gallery manager and the catering staff remained, all occupied at various cleanup chores. He raised his glass to Whitney.

"What are you babbling about?" she asked, sinking into a wooden folding chair. She did little to mask her annoyance at his drunken behavior.

Roger had acted outrageously all evening. Insulting one guest after another, he had successfully destroyed everything she'd accomplished over the past several weeks. How could they ever hope to regain control of the company if he couldn't even conduct himself in a fitting manner for four fucking hours? She shuddered to think what the society columns would say tomorrow morning. Several unpleasant headlines sprang to mind.

"To your success, Mrs. Montgomery." He drained his glass, then scowled at her. "And our financial ruin."

"Either make sense or shut the fuck up, Roger! You're giving me a headache."

"Forgive me, darling." He strode across the wooden floor and leaned over her chair, his alcoholic breath chasing away the surrounding oxygen. "Let me spell it out for you in the simplest of terms. While you were busy trying to charm your way up the social ladder with this little fundraiser we were forced into, you forgot two important facts."

"Such as?"

He held up his index finger. "One. Every one of these damn photographs belonged to us, and we don't get a dime from their sale. And two." His middle finger sprang up alongside his index finger. "You and I both have to cough up an amount equal to tonight's receipts. From the looks of it, that's a sizable chunk of change."

Whitney groaned.

"Feeling a bit queasy, my love?"

She pushed him away and rose to her feet. "I need some air."

Roger stared down at the empty glass still in his hand. Depositing it on the vacated chair, he followed Whitney toward the exit. "I need another drink. That bitch Caldwell brought with him tonight gave me the creeps."

You're not the only one, thought Whitney, but she refused to give Roger the satisfaction of knowing how unsettling she had found the woman's likeness to Sarah.

Instead, she tossed a snide remark over her shoulder along with a hostile sneer. "And you handled the situation so well, darling. Sarah's dead. Even Trent Caldwell with all his power and money can't bring her back."

But even as she uttered the words, Whitney wondered whom she was trying to convince, herself or Roger. She stepped out onto the sidewalk. The temperature had dipped considerably since early evening. A brisk wind swirled leaves and assorted debris around scurrying pedestrians.

Roger grabbed her arm and swung her around. "If Sarah's really dead."

Whitney shivered, from the thought as much as the weather. "No." She shook her head, dismissing the suggestion that had plagued her as well. "No. You saw the photos of the wreckage. No one could have survived that crash."

"No one who was in the car."

That was a possibility even she hadn't considered. "Are you suggesting Sarah faked her own death? And Trent Caldwell is somehow in on it?"

Roger stepped off the curb to hail a cab. "I'm not sure what I'm suggesting," he said, opening the door for Whitney after a taxi pulled to a stop in front of them. "All I know is staring into that woman's eyes tonight was like seeing a ghost. She might not look exactly like Sarah, but those were Sarah's eyes staring back at me."

"You're drunk, Roger. The alcohol is making you fucking paranoid."

"Drunk or sober, I know what I saw. Besides, I wouldn't put anything past Caldwell."

Leaning back against the seat, Whitney mulled over his words. Was it coincidence that Trent Caldwell initiated his takeover of

Montgomery Aeronautics moments after Sarah's death, or was it part of a master plan? Was the woman with no memory really Roger's dead wife, and if so, was the amnesia a smoke and mirrors ruse? But for what? Why the complicated conspiracy? Whitney could come up with no possible explanation.

"It doesn't matter," she muttered to herself. It was apparent to her now that they couldn't risk the possibility. They had to do something before Caldwell destroyed them.

TWENTY-ONE

Rafe glared down at the bills in his fist. "You promised me ten Gs and a ticket to L.A. There's only a measly grand here." He waved the wad of money in the stranger's face. "And no ticket."

"You get the rest after you finish the job. The balance and the ticket are waiting for you in Nome."

He shoved the money into the pocket of his jeans. It wasn't like he hadn't expected something like this. No one paid a hundred percent up front. Hell, he wouldn't, and he'd been in the business a long time. Knew people he could trust to do a job and do it right. Like him.

Still just once it would be nice, but in his line of work it was all about performance pay. If you didn't perform up to specs, you could kiss the *dineros adios*. And sometimes you kissed a lot more than *dineros adios* if you weren't careful. This job he could do blindfolded with one hand behind his back, though. Ten Gs for a few hours work and no risk. "So what am I supposed to do with the broad once I get her to Alaska?"

"I don't really care. As long as she never leaves."

Rafe shrugged. "Not much chance of that unless she sprouts wings." He studied the stranger. "Pretty damn cold up there this time of year. A person could freeze to death without the proper gear."

His comment went ignored.

"Here's everything else you'll need. ID for both of you. Two tickets departing from Newark Liberty tomorrow evening with a stopover in Seattle and a connecting flight in Anchorage. I typed up your cover story. Memorize it, then burn it."

Just like the old days, thought Rafe, resisting the impulse to salute. Only this time of year he'd much prefer gunrunning in Central America to freezing his butt off on Norton Sound. The sooner he ditched the broad and got the hell out of there, the better. Rafe hated winter. He hated Alaska. And he *really* hated winter in Alaska.

He stuffed the papers into his jacket pocket and studied the stranger with an appreciative eye. Funny thing about hate. It could bring scrapple and caviar together in the most peculiar ways.

* * *

Trent hung up the phone and slumped back in his chair. *Her husband!* After all this time it didn't seem possible, but the man had a plausible explanation for not showing up sooner.

"Been off cappin' whales in Saudi," he said with a deep Texas twang.

Trent knew little of the whaling industry, but he was reasonably certain it was *not* part of the Saudi economy. "There are no whales in Saudi Arabia," he said, ready to slam the phone down on the crank caller.

"Not big fish whales!" The man yelled from the other end of the connection. "Oil whales! I troubleshoot for International Petroleum. Been gone over three months this time 'round."

He went on to explain how he'd come across a two-week-old copy of *People* magazine during a layover at Heathrow. "Nearly blew my socks off. That's my sweet Billie Sue you've got there, Mr. Caldwell."

"You mean to tell me you leave your wife for three months at a time and don't stay in touch?"

"Ain't that easy what with where I am. Hell, man. This is grueling work. Half the time I don't even know what day it is!" Trent heard him exhale. "Besides, that ain't none of your business, now, is it? I've got a flight out of here that brings me into JFK early tomorrow afternoon. Tell Billie Sue I'm on my way."

"She may not recognize you," warned Trent.

"She'll be fine once I get her home." And then the phone went dead.

Her husband! He couldn't picture Angel—Billie Sue—with a man who sounded like...what was his name? Trent scanned the notepad in front of him, searching through his scribbles. Rafe. Rafe Faber. And he was coming to claim Angel.

"Earth to Trent. Are you there?"

Felicia's high-pitched nasal soprano startled him back into the present. "Don't you ever knock?"

"I did knock. Several times. And I've been standing here a full minute waiting for you to return to the planet. What's going on?"

"Angel's husband showed up. He's on his way here from London."

The corners of Felicia's mouth turned up into a devilish smile.

Her voice took on a sing-song lilt. "Well, isn't that nice? All's well that ends well."

"I'm not so sure," said Trent. "I'm going to have Security run a check on this guy." He jotted down the name on a separate piece of paper. "There's something about his story that just doesn't add up."

"I'll contact them for you," she said. Snatching the note from his hand, she deposited several manila folders in front of him. "I need you to okay these changes so we can proceed with cleaning up the Chicago mess."

Trent ignored the files, pointing instead to the slip of paper as she typed something on her iPhone. "Don't bury that, Felicia. I want a full report by six."

"And you'll have it," she replied, flashing him a too-sweet smile. "I've already sent an e-mail to Security. Really, Trent. What did you think I'd do?"

Anything to get rid of Angel, thought Trent, frowning at her. "Still think she's after my money?"

Felicia crumbled the note and tossed it into the waste basket next to Trent's desk. With a shrug she said, "Anything is still possible. Who knows? Her husband could be her partner in crime."

* * *

An hour later Trent knew more about Angel than she did. According to the fax sent up by his head of Security, Rafe Faber's story checked out. A former, decorated Green Beret, he leap-frogged across the world from one oil rig to the next while his wife stayed at home in Big Sandy, Texas. The report contained no red flags. No police records. No bad credit ratings. Not even an outstanding parking ticket.

Only Trent couldn't reconcile himself to the news. Angel was *not* Billie Sue Faber from Big Sandy, Texas. He felt it in every cell of his body. She didn't look like a Billie Sue from Big Sandy. She didn't speak like a Billie Sue from Big Sandy. No way was anyone going to convince him she *was* Billie Sue from Big Sandy. Something just didn't add up, and in Trent's world if things didn't add up, his suspicions went into overdrive.

Could amnesia cause a person to lose her accent as well as her memories? He wasn't sure that was possible, but it hardly mattered. He knew his reaction to her husband's call was based more on irrational feelings than rational thought. The truth was, he didn't want Angel to be Billie Sue Faber from Big Sandy, Texas because he didn't want her to leave. There. He'd admitted it to himself.

But she would leave. He stared at his Rolex, following the second hand as it swept past each consecutive number. In less than twenty-four hours Angel—Billie Sue—would walk out of his life forever, and he was powerless to stop her.

* * *

Angel had waited for this moment. Hoped for it. Prayed for it. But now that it was here, a blanket of foreboding settled over her. She reached up and worried a lock of hair between her thumb and index finger. "Texas?"

Trent nodded.

"How did I get to New York?"

"I don't know, Angel. I mean, Billie Sue." He grimaced. "Damn I can't get used to that."

"Neither can I." She sprang to her feet and paced across the living room, her arms hugging her torso. "And I'm married? To a man named Rafe?"

"Rafe Faber. I had him checked out. He's telling the truth."

I don't want to leave you. The words threatened to bubble up from where she kept her feelings for Trent buried. She swallowed back her emotions and stared out the window at the Manhattan skyline—the skyline whose familiar silhouette had comforted her during those first frightening hours in the hospital. But how was that possible? She was Billie Sue Faber. From Texas. The very thought seemed like a cruel hoax.

A nightmare.

A prison sentence.

She turned back to look at Trent and wondered what he really thought of all this. His face showed no emotion. Would he miss her? Or was he glad to be rid of the burden of her? She had disrupted his well-ordered world.

Her very presence stripped away the veneer that hid his deepest, most painful wounds, but it had also caused Trent to undergo a metamorphosis of sorts. Gradually, he had shed his shell of aloofness, and exposed her to the warm, caring soul that still lived within him—a soul kept hidden from the rest of the world since Caitlin's death.

A soul that touched her own soul.

In the background she heard Mrs. Kearn taking her frustrations out on her copper-clad pots and pans. The housekeeper did little to hide her feelings as she prepared a dinner which in all likelihood, would go uneaten by all three of them.

Poor Mrs. Kearn. Angel was well-aware of the not-so-subtle ways the Irishwoman had manipulated her and Trent. With the best of intentions, she had tried to maneuver them into a relationship, but none of that mattered any longer. Angel had a husband, and he was on his way to claim her.

* * *

Dinner was a near silent affair, a last supper of sorts. "I don't know how to cook," Angel whispered, staring blankly at the stuffed pepper on her plate. She hadn't taken a single bite, and she felt badly about that because of the time Mrs. Kearn had taken to prepare the meal. But under the circumstances how could she eat anything? She could barely breathe from the constriction in her throat, let alone chew and swallow food. "He's going to expect me to cook his meals."

Mrs. Kearn reached over and patted her hand. "'Twill come back to you, lass."

She bit down on her lip and shook her head. "He's going to expect other things, too." She looked over at Trent and saw her own anguish mirrored in his eyes. Some emotions even he couldn't hide.

He slammed his fork onto his plate. "You're not chattel, damn it!"

"No, I'm his wife." The resignation she heard in her own voice sent a lone tear trickling down her cheek.

* * *

That night Angel curled up on the wide windowsill in the floral bedroom and watched the full moon slowly arc its way across the night sky. Eventually, the melancholy sounds of Trent's saxophone crept like fog down the long terra cotta hallway, seeping under the door of her room. The notes called to her, beseeching her to follow them, but Angel stayed huddled against the window frame, her knees pulled up to her chest. Joining him in the study at such a late hour now seemed inappropriate. She was another man's wife.

Another man's wife. The thought sobered her. She wondered if seeing her husband might finally unlock her memory, but the question opened a Pandora's box of fears that sent shudders up and down her spine. Had she, as Dr. Pierce suggested, deliberately suppressed her memories? Had she run off to New York to escape her past? Escape Rafe Faber?

Maybe you were happy in Texas. Maybe you love Rafe Faber, and he loves you.

Trying to convince herself of that only led back to the same nagging question, though. Why was she in New York? Not to visit friends or relatives. She already knew that from the extensive investigations. No one had come forth to claim her after the accident, and none of the area hotels had reported a missing guest.

She tried to imagine herself in Texas, but when she closed her eyes, all she saw was a scene from some old Western—sagebrush and tumbleweed peppering an endless, desolate prairie. Was that what awaited her?

Be careful what you wish for.

For well over two months, she had clung to the hope that someone would come along to free her from the nameless abyss she'd fallen into. Someone who would claim her as family or friend. Yet, now that he approached, she dreaded his arrival. Dreaded learning the answers to the countless questions that plagued her.

* * *

Trent remained in the apartment the next morning, spending much of his time closeted in his study. Mrs. Kearn busied herself packing Angel's clothes.

"I'm sure I have clothes in Texas," she said. "You should donate these to a homeless shelter."

"He wants you to have them."

Angel nodded her acceptance. "Strange," she said, drifting over to the wall that held Sarah's photographs, "the one clue to my identity turned out not to be a clue at all, and yet, I still feel a powerful connection to these photographs."

Behind her Mrs. Kearn grunted.

"I could understand if they were scenes of Texas," she continued, "but I have a feeling Billie Sue Faber has never seen Provence. Or much of anything outside Texas."

"You talk like she's someone else," said Mrs. Kearn, snapping closed the lid of the Tumi suitcase Trent had ordered up from the luggage shop in the building's lobby.

She turned toward the housekeeper. Her chin began to tremble. "I can't help it."

Mrs. Kearn held out her arms, offering the comfort of a warm, motherly embrace. Angel accepted without reserve. "I'm going to miss you," she said between soft sobs.

"And I you, lass."

TWENTY-TWO

Rafe Faber sailed into the apartment like a little boy diving into a pile of presents on Christmas morning. He swept Angel up in his arms and twirled her so furiously that the room continued to spin long after he set her down.

"I've missed you, sugar." He pulled her close and covered her face with kisses.

Angel wrestled her way out of his arms, taking several steps backwards. "Please," she said, holding up her hands to fend him off.

Rafe's eyes grew wide with hurt. His jaw dropped open. "You really don't know me, do you, Billie Sue?"

Angel shook her head. The man standing before her was tall and muscular with dark hair that fell slightly below his collar and a bushy, bristly mustache covering his upper lip. He wore black tooled cowboy boots, a body-hugging pair of extremely worn

Levis, and a brown leather bomber jacket over a denim cowboy style shirt, the kind that fastened with pearl snaps instead of buttons.

Rafe Faber looked like a cross between an Abercrombie and Fitch poster boy and the Marlboro man. A navy baseball cap with the International Petroleum logo instead of a Stetson was the only indication that his line of work involved chemicals and not cattle. Along with looking tough and weathered, Rafe Faber possessed a dangerous sex appeal that seemed to ooze out of every pore. His *aw shucks, ma'am* attitude struck Angel as both forced and phony. Nothing about him triggered any memory in her. As far as she was concerned, the man was a complete stranger.

"I'm sorry," she said.

Rafe rubbed his hand across his stubbled jaw. He turned his attention for the first time to Trent. "She doesn't remember anything?"

"Not a thing."

"Damned if that don't beat all." He shoved his hands into his back pockets and circled around her as if sizing her up like some prized heifer at a county fair. "Looks like I've got my work cut out for me, don't it?"

"Yes, I'm afraid so, but would you mind clearing up a few questions, Mr. Faber?"

Raising an eyebrow, Rafe eyed Trent with suspicion. "Such as?"

"Your wife doesn't speak with a Texas accent."

"Course not," he said, a huge grin replacing the wary expression. "Billie Sue's not a native like me."

"Then where am I from?" asked Angel.

"All over, sugar." He ticked off a long list of cities, punctuating each with a raised finger. "Billings, Tupelo, Casper, Wausau, Spokane, Hastings, Boise. Let's see. Did I leave any out?" He removed his baseball cap and scratched his temple with an index finger. "Oh, yeah, Provo, Little Rock, and Pueblo."

"We've lived in all those places?"

"Not me, sugar. You."

"Why?"

"Your Daddy never could cotton to putting down roots in any one place for too long."

"I have a father?"

Rafe shook his head. "Hell, Billie Sue. We all got fathers. Don't you remember any basic birds and bees, either?"

He turned back to Trent. "That answer your question?"

"Billie Sue's a long way from Big Sandy. How do you explain how she came to be in New York?"

Irritation settled over Rafe's face. He obviously didn't appreciate Trent's grilling, but Angel welcomed it. His answers, on the other hand, were far from welcome.

"Well, I guess she got a hankering to do some big city shopping, Mr. Caldwell. You know how women are, they just love to spend money. Billie Sue's real good at that. But I don't mind. In my line of work the money flows as thick and fast as the crude. Besides, Billie Sue's real talented at a few other things that more than make up for all that spending." He wrapped his arm around Angel's shoulders and threw Trent a wink. "Know what I mean?"

Angel cringed. She cast a pleading look in Trent's direction and held her breath.

As she hoped, he stepped in, offering her a lifeline. "Under the circumstances, perhaps, Ang...Billie Sue should stay here for a few more days to give you both time to get reacquainted."

Rafe shook his head, dashing any hopes Angel held for a stay of execution. "No can do, pal. Duty calls. I was damn lucky to get us on a flight leaving Newark—" He flipped his wrist over and glanced at his watch. "—in just under three hours. La Guardia was all booked, and I can't afford to hang around until tomorrow. I got me a gusher a'waiting. The bosses ain't really pleased about this here little stopover in the Big Apple." He reached for Angel's hand. "Say your goodbyes, sugar. It's time to hit the trail."

Once more Angel found herself engulfed within Mrs. Kearn's plump torso. "Godspeed, lass. You keep in touch."

Angel nodded, too choked up to answer. She stepped from the housekeeper's embrace and locked eyes with Trent. There was so much she wanted to say to him and so much she couldn't. She swallowed hard and managed a soft, "Thank you."

Trent placed his palm against her cheek. His touch threatened to shatter the fragile thread of composure holding her together. "Be well, sweet Angel."

She raised her hand to her cheek, and for the briefest of moments their fingers laced before Trent withdrew his, and Rafe nudged her toward the door.

* * *

Trent had offered the use of his car and driver for the ride to the airport, but Rafe declined.

"I didn't get a chance to say goodbye to Mr. O'Hara," said Angel after they stepped from the elevator into the lobby of the Trentwell Arms.

"Who's Mr. O'Hara?" asked Rafe, his voice tinged with suspicion.

"Trent's driver. He's probably around back," she explained. "He was very nice to me. I'd really like to say goodbye, if you don't mind."

"I do mind," he said, grabbing her hand. "We ain't got time for anymore teary farewells." He dragged her across the polished marble lobby and out the main doors.

Within seconds an empty cab pulled up to the entrance. "This one's ours," he said, shouldering his way past the elderly couple next in line at the taxi stand. Before the doorman could react, Rafe pushed him aside. Yanking open the back door, he tossed the suitcase across the seat, then shoved Angel in after it.

"How could you do that?" she cried after he climbed in beside her and slammed the door shut. She twisted around and through the back window mouthed an apology to the startled doorman.

"You snooze, you lose. Newark Liberty," he told the cabby, "and don't try goin' by way of Schenectady, hear? I ain't no hayseed tourist."

Horrified, she turned to study him. Gone were all traces of the effusive southern charm he had displayed in the apartment. Rafe Faber now radiated nothing but belligerence and hostility. How could she possibly be married to this man?

"What are you gawking at?"

Angel jumped. "I...I don't remember anything about you. About us. How we met. How long we've been married. If we have—"

"Enough!" Rafe barked the word at her. "Jesus H. Christ! What do you think I am, a fucking encyclopedia?"

Angel cringed at his words, but unwilling to be cowed by them, she forced the issue. "No, I think you're my husband," she said, "but you certainly aren't acting like one. Especially under the circumstances. You're not at all curious as to how I wound up in New York, and you don't seem to care that I was nearly killed by a cab and have amnesia!"

Ignoring her outburst, he pulled a crumpled pack of Marlboros from his jacket pocket and fished for a cigarette. "Hey, buddy, got a light?" he asked the cabby.

"No smoking in the taxi, mon. City ordinance."

"Fucking Eastern liberals. Give 'em the chance, and they'll legislate all our goddamn rights away." He scowled at Angel. "You're alive, ain't you?"

She stared at him in wide-eyed disbelief.

"You'll know everything you need to know soon enough," he said, shoving the pack back into his pocket.

While the taxi navigated through midtown traffic, inched its way into the Lincoln Tunnel, and sped down the New Jersey Turnpike, Angel mulled over her options. By the time the cab pulled up to the curb at Terminal C of Newark Liberty Airport, she'd made up her mind. She had no intention of returning to Texas with Rafe Faber.

She was now convinced that Dr. Pierce had been right. She had willed herself to forget her past. The surly proof was seated beside her. The accident had given her a chance that few people ever get—to start over with no strings attached, and her brain refused to deny her that opportunity.

Rafe glanced at the cab meter. "Fucking vultures." He pulled a wad of bills from his pocket, counted out the exact amount and tossed the money through the window in the Plexiglas partition that separated the front and back seats.

The driver glared at him. "Hey, what the fuck, mon. You no give me a tip?"

"Sure, pal. I'll give you a tip. Don't bet on the horses." Rafe laughed at his own joke as he dragged Angel and her suitcase from the cab over to the curbside check-in.

Angel stood in silence as Rafe checked her bag, noting that he also stiffed the Skycap. He then half-led, half-dragged her through the terminal toward Security.

Angel's mind continued to race, desperately searching for a way to avoid getting on the flight that would take her back to Texas. "I don't have any identification," she said as they stood in line waiting to go through security. He may have used his own ID to check her bag, but they'd both need identification to pass through the security checkpoint. "They won't allow me through without any."

"Don't worry about it," he said.

"But—"

He turned and glared at her. "I said, don't worry about it, didn't I? So just shut the fuck up." When they'd inched their way up to the front of the line, Rafe handed over the tickets and two driver's licenses. A dour faced TSA agent scrutinized the licenses against the names on the tickets, then handed them back to Rafe.

Once through the checkpoint, he dragged her down the long corridor to gate twenty-eight. Pointing to a bank of chairs against the window, he said. "Sit there while I see if I can get bumped up to first-class."

She noticed he didn't say 'us.' Was he planning to take an available first-class seat and leave her in coach? Nothing would surprise her at this point.

She glanced at the ticketing counter. *United Flight 902— Seattle-Anchorage* traveled across a digital display in large red letters. Deciding Rafe was not a man who liked having his mistakes pointed out to him, she walked over to the chairs and sat down in one.

Her uneasiness grew as she watched him flirt with the ticketing agent. The woman wasn't directing him to another gate. Instead, she glanced first at something Rafe showed her, then over in Angel's direction after Rafe pointed her out. Angel felt the hairs on the back of her neck stand on end. *How did he get her ID, and why were they going to Seattle, or worse yet Anchorage, if they lived in Texas?*

By this point she knew better than to ask him.

A few minutes later Rafe sauntered over and sank down into one of the few remaining empty chairs facing her.

Gate twenty-eight was at the extreme end of the concourse, one of a half dozen gates that dotted the circumference of a circular area. Several flights were experiencing delays. The seating area filled up quickly. Within fifteen minutes of their arrival, there were no available seats left in the communal waiting area. People stood or leaned against the windows and walls. The floor was littered with carry-on luggage and strollers with babies. Unruly children ran willy-nilly, bumping into passengers, tripping over duffels, and knocking over luggage.

A steady stream of travelers scurried in one direction to catch flights or in the opposite direction to claim baggage. Adding to the congestion, a Starbucks kiosk stood in the middle of the circular area. A long line of people in need of caffeine snaked around the rows of seats.

A person could easily disappear within this mass of humanity, Angel thought, as she studied the area. Rafe sat facing the runway, his back to the crowd. She'd have no difficulty slipping away. He couldn't very well follow her into the bathroom. She didn't think he'd escort her to the entrance. That would mean forfeiting his seat, and Rafe Faber didn't look like a man who would give up his seat for anyone.

Angel could see two major problems: First, how would she get from the airport back into the city? She had no money. And how would she do it without freezing to death? November was no time to walk around with only a silk shirt as protection against plunging temperatures and whipping winds.

Taking her coat was not an option, though. Rafe would immediately know something was up. She needed to keep him blissfully in the dark for as long as possible while she made her escape.

"I need to use the restroom," she said, rising from her seat and stretching. Time was running out. Their flight would be boarding in twenty minutes. If she had to, she'd beg a ride into the city.

Rafe glanced at his watch, then nodded. "Bring me back an order of cheese nachos and a Dr. Pepper."

"I have no money."

He grimaced, then fished inside his jacket and withdrew the wad of bills. "I ain't got nothing smaller," he said, handing her a fifty.

Fifty dollars! Angel could hardly contain herself. Not wanting to appear too eager, she hesitated before taking the bill. "I think I saw a currency exchange booth back near the food court," she said. "I can break this there if the cashier can't make change."

"Don't take all day." He crossed his arms over his chest and slumped down in his seat, stretching his long legs out in front of him.

With her heart pounding like a kettle drum against the walls of her chest, Angel stepped over Rafe's legs and around the carry-ons and people scattered throughout the waiting area. She couldn't do anything that would raise his suspicions. She forced herself to keep a calm, steady pace even though her heart wanted her to sprint as fast as she could away from gate twenty-eight and Rafe Faber.

Once she'd put a good ten yards or so between them, Angel hazarded a glance over her shoulder. Through the crowds she spied the back of Rafe's head slumped across his left shoulder. He wasn't watching her! She stepped up her pace. With luck, by the time he realized she was gone, she'd be halfway back to Manhattan.

Angel plunged into the crowd heading down the concourse. Walking as fast as she thought prudent without drawing attention to herself, she followed the signs pointing the way to Ground Transportation.

TWENTY-THREE

Whitney popped a Xanax, washing the pill down with a glass of Mouton Cadet. Tranqs and wine. She knew better, but she no longer cared. Frowning, she refilled the glass, carrying it and the bottle out to the gazebo. The dismal November day matched her mood—fucking cold and colorless. An icy wind whipped the branches of the barren oaks and maples that swayed like skeletons against the gray sky. Not bothering to brush the dead leaves from the cushions, she sank into a chaise lounge at the center of the gazebo and stared sullenly at the house. She wasn't overly fond of the Greenwich estate, but it offered her the solitude she craved. At present, the sprawling West Side apartment was too cramped for both her and Roger.

Thanks to Trent Caldwell, nothing was going as planned. Damn the man! And damn Roger! His erratic behavior added to their precarious situation. She could no longer trust his judgment,

LOIS WINSTON

never knowing for certain when it was clouded by alcohol.

Too late she'd realized his limitations. When he controlled events, he functioned superbly, manipulating people with a skill that amazed her. But throw a monkey wrench into his well-orchestrated plans, and he fell apart, seeking solace in case after case of imported Scotch. Roger Caine was incapable of functioning when he hadn't worked through all the variables down to the most-minute detail ahead of time.

Except he hadn't this time, had he? He'd been too convinced of his own genius and his own superiority over Abel's flunkies. After all, he was Roger Caine. He didn't make mistakes. He never had. Until now.

So when the plan began to crumble around them, thanks to Trent Caldwell, the seismic variable neither of them had seen coming, Roger became useless and worthless. And a fucking sloppy drunk. Now it was up to Whitney to figure out how to keep them one step ahead of Caldwell, not to mention the law.

Whitney knew that if Trent Caldwell dug deep enough, she and Roger would wind up wearing neon orange jumpsuits for years to come. And orange was definitely not Whitney's color.

She seethed when she thought of the way Trent had toyed with her at the gallery, as if he were privy to some private joke—a joke made at her expense. His words had given away nothing of his plans, but his eyes had conveyed a chilling message: *I'm going to enjoy destroying you.*

Not if I destroy you first, Trent Caldwell.

"Mrs. Montgomery?" The housekeeper called from the back porch.

Whitney ignored her, but the woman persisted, her shrill voice carrying over the wind and stabbing at the cloak of numbness

Whitney was desperately trying to induce. "Damn it! What the fuck is it, Bridey?"

"A package for you, mum. Delivered by special messenger," said the woman, trudging out to the gazebo. "I thought it might be important." She deposited the box in Whitney's lap.

Whitney scowled at the package. She hadn't heard a car pull up to the house, but then again, she'd been busy numbing her mind. She glanced at the bottle nestled in the crook of her arm. *Must be working.* Pushing the package to the foot of the lounge, she dismissed its importance.

"If you won't be needin' anythin', mum, I thought I'd do the marketin'."

Whitney waved the maid off as if she were a fly. "Go. I don't want you here, anyway."

"Are you sure, mum?"

Whitney caught the maid's disapproving glance at the half-empty bottle. "I said leave! Get the hell out of here. I want to be alone!"

"Yes, mum."

Whitney watched the housekeeper scurry back to the kitchen. Several minutes later she heard Bridey Callahan's fifteen-year-old Ford Escort sputter its way down the driveway.

Damn immigrant trash, thought Whitney, reaching for the cardboard box. She ought to fire the disrespectful bitch, but Bridey had worked at the estate for years and knew it inside-out. For that reason, her job remained secure. That and the fact that it was near impossible to get English-speaking help anymore.

Nowadays they all came from whatever Godforsaken Third World country was disgorging its riffraff onto American soil on any given day. How the hell was she supposed to give orders to a housekeeper who didn't speak English? No, she'd have to put up with Bridey Callahan and her scornful looks. Either that or learn Spanish, and going back to school was definitely not on Whitney's to-do list.

She placed the wine bottle on the gazebo floor next to her lounge chair and turned her attention to the carton. It contained no identifying markings other than her own name. She picked at the packing tape, cursing out loud when the adhesive side of the cellophane fell back against her nail, destroying a fifty-dollar French manicure. "Shit!" She scowled at the offending finger, now half-stripped of its polish. "This damn well better be worth it," she muttered, tearing open the corrugated box.

The carton was filled with hundreds, if not thousands, of beige plastic foam pellets. Whitney scowled first at the pellets, then her nails before plunging her hands into the packing material. She dug around until she felt a smaller package nestled within the protective material and withdrew a silver gift-wrapped box. Pellets clung to the box, her arms, and hands. Irritated, she vigorously shook her arms and brushed off the package, sending the debris sailing across the yard.

Finally free of the annoying packing material, Whitney stared inquisitively at the box. Too late for her birthday. Too early for Christmas or Valentine's Day, and Roger wasn't prone to buying spur-of-the-moment gifts. However, she did expect a show of appreciation from the owner of the gallery where Sarah's exhibition was held. The woman had netted a sizable chunk from her cut of the sales. A thank-you gift was certainly in order.

Whitney grabbed the shipping carton and upended it in search of a card, but except for the remaining pellets which flew away with the wind, the box proved empty. With a combination of mounting curiosity and impatience, she tossed the carton to the floor of the gazebo, swept the remaining pellets off the chaise, and tore away the wrapping paper.

Inside the gift box, hidden under several layers of yellow tissue paper, she found a delicate creamy ivory porcelain box adorned with tiny green shamrocks. Whitney recognized the trademark Belleek china. Expensive, but not exactly her taste. She never could understand why anyone would set a table with weed-covered dishes.

Thinking the card must be inside the box, she lifted the hinged lid. Music filled the air. Whitney listened to the first few notes, unable to place the familiar sounding tune. Finally, it came to her. *Danny Boy*. Sentimental Irish drivel.

It was her last thought before a massive explosion ripped through the gazebo.

* * *

Clutching the fifty-dollar bill in her fist, Angel scanned the transportation signs and weighed her options. The bus into the city only cost a few dollars, but it wasn't scheduled to leave for fifteen minutes. What if Rafe came searching for her before it pulled away? She'd seen a sign for a train as she raced through the terminal, but there, too, she ran the risk of him catching up with her before the next scheduled one departed. Taking a taxi would eat up a sizable chunk of the fifty dollars, but within seconds she'd leave the airport far behind.

Angel glanced over her shoulder. Throngs of people converged around the baggage carousels. Others headed in her direction, suitcases in hand. But Rafe was nowhere in sight. Without further hesitation, she raced out the double doors and onto the sidewalk, jumping into the back seat of a waiting yellow cab.

"Where to, lady?" When she failed to answer, the driver twisted his head around and stared at her, his brusque expression implying she'd better make up her mind or relinquish the taxi to a customer with a destination.

"Uhh…Manhattan."

"Right. Mind clueing me in on where. It's a big island, you know?"

"Umm…" Just her luck to get the one cab driver in all the tri-state area who spoke English! *Where?*

She couldn't go back to Trent's apartment. That's the first place Rafe would look for her. But how long could she survive on the ten or fifteen dollars she'd have left after she paid the cabby? "Just drop me off as soon as you get through the tunnel," she said.

"Which one?"

"What?"

"Which tunnel, lady? Lincoln or Holland?"

"Holland." She thought that one was closer to Newark, even though the driver coming from the city had taken the Lincoln. He'd probably done so on purpose to squeeze more money out of Rafe.

Every penny counted. Once downtown, she'd hop a bus or subway or walk. But to where?

Angel lowered her head onto her hands and took deep breaths, fighting to control the panic rising inside her. She had escaped with the clothes on her back and enough money for one less-than-decent meal after she paid the cab fare. Maybe. As the taxi sped away from the airport, she began to question the wisdom of her impulsive decision.

Closing her eyes, she tried to remember, then analyze each verbal exchange, every scene and nuance, from the moment Rafe

Faber entered Trent's apartment until she left him sitting at the gate. No matter how objectively she tried to view the last few hours, she still came to the same conclusion. Husband or not, Rafe Faber scared the crap out of her.

So, now what?

The taxi stood in bumper-to-bumper traffic in Jersey City on the approach into the Holland Tunnel. Angel watched in dismay, her minimal funds dwindling ever lower as the meter marked time with a steady tick-tick-tick.

Sighing in resignation, she realized she had but one option open to her.

* * *

Trent couldn't shake the fear in Angel's eyes from his mind. Nor his own feelings of misgiving. But he knew he had done all he could. Her husband had come to claim her. Several hours from now Angel would be back in Texas, and hopefully, the familiarity of the setting, along with family and friends, would break through her wall of amnesia. Faber seemed genuine enough in his affection for his wife, even if those feelings smacked of chauvinism. But considering his background, Trent could hardly expect otherwise.

He needed to purge Angel from his soul. He never should have let her enter, but her sweet innocence had wormed its way inside him, releasing long-suppressed yearnings. Angel had made him come alive again, and he had no right to that particular happiness. Not after what he'd done to Caitlin.

"Don't bother fixing dinner for me tonight," he told Mrs. Kearn. I'm going to work late."

"Could've predicted that one," she muttered under her breath.

Trent whipped his head around in time to see the accusation in her eyes. "What could I do?" he demanded. "She's the guy's wife!"

"She didn't want to go with him."

"Did she say that, Moira? She left willingly."

"The lass was scared to death, and you know it!"

Yes, he knew it. Not that it mattered. She could have told Faber to take a hike. She didn't have to leave with him. "Of the uncertainty, not him," he said, attempting to convince himself as well as his housekeeper. "You saw how he greeted her."

"A fine piece o' actin', if you ask me."

Trent reached back and grabbed for the knot growing between his shoulder blades. A steady pounding erupted inside his head. What if Moira were right? Women were far more intuitive than men when it came to reading beneath the surface. Had she sensed something ominous, or was she merely acting churlish? Mrs. K.'s attempts at playing Cupid had been far from subtle. She had doted on Angel. Unfortunately, Rafe Faber's arrival thwarted her matchmaking plans. "God, I hope you're wrong."

His ringing cell phone kept her from responding. He pulled the phone from his pocket and glanced at the display before answering. "Trent Caldwell." After listening for a minute, he asked, "Are you certain?"

A minute later, he ended the call and turned to his housekeeper. "Whitney Montgomery is dead."

Mrs. Kearn acknowledged the news with nothing more than a slight incline of her head. "As I've told you before, the Lord works in mysterious ways."

"The Lord had nothing to do with this, Moira. She was murdered."

With a shrug of her shoulders, Mrs. Kearn spouted another homily. "The Lord giveth, an' the Lord taketh away."

Trent wasn't certain which shook him more, Whitney Montgomery's murder or Moira Kearn's calm acceptance of the righteousness of the act—an act that validated her unyielding belief in divine retribution. He left the apartment without another word, the murder relegating his worries over Angel to a back corner of his mind.

* * *

The news of Whitney Montgomery's death spread through corporate headquarters at both Montgomery Aeronautics and Trentwell International like an Australian brush fire. By the time Trent arrived downstairs at his office, his secretary had fielded over two dozen calls from worried board members, nosy reporters, and one very hostile and extremely accusatory Roger Caine who was bent on pinning Whitney's murder on Trent.

TWENTY-FOUR

Seamus Hurley lowered the newspaper to the table, removed his reading glasses, and turned to his friend. He kept his voice low, the whispered words an equal mix of gravel and rasp barely heard above the raucous sounds of the Friday night pub crowd. "I see you've been up to your old tricks."

Devon took a long draught of stout, draining the pilsner, before acknowledging the comment. "'Tis all in God's plan, Seamus. I'm no more than an instrument o' the good Lord. Like yourself."

"Aye," he agreed. "We must all do His work in His name." He lifted his arm, signaling the barmaid for another round. While they waited for their refills, he pulled a handkerchief from his breast pocket and began polishing the lenses of his glasses. "You're near done now, are you not?"

"Soon. Quite soon."

"And then what?"

"Then, Seamus, surely the angels will raise their voices in sweet song, and the souls of the departed will finally rest in peace."

The barmaid arrived with their stout. "Anything else, Seamus?" she asked, setting the tall glasses in front of them.

"Not now, Meggie." He waited until she left before resuming the conversation. "If you should need any help—"

"I know where to turn."

Seamus lifted his glass in a toast. "Health to your enemies' enemies, my friend!"

"*Go mbeannaí dia dhaoibh*, Seamus."

TWENTY-FIVE

Angel stood on the sidewalk staring up at the small brass nameplate attached to the wall of the unassuming brownstone. A soft overhead light above the door illuminated the raised letters. *Haven*.

When the cab dropped her off near Hudson Street, Angel had walked several blocks until she found a pay phone and called 311, the New York City information hotline. After telling the operator where she was and that she needed directions to the nearest women's shelter, the woman had told her to walk one block north and three blocks east.

Haven. Angel hugged her arms around her body. With the coming of darkness, the temperature had plummeted. A cold wind whipped at her face, stinging her cheeks and bringing tears to her eyes. Her entire body shivered. She desperately needed a haven. From the cold. From the dark. From her fears.

"You comin' in, or you gonna stand out here all night freezin' your ass off, girl?"

Angel spun around, nearly crashing into a tiny, rail thin teenager, her head a mass of cornrows. A multitude of piercings traveled down both ears, across one eyebrow, and through her left nostril.

"Well?"

"I...I'm not sure."

"Ain't nobody gonna hurt you. Come on. Sister don't never turn nobody away." The girl grabbed her arm and yanked her up the five concrete steps leading to the door.

"You're late, Charmaine." The stern voice came from a room at the opposite end of the mahogany paneled hall as soon as the girl closed the heavy front door behind them. A moment later a middle-aged woman dressed in a plain gray wool A-line dress and white wimple appeared through the doorway. A large silver crucifix hung from her neck. Her arms crossed over her chest, her expression somber, she confronted the young woman whose fingers still circled Angel's arm. "Class ended over two hours ago. What kept you?"

"Yeah, um, well." Charmaine shuffled her feet and stared at the floor.

"You were with Julio again, weren't you?" When the girl refused to answer, the nun shook her head and sighed deeply. "Hasn't he hurt you enough, Charmaine? Isn't that why you came to me?"

"Mama! Mama! Mama!" A pint-sized whirlwind in bright pink overalls, a pastel rainbow striped polo shirt, and an untamed mop of light brown curls ran down the hall and hurled herself into Charmaine's legs.

"Hey there, precious bundle!" Charmaine lifted the child into her arms and covered her face with kisses. "You come to rescue you're mama from the Grand Inquisitor?"

The sister's features softened as she watched the display of affection between mother and child. She raised an eyebrow and fought to suppress a chuckle. "Grand Inquisitor?"

"Yeah, like that Spanish dude, Father Torquemada. We learned 'bout him in history class. He was always askin' questions, too. And if he didn't like your answers, forget it. You's toast. Like for real."

The nun scowled. "Well, I'm certainly not thrilled with the comparison, Charmaine, but at least you're paying attention in school."

Finally, she turned to Angel for the first time. "Are you a friend of Charmaine's?"

"Nah." Charmaine settled her daughter on her hip and answered for Angel. "She's just some stray pup was standin' outside lookin' lost and scared. Our kinda people. Right, Sister?"

The nun studied Angel for a moment. "Do you need shelter, my dear?"

Angel hesitated. Dressed in Donna Karan slacks and a silk shirt, with a pair of Ferragamo suede boots on her feet, she knew she appeared better suited to a suite at the Waldorf than a homeless shelter for abused women and children.

As if reading her mind, the nun took her hand and led her down the hall. "Let's talk in my office, shall we?"

The office, which Angel assumed was once a back parlor, was crammed to overflowing with a battered oak desk, a well-worn leather office chair, half a dozen beige file cabinets, a floor-to-ceiling bookcase, and two straight-back wooden chairs. Every available horizontal surface was covered with stacks of papers and manila folders. The sister lowered herself into the chair behind her desk and motioned Angel to take one of the wooden chairs on the opposite side of the desk.

"I'm Sister Margaret Mary," she said, "but my girls call me Sister Mags. And you are?"

Angel tensed, unsure how to respond. She couldn't lie to a nun, but neither could she bring herself to utter her name. It didn't sound right on her tongue or to her ears. And yet, she *was* Billie Sue Faber.

And what would happen to her if she told the sister her name? Her story? She couldn't claim she had suffered abuse at the hands of her husband. She didn't know anything about her life with Rafe. Only that the thought of leaving New York with him scared the shit out of her. Although she probably shouldn't use such graphic language in front of a nun.

Sister Mags clasped her hands together on her desk and offered Angel an understanding smile. "Trust comes with time, my dear, but rest assured, anything you tell me will be kept in the strictest of confidence. Haven is a sanctuary. No one is ever turned away, and no one will know you're here."

Slowly the tension drained from Angel's body. She nodded in understanding. "Angel," she said. "I'm called Angel." Not her given name, but not a lie.

Sister Mags stood and extended her hand in greeting. "Then welcome, Angel. Come. I'll bet you're hungry. I know I am."

She asked no further questions. Made no demands. Angel followed her from the office, down the hallway, and into a large, brightly lit dining room with mahogany wainscoting and pale gold painted walls. Two dozen children, young girls, and women of various ethnic backgrounds crowded around an enormous table draped with a white linen tablecloth.

Several of the girls and women were visibly pregnant. Others held babies on their laps. Toddlers, nursing bottles of milk, perched in highchairs alongside their mothers. Chatter and laughter rang through the room, but all stopped and respectfully turned their attention to Sister Mags when she entered.

"Girls, we have a new family member." She motioned to Angel. "This is Angel. I know you'll do your best to make her feel welcome."

Hands waved, and a dozen voices filled the room with enthusiastic greetings.

"Over here, girlfriend." Charmaine called from the far end of the table. "Already got you a place set right by me an' Sunshine."

After both Angel and Sister Mags had taken their seats, all bowed their heads and held hands while the sister said Grace. "Thank you, dear Lord, for this beautiful day you have given us and the abundant feast set before us. Thank you for filling us with your love and for sending us our generous benefactor who makes so much possible for these, your children. And thank you, Lord, for leading Angel to our door. In the name of The Father, The Son, and The Holy Spirit, Amen."

"Amen." The word echoed from all in unison.

Heaping platters and bowls of food were then passed around the table, each girl serving herself and any children seated on her lap or beside her. As they ate, one-by-one they related the events of their day to the Sister. Even the smallest children contributed to the mealtime conversation.

Angel quickly learned that Haven operated as both a shelter for these women and a day care for their children. While the younger girls attended school and the older ones went to job-training classes, Sister Mags, along with several other nuns who came in during the day, tended to the infants, toddlers, and preschoolers. All the women were responsible for caring for their own children in the evening as well as taking on one housekeeping chore at Haven.

"We have plenty of cooks, laundresses, and cleaning crews," explained Sister Mags, "but I am a bit shorthanded in childcare at present." She motioned towards three newborns asleep on their mothers' shoulders. "We had a series of blessed events last month, and I'm afraid the other sisters are getting too frail to handle so many lively souls."

Angel felt a tug at her sleeve from Charmaine's daughter. "We gots new babies."

"So I see."

"I helps sisters wiff babies."

Angel smiled at the child. "I bet you're a big help. Is your name really Sunshine?"

The child nodded vigorously. "Uh-huh."

Angel caught Charmaine's sheepish grin over her daughter's head.

"I big girl now," said Sunshine. "I's free." She held up three mashed potato covered fingers from one hand and carefully counted them off with the index finger of her other hand. "See? One. Two. Free."

"My! You're all grown up!" Angel bent down and kissed the top of Sunshine's head, then turned her attention back to Sister Mags. "I'd be happy to care for the children, Sister, especially if Sunshine can be my helper."

"I helps Angel, Sister!"

"First you eat them peas, young lady." Charmaine pointed to the small pile of vegetables left on her daughter's plate. "Every last one of 'em. You hear me?"

Sunshine scrunched up her nose. "Does I gots to?" She cast pleading eyes at first her mother, then Angel, and finally Sister Mags. When all three nodded, she let loose a dramatic sigh before slowly feeding one pea at a time into her mouth, chewing and swallowing with exaggerated deliberateness.

Angel caught the twinkle in Sister Mags's eyes as she watched Sunshine clean her plate.

"Our little thespian," said the nun.

* * *

Angel settled easily into the routine at Haven, taking care of the children during the day while their mothers, many of them little more than children themselves, attended school. In the evenings, with the blessing of Sister Mags, she tackled the nun's office, creating order from chaos within a matter of days.

Caring for colicky infants and sorting through casework reports kept her mind from dwelling on her own problems and how she had run from them. As time passed, she grew increasingly convinced she had made the right decision in fleeing from Rafe Faber.

For the first few nights at Haven, she had avoided the evening news, but others watched religiously after dinner. Angel held her breath, expecting someone to see an account of her disappearance, but none of the residents mentioned anything. She found the lack of media coverage puzzling. Logically, Rafe should have gone looking for her at Trent's apartment, then notified the police. Apparently, he hadn't. Not from what she could tell. It made no sense to her, but then again, nothing had made much sense since she had awakened in that hospital bed months earlier.

She tried not to think about her circumstances. Or about Trent, attempting to banish those feelings to the vast emptiness that housed what little memory she possessed. She discovered the more she exhausted herself during the day, the less time she had to dwell on how much she missed him.

The extreme fatigue had another benefit, as well. The more she pushed herself during the day, the less disturbed was her sleep. Her nights were now often devoid of the terrifying, fiery nightmares which had plagued her since the accident.

Gradually, Angel became acquainted with each resident and learned their stories. She heard about the alcoholic fathers and crack-addicted mothers. The physical and often sexual abuse. The pimps and prostitution. Although she inwardly cringed at the brutal accounts, she found herself filled with admiration for the young women who fought with such tenacity to overcome their pasts and make better lives for themselves and their young children.

Charmaine's story was not unlike many of the other girls' tales. When her mother O.D.'d on heroin, Children's Services placed Charmaine with a foster family. Raped the first night, she didn't stick around for night two. She was cold, hungry, and scared when Julio Rivera found her huddled in an alley and taught her how to earn a living on the streets. She was thirteen years old. By fourteen she was a mother.

"Julio threw me out when I got knocked up and wouldn't have an abortion," she confided to Angel while folding laundry one evening. "That's when I found Sister Mags. She took me in."

"Is Julio Sunshine's father?"

Charmaine shrugged. "Could be, but I doubts it. She don't

look nuffin like him."

"Then who is?" asked Angel.

"Shit, girl! How should I know? I was pullin' down a dozen tricks a night back then. Ain't no way of tellin' who's her daddy." She picked up a pair of socks from the laundry basket and rolled them into a neat ball. After adding the socks to the growing pile of folded clothes on the bed, she offered Angel a devilish grin. "I bets he was some smart honky, though. Cause of her light brown hair and blue eyes. And she's real bright, y'know?"

Angel nodded in agreement. She was well-aware of the little girl's intelligence. Sunshine had attached herself to Angel like a spare appendage, leaving her side only after Charmaine returned each afternoon. From interacting with the child, Angel knew her mother's boast was well-founded. At three years of age the sweet little bundle of energy was already beginning to read.

"But that's not as important as her bein' healthy," continued Charmaine. "Sister Mags says that's a miracle, considerin' I was doin' nickel bags pretty regular before I knowed I was preggers."

When Angel heard about Charmaine's former drug habit, she worried what would become of the young mother and her daughter. She had learned that after graduating high school or completing job training, the residents left Haven. With the help of Sister Mags they found jobs, suitable housing, and day care for their younger children. But for all her bravado and street smarts, at seventeen Charmaine was still more child than adult. How would she deal with the day-to-day stresses of single parenthood once she was on her own?

"You haven't used drugs since then?" Angel asked, grabbing one of Sunshine's footed sleepers from the laundry basket.

"Been clean for over three years," Charmaine bragged. "Got no choice if I wants to stay here. Sister's real strict 'bout that. Makes us take pee tests every week." Charmaine scrunched up her nose. "She don't kick no one out, but you gets caught, you's shipped off to rehab, and social services takes your kids. Ain't no way they gettin' their hands on my baby. Not after what they did to me."

Angel prayed Charmaine had the courage of her convictions, although she doubted it. When she raised her concern with Sister Mags, the nun admitted to the same reservations.

"We have a very high success rate at Haven," she explained to Angel, "but unfortunately, it's not one hundred percent. I never turn away any girl who falters and asks to come back. Sometimes all it takes is knowing there's a candle in the window if it's ever needed. But I have lost some."

She sighed, her shoulders slumping from the weight of her burden. "Unfortunately, sometimes the lure of their old lives is just too much for them to overcome.

"With Charmaine it's Julio, her former pimp. She's never been able to break completely free of him. He's woven a charismatic spell around her that's as addictive as any drug I've ever seen. I know she sneaks off to see him, but there's not much I can do about it except pray."

"And Sunshine?"

Sister Mags offered Angel a sad smile. "I pray especially hard for her."

* * *

For two weeks following Whitney's murder Trent shuttled between both companies, calming fears, bolstering morale, placating nervous stockholders, and seeking advice from his attorneys. In between, he gave statements to the press and made himself available for questioning by both the FBI and local

Connecticut law enforcement officials, neither of which gave much credence to Roger's accusations of Trent's involvement in Whitney's murder.

In a twisted way Trent welcomed the melee caused by Whitney's death. Dealing with the aftershocks of the murder kept his mind from dwelling on the hollowness he felt over Angel's departure. Not until she was no longer part of his daily life did he realize just how much he had come to depend on her presence to lift his spirits.

Now his bitterness had returned. With a vengeance. He hated returning to the apartment each evening, knowing that he would no longer hear her sweet laughter or be greeted by her smiling face.

Mrs. Kearn's suspicions about Rafe Faber and Angel's level of anxiety haunted him. He worried over her adjustment to a husband and life she couldn't remember. Had returning to Texas helped her regain her memory? Was she happy? He wished she'd contact him—if only to ease his troubled mind.

Making matters worse was Felicia's triumphant return from Chicago. Although he detested her boastful attitude, she certainly had earned the right to gloat. She had defied the laws of business and the predictions of countless financial analysts, lifting his Chicago holding from the ashes of near-bankruptcy to solvency in less than a month. The woman was a damn genius, and he intended to reward her amply for her efforts.

Unfortunately, if Trent was reading her signals correctly, Felicia had an altogether different idea for her bonus—one which he thought he'd previously, and permanently, squelched. Since her return, however, her behavior had grown increasingly more brazen. Her wardrobe more seductive. Her vocabulary more suggestive. Had the situation been reversed, it would qualify as sexual harassment.

Another man might have reveled in the attention, taking Felicia up on her offer. She was a beautiful, intelligent woman—a living, breathing fantasy for most men. Just not him.

"Get rid of her," said Mrs. Kearn after he made the mistake of voicing his concerns to her one morning.

"I can't. I need her."

"Like you need an abscessed tooth, maybe?"

Trent scowled. Breakfast this morning would be one-part Western omelet, one-part Irish advice. "You don't understand, Moira."

She shook her head, slamming a plate of buttered toast down in front of him. "No, 'tis you who don't understand. That one's as transparent as the day is long. I'll bet she goes 'round creatin' troubles behind your back just so's she can fix 'em and make herself look like some kind o' miracle worker."

"That's pretty damn cynical, even for you."

Mrs. Kearn shrugged her shoulders. "Call it what you will, lad. She's got you believin' she's a saint. And trust me, there's nothin' holy about that woman."

Having made her dislike of Felicia clear from the moment she first met the woman, Trent dismissed his housekeeper's insinuations without another thought. After all, what did an uneducated Irish immigrant know about the complex financial workings of the corporate world? Even Felicia wasn't enough of a genius to accomplish the slight-of-hand Mrs. Kearn accused her of committing.

* * *

Later that morning after returning from a meeting downtown, Trent found himself sharing an elevator with his head of Security.

"I never got a chance to thank you for that rush job you handled for me a few weeks ago, Arthur."

"Excuse me, sir?" The man gave him a quizzical look. "I'm not sure I know what you're referring to, Mr. Caldwell."

"Rafe Faber? Ms. Sutton asked you to do a background check for me."

The man scratched his balding head and thought for a moment. "Wasn't me, Mr. Caldwell. I can't remember the last time I spoke with Ms. Sutton. Haven't been asked to run any background checks on anyone, either. Not for at least a month." The elevator came to a stop, and the doors opened. "Maybe she had Grant run it," he said, stepping out.

"I suppose so, Arthur. I guess I just assumed she had gone directly to you."

But Trent remembered the report all too well. Arthur Page's signature had been scrawled at the bottom of that report. As the elevator continued its ascent to his office, he felt the seeds of doubt Mrs. Kearn had sown earlier take root within him. With mounting uneasiness, he strode from the elevator and headed for Felicia's office.

At his approach her secretary glanced up from her desk. "She hasn't come in yet this morning, Mr. Caldwell. She had several onsite meetings scheduled."

"I know. Is her office unlocked?"

"Yes, sir. Is there something I can help you with?"

"Just see that I'm not disturbed."

Trent entered Felicia's office and locked the door. Sitting behind her desk, he switched on the computer and began a systematic search of the drawers while waiting for the machine to boot up. Nothing seemed out of the ordinary, but he hardly expected her to leave incriminating evidence lying out in the open. What he was looking for would be well-hidden within her computer, a computer which Felicia believed to be password protected.

And it was. From everyone in the company except him. Unbeknownst to his employees, Trent's password overrode all others, giving him access to every system and file. It was an entitlement he rarely exercised.

He didn't want to believe Felicia capable of such duplicity. As he opened and scanned one file after another, he prayed he was wrong in suspecting her, but his thoughts kept drifting back to the day he told her about his call from Rafe Faber. He remembered the twinkle in her eye on hearing the news. Then there was her eagerness to play secretary and expedite the background check. Such an offer was totally out of character. Felicia balked at performing any menial task which could be relegated to a subordinate.

He knew his vice-president harbored a strong dislike for Angel, but her jealousy had been confined to verbal barbs.

Until now.

As Trent stared at the document on the screen, all hope of having jumped to the wrong conclusion evaporated. There, in a sub-directory she had named Apollyon, lay the proof of Felicia's dirty deeds. Trent remembered enough from years of Sunday school at Our Lady of Peace to recognize the word.

Apollyon, an evil spirit.

Apollyon, an obscure term for the Devil.

Apollyon, the opposite of Angel.

Felicia had documented every step of her devious plan. Research into finding a mercenary. Acquiring false identification.

The mercenary's cover story. Transportation arrangements. Transfer of funds. So like Felicia—every aspect of the operation planned down to the most-minute detail. And judging from the file creation date, begun the moment Angel entered his life.

Trent lowered his head into his hands. Rage roiled and churned inside him, mixing with fear and helplessness. Two precious weeks had already slipped away. Whatever trail Faber may have left—and judging from the man's unsavory background, Trent doubted there would be much of one—was now ice cold. Like the frigid wasteland where he had been instructed to dump Angel.

My God, Felicia! What have you done?

TWENTY-SIX

Trent glanced around at Felicia's office. When he'd hired her, he'd given her the freedom to redecorate, but Felicia had declined, saying that the office was fine the way it was. She'd kept the masculine trappings of her predecessor, a man partial to severe minimalism—glass, chrome, and black leather. She had no personal knickknacks on the shelves, no photos of family. Everything about the room was cold and business-like, a perfect reflection of the woman usually occupying the chair behind the desk.

Trent felt like Julius Caesar confronting his treasonous comrade on the steps of the Senate. *Et tu, Brute?* He swiveled the desk chair around and stared off across the dull gray November cityscape. *Et tu, Felicia?*

He heard the metallic click of her key in the lock, the creak of the heavy oak door as it swung open.

He swiveled the chair around to confront her.

"Trent?" She stood in the doorway, her hand lingering on the knob, her body frozen in place as she gave him a quizzical look. He could tell her mind was spinning, trying to run through all the permutations that might account for why he would be in her locked office, sitting at her desk. Sorting through scenarios like she sorted through facts and figures until she came up with the right answer for the given problem set.

He kept his voice calm, his face as clueless as a master poker player. "Close the door, Felicia."

"Is something wrong?" She couldn't mask the anxiety in her eyes. Or her voice. She knew something was up, but she didn't know what. Was she standing there worrying that he'd uncovered her treachery? He'd sent her secretary on an errand to keep from alerting Felicia to his presence in her office when she arrived. He wanted to take her by surprise, catch the ungrateful, traitorous bitch off guard. And he had.

"Take a seat." He motioned to one of two Eames chairs in front of the desk. At the same time, he fought to control the timbre of his voice, the vehemence in his heart, but the longer he looked at her, the more he wanted to tear her limb from limb.

"What's going on? Why are you in my office?"

"Apollyon," he said.

Felicia's step faltered as she walked toward the desk. She reached out and grabbed hold of the back of one of the chairs to steady herself. The color drained from her face, but she quickly recovered and feigned ignorance as she took a seat in front of him. "Excuse me?"

Trent repeated the word, this time slightly louder and more menacing. "Apollyon."

Felicia raised an inquisitive eyebrow as she brushed an imaginary speck of lint from the collar of her navy suit. "What is this, Twenty Questions?" She offered him a look of concern. "Are you feeling all right? Have you been drinking, Trent? You don't look well, and you're not making any sense."

But he could tell he had her. He saw the fear building inside her.

He jumped to his feet. Bracing his hands against the desk, he leaned over and roared at her. "Apollyon, Felicia! Apollyon! Don't play the innocent with me. I read your files. I know what you've done." He rounded the desk and grabbed her arm, yanking her to her feet. "Where is she?"

She struggled in his grasp. "Let go, Trent! You're hurting me!"

He tightened his grip, his fingers digging into the soft flesh of her upper arm. With his free hand he grabbed her jaw. "Tell me what you've done with her!"

Before he had time to react, Felicia raised her leg and kneed him in the groin. As Trent doubled over in pain, she slipped from his hold.

"I refuse to subject myself to such lunacy," she said, rubbing her arm. "I don't have to take this kind of abuse from you."

"Very...well." Still reeling from the painful jab, his words came out between pants. He wiped the beads of sweat from his brow and reached across the desk for the phone. With one hand he lifted the receiver and punched in a series of numbers. "Send them in."

Felicia spun around to face the door. Two men entered, both flashing badges. Her gaze shifted between the men and Trent. "What the hell's going on?"

Trent answered her question with one of his own. "Why,

Felicia? She was no threat to you."

Her body stiffened. Her eyes grew dark with hate, her lips tightening into a thin line. "Wasn't she?"

She turned back to the detectives, the bravado seeping from her as the gravity of the situation took hold. "I want to speak with my attorney," she said.

* * *

"Find her." Trent paced back and forth in front of his desk, his hands flailing at his sides in a combination of frustration, anger, and pent-up nervousness. After twenty-four hours he was still reeling from the shock of Felicia's betrayal. Unfairly, he lashed out at the detective giving him an update on the police investigation. "I don't care what it takes. Just find her before something happens."

The detective, a man closing in on middle age, remained calm in the face of Trent's outburst. "I'm afraid that might already be the case, Mr. Caldwell."

Trent stopped dead in his tracks and stared in disbelief at the detective. "No! I won't accept that."

The man dropped into one of the two chairs across from Trent's desk and rested beefy forearms on his thick thighs. "This isn't a pissing match, Caldwell. We're both on the same side here."

Trent took the chair behind his desk. "You're right. I'm sorry."

For several long seconds the detective stared at Trent before he spoke again. "Here's what we know, sir. The woman's luggage was checked through to Alaska, and the computer indicates boarding passes were issued to both her and Faber for that flight, but she wasn't on it. Only him."

The implication slammed into Trent like a careening eighteen-wheeler.

The detective continued. "We tracked Faber to Nome, Alaska where he picked up a package, presumably the balance of the payoff, at a private mail drop. After that he disappears."

Trent shoved his hands through his hair, then reached behind his head and grabbed at the knot between his shoulder blades. "You lost him?"

"My guess is he hopped a plane back to the lower forty-eight."

"In other words, you lost him. Damn it! We're talking winter in Nome, Alaska! How many people fly in and out? How hard could it be to track him?"

The detective grimaced. "Are you aware that nearly everyone in that part of the country has his own plane, Mr. Caldwell? There are few roads up there, more sea planes than cars and trucks. Everyone flies in and out. If the guy booked a commercial flight, we'd have a chance of finding him. But he didn't. We've checked.

"Besides, as you yourself discovered, Rafe Faber doesn't exist. The name's an alias. For what, we don't know. The name Ms. Sutton had for him was just another alias. It's not like we're not trying, sir, but you gotta understand, we're stumbling in circles here. We've got a missing person with no identity, a suspect with a phony one, and an uncooperative accomplice who claims she's being framed."

"Felicia framed herself," mumbled Trent.

The detective shrugged. "Doesn't much matter. She ain't talking."

"Then let her rot in jail!"

Felicia! The moment he uttered her name Trent's hands balled into tight fists. His limbs went rigid. How could she mastermind such a heinous act? Had jealousy pushed her over the edge? She had thrown away a brilliant career and for what? One way or another Felicia Sutton faced a long sentence—at best, for kidnapping. At worst, for murder.

Trent wasn't about to give up, and he refused to believe what the detective had implied, but not voiced—that Faber had killed Angel before he boarded the flight to Alaska. "It doesn't make sense," he insisted. "Why would he go to the trouble of bringing her to the airport, checking her luggage, and picking up both boarding passes if he planned to kill her before they boarded the plane?"

"We don't know that he did bring her to the airport. Maybe he had an accomplice, someone he planned to travel with, and for some reason they changed their plans at the last moment. Maybe the accomplice took a separate flight to their rendezvous point. As for the luggage, he probably figured it was safer to check it through rather than dump it somewhere in the city."

"What about the gate agent?" asked Trent. "Maybe she remembers seeing Angel."

"We already interviewed her. Showed her a picture of the victim, but she could neither confirm nor deny seeing her. And she didn't recognized Faber from the police sketch."

Trent felt his gut tying into knots. A groan escaped his throat.

"That doesn't necessarily mean anything, though," offered the detective. "They handle so many passengers each day that you can't expect them to remember any one face in a crowd of thousands—especially after two weeks."

Two weeks! Might just as well be two years, thought Trent, the knot in his stomach twisting tighter. A vision of Angel's anxious face passed before him. Too late he realized she had sensed something amiss. If only she'd refused to leave, voiced her fear to him, demanded more proof of her connection to Faber.

Something. Anything.

"We're calling a press conference for later this afternoon," said the detective. "The victim's picture and the police composite of the suspect will be flashed across all the evening newscasts and be in the morning editions of the papers. That might produce some fresh leads."

"It's Thanksgiving eve," said Trent, glumly. "People are traveling tonight. How many of them will be watching the nightly news? Or reading tomorrow's paper, for that matter?" He pounded the desk with his fists, a less-than-adequate outlet for the frustration building inside him. "Offer a reward," he said. "Ten thousand dollars." The same amount Felicia had paid Faber to get rid of Angel.

The detective nodded. "Not a bad idea. Money's a powerful incentive. Especially this time of year. Just might shake loose a few memories."

* * *

Haven buzzed with excitement. Every year on the day before Thanksgiving Santa arrived for his yearly visit. Like his department store counterparts, he sat each child on his lap and listened solemnly to one Wish List after another. Only Sister Mags, taking notes off to the side, was privy to Santa's true identity.

"You look tired," she said, helping him adjust the padding layered beneath the red suit. As in past years, he'd come carrying his costume and all its accouterments in a large suitcase. The routine never varied. At a pre-set time, he entered the brownstone through the back service entrance and slipped into her office while she distracted the children and their mothers. "I'm not used to seeing dark circles under your eyes."

He clasped one of her hands in both of his and held it for a moment. "Can't hide anything from you, can I, Mags?"

She stepped back and studied him, nodding her approval over the transformation of man into myth. "Does this have anything to do with the young woman the taxi hit?"

Trent nodded.

"Want to talk about it, Santa?"

"Maybe later. This getup is closer to a sauna than a costume." He bent down and picked up the jacket and shoes he'd discarded, dropping them into the empty suitcase. Then he deliberately changed the subject. "So how are things here?"

"Quite well." She opened a closet and pulled out several large shopping bags brimming with candy and small toys. Santa passed his empty sack over to her, and she began transferring the contents of the shopping bags into it. "I took in an interesting young woman a couple of weeks ago. A bit of a mystery, actually. Not the typical case we get here."

"In what way?"

Sister Mags finished filling the sack and sat down. "In every way. For one thing she was stylishly dressed. And she's obviously well-educated."

"You of all people should know abuse doesn't restrict itself to the lower classes, Mags."

"That's just it," she said. "I've seen all forms of abuse over the years. Nothing shocks me anymore. I just don't think she's been abused. She's running from something, though—something that's frightened her nearly to death, I'm afraid. But she won't talk about it. Other than her first name, she's offered no information about herself."

Santa stroked his fake beard. "Maybe she's running from the

law."

"I thought of that, but my intuition tells me otherwise." She rose and passed the sack over to him. "At any rate, she's been a Godsend to me."

"How so?"

"She's become more assistant than resident. I'm beginning to wonder how I ever ran this place without her. Look around." She swept her arms across her body to encompass the room. "Have you ever seen my office so organized?"

He scanned the room, noticing for the first time the absence of the nun's ever-present lopsided towers of files and assorted paperwork. "No piles," he said, shaking his head in amazement. "She did this?"

"She did."

"I'm impressed. But are you certain she didn't just trash everything?"

"She did, in a manner of speaking. But with my complete permission and blessing."

"What?"

Sister Mags laughed. "Calm down. They're all packed away in cartons in the basement. You, dear boy, are looking at an old dog who has learned a new trick. The Lord sent me a computer literate angel. She spent a full week entering my files into data bases every night after dinner. Then she taught me how to use that computer you forced on me last year."

"Well, I'll be!" He swung the sack over his shoulder. "I think I'll have to meet this miracle worker of yours, Mags."

"I thought you might want to. I'll introduce you later, but only if you promise to tell me what's bothering you."

He shook his head and grimaced. "It's a long story."

"I'm not going anywhere."

* * *

"I don't know who the dude is," Charmaine whispered to Angel. She quickly scanned the room, making sure Sunshine wasn't within earshot. "But he shows up here every year, and the kids all gets what they asks for. Sorta."

Angel finished diapering one of the babies and settled him onto her shoulder just as his mother walked into the nursery.

"Thanks," she said, relieving Angel of the infant.

"All finished studying?" asked Angel.

"For now. Don't want to miss Santa's visit. It'll be Tyrone's first." She snuggled the baby's cheek, at the same time dangling a disposable camera in front of Angel. "Will you take a picture of us with Santa?"

"Of course." Angel reached for the camera, then turned back to Charmaine. "What did you mean by 'sort of?'"

"Well, last year Sunshine, she asks Santa for a real-live pony."

Angel chuckled. "I can see where that might present a problem given that Haven has no stables. What happened?"

"She got a rocking horse."

"The one in the playroom?"

"Yeah. That's the one."

A very generous Santa Claus, thought Angel, remembering the beautiful hand-carved wooden rocking horse with its genuine horsehair tail and mane. "Was she upset when she didn't get a real pony?"

"Nah. Santa tol' her he'd bring her a pony she could ride, but we's not allowed to have real animals in Haven 'cause we ain't got no barn."

Generous and quick thinking. Angel wondered if Santa were

the mysterious benefactor Sister Mags always remembered to thank when she said Grace at each meal. "And what does Sunshine want this year?" she asked as she and Charmaine headed toward the living room.

Charmaine stopped walking and turned to face Angel. An expression half sheepishness and half guilt spread across her face. "A baby brother?"

Angel grabbed the young girl by the shoulders. "Oh, Charmaine, you're not!"

Charmaine ducked her head and bit down on her lower lip.

"Does Sister Mags know?"

"I was hopin' you might tell her for me," she said, raising her head slightly to cast a pleading glance at Angel.

Angel groaned. "Julio?"

"Uh-huh."

"Oh, dear." Angel tugged at a lock of her hair. Settling her other arm around Charmaine's shoulder, she led her the rest of the way to the living room. The residents were already assembled, mothers and children anxiously awaiting Santa's arrival.

Sunshine scampered over to them, wrapping her arms around one of Charmaine's legs and one of Angel's. "Santa's coming! Santa's coming!" she cried.

"Go on in with Sunshine," Angel said, giving Charmaine a comforting squeeze. "We'll talk more later."

She turned and headed down the hall toward the office, anticipating the nun's reaction to the bombshell Charmaine had just dropped. *How could the girl be so stupid?* Angel shook her head, but what she really wanted to do was shake some sense into Charmaine. Only it was too late for that. When it came to Julio, Charmaine couldn't see any farther than her stud-pierced nose.

Convincing Charmaine to stay away from Julio would meet with about as much success as trying to convince the devout nun to spike the morning orange juice with birth control pills.

Angel stopped at the entrance to Sister Mags' office. Taking a deep breath, she forced a smile onto her face. Now was not the time to divulge Charmaine's secret. Not with Santa waiting in the wings. She rapped on the door. "Sister? Everyone's gathered in the living room."

The door swung open. "Come in, my dear. There's someone I'd like you to meet."

TWENTY-SEVEN

She stood in the doorway, clad in a blue flannel shirt frayed at the collar and cuffs and a denim jumper too large for her small frame—garments obviously rummaged from the bags of second-hand clothes donated to the shelter. For a moment Trent thought he was seeing a ghost. He stared at her, unable to speak, then finally gasped out her name. "Angel!"

She regarded his overstuffed body and bewhiskered face with apprehension before recognition slowly dawned, and she answered him in a questioning whisper. "Trent?"

Relief flooded through him. He crossed the small office in two strides and pulled her into his arms. "Thank God," he cried. "You're alive."

He held onto her like a lifeline, afraid to let go for fear of losing her once more. She raised her face to him, and he cupped his hand against her cheek, needing to feel flesh against flesh to assure himself that she was truly safe.

"He didn't harm you?" he asked, steeling himself against an answer he feared.

She shook her head.

Trent released his breath in a rush of air. He loosened his grip on her and held her at arm's length, searching her face for answers to the many questions that filled him. But he asked only one. "Why didn't you come back?"

Angel's lower lip quivered. Her eyes filled with tears. All at once large droplets spilled down her face as the words tumbled from her mouth. "He scared me, Trent, from the moment he came to get me. Something felt wrong. And when we left the apartment, he became belligerent and ugly. And we weren't going back to Texas, and the more I thought about it, the more frightened I became. I panicked and ran. I knew he'd go back to you looking for me, but he didn't, did he? There was nothing on the news, and I didn't understand why, and I don't want to be Billie Sue Faber..." She couldn't continue. Her words became lost in her sobs.

He drew her back into his arms and stroked her head, running his fingers through her short, springy curls. "You're not Billie Sue," he said, trying to break through her pain with soothing words. "Listen to me, Angel. There is no Billie Sue. She doesn't exist." He lifted her chin and brushed at the cascading tears with the pads of his thumbs.

He watched her face as his words penetrated. Slowly the tears subsided, and Angel's eyes filled with a combination of hope and skepticism. "I...I'm not?"

"No." He swiped at another group of renegade tears that streamed down her cheeks. "You are most definitely not." He sighed, his heart heaving with guilt. "I was so blind. I should have seen it. I could have stopped her."

"Her?"

Trent led her over to the chair. "Sit." When she complied, he knelt on one knee beside her, clasping her hands in both of his. "Until yesterday I thought you were in Texas. I kept wondering how you were getting along, but I had no idea anything was wrong." He closed his eyes, pausing for a moment, the memory of Felicia's betrayal still painfully fresh.

Angel withdrew one hand and placed it against his cheek. "Whatever happened, Trent, I know you're not to blame."

He opened his eyes. She was looking at him with a trust he didn't deserve. He had failed to protect her. First Caitlin. Now Angel. At least Angel had survived.

He took a ragged breath and slowly related the bizarre tale he had uncovered. She listened silently, an expression of disbelief settling over her face.

"Felicia's in jail. Rafe, or whoever he is, has disappeared," he concluded. "And at this moment the police are holding a press conference about your disappearance." He lifted her clasped hands and brushed his lips against them. "Thank God, you're safe," he whispered, a part of him still needing to hear the spoken words as reassurance of the fact.

"Trent." A hand settled on his shoulder. He looked up at the sound of his name, startled to see Sister Mags standing over him. He'd forgotten she was in the room. "The children," she reminded him.

"The children," he repeated, remembering the reason for his visit.

"I'll meet you in the living room." Sister Mags left the office, closing the door behind her.

Trent turned back to Angel. "Are you okay?"

"This is so strange, so unbelievable. I'm shocked. Confused. Overwhelmed. But...," She paused and smiled at him, "oddly enough—and I know this is going to sound totally weird—mostly relieved by what you've told me."

"Relieved? Angel, he could have killed you!"

She shook her head. "You don't understand. Staying at Haven, learning about the abuse these women have suffered, made me realize that I, too, must have suffered horrible abuse—abuse that caused me to flee Texas and block out my past. But that never happened. It couldn't have because I'm not Billie Sue." She thought for a moment, then smiled. "Yes, I'm all right. Now."

She paused once more, then added, "You're the benefactor Sister Mags speaks of, aren't you?"

He stood and straightened his suit. Averting his eyes as he spoke, he forced the words out in terse sentences. "Caitlin was a social worker. Haven was her dream. After we married, I set up a foundation to finance it."

"And every year you come to play Santa Claus." It was a statement, not a question. She stared up at him, trapping him in an intense gaze. "I think you're a wonderful man, Trent Caldwell. Kind and generous. It's time you stopped blaming yourself for what happened to Caitlin. And me."

Trent turned away and headed for the door. "The children are waiting," he muttered, reaching for the filled sack. Without another word he opened the door and strode down the hall, forcing out a jolly ho-ho-ho before entering the living room.

* * *

Saddened by Trent's reaction, Angel stared after him. "You're not God, Trent Caldwell," she muttered under her breath. "There are

240

some things even you can't control."

"Sometimes powerful men find that difficult to accept."

Angel jumped, startled by the response. Sister Mags had preceded Trent out of the office. Angel assumed the nun was already in the living room. Instead, she found her standing behind her, just outside the doorway in the shadows of the hall.

Sister Mags reentered the office and approached her. "Go wash your face, my dear. You don't want the children to see you've been crying."

The nun wrapped an arm around her shoulders and led her from the room. In the hallway, before parting, she placed a hand on Angel's forearm. "You're right about one thing, Angel."

"What's that?"

"He's a very good man."

* * *

Joining the others in the living room, Angel mechanically ushered the children on and off Trent's lap, her attention fixed on the man himself. Only minutes earlier she'd witnessed him turn inward and close off the world. Now she watched in amazement as he lavished love and attention on each child, even remembering the names of those he'd seen the year before.

He would have made a wonderful father, she realized. Although he never mentioned his unborn child, Angel now comprehended the full magnitude of Trent's loss. His was a double tragedy, and only someone familiar with his suffering could see the anguish he hid behind those twinkling hazel eyes.

She glanced over at Sister Mags, hard at work jotting down each child's Wish List, but also keeping one eye on Trent. She knows, too, thought Angel, catching the concerned expression on the nun's face.

A familiar tug on her skirt drew her from her thoughts.

"My turn! My turn!" sang Sunshine.

"Your turn," said Angel, lifting the child into her arms. She quickly scanned the room, searching for Charmaine. "Where's your mama?"

"Mama gots go pee-pee."

Or Mama's suffering a little ill-timed morning sickness, thought Angel, certain that Charmaine would control a full bladder long enough to see her child's visit with Santa. She glanced down the hall. The powder room door stood open, the light off.

Turning back, she caught Sister Mags watching her. The nun was frowning. Was it over Charmaine's sudden disappearance or did she already suspect the girl's pregnancy? In her line of work she must have considerable experience with such things. Angel had no idea how far along Charmaine was, but the sister may have already noticed the telltale signs.

Angel gave Sunshine an extra hug before placing her on Trent's lap. She drank in the child's baby powder innocence and prayed the extra attention she gave her would help ward off whatever bitter realities awaited her. Glancing once more at Sister Mags, she saw a reflection of her own sadness and frustration in the nun's eyes.

Charmaine was a sweet kid. Fate and the system had tossed her into a cesspool. Sister Mags had lowered a ladder, but Charmaine's own self-destructive nature might prevent her from climbing out.

Angel sighed and turned her attention to the affectionate interplay between Trent and Sunshine. The youngster was regaling him with an account of her day—down to the colors of the feathers she had glued on her paper plate turkey during an arts and crafts session in day care.

"I shows you," said Sunshine, scampering off his lap.

She raced out of the living room and scurried down the hall. Moments later Angel heard the unmistakable sound of tiny sneakers padding up the wide oak staircase.

"That one could charm the devil, Mags."

Hearing the murmured comment, Angel glanced over her shoulder and caught Trent's sad smile, partially hidden by the fake whiskers. Sister Mags was resting her hand on his shoulder. She bent down and whispered something in his ear. Trent patted her hand and nodded. Without hearing the nun's comment, Angel understood. Had his unborn child survived, she would have been near Sunshine's age.

* * *

"You're being foolish!" shouted Trent. He paced back and forth within the limited floor space of the nun's small office.

"And you're not?" Angel crossed her arms over her chest, adamant in her decision. "I'm not your responsibility. I can't stay in your apartment indefinitely."

"Why the hell not?"

"Trent!" Angel's eyes flew to the large, wooden crucifix hanging on the wall behind Sister Mags's desk. "Remember where you are!"

He sank into Sister Mags's chair and leaned his elbows on the desk. Lowering his head into his hands, he expelled a sigh heavy with frustration. "Damn it, Angel, this isn't a church!"

"Please try to understand," she said, steering the argument back on course. "It's been nearly three months. I may never get my memory back. I need to make a life for myself."

Trent raised his head and scowled at her. "In a homeless shelter? What kind of life is that?"

"One where I feel useful. Where I'm doing something besides sitting around a penthouse hoping someday I'll remember who I am."

"Is that the only reason you won't come back?"

Angel hesitated. There was another reason, but she had no idea how to tell him without her answer deeply wounding him. The man had shown her such generosity, even if his actions had been dictated by some misguided notion of penance.

He'd suffered too much. She couldn't hurt him further by accusing him of using her to absolve his guilt over the death of his wife and child. No matter how much Trent did for her, it would never bring back Caitlin and their baby. And he'd never be free of his pain until he stopped blaming himself for their deaths.

"It's Mrs. Kearn, isn't it?" he asked.

His question startled her. "What do you mean?"

"I think we both know she's been trying to play Cupid. If that's what's bothering you, Angel, you needn't worry."

The harshness of his tone shocked her. She studied his features, his mouth set in a firm line, his eyes unreadable. Once again, Trent Caldwell had yanked the yo-yo string and reined in his emotions. Angel felt like pummeling him with her fists and screaming.

But she didn't scream. Instead, she stooped to the floor and retrieved the Santa jacket he'd discarded earlier. Forcing an indifference into her voice which she didn't feel, she calmly folded the garment and answered, "I'm not worried."

Stupid, blind, arrogant man! If he wanted to continue denying his feelings for her, let him go on fooling himself. She knew otherwise. She felt the electricity that surged between them, no matter how they each fought to deny it.

Mrs. Kearn was merely a conduit. But it didn't matter. A

woman struggling to discover her past had no business competing with the ghost of a dead wife—especially one whose husband refused to bury her.

Angel realized Trent was not going to let her go without a fight. The man was used to getting his way. The tension radiating from his body filled the room and bounced off the walls. He stood and walked around the desk. She dropped the folded jacket into the open suitcase and picked up the pants. Keeping her eyes averted, she forced herself to concentrate on matching the huge red leg seams and not on the man walking toward her.

He stood so close, she could feel the heat from his body, but she continued fussing over the trousers until he pried them from her grasp. Only then did she raise her head and confront him. "You're trying to bully me."

Her words pierced the barrier around his emotions. The yo-yo slipped down its string, and his eyes filled with hurt. "Never. "I've hurt you so much already. Please come back. I can't undo what's done, but let me give you a comfortable place to stay. Not here." He touched the frayed collar of her shirt. "Not in rags."

Angel felt her resolve crumbling. His pain overwhelmed her. "Please, Trent. I need to do this. It helps fill the emptiness inside me."

"Then do it," he said. "During the day. But come home at night."

Home. The word released a nervous flutter that raced helter-skelter inside her. She automatically reached for a curl, accidentally brushing against his knuckles. He captured her hand, lacing their fingers together, then covered them with his free hand. She dared to look into his eyes again and saw the anguish he thought he hid from her.

Home. His was the only home she remembered, but it *had* been home—with people who cared about her, people she had grown to love.

She glanced over her shoulder at the closed office door. Down the hall were other people whose lives were now entwined with hers, but they filled a different need within her. Haven was not *home,* its residents not *family.* The emotional bond she had with them could not replace the one that had grown between her, Trent, and Mrs. Kearn. They had developed into an odd little trio, but they *were* family, and suddenly, she realized she needed that connection as much as she needed air to breathe and food to eat.

"I can come help Sister Mags during the day?" she asked, making sure she understood his offer.

"I'll have O'Hara drop you off each morning and pick you up at the end of the day."

Her one hand was still nestled within his. She added her free hand to their joined ones and smiled up at him. "All right," she agreed. "I'll come home, but I want to be here tomorrow to help with Thanksgiving dinner. I'm sure you and Mrs. Kearn have plans of your own, anyway."

"We do. Here."

Angel shook her head and chuckled softly. "I should have known."

* * *

The ride uptown took longer than normal, but as far as Angel could tell, Trent, who was always rushing from one point to the next, barely noticed.

"Sorry 'tis takin' so long, sir," said O'Hara, apologizing for the gridlock. "Everyone rushin' to leave the city, I s'pose."

"I suppose," echoed Trent, his voice distant, his eyes never leaving her. He reached for her hand. "I was so worried about you."

"I know," she said, gently squeezing his hand, "but it's over now. I'm fine."

But Trent wasn't fine. Angel realized, as much as he tried to hide it, he was reeling from the events of the last two days. She had come to realize that although personally his relationship with Felicia Sutton had teetered on a love-hate precipice, professionally he had always admired and respected her. He had treated her more like a partner than an employee, continually taking her into his confidence. Felicia's betrayal affected him deeply.

Now was not the time to discuss such things, though. A chink had appeared in Trent's emotional defenses. He'd dropped his guard, and his imprisoned feelings were pushing through. If she pressed, he might clam up and retreat once more behind his fortress. As much as she ached for him, she kept her voice cheerful and directed a question to the chauffeur. "Do you have plans for the holiday, Mr. O'Hara?"

"'Tain't my holiday, Miss Angel. I says me thanks on Saint Paddy's Day."

"You mean you're going to be all alone tomorrow?"

"Oh, no, lassie. Don't you go worryin' yourself 'bout that."

"But—" She turned to Trent.

He smiled and patted her hand. "I doubt O'Hara will be alone."

"Right you are, sir." The driver chuckled. "I'm sure me old mate Seamus is plannin' somethin'. Maybe we'll have ourselves a green turkey."

TWENTY-EIGHT

The succulent aroma of freshly baked pies seeped under the threshold of the apartment's front door, greeting Angel before Trent slipped his key into the lock. The sweetness of peaches and blueberries, the tangy tartness of cinnamon dressed apples and cranberries, nutmeg spiced pumpkin—all mingled together bidding Angel welcome. Welcome home.

She drew in a deep breath. "Hmm!"

"Every year I tell her not to bother," said Trent, "but she insists. Claims Thanksgiving from a caterer isn't a true Thanksgiving."

"She doesn't do everything herself, does she? There are over two dozen people living at Haven."

Trent's mouth curled up in an apologetic smile. Pushing the door open, he stepped aside, allowing Angel to enter. "The woman would figure out a way to make turkey-flavored formula for the infants if she could."

The sounds of Mrs. Kearn's rich soprano voice filtered down the hallway from the kitchen. Angel recognized the sad Irish ballad as one the housekeeper sang often. Frowning, she turned and confronted Trent. "How can you let her do all that work by herself?"

He choked on a laugh. "Let her? Angel, you've seen how stubborn she gets. A gale force wind couldn't sway that bullheaded Irish head of hers once she's made up her mind."

Angel sighed. "I suppose, but I'm going to do my best—if she hasn't already finished everything."

"Another bullheaded woman," muttered Trent, but Angel caught the amused expression on his face.

By mutual agreement she hung back as he entered the kitchen.

"Anything to eat?" she heard him ask.

Mrs. Kearn grunted. "Didn't expect you and get your hands out o' there." She swatted at him with a dishtowel as he grabbed a pumpkin shaped cookie off the cooling rack. "Them's for tomorrow."

He placed the cookie back on the rack. "So what's for tonight?"

"I'll fix you a sandwich when I get a chance," she said as she stooped to remove a pie from the oven.

"Hardly fitting fare to serve company, Moira."

"You're hardly what I'd consider company, even if you're rarely 'round o' late."

"I wouldn't mind a sandwich," said Angel, stepping into the kitchen.

"Sweet Mother o' God!" cried Mrs. Kearn. "Angel!"

Trent grabbed a pair of potholders off the table and lifted the pie from his housekeeper's trembling hands before she dropped it on the floor. Immediately, Mrs. Kearn bounded across the kitchen and engulfed Angel in a smothering hug. Tears streamed down her cheeks. "Oh, lass, praise be to God and all the saints!"

When she finally loosened her embrace, she stepped back and held Angel at arm's length. Without leaving go, she used her shoulders to shrug the tears from her face. Then she scrutinized Angel from head to toe, examining her as carefully as a mother would a newborn. "Did he hurt you?" she asked, her voice a mixture of gruff emotion and hard anger.

Angel shook her head. "No. He never had the chance."

Mrs. Kearn raised one hand and gently pushed the curls off Angel's face. Motherly love shone in her watery emerald eyes. Trent came up from behind and placed his hands on his housekeeper's shoulders. "It's over, Moira. She's safe now."

The love in Mrs. Kearn's eyes grew dark and wary, like a lioness about to defend her cub from a predator. "That woman will pay for what she's done. Mark my words."

The anger in her voice sent a shiver up Angel's spine. Felicia Sutton was in jail. She had already lost everything, as far as Angel could see—her career, her freedom, her respect. And Trent. "I think she's already paying for what she did," she told Mrs. Kearn.

"Not any longer."

"What do you mean?" asked Trent.

She lifted her chin in the direction of a small television mounted under one of the kitchen cabinets. "Accordin' to the news, she's out. Got herself a fancy lawyer."

"She's only free on bail," Trent assured her. "She won't escape justice."

"No," agreed the housekeeper, "she won't."

TWENTY-NINE

An eye for an eye, he thought, admiring the results of his labors. Leave justice to the law, and the lawless avoid justice. But not this time. He pulled the hammered silver flask from the inside pocket of his overcoat. His hands shook as he removed the cap, but he convinced himself it was from the powerful surge of electricity flowing through him and not fear. No, she'd be proud of what he'd accomplished. Revenge. In her name.

He scanned the room, searching for telltale signs which might alert someone to his presence. He was confident no one had seen him enter. He'd make sure no one saw him leave. He heaved a sigh of relief. She was so much better at this sort of thing than he was. She had nerves of steel. But she wasn't here. It was up to him.

Confident of his success, he raised the flask to his lips and took a long swig. The smooth amber liquid spread quickly to his limbs, stilling his tremors. He was amazed at how easy it had been. And how exhilarating. He stared at his hands, admiring the Godlike instruments and remembering the rush that had consumed him. Better than sex, he realized, a sheepish grin spreading across his face. Much better.

THIRTY

Mrs. Kearn had left little undone except cooking the turkeys and making the salads, both of which had to wait until the next morning. As Trent predicted, she adamantly refused to let Angel help with anything.

"You've been through enough, lass. Besides, you don't know how to cook, remember?"

Angel blew out a lungful of frustration. "I *can* cut up salad!"

"No need. 'Tis already done. I had to be up with the roosters to put the turkeys in the oven, anyway."

Angel raised an eyebrow. "Roosters? In Manhattan?"

"I'm sure there must be some somewhere." She tossed Angel a mischievous smile. "If'n it bothers you so, you can toss the salad all together once we get to Haven. Everything's in them zipper bags right now."

"I will."

And aside from filling the refrigerator with the canapés, cranberry relish, and whipped cream for the pies, tossing and dressing the salad was all anyone allowed Angel to do once she, Trent, and Mrs. Kearn arrived at Haven shortly before noon. She watched as Mrs. Kearn loaded the three stuffed and cooked birds into one of Haven's two commercial ovens to keep warm while Sister Mags heated up the candied yams and string bean casseroles in the second oven.

The room soon filled with the aroma of roasted turkey and chestnut dressing. Angel knew when she wasn't wanted. She drifted into the dining room, only to find the table already set. Cardboard turkey napkin holders, made by the children earlier in the week, decorated the plates. Inside each was a festive holiday napkin folded to resemble turkey feathers. An arrangement of golden mums, gourds, and acorns with a tall burgundy taper extending from either side, graced the center of the table. Ordered from the florist by Trent, no doubt.

"Give up," he advised, coming up behind her. "She's bent on treating you like a princess, and you're outmatched." He offered her a glass of sparkling wine with an apology. "Non-alcoholic, I'm afraid. Too many ex-addicts here."

"Of course." She reached for the long-stemmed crystal flute and studied it before taking a sip. "Pretty fancy for a homeless shelter."

Trent shrugged. "I have no use for them. Even if they're only used for 7-Up, it makes the girls feel special."

Angel shifted her gaze from the glass to Trent. He was sipping from his own glass, trying to mask the faraway, pained look in his eyes. She desperately yearned to reach out and comfort him in some way but wasn't certain how. Any words that came to mind sounded like hollow platitudes. Besides, a large lump had formed in her throat. Before she could force it down, Sunshine ran into the room.

"Angel!" She hurled her small ruffle-clad body against Angel's legs.

Trent grabbed for the glass but not before some of the beverage sloshed over the rim and landed on Sunshine's head. She stopped short and patted her curls. Glancing upward, she frowned, her brow creasing in puzzlement. "It raining," she finally declared. "I gets 'brellas."

"Whoa!" Angel grabbed her before she could take off back down the hall and swung her up into her arms. Sunshine rustled, her body a mass of stiffened crinolines, red velvet, and starched white lace. Charmaine had struck gold in one of the donation bags. "It's not raining, you silly goose. You spilled my drink on your head."

The toddler's face crumbled. Her lower lip trembled. She wrapped her arms around Angel's neck and buried her tiny head against her shoulder. "I sorry, Angel. You mad ats me?"

Sister Mags had called it, thought Angel. Sunshine was definitely a little actress. "Of course not," she assured the child, kissing her damp curls. "Hmm. You taste like fine champagne."

Sunshine lifted her head. Eyes wide with confusion, she gaped at Angel. "I does?"

"I think so, but maybe we need a second opinion." She offered Sunshine to Trent who was observing with a bemused expression.

He leaned over the child and inhaled deeply. "Definitely champagne," he agreed, struggling to keep from laughing.

Sunshine cocked her head and studied him. "You sounds like Santa," she said.

Trent raised an eyebrow. "Doesn't miss a beat, does she?" he whispered to Angel.

Two pudgy hands clasped themselves on either side of his face. Squinting her eyes in concentration, Sunshine tilted Trent's head, first one way, then the other. "You not Santa," she finally decided, shaking her head. "Santa gots a big fluffy beard." She dropped her gaze to his chest. "An' a fat red belly."

"Where's your mama?" asked Angel.

"Mama gots go pee-pee." She scrunched her nose. "Mama gots go lots pee-pee."

Angel scowled. Trent's arrival yesterday had kept her from speaking with Sister Mags about Charmaine's condition. She had already confided Charmaine's predicament to Trent the previous evening after Mrs. Kearn kicked them out of the kitchen. "I can't put this off any longer," she mumbled.

He lifted Sunshine from her arms. "Go. I'll keep her occupied."

The man flips his emotional switch as easily as a chameleon changes color, thought Angel, watching him play a finger game with Sunshine. She headed towards the kitchen. She wondered if anyone besides herself, Mrs. Kearn, and Sister Mags knew the gentler side of Trent Caldwell. Certainly not anyone in the business world. From what she gathered, Trent had a reputation for devouring other corporate barracudas as if they were minnows. She didn't doubt the reputation was well-founded—certainly not after witnessing his confrontation with Roger and Whitney Montgomery at the art gallery. But she couldn't help wondering if that side of him had developed as a defense mechanism against the pain of his loss.

Friendly bickering greeted her at the entrance to the kitchen, interrupting her brooding thoughts. From what Angel had observed earlier, Mrs. Kearn and Sister Mags maintained a long-standing, but amiable rivalry. The barbs they hurled back and forth across the kitchen were wrapped in feathery down and delivered with a twinkle and a wink.

"I thought I chased you out o' here," said Mrs. Kearn, spying Angel in the doorway.

Angel suppressed the giggle fighting to free itself from the back of her throat. "You did. Could I borrow Sister Mags for a few minutes? Unless, of course, you need her."

"Need her?" Mrs. Kearn snorted. "Take her. And keep her. She's only gettin' in my way."

"Some things never change," said Sister Mags, dropping a turkey baster into a sink full of soapy water, "and you, Moira Kearn are one of them!"

She turned to Angel and winked. "Every holiday, the same thing. You'd think it's her kitchen the way she bosses everyone around."

"Humph!" Mrs. Kearn spun around, pointing a large-pronged fork at the nun but directing her comment to Angel. "She's just jealous. Never could cook to save her life."

"Truce!" Angel raised her hands palms outward and lost her battle with the giggles.

With one last scowl for Mrs. Kearn, Sister Mags grabbed Angel's arm and led her from the kitchen. "My office?"

Angel nodded, her expression sobering.

Women and children were beginning to filter down from the upstairs rooms and congregate in the large living room. From down the hall Angel heard Trent laugh, the boisterous sound rising above the chaotic chatter.

Sister Mags smiled. "I love to hear laughter fill these rooms. It's a healing sound."

"We all need to laugh more, then," said Angel. She could hear the wistfulness in her own voice. A quick glance to her left showed her that Sister Mags had, too.

The nun tilted her head and frowned, closing the office door behind them. "So, my dear, what's troubling you? If you're uncomfortable uptown with that Irish harridan, you know you're always welcome back here."

Angel shook her head. "No, it's not about me." She paused for a moment, then continued. "It's Charmaine."

"Ah." Sister Mags leaned against her desk and pointed to one of the chairs. "Have a seat, and tell me something I don't already know."

Angel sank into the chair and expelled a deep sigh. "She's pregnant."

Sadness crept across the nun's face as she silently contemplated Angel's words. She crossed her arms over her chest and matched Angel's sigh with one of her own. "I thought as much," she finally said. Deep frown lines settled across her brow. "I prayed I was wrong, but—"

"She's not going to be one of the one's that makes it, is she, Sister?" Plead as she might, Angel knew the answer to that question before she asked it.

When Sister Mags shook her head, she wasn't surprised. "God might have a miracle up his sleeve, but Charmaine's doing her best to prevent Him from executing one."

"What happens now?"

"First, we make certain she has excellent medical care. Then we pray harder than ever." She rose from her chair and walked around her desk. Her fingertips planting a butterfly kiss against Angel's cheek. "I'm glad she has you to confide in. Perhaps, you'll succeed where I've failed."

"You mean with Julio?"

Sister Mags grimaced. "Julio. You don't by any chance know any hit men, do you?"

Luckily, Angel knew she was joking. All the same, she shook her head. "Actually, I think I may have crossed paths with one recently."

"So I hear."

After Trent's arrival at Haven yesterday, Angel had planned to fill Sister Mags in on the events leading up to her coming to Haven, but there'd been no time. "How did you—?"

"Moira."

"Of course."

No wonder Mrs. Kearn hadn't wanted Angel in the kitchen. In-between the bickerfest, she'd filled Sister Mags in on all things Angel. Knowing Mrs. Kearn, she'd probably also elicited the Sister's aid in her matchmaking scheme.

She grew sober. "I don't know anyone, Sister. And apparently, no one knows me. That's *my* problem."

"And that's something else we continue to pray about, my dear."

As they left the office, Angel and Sister Mags discovered Charmaine, fearful as an injured sparrow, waiting on the other side of the door. Without a word Sister Mags drew her into her arms, and Angel knew the feisty nun would fight the devil himself to try to save the young girl.

* * *

Thirty grateful bodies, ranging in age from six weeks through multiple decades, crowded around the large oak dining room table for Thanksgiving dinner. Two hours later, after the last slice of pie had been devoured, the young women of Haven staged a coup. First, they forced Mrs. Kearn to join Sister Mags, Trent, and Angel in the living room. Then they settled the infants down for naps and organized a massive cleanup detail, drafting all but the youngest into action. Camaraderie reigned; no one complained. Women and children alike tackled each task with a sense of pride and accomplishment.

From a comfortable seat in the living room Trent maintained a surreptitious watch over the frenetic activities while he bounced Sunshine on his knee. "You're doing a fine job, Mags," he said. "I'd be privileged to have any one of them work for me."

"Good thing," she said. "I've got several graduating computer school the end of next month."

No wonder Sister Mags has little trouble placing her graduates, thought Angel. *And I'll bet they're some of the finest, most loyal employees Trent has.* She wondered whether the women of Haven knew just how much of their salvation they owed to the man who had carved their Thanksgiving turkeys.

The *briiing* of Trent's cell phone caused all heads to turn his way. "Who the devil would be callin' on Thanksgivin'?" muttered Mrs. Kearn.

"The majority of the world is not celebrating a holiday today," he reminded her, handing over the child.

"Well, you are, and the rest o' the world should recognize that. Let you enjoy it in peace!"

"I'll mention that to the caller," said Trent, answering the phone. "Trent Caldwell."

As Trent listened to the voice on the other end of the line, the color drained from his face. His body stiffened, his knuckles growing white from their grip on the phone and the arm of his chair. He continued listening, not saying a word, the seconds ticking into minutes.

The room had grown still, all attention riveted on him. Angel, Mrs. Kearn, and Sister Mags watched. Waited. For what they didn't know. Even the toddlers, sensing the gravity of the call, quieted.

Finally, Trent ended the call and placed the phone back in his pocket. Without a word, without making eye contact with any of them, he stood and left the room. His face contorted in anguish; he looked as though he had just heard the most devastating news of his life.

Excruciating minutes dragged by, one after another. In the background Angel heard the commotion drifting in from the kitchen—the dishwasher chugging through a cycle, the clatter of pots, the swish of a broom sliding along the linoleum. Above it all, came the chatter of the women and laughter of the children as they worked side by side, unaware of the tension that gripped the occupants of the living room.

Sister Mags was the first to break the strained silence. "Something awful's happened. We should go to him."

"Leave him be," said Mrs. Kearn, glaring at the nun. "Whatever 'tis, he wants no meddlin' from anyone just now."

"Really, Moira!"

They continued to bicker back and forth. At first Angel watched in horror, wanting to scream some sense into the two of them. How could they act so petty and self-centered while Trent wrestled with some unknown hell? And one of them a nun, no less!

However, when the first of the kitchen crew entered the living room, the squabbling came to an abrupt halt, and the two older women began chatting with the younger ones as if nothing contentious had passed between them. Angel realized then that their aberrant behavior was nothing more than a release mechanism for the anxiety they felt. Trent's abrupt departure from the room worried them beyond reason.

And worried her. Angel thought she had grown accustomed to Trent's see-sawing personality—open and feeling one moment, shut down the next. She had witnessed his blacker moods, when the grief overwhelmed all else and threatened to close him off to life and hope forever. But that was an old pain, one he'd lived with for many years. The anguish she saw in his eyes as he left the room was fresh. What could have possibly happened to cause such utter bleakness?

As the room filled with people, temporarily diverting both Sister Mags and Mrs. Kearn, Angel slipped away. Somewhere within the large brownstone Trent was alone with his misery, and contrary to Mrs. Kearn's opinion, he needed human comfort, not solitude. Whether he knew it or not.

She found him in the first place she looked.

THIRTY-ONE

Trent sensed Angel's presence before he saw her. From the corner of his eye, he followed her progress down the center aisle of the room which was once a library and now served as Haven's chapel.

Trent had outfitted the chapel himself, salvaging the furnishing from an old church slated for demolition. The room's original dark mahogany paneling still remained. The shelves that once contained hundreds of books now held a few dozen Bibles and hymnals and framed religious postcards from trips Sister Mags had taken to the Vatican and various religious shrines throughout the world. Five rows of high pews on either side of the aisle faced the simple altar that stood in front of the room's original marble fireplace. A large wooden crucifix was mounted above the mantle. He'd hired a stained glass artisan to replace the three paned windows on the right side of the room with depictions of Mary, Joseph, and the baby Jesus.

Trent watched Angel genuflect and make the sign of the cross before entering the pew and seating herself beside him. He wondered if she somehow sensed she was Catholic or if she'd merely taken on the trappings and customs of the religion since arriving at Haven. She neither looked his way, nor said a word to him, simply sat there beside him while he continued to flog himself.

Eventually, he reached over and rested his hand on the top of hers. Only then did she speak.

"Want to talk about it?"

"No. Talking gives it life." He hated to think his actions had set in motion a chain of events that precipitated such a heinous act. Perhaps, if he had handled the situation differently....

Respecting his wishes, Angel said no more. She laced her fingers through his and continued to sit in silence beside him. The physical connection comforted him. He felt as though she were willing a part of herself, the sweetest part, to flow through her fingertips and infuse him with courage to confront this new horror.

"Not talking about it won't make it go away," he finally said.

"No."

Her voice was feathery soft. Angelic. She said nothing beyond the one word. No questions. No prodding looks. Her only communication, the slight pressure of her slim, pale fingers entwined with his. Trent focused on their joined hands, nestled on the burgundy cushioned bench in the space between them and anguished over his culpability in the events which had devastated her life.

Sweet Angel, victim of a cruel twist of fate. If he hadn't insisted on her staying with him, none of this hell would exist. But he had. And it did. Even when he tried to atone for his sins, people wound up getting hurt. Innocent people. Like Angel. He threw his head back against the pew and took a deep breath. Without preamble, he blurted out the news. "Felicia's dead."

Angel gasped. "What happened?"

"The police received an anonymous tip. They found her hanging in her apartment."

"My God! She killed herself?"

Trent shook his head. As repugnant as suicide was, what had actually occurred was far worse. "That's what the police believed at first."

"But?"

"She was murdered—strangled, then strung up to make it look like she'd hanged herself."

He felt Angel's hand trembling beneath his. Her voice quivered as she spoke. "Who would do such a thing?"

"I wish I knew. Rafe, maybe?"

Angel shook her head. "That makes no sense. He'd be crazy to contact Felicia. He swindled her. Wouldn't she demand her money back?"

"I suppose." But if not Rafe or whoever he was, then whom? He stared ahead into nothingness, attempting to sort through his conflicting emotions. What else was Felicia involved in that could have led to her murder? How many Rafes had she crossed paths with over the years? "You think you know someone..."

Trent sat brooding on that thought for several minutes before Angel spoke again.

"Why are you blaming yourself for her murder?"

No point denying it. Angel had read him like a cheap novel. He could maintain a poker face in the most crucial of situations, never allowing anyone to know his thoughts. Presidents and kings.

Titans of industry. He dealt with them all without showing his hand. What magical powers did this woman wield that suddenly broke through his defenses?

Trent grimaced. If she sat opposite him at the negotiating table, he'd wind up living out of a cardboard box on Skid Row. "If I had dealt with her differently—"

Angel completed the thought. "She'd still be alive?"

He nodded, his lips pursed in a tight line. "What Felicia did was despicable, but she didn't deserve to die for it."

"Even if Rafe had succeeded?"

Her question caught him off guard. What had he been thinking? If Angel hadn't fled from Rafe at the airport, she may have met a similar fate. Or worse. All because Felicia wanted to eliminate what she perceived as her competition. Trent shuddered at the thought. "I didn't mean—"

"I know."

Searching past the ever-present sadness in her eyes, he found undeserved acceptance. It compelled him to explain his complex relationship with Felicia. Maybe then she'd understand. "Felicia was the polar opposite of Caitlin. Cold, ruthless, completely lacking in compassion. The perfect business associate for the world of corporate takeovers. Being with her was safe."

"So you used her."

Although her words remained soft, her tone calm, the accusation stung. "No! Not like that. Our relationship was strictly professional. Or so I thought. Until..." He threw his head back again and stared up at the hammered tin ceiling. "I'm supposed to be an intelligent, perceptive man. How the hell could I have been so blind?"

"You never realized she was in love with you?"

Trent lowered his head and stared at the kneeling cushion for several long seconds. "We were on a business trip last year. February thirteenth. It would have been Caitlin's thirty-fourth birthday. I was in an exceptionally black mood. After an unproductive, tedious business dinner, I retired to my room with the sole intention of drinking myself into oblivion."

He squeezed his eyelids closed, embarrassed by the memory of that dismal winter night. "I had already polished off half a bottle of Jack Daniels when Felicia knocked on the door."

"And she offered herself in place of the whiskey?"

He pounded his fist repeatedly into the pew cushion, emphasizing each agonizing sentence. "Yes, damn it. I used her. That night. Over and over again. I hated myself for doing it, and I hated her for being there. For not being Caitlin."

He hung his head and took a deep breath. Offering Angel an apologetic look, he finished his sorry tale. "Afterward, the relationship changed. In her mind. Not mine. Nothing I said or did dissuaded her. I guess she deluded herself into thinking I'd eventually come around. Caitlin was a ghost. Maybe she decided she could deal with that, but not you. You were too real a threat to her."

Angel studied him with a pensive gaze before responding to his confession. "There is the distinct possibility that Felicia's murder had nothing to do with you. Or me. Think about it, Trent. There are countless other possibilities. For all you know, she may have picked up some psycho in a bar. Or gotten herself mixed up with the wrong people. Did she gamble? Do drugs?"

Trent dismissed the suggestions with an impatient wave of his hand. "She wasn't that stupid."

A touch of annoyance permeated Angel's next words. "No, she

was just stupid enough to hire a kidnapper. Or was he a hit man?"

She scowled at him. "We'll never really know, will we? Think about it, Trent. If Felicia had the kind of connections that would enable her to hire Rafe—or whoever he is—and orchestrate my kidnapping, she had to know some pretty scary characters."

He shook his head. Tight lines etched into his jaw and around his mouth. "I know. I just don't want to believe that of her. It was hard enough accepting she'd acted out of jealousy of you."

"Rafe had a fake ID for me. ID that stood the scrutiny of the TSA agents at the airport. Maybe he got the ID through his connections, but Felicia knew how to find Rafe, and I doubt it was as simple as Googling *hit man* on her computer."

Trent stared at the crucifix. He'd been so damn blind about so many things. How could he ever again trust his instincts about anything?

"What do you really know about Felicia's life outside of her work?" asked Angel. "How she spent her evenings? Her weekends? Her vacations?"

"Felicia's work was her life. She never spoke of anything else, and I made a point of not asking."

"Everyone has a life outside the office, Trent. Even you. Even if it's not much of one."

He snorted but gave her a look that said she'd made her point. "I guess I never really knew her, did I?"

"Guess not."

Shifting sideways in the pew, Angel confronted him. "Sister Mags told me that powerful men often can't accept their own limitations. You're not God, Trent. Stop trying to nail yourself to a cross.

"Felicia's misguided jealousy set in motion a series of events that neither you nor anyone else could have foreseen. They may or may not be connected to her murder, but don't forget, *she's* the one who contacted Rafe. She had to know what he was capable of doing. After all, she hired him to do it. You are no more to blame for her downfall or her murder, than you are for my accident."

She paused for a moment. Her voice lowered to a near-whisper, she added, "Or Caitlin's death."

Pulling her hand out from under his, she rose. "You have two alternatives. You can sit here sulking and praying and cursing yourself for all eternity, or you can accept the fact that you're only human, like the rest of us, and get on with your life. Either way, the choice is yours, but for what it's worth, I much prefer you as a man, flawed like the rest of us, than a morose, self-flagellating god-wannabe."

She spun on her heels and stormed out of the chapel.

Her words echoed within him long after her footsteps faded. Angel was no longer the timid, frightened mouse who cowered at his approach. Feistiness now sprinkled her sweet nature, adding dimension to her gentle disposition. Over the past few months, she'd grown comfortable enough in his presence to challenge him. And had she ever done just that.

Stunned by her verbal assault, Trent sat alone in the semi-dark chapel, staring at the linen-draped altar. He had come seeking comfort and answers. In an unconventional way Angel had delivered both. Blunt and to the point, she'd held up a mirror and forced him to examine himself in the harsh light of reality. He wasn't happy with what he saw. The reflection was neither the man he used to be nor the man he wished to be.

Mark my words, Trent. That one's your salvation. Unbidden, Moira's words insinuated themselves into his thoughts. Early on she'd concluded that the young woman with no memory *was* an angel, sent by God to bring him back to life. He'd scoffed at her. Absurd nonsense. Or was it?

* * *

What in the world had possessed her to lash out at Trent like that? One moment she's sympathetic, and the next, she's rebuking him. *My God, how cruel!* The man bares his soul to her, and all she can do is accuse him of being a martyr! The moment the words spewed from her lips, she regretted them. But it was too late. Mortified, she fled the chapel, taking refuge in the powder room.

Sinking to the tile floor, she drew her knees up to her chest, buried her head in her hands and continued to curse herself. *Way to go, Angel. Trent Caldwell has offered you every kindness, and how do you repay him? With callousness and insults!*

A frightening thought grabbed hold of her, sending a chilling shudder along her spine. "Oh, God," she moaned out loud. Was this nasty side her true personality trying to resurface? Her eyes filled with tears, and she began to cry.

Angel had no idea how long she sat huddled on the hard tile floor, tears streaming down her cheeks. Eventually, she cried herself out. When she pulled herself to her feet, her muscles screamed their discomfort. Rubbing the kinks from her neck and shoulders, she caught sight of herself in the mirror above the sink and winced at her tear-stained reflection.

You brought this on yourself, she castigated the image. *Stop acting like a coward, and go apologize.* But first she needed major damage control. Cupping her palms under the faucet, she splashed handful after handful of cold water over her face, blotting herself dry with several coarse paper towels. Taking a deep breath, hoping to suck in some measure of courage, she reluctantly swung open the door.

And came face-to-face with Trent.

Startled to find him standing there, her step faltered. He reached out and grabbed her arm to steady her.

"Are you all right?"

She nodded, backing up against the door jamb while her tongue tripped over the words of apology that had deserted her. "I...I'm sorry. I had no right to...no right...I mean...I...you..."

Trent reached out and brushed an errant lock of damp hair off her cheek before placing his index finger against her lips. "Shh. Don't. You owe me no apology."

"But—" The word kissed the tip of his finger.

"No buts. I came to thank you."

Angel stared at him in wide-eyed disbelief. "Thank me?"

"For your courage. And your honesty. You spoke from your heart and forced me to take a long, hard look at myself. To see myself through your eyes."

She shook her head fiercely, her damp curls whipping around her head and slapping at her face. "No. I was mean. You were hurting, and I made it worse."

"You spoke the truth, Angel. Sometimes that's painful. But, all the same, I needed to hear it." He placed his palm against the wall and leaned closer to her. "I've always believed a man has to take responsibility for his actions."

Angel nodded. "An admirable trait."

Trent raised one eyebrow in question. "I hear a but hidden somewhere in there."

She squirmed, unable to make eye contact.

"Go on," he prodded. "Say what you're thinking."

"You take responsibility for the actions of others," she

mumbled, her gaze downcast, her voice filled with apology.

"For events out of my control?"

"Yes."

"A bad habit?"

Angel raised her chin and stared into his hazel eyes. Warm and smiling, they held not a trace of annoyance or anger. Only sincerity, coupled with an abundant dose of melancholy. She offered him a slight nod.

"I suppose I could argue otherwise," he said. "In business, management is always held accountable—for both successes and failures." He chuckled. "But you're not going to buy that, are you?"

"Your soul is far more important than a business deal, Trent."

"My soul." He echoed, turning into himself. "My soul died with Caitlin, Angel."

"I know better," she argued. "I've seen it. On more than one occasion."

Trent watched as she reached for a lock of hair, nervously worrying it between her index finger and thumb. He appreciated the difficulty with which she forced herself to tear at the barbed wire he'd wrapped himself in since that fateful wintry day. To his surprise, Angel was successfully stripping the killer spikes from his soul. And his heart. But at what price? To both her and him.

She was everything missing in his life. Sweetness and laughter. Warmth and caring. Everything Caitlin had once been. Everything he'd extinguished with the twist of a steering wheel. With sudden clarity Trent realized that if he let himself, he could easily fall in love with Angel. But of course, he could never let that happen. For her sake as well as his.

"We should go join the others," he said.

* * *

Trent couldn't shake the shock of Felicia's death. He brooded over it throughout the ride back uptown in the hired car, saying little to either Angel or Mrs. Kearn.

"What's eatin' you?" asked his housekeeper, shattering the tense silence.

When Trent ignored her question, Angel provided a brief explanation.

"The world's gone mad," he muttered under his breath. "First Whitney. Now Felicia."

Angel's body stiffened. A worrisome crease settled across her brow. "Whitney Montgomery? Something happened to her? When?"

Trent blew out a lungful of irritation. Part of him wanted to shield Angel from yet another violent act, but she had a right to know. "The day you disappeared," he said. "Someone sent her a deadly gift."

"Blew her to Kingdom Come," offered Mrs. Kearn.

"A bomb? My God!"

"It gets worse," said Trent, realizing there was no turning back. If he didn't tell her, Moira would. "Remember Roger Caine? Sarah Montgomery's husband?"

Angel shuddered, recalling their encounter at the gallery opening. "Of course. Nasty beady-eyed drunk."

"He tried his damnedest to convince the police that I was responsible for Whitney's murder."

Angel's eyes grew wide with horror. "But...they couldn't believe...you would never—"

"No," he assured her, reaching over and patting her hand. "They don't, and I wouldn't. But Roger did have a list of witnesses who overheard my brief altercation with Whitney at the gallery."

"How convenient," said Mrs. Kearn. "I'll bet he did her in himself."

"Why?" asked Angel.

The housekeeper shrugged. "Money. That's all them Montgomerys ever cared about."

"Roger's not a Montgomery," Trent reminded her, "but he did have the most to gain from Whitney's death. The entire Montgomery fortune. There's no one else left alive." He shook his head. "So many deaths."

"There are some what deserves to die," said Mrs. Kearn. "Don't you be forgettin' that, lad."

"Don't start, Moira," muttered Trent. "Not tonight."

* * *

Two a.m. *The more things change, the more they remain the same.* Angel shook the fiery vision from her head and rose from the bed. Draping one of Mrs. Kearn's crocheted afghans around her shoulders, she curled up on the wide windowsill and stared out across the towering shadows of the city. Saxophone music drifted down the hallway, seeping under the closed door and into the floral bedroom. *The same, yet different.* Angel closed her eyes and allowed the notes to fill her soul. *Much different.* This was not the same mournful melody she'd heard Trent play in the past. No. This tune spoke of tomorrows and held a promise of hope.

Angel hugged her knees to her chest, the corners of her mouth curling up in a satisfied smile.

THIRTY-TWO

Who am I?

As she filled her days at Haven, the question, although ever present, now taunted Angel less and less. Her own predicament paled in comparison to the problems faced by the members of Sister Mags's little family. These women had fled intolerable situations. They and their children would carry brutal memories and physical scars with them the rest of their lives. Ironically, or maybe because of their own pasts, many of the women envied her lack of memory.

Prior to finding Haven, Angel had worried she might never regain her past. Now, striving to help Haven's residents overcome theirs, she began to accept her situation as a mystery which might never be solved.

Only in the quiet moments of early morning, when the sun streamed through the Irish lace curtains in the floral bedroom and illuminated Sarah Montgomery's French landscapes, did she feel a twinge of emptiness and longing for a life she couldn't remember.

And then there were the recurring fiery visions. Always lurking on the fringes of her mind, they continued to invade both her sleep and her waking peace. Although they subsided for a while during her brief stay at Haven, they'd now returned with a vengeance. Powerful undefined images, they forced their way into her conscious mind—anytime, anywhere—leaving her frightened and confused.

"Bad night?" asked Trent one morning after a visibly shaken Angel entered the kitchen.

She nodded. Having already seen herself in the bathroom mirror, she knew there was no point denying it. Her eyes were bloodshot, her face drained of color.

How many times during the night had she fallen asleep only to be awakened by desperate screams? The conflagration had become so real that she could feel the heat blistering her skin, the thick black smoke stinging her eyes and choking the air from her lungs.

"I think you should go back to Dr. Pierce." Trent rose from his seat to pour her a cup of coffee.

Angel dropped into one of the ladder-back chairs, propped her elbows on the table, and cradled her forehead with her palms. Her head throbbed from lack of sleep. "No. It's a waste of money."

"Damn the money!" Placing a cup in front of her, Trent seated himself at the table and downed the remainder of his coffee in one long gulp. "These visions are tearing you apart. You need to find out what they mean and how to stop them."

"I can't."

"Angel—"

"Leave her be," said Mrs. Kearn, turning from the stove, one hand on her ample hip, the other waving a spatula. "She'll remember when the good Lord wants her to remember. Not from talkin' to any fancy-pants psycho-babble crackpot spewing mumbo-jumbo."

Angel cast a pleading look in Trent's direction, stopping him from responding to Mrs. Kearn. She reached across the table and placed her hand over his. "I appreciate your concern, Trent, but I don't think Dr. Pierce can help me any further. That's why I stopped seeing her."

"Fine. Dr. Pierce isn't the only psychiatrist in New York. I'll send you to someone else."

Angel shook her head. "It's my problem. I can deal with it."

Trent set his empty cup on the table with enough force to rattle the dishes and cause the pepper mill to sway precariously. "Yes, I can see how well you're dealing with it. You look like death warmed over this morning."

"Leave the lass be!" Mrs. Kearn slammed a plate down in front of him. Once more the dishes clattered a response, and this time the pepper mill lost its battle with gravity, landing on the table with a loud bang.

Trent righted the pepper mill as he scowled at first the food, then his housekeeper. "Fine. I'll be damned if I'm going to fight you both." He grabbed a fork and attacked the stack of waffles Mrs. Kearn had placed in front of him. "One's more pigheaded than the other."

After cleaning his plate in several quick mouthfuls, he pushed his chair back from the table and rose. Turning to Angel, he said. "I need O'Hara all morning. If you want a ride to Haven, I'm leaving in ten minutes."

"I'll be ready," she answered.

* * *

A shiver of fear crept through Angel as Mr. O'Hara pulled the car up behind a police cruiser parked in front of Haven. "Something's wrong," she said.

O'Hara slipped out from behind the wheel and opened the back door for her. "I'm sure 'tis nothin'," he said. "Probably just one of the beat coppers droppin' off some donations to the good Sister. The local precinct is right around the corner."

Angel stood on the sidewalk and stared at the front door. A rope of evergreens outlined its perimeter. A Christmas wreath, trimmed with a large burgundy and gold velvet bow, hung from the center of the heavy oak door. But neither the festive holiday decorations nor O'Hara's reassuring words could dismiss the sense of foreboding creeping through every nerve in her body.

The door opened, and two grim-faced officers stepped out onto the brick landing. The younger of the two hurried down the stairs. Pausing at the base, he made quick eye contact with first Angel, then the chauffeur, before crossing the pavement, jumping into the cruiser, and starting the engine.

"I'd best be goin'," said O'Hara. "Mr. Caldwell has a busy schedule today. Can't keep him waiting."

Angel nodded, paying little regard to the driver as he slipped behind the wheel of the black limo and drove off. Her attention was focused on the remaining policeman who lingered on the narrow landing. Considerably older than his partner, the man looked like he'd seen more than his share of crime and violence over the years. Sister Mags, her face drawn, her forehead creased with worry lines, stood in the doorway listening as he spoke.

His words carried down the short flight of stairs to where Angel stood. "I'll put a call in to ACS for you, Sister. They'll be out to get the little girl sometime this afternoon, I should think."

Sister Mags nodded. "Thank you, Tony. I appreciate your coming to tell me yourself."

The policeman dropped his chin onto his chest and shook his head. A deep scowl settled across his face. "It's the worst part of the job, you know? Bringing bad news. Even worse than the crime scenes themselves. Especially this time of year."

The nun placed her hand on his forearm. "The city needs more caring souls like you, Tony. God bless you."

"And you, Sister." He turned and lumbered down the steps. A moment later the police car pulled into traffic and headed up the street.

Time seemed to stand still. Angel watched Sister Mags watching the cruiser weave its way through a street full of cars, delivery trucks, and taxis until it turned out of sight. Her feet remained frozen to the sidewalk in front of Haven. Once she mounted the steps to the entrance, she was certain the dread she sensed would turn into a brutal reality. Something had happened to one of Haven's young mothers. That much Angel was certain of from the officer's comment to Sister Mags. And Angel feared she knew which mother.

"Come inside, Angel," said Sister Mags, her voice devoid of the cheerfulness that usually greeted Angel each morning.

Angel climbed the handful of steps as though she were ascending a guillotine, each stair bringing her nearer to a truth she didn't want to know. When she reached the top, the nun led her across the threshold, closing the door behind them. In the dim foyer light Angel's gaze locked onto Sister Mags. Tears swam in the nun's sad eyes, and Angel knew, without a word spoken between them, that fate had finally caught up with Charmaine.

She fell into Sister Mags' arms. "No! No! No!"

"Shh! Don't," she said, wrapping her arms around Angel. "The children."

Angel choked down a sob and brushed the tears from her cheeks. The nun was right. She had to compose herself. "Where's Sunshine? Does she know?"

The sister shook her head. "Not here. We'll talk in my office." She led Angel down the hall.

"What happened?" asked Angel, sinking into one of the two chairs opposite the desk.

Sister Mags leaned against the closed door and sighed. "I wish I had eyes in the back of my head, Angel, but the dear Lord didn't see fit to so equip me."

"You can't be blaming yourself!"

"No. I just wish I had gotten through to her, but I guess it wasn't meant to be. God had other plans."

"Are you saying God wanted Charmaine to die? Wanted Sunshine orphaned?"

Sister Mags crossed the tiny room and collapsed into her desk chair. "It's not for us to second guess Him."

Angel shook her head with such force that her curls slapped her cheeks. "No. I can't accept that." Her gaze raked Sister Mags. "But you do, don't you? How can you?"

"Faith."

"Faith," echoed Angel, the word more a question than a statement. This was no time for a theology debate. She closed her eyes and repeated her earlier query. "Tell me what happened."

"She sneaked out last night. After everyone had gone to bed. Maybe she'd been doing it for some time. Maybe last night was the first. I don't know."

Sister Mags steepled her fingers, resting her index fingers beneath her lower lip. "I was on my way to the chapel for my morning prayers when I discovered Sunshine wandering around downstairs. She was barefoot and clutching that tattered stuffed bunny of hers. Tears spilled down her cheeks. She was whimpering that she couldn't find her mama, that she'd looked everywhere."

"Sunshine meant the world to Charmaine," argued Angel. "She'd never risk her daughter's future."

Sister Mags shrugged. "Maybe she was trying to insure the child's future. And hers."

"How do you mean?"

"Julio." Sister Mags nearly spit out the name. "Charmaine romanticized him. She refused to believe he was using her. Maybe the poor girl thought if she got herself pregnant again, he'd marry her."

"And they'd live happily ever after in a three-bedroom colonial with a picket fence, a cocker spaniel, and a swing set in the backyard?"

Sister Mags scowled. "Absurd, isn't it? Julio's a two-bit pimp. He threw her out when she became pregnant with Sunshine and refused to get an abortion. You'd think that would tell her something, but to Charmaine he was always the knight in shining armor who rescued her from the streets."

"You rescued her," said Angel. "The way I heard it, Julio enslaved her. My God, she was only a child herself when he forced her into prostitution!"

"Obviously, Charmaine chose to remember a more romanticized and fictionalized account of her past. She wound up paying for it with her life."

"Have the police arrested Julio?"

"They picked him up for questioning. Tony...Officer Fernandez...said they don't have enough evidence to book him yet."

Angel braced herself, afraid of the answer to the question she had to ask. "What did he do to her?"

Sister Mags sucked in a sharp breath. Squeezing her eyes closed, she shuddered. "He used a knife. Brutalized her in ways you don't want to hear, trust me. Then he left her to bleed to death in a garbage strewn alley. A trash hauler stumbled across her body early this morning."

The viciousness of the act severed the thin thread holding Angel together. "Why?" she kept asking over and over again. "Why?" What had Charmaine done to deserve such a fate? And what about Sunshine? What would happen to her?

Angel thought back to the conversation she'd overheard between Sister Mags and the police officer. *I'll put a call into ACS for you, Sister. They'll be out to get the little girl sometime this afternoon.*

ACS. Administration for Children's Services. As far as Angel was concerned, the agency was directly responsible for Charmaine's death. If they hadn't placed her in a home where she was raped, she wouldn't have run away and wound up on the streets where she quickly became fresh meat. If she hadn't met Julio, she would have fallen in with some other pimp. Charmaine had no other way to survive.

"You can't let Children's Services take her. They failed Charmaine. How do you know the same thing won't happen to Sunshine? Or worse?"

"I have no choice. My hands are tied."

Angel rose to her feet. "I can't accept that! Charmaine is dead because of their incompetence. They're not getting Sunshine!"

"We have to pray that the system works for Sunshine the way it was intended."

Prayer hadn't work for Charmaine. There was no guarantee it would succeed for her daughter. Angel wasn't willing to risk Sunshine's life to an overburdened, understaffed bureaucracy with a history of failure. "We owe her more than that, Sister. *I* owe her more than that."

Sister Mags rose from her chair and began pacing back and forth between her desk and the file cabinets. The agony of the situation was carved into every crease and worry line in her face. "I can't keep her here, Angel, and ACS would never release her to you. Not with your unusual circumstances." She threw her arms up in defeat. "I'm afraid there's nothing either of us can do, my dear."

"Maybe not. But I know someone who can." She reached across the desk, grabbed the telephone, and dialed Trent's personal cell phone number.

* * *

Trent and a select number of board members from Montgomery Aeronautics were huddled in a private meeting called by John Ferguson, attorney for the late Abel Montgomery.

"I always suspected Caine wasn't telling the truth about the embezzlement scheme," said the lawyer. "Perhaps, I should have brought my suspicions to you sooner."

"Why didn't you?" asked Trent.

Ferguson shrugged. "When I heard you were moving to oust him, I figured you'd already unearthed enough evidence on your own."

"I surmised incompetence, not malfeasance. Why now,

Ferguson?"

"Whitney Montgomery's murder. Rumors of Caine's erratic behavior. He's a dangerous man, Caldwell. I'm convinced of that. Besides, I owe it to Abel." He paused before adding, "And Sarah."

Trent tapped his pen on the legal pad in front of him. Frowning at the notes he'd scrawled, he pondered the lawyer's words. John Ferguson had nothing to gain by accusing Roger Caine of fraud. Or murder. "You have no concrete proof of the theft?"

"No. Abel insisted on keeping the evidence. After his heart attack and subsequent death, it disappeared."

"You didn't have copies?"

Ferguson shook his head and grimaced. "Stupid, wasn't it? Abel's orders, though. He didn't want word leaking out until he confronted Caine himself. I'm sure he was hoping it was all a big misunderstanding. Some sort of mistake. For Sarah's sake. After Abel's death Caine supposedly uncovered the evidence himself."

"Framing an innocent man?"

"In my opinion."

"What about Osbourne? I can't believe he didn't keep a copy of the report detailing what he'd uncovered."

"He did," said John, "but Caine had enough time to go back into the system and manipulate the data to his advantage. Assuming he had the report I left with Abel, he knew exactly what he needed to destroy or tweak. Osbourne's the best there is when it comes to computer forensics, but apparently not good enough. Caine got the better of him. He's one sly bastard when he's not shit-faced drunk."

Trent refrained from using the expletive at the tip of his tongue. He'd suspected Caine of deceit, but only as a means of covering up his own ineptitude, not the crime Ferguson suggested. He hadn't given the bastard enough credit. If these accusations were true, Roger Caine was both cunning and resourceful. Not to mention, as Ferguson implied, very dangerous.

When Moira had insinuated Roger killed Whitney, he'd dismissed the accusation without a second thought. Mrs. Kearn's perception of the Montgomerys was colored by a blinding hatred stemming from a grief that grew more severe with each passing year.

Still, Trent had made certain he was kept apprised of the police investigation into Whitney Montgomery's murder. Although Roger was a suspect, to date the police had turned up only circumstantial evidence, nothing concrete enough for an indictment. However, Trent had no way of knowing how much the police and district attorney were keeping to themselves. His source only went so far before smacking up against that solid blue wall.

Abel died shortly after discovering Roger's duplicity. Roger's wife died the day Abel's will was read. Whitney was murdered shortly after his confrontation with her and Roger at the gallery opening. Was it possible that Abel's and Sarah's deaths were actually homicides made to appear otherwise? Was Roger Caine a coldblooded murderer?

Trent scribbled all three names on his legal pad, then scratched out Sarah's and Whitney's. There was no doubt of Whitney's murder, and there was no possibility of an autopsy on Sarah. What had been left of her charred remains were now ashes in an urn.

Abel, however, was a different story. His exhumed body just might unravel a mystery and catch a killer. Trent circled the name. He'd call his contact at the district attorney's office as soon as he returned to his own office.

Then he noticed a fourth name he'd scrawled in the margin next to the first three. A question mark flanked it. Felicia. Another murder victim. When had he written her name? And why? Could Roger Caine somehow be connected to her murder, as well? And to what end? Revenge instantly came to mind.

Felicia Sutton had been one of Trentwell's greatest assets. Many companies routinely courted her, hoping to lure her away. Had Caine killed Felicia in an attempt to hurt Trent and cripple his empire?

Trent's head spun. Ferguson's revelations had unleashed a host of suppositions—all of them frightening possibilities. The sooner he turned this information over to the authorities, the better. Even if it were all circumstantial, a pattern existed—one that bore scrutiny. If the monster had committed one, and possibly several murders, he could strike again. Soon. At anyone. Trent suppressed a shudder. Who would be his next victim?

His ringing cell phone interrupted the conjecture. "Excuse me, gentlemen," he mumbled, withdrawing the phone from his pocket. "Trent Caldwell."

Angel's hysterical voice greeted him.

"Wait! I can't understand you. Hold on." He turned to Ferguson. "Is there somewhere I can take this in private?"

"Use my office." He pointed to a door at the side of the conference room.

"All right, Angel," said Trent after entering the office and closing the door behind him. "Slowly and from the top."

He heard her take a deep breath. "Julio killed Charmaine, and ACS is coming to get Sunshine, and Sister Mags says there's nothing we can do, but I *know* you can, Trent! Please!"

"Please what?" He had a sinking feeling he already knew the answer to that.

"Keep them from taking her!"

"Contrary to popular belief, I don't run the city, Angel. Just how do you expect me to do that? And where would Sunshine go if not into a foster home? She can't stay at Haven by herself."

Again, he heard her suck in a deep breath and then expel it before answering. "She could live with us. I'd take care of her, but Sister Mags says they'd never give me custody, not with my amnesia, but they'd never object to you, Trent. They couldn't. Please?"

Christ! He was afraid of this. "Angel, this is not a good time. I really—"

"You're right. It sure wasn't a good time for Charmaine to get herself killed. But it happened, and you can't let them do to Sunshine what they did to her mother. The system doesn't work. You know that, Trent. Caitlin knew it. That's why she started Haven."

Angel hit him below the belt with that one. "Angel, you don't know what you're asking."

He closed his eyes and saw the toddler he'd bounced on his knee only two weeks ago. He could lose his heart to that little girl. If he still had a heart. No. He'd already caused too much pain to those who had loved him. She was far better off taking her chances elsewhere. He'd see that she got placed with good people. That much he *could* do. "I'll make certain she's sent to a loving family."

"For how long? A month or two before she's bounced to another home? And another? And another? Not good enough, Trent!"

"Angel, please understand—"

"Damn it, Trent, I've never asked you for anything. Everything you've ever done for me was to assuage your own guilt. Well, I'm asking now. No, I'm demanding. You *have* to do this, Trent. For Sunshine. For me." She paused, then added in a whisper, "For yourself."

She hung up before he could respond.

Damn her! Trent paced back and forth across the large expanse of John Ferguson's office, but he hardly noticed the plush surroundings. He punctuated each stride by pounding a tightly balled fist against his left thigh. Who the hell appointed Angel as his moral barometer?

We have to do this, Trent. We have so much, and they have so little. If we can save just a handful from falling through the cracks... Caitlin's words. And he had agreed with her.

You have to do this, Trent...For yourself. Angel's words. And he knew in that nonexistent heart of his that she was right.

Damn her!

He pushed the speed-dial that connected him directly to his secretary. "Cancel the rest of my appointments for today."

THIRTY-THREE

Two caseworkers were already at Haven when Trent arrived. He heard them. And Angel. Arguing. Loudly. Following the sounds of their escalating voices, he strode down the hall to the office. He wondered why they'd bothered to close the door. The heavy oak was no match for their heated words.

"About time you got here," said Sister Mags, coming up behind him.

"Miracles take less time than dealing with City Hall," he said. "Even for me." He nodded toward the door. "How long has she been fending off the cattle rustlers?"

"Long enough but I wouldn't go in there unless you've brought her a miracle."

"Where's Sunshine?"

"I arranged a spur-of-the-moment outing for the preschoolers. Sister Catherine and Sister Agnes took them to my cousin's bakery to watch them decorate gingerbread houses." She glanced at her watch. "They'll be gone for at least another half hour."

"No one's told Sunshine about her mother?"

Frustration settled across the nun's face. "How do you explain death to a three-year-old, Trent? A toddler can't understand the concept of forever."

"So she knows nothing?"

"She knows her mama is with God, but she left for the bakery as excited as the rest of the children. I'm sure she expects Charmaine to be waiting for her when she returns."

"Damn." He reached for the doorknob.

The nun stopped him with a gentle touch of her hand on his forearm. "About that miracle Angel's expecting?"

He offered her a sad smile. "Could I do any less, Mags?"

Trent opened the door to the battlefield. Neither Angel nor the caseworkers gave any indication that they heard him. They were too wrapped up in the drama playing out in the room.

"You're being unreasonable," pleaded one of the caseworkers, a slightly balding man in his early forties with a reedy voice and a wardrobe that bespoke how little social workers were paid. Trent couldn't help but notice that the man's collar and cuffs were frayed, his suit pants shiny from wear, his fringe of hair in need of a good trim. "We're only doing our job," said the man.

"No," replied Angel, her voice climbing higher as she built up a good head of steam. "You definitely are *not* doing your job! If you had done your job, Charmaine wouldn't have run away from an abusive foster home. She wouldn't have wound up turning tricks on the street in order to survive. And she sure as hell wouldn't be dead now. So don't you dare tell me you're doing your job."

Feisty as ever, thought Trent. But because of Caitlin, he had a perspective that Angel didn't. Kids fell through the cracks because caseworkers were juggling too many cases. His wife had often bemoaned the fact that she couldn't visit every child as often as she'd like, even working sixty-hour weeks. There were just too many kids and not enough caseworkers to go around.

"You can't blame the mother's death on us!" yelled the man.

"I believe I just did," said Angel.

"This is insane." The second caseworker stormed across the room and accosted Angel. A large woman who seemed comfortable using her size to intimidate, she planted herself toe-to-toe with Angel, jabbing a chubby finger inches from Angel's face as she spoke. "Who the hell do you think you are? We don't need your permission. When the kid gets back, we're taking her. Period. And if I have to climb over your uptown designer butt to do it, I will. You got a problem with that, lady, go tell it to the judge."

"That won't be necessary," said Trent, stepping into the already crowded room and closing the door behind him. He gently pulled Angel away from the caseworker and inserted his body between them.

"Trent Caldwell?" The first caseworker gaped at him, awestruck. The second placed her hands on her extremely large hips and eyed him suspiciously.

Trent removed an envelope from his breast pocket and held it out to her. "I have a court order releasing the child into my custody."

The woman snatched the envelope from his hand, withdrew the paperwork, and studied it. "So it appears." She lifted her chin and scrutinized him. "Why? What's your interest in some nappy-haired little bastard?"

Angel gasped.

Trent gritted his teeth to keep from saying what immediately sprang to his mind. Instead, he kept his voice as controlled and level as possible and said, "That doesn't concern you." He opened the office door and stepped aside. Sister Mags was standing in the hall. "Sister will see you out."

The woman shrugged. "You got some white liberal guilt you need to assuage, I'll be damned if I give a rat's ass." She picked up her briefcase and headed out the door. "That's one less brat we need to deal with. Let's go, Harold."

Without saying a word, the other caseworker followed quickly behind her.

"Thank you," said Angel after Trent closed the door behind the caseworkers. Her eyes shone with happiness and tears of gratitude.

Trent slowly shook his head and shoved his fingers through his hair. "You left me little choice. I hope you know what you're doing. She's your responsibility."

Angel reached for the court order the caseworker had dropped onto Sister Mags's desk and handed it to him. A shy smile danced at the corners of her mouth. "Says here she's yours."

False bravado. Her nervous fingers betrayed her. As they fidgeted with a curl, they told him what her words tried to hide. She was scared to death she'd pushed him too far.

"You're turning into one hell of a little manipulator," he said, plucking the papers from her fingers. Then he laughed. "And to think once upon a time you were afraid to be in the same room with me."

Angel released the figurative breath she'd been holding since she hung up on him hours before.

* * *

Sunshine accepted the move to Trent's apartment as a great adventure. With her ragged, floppy-eared bunny and a cellophane wrapped miniature gingerbread house balanced next to each other on her tiny lap, she sat sandwiched between Trent and Angel for the ride uptown. Unaware of the life-altering events which had precipitated her first car ride, she chattered away nonstop. "I gots this for Mama," she said, carefully lifting the decorated confection and showing it first to Angel, then to Trent.

Angel inwardly cringed at the scowl Trent delivered over the toddler's head. She wrapped her arm around Sunshine and hugged her. "Don't you remember, sweetheart? Sister Mags told you Mama had to go be with God."

"We saves it for her," answered Sunshine, carefully setting the package back down.

"Who's this?" asked Trent, lifting the bedraggled, stuffed animal from the child's lap.

"Bun-Bun."

"Is Bun-Bun your special friend?"

Sunshine shook her head and giggled. "No, silly!" She reached over and grabbed one of Trent's hands and one of Angel's. "*You* my special friends. Bun-Bun my nighty-night friend." Growing sober, she leaned as far forward as her seatbelt allowed. Twisting her body, she studied Trent with the same intense scrutiny she had on Thanksgiving, then cocked her head to one side and asked, "You gots a widdle girl?"

"No."

"Good," she said, leaning back against the seat and nodding matter-of-factly. "I don't gots a daddy. Mama want Julio to be's my daddy."

Angel suppressed a shudder. For the hundredth time that day she wondered how Charmaine could have been so blind.

Sunshine wrinkled her nose. "Julio scary," she continued, "and mean." She slipped her hand into Trent's. "You nice. I be's your widdle girl. You be's my daddy. We tell Mama when she come back from visiting God."

If only the mother had seen as clearly as her three-year-old, thought Angel. But fate had interceded. Or God, if you possessed the resolute faith of Sister Mags. She glanced over at Trent. He was smiling down at Sunshine, his eyes filled with a combination of sadness, warmth, and awe. She could almost see his heart melting. Maybe Sister Mags was right. Maybe God had a grander plan in mind. For Sunshine *and* Trent.

* * *

"You turkey lady!" Sunshine pointed a chubby finger at Mrs. Kearn. Her face lit up like a Christmas tree.

"We prefer to call her Mrs. Kearn," said Trent, stifling a laugh. Sunshine still clutched his hand. Both Bun-Bun and the gingerbread house were firmly tucked under his free arm.

His housekeeper's emerald eyes twinkled with delight. A smug satisfied expression settled across her face as her gaze traveled from him to Sunshine to Angel.

"Don't get too attached," he warned her.

"Wouldn't dream of it," she said. "Least no more'n you already have." She stooped to unfasten the child's coat. "First an angel. Now some sunshine," she whispered loud enough for him to hear her. "All in the good Lord's plan."

* * *

Everyone at the company was whispering behind Roger's back.

They thought they hid it from him, but he knew what they were saying even if he couldn't hear their words. Their quickly terminated conversations, their averted eyes each time he approached, spoke volumes. They thought his days at Montgomery Aeronautics were numbered, but he'd show them. All the disloyal bastards who had turned against him and sided with Caldwell—they'd be sorry they ever messed with him.

He still had a few tricks up his sleeve and the genius to execute them. Neither that holier-than-thou bastard nor all those turncoat directors were going to keep him from what was rightfully his. When the ashes settled, Roger Caine, not Trent Caldwell, would rise victorious. *Maybe I should relocate corporate headquarters to Phoenix*, he thought, chuckling out loud at his own joke.

Too bad Whitney wasn't around to see it. He would have enjoyed gloating in front of the haughty bitch. She'd taunted him, claimed he didn't have the balls to succeed without her. Well, he'd prove her wrong. He'd prove them all wrong.

He pulled a silver flask from the pocket of his overcoat and took a long swig. As the liquid courage slid down his throat, the cab rounded a corner and came to a stop at the front entrance of Montgomery headquarters.

"Keep the change," he said, handing the driver a ten-dollar bill for a six-dollar fare.

"Thank you, sir. Merry Christmas."

"Yeah, Merry-Fucking-Christmas." Roger grunted. He stepped from the taxi and slammed the door shut. The odor of burnt chestnuts clung to the icy air. God, he hated that stench. The streets teemed with holiday shoppers and too many damn rubbernecking tourists. But the lobby of the high-rise office building was empty except for the lone guard stationed at his desk near the bank of elevators.

With only two Saturdays left before Christmas, Roger expected to have the floor housing Montgomery corporate headquarters all to himself. He only needed a few hours. Three or four tops. Come Monday morning, Caldwell and the others would be reeling from the fallout, but by then it would be too fucking late for any of them.

Roger sauntered across the cavernous marble lobby and approached the guard. *Act natural. Don't arouse suspicion.* "Morning, Bill," he said, flashing his ID card. He couldn't stand the donut-bellied retired cop-turned-gatekeeper, one of dear-departed Abel's loyal flunkies, but he flashed the asshole his pearly whites.

"Oh, Mr. Caine." The guard swallowed, his Adam's apple bobbing up and down. "I...I'm afraid I can't allow you upstairs, sir." He stepped out from behind his desk, blocking access to the elevators.

Roger sneered. "I hardly need your permission," he said, attempting to brush past the guard. "Out of my way."

The security officer refused to budge. He rested one hand on the leather holster housing his firearm. His other hand reached for the phone. "I have my orders, sir. If you don't leave peacefully, I'm instructed to summon the police."

Taking a step backwards, Roger glared at the man. "Says who?"

"Mr. Caldwell, sir."

White hot anger roared through Roger. "This is *my* company, not Trent Caldwell's! You take orders from me!" He threw his weight against the guard's bulky torso, but the man's feet remained firmly planted on the marble floor.

The guard withdrew his gun but kept it pointing toward the floor. "You'd be doing us both a favor if you left peacefully, Mr. Caine."

Roger erupted, rage spewing from his eyes, his mouth, his tensed limbs. "You're fired! You hear me? Fired!"

"You don't have the authority, sir. I'm not a Montgomery employee."

Roger grabbed a large potted arrangement of holiday flowers and hurled it across the lobby. Slamming into a marble column, the planter shattered, sending dirt, poinsettias and shards of pottery skidding across the polished floor.

The guard simultaneously leveled his gun and pressed the speed dial on his phone. Roger ran from the building before the call connected.

THIRTY-FOUR

Thump! Trent listened intently, trying to determine if the noise which had wakened him was dream or reality. He reluctantly raised one eyelid and cast a bleary gaze in the direction of his clock-radio. Six-thirty? *Thump-thump!* Definitely reality and coming from the direction of his study. Who was up this early on a Saturday morning, and what was she doing in his study? *Thump! Thump! Thump!* What the hell—. He tossed back the quilt and reached for his robe. *Thump-thump-thump!*

"What's going on in here?" Standing in the doorway, Trent surveyed the room. Not a single volume remained on the bottom two shelves of his wall of bookcases. Scattered in haphazard piles, the books surrounded a little girl clothed in a red footed sleeper. She sat cross-legged in the center of the mess, her pudgy hands flying as she rapidly flipped through the book on her lap then, with a dramatic sigh, consigned it to the nearest heap. *Thump!*

Sunshine glanced up at him, her brows knit together, the corners of her mouth turned down in a determined frown. "Daddy, you gots a problem."

"I'll say." *Daddy.* He wasn't sure he'd ever get used to *that*, but the precocious three-year-old had made up her mind, and he was quickly learning she possessed a stubborn streak that put both Moira and Angel to shame. He knew he'd do well to heed the advice he'd given his housekeeper, but the truth was, the little imp had already wormed her way into his heart. Stifling a chuckle, he folded his arms across his chest in an attempt to affect a stern, disapproving demeanor.

Sunshine scrambled to her feet and spread her arms to encompass the stacks of books. "These books all very, very silly."

Trent raised an eyebrow. "Silly?" He glanced at the volume she had cast aside. Melville did have his critics, but Trent couldn't remember any of them ever accusing Ahab or Ishmael of silliness.

"No pictures!" She planted her hands on her hips and stamped her foot. Her lower lip jutted out in a full-fledged pout. "Books gots to have pictures!"

Well, of course. His gaze inspected the room once more, this time taking stock of the contents and not the mess. No picture books. No toys. Hardly a fitting environment for a three-year-old. Judging from the sight before him, Trent figured Sunshine had risen well before daybreak, silently wreaking havoc while he and the rest of the household slept peacefully unaware.

In the distance he heard the sounds of running water. "Does Angel know you're awake?"

Sunshine shook her head. "Angel night-night. Bun-Bun an' me wakes up and be's quiet."

Stepping from the study, he marched down the hall, into

Angel's bedroom and pounded on the bathroom door. "Angel!"

Within seconds he heard the flow of water abruptly end. A moment later the door flew open. "What's wrong?" she asked, hastily cinching her robe belt around her waist. A look of panic covered her face.

"We have a problem," he said, taking hold of her elbow and escorting her from the steam-filled room and back toward his study.

"Sunshine! Is she hurt?"

"Hardly." When they reached the study, he stood aside and waved her into the room.

Angel poked her head through the doorway and groaned. "Oh, no!" She turned back to him. "I'm sorry, Trent. I didn't know she was awake. I—"

"You *said* you'd take care of her."

"Yes. I did, and I should have told her she's not allowed to touch anything without your permission."

Angel frowned at Sunshine. The child had returned to her seat on the floor. Absorbed in her quest for an illustrated tome, she ignored the adult conversation, preferring instead to hold a one-sided dialogue with the bedraggled Bun-Bun as he helped her search through yet another book.

"You haven't lived up to your end of our agreement," he continued. "This apartment is not a suitable place for a three year old."

"I understand. I promise I'll—"

"The books have no pictures."

"What?" Angel's head whipped around.

"The books have no pictures," he repeated, maintaining his stern attitude.

Angel eyed him suspiciously. "You don't look very angry."

"Did I say I was angry?"

"But...the mess...I thought—"

"I think you'd better get that child dressed and fed. And wake Mrs. Kearn. It's obvious you and I both need an education, and she's the only one among us with any experience in this area."

Angel stared at him.

"Well, what are you waiting for?"

"You're not making any sense, Trent."

He shrugged his shoulders and laughed at her confusion. "The books have no pictures, Angel. We're going shopping, the four of us, for picture books." He paused and thought for a moment, then whispered, "And call Sister Mags. Find out what Sunshine asked Santa to bring her for Christmas."

Angel tilted her towel-wrapped head and smirked. "Isn't Santa supposed to remember such things?"

* * *

"Hold still," said Angel, attempting to fasten the squirming child's coat. She had barely slipped the last button through the buttonhole before Sunshine darted under her arm and made a beeline for Trent.

"I's ready, Daddy." She slipped her tiny mitten covered hand into his and tugged. "Let's go."

Trent smiled down at her.

He's glowing!, thought Angel, herself filling with a warm sense of satisfaction.

"*Whoso shall receive one such little child in my name receiveth me*," whispered Mrs. Kearn, coming up behind her.

"An Irish proverb?" asked Angel.

The housekeeper scowled at her. "Matthew eighteen five. You

304

should read your Bible, lass. Of course, there's somes what believe the good Lord couldn't be anything but an Irishman."

Angel caught the twinkle of mirth in Mrs. Kearn's eyes. It danced along with the love the older woman radiated for her, Trent, and Sunshine.

"You did good, lass, bringin' that wee one into his life. 'Tis years since I've seen him smile like that. *Go raibh mile maith agat!*"

"What does that mean?"

"'Tis an Irish blessing—wishin' you a thousand good things."

Angel gazed at the unorthodox little family surrounding her and sighed. She already had nine hundred and ninety-nine. If need be, she could live with that. Better to have a future without a past, than a past without a future.

She glanced over at Trent as he held the apartment door for them, and she sighed again, but this sigh was far from content. Nine hundred and ninety-eight, she corrected herself. But friendship was better than nothing at all.

"Did you reach Sister Mags?" he whispered as she crossed the threshold.

Angel nodded. "You're off the hook, Santa. She's already got what she asked for. Funny you didn't remember."

"What?"

"A home."

His mouth twisted into a smirk, but his eyes sparkled with amusement. "I think Santa had a bit of help from a certain manipulative elf on that one." Trent ushered them towards the elevator, then lifted Sunshine so she could reach the button.

He chuckled to himself throughout the short descent to the main lobby.

The grand concourse of the hotel was festooned in holiday

splendor. A majestic silver and gold-clad evergreen, its stature rivaling the one at Rockefeller Center, held center court in the glass-enclosed atrium. Spread beneath its garlanded bows was an ever-growing pile of donated food, clothing, and toys awaiting distribution to the city's less fortunate inhabitants. Off to one side a chorus of local school children serenaded visitors with a selection of holiday favorites. Shoppers, their arms laden with packages, scurried in and out of the designer boutiques that lined either side of the lobby or headed for the coffee shop or one of several restaurants.

Trent paused and nodded in satisfaction at his creation. Once an empty, rat-infested shell, the building was now a showplace. Home to a five-star hotel, an award-winning restaurant, and dozens of exclusive shops and cafes, as well as his corporate headquarters, Trentwell Arms employed nearly a thousand people and was listed as a must-see in every New York visitors' guidebook.

"Caldwell!" An enraged cry shattered the moment of peaceful reflection. From across the lobby a man, his face purple with hate, bulldozed his way past the startled crowds, knocking off-balance anyone unlucky enough to be in his path.

"Caine," he said, handing Sunshine to Angel.

"My God," she cried. "Look at him. He's mad!" And she knew why. Moments before she'd pleaded with Trent to save Sunshine from the Children's Services people, he'd learned of Roger Caine's treachery. Although he lacked solid evidence, John Ferguson's revelations became the catalyst Trent needed to rid Montgomery Aeronautics of Roger Caine. Apparently, Roger had somehow gotten wind of Trent's plans.

"You son-of-a-bitch!" Roger stopped abruptly, inches from Trent, but the verbal rampage continued. A large blue vein pulsed along the side of his neck. His hands clenched in tight fists, he waved one under Trent's nose, the other pounded an agitated staccato rhythm against his thigh. "Who gives you the fucking right to keep me out of my own offices?"

Although she suspected Trent's own rage fomented just beneath the surface, Angel watched in awe as he maintained an emotionless posture, keeping both his words and limbs tightly controlled. "Lower your voice and your fist, Caine. You're creating a scene."

"Don't tell me what to do, you motherfucking bastard!"

Angel gasped.

Mrs. Kearn reached over and clamped her hands over Sunshine's ears. Under her breath she uttered something in Gaelic which Angel suspected needed no translation.

Off to the left two security guards rapidly approached, but Trent held up his hand, halting their progress. Like well-trained attack dogs they remained poised and ready to strike at their master's command.

"Remember where you are, Caine."

Roger scoured his surroundings with a glare of contempt. "I know damn well where I am, you thieving piece of shit, and by the time I'm through, this palace of yours will be a pile of rubble at your fucking feet. Count on it!"

A crowd had gathered around them—curious shoppers, hotel guests, a handful of employees. Angel could hear the background rumble of speculative conversation. Some pointed toward Trent, his name floating above the undertone. Others shouted words of encouragement or advice. Several even offered to take care of Roger for him.

Trent didn't flinch so much as an eyelash throughout Roger's

307

tirade. He seemed oblivious to the assembled throng. "It's over, Caine. I know what you did and how you did it."

"You don't know shit!"

"I've spoken with John Ferguson."

Roger scoffed with derision at the mention of the name. "You'll try anything to steal Montgomery Aeronautics from me. How much are you paying that washed-up lawyer to say what you want to hear, Caldwell? Everyone knows that's how you operate. You're nothing but a two-bit thief in a custom-made suit."

"I know about the embezzlement."

"Lies! All lies! Ferguson never liked me. He wanted Sarah for himself. When she married me, he tried to turn Abel against me."

Trent delivered his next sentence in the same calm tone he'd managed to sustain throughout Roger's verbal diatribe. "I have a copy of the report Ferguson gave Abel Montgomery the night Abel died."

The color drained from Roger's face and neck. Beads of sweat broke out across his brow. The bulging vein that ran from his neck up the side of his head and into his temple increased its percussion beat. "You're bluffing!"

"Are you willing to take that chance?"

The choir had long since ceased its singing, its member's swelling the circle that continued to grow around the commotion in the hotel concourse. Angel cast a nervous glance around the crowd, finally making eye contact with one of the guards.

He broke away and came up behind her. Lowering his head, he whispered in her ear. "We've got the situation under control, miss."

She twisted her neck to face him. "No. There are too many people here."

"And many more security personnel than you realize. No need to worry." He disappeared into the crowd. Seconds later she saw him slip into position at his previous location.

Mrs. Kearn placed a hand on her shoulder. "Trust him," she said.

Angel chewed on her lower lip. "Trent or the guard?"

"Both."

Not that she had any choice. The bizarre confrontation continued to unfold in front of her.

"You can't have any proof, you arrogant bastard."

As far as Angel knew, Roger was correct in his assumption—unless Trent had unearthed something significant since he last spoke to her about his investigation. Her gaze darted to his grave features. Was he bluffing?

"Would you care to bet your future on that?" Trent asked Caine.

Sunshine began to squirm in her arms. "I don't like hims," she said, pointing to Roger. "Hims mean."

"Yes, very mean," Angel agreed.

Sunshine continued to fidget. Angel set her down but kept the child firmly clasped against her body. Wiggling an arm free, Sunshine reached over and tugged at Trent's trouser leg. "Why dat mean man yelling at you, Daddy?"

Roger abruptly broke off his latest stream of invectives. "*Daddy?*" His piercing gaze zeroed in on Sunshine, raking over her tiny body. He stepped closer, bending down to examine her further.

An ominous chill slithered up Angel's spine. "Leave her alone!" She took a step backwards, pulling Sunshine along with her, then lifted the child back into her arms.

Caine pierced her with a malicious grin. Rising, he grabbed her upper arm and squeezed hard while he whispered in her ear. "If this *memory loss* is some kind of trick to get back at me, *Sarah,*—"

Trent yanked him away from her before he could finish his sentence.

With smug disdain, Caine turned to Trent and sneered. "Well, well, well. Looks like the self-righteous Trent Caldwell has a chocolate skeleton in his closet."

Push the right buttons and even the most tightly controlled man will lose his resolve. Trent's fist connected with Roger's jaw. A woman screamed, but the remainder of the onlookers stared in stunned silence at the man sprawled on the floor.

Someone in the crowd began to applaud. Then another, and another until a groundswell of cheering echoed throughout the lobby.

The guards rushed forward. Two of them jerked Roger to his feet. The rest began dispersing the crowd.

"Get him out of here," said Trent.

"Should I call the police, sir?"

Trent shook his head. "See that he gets back to his apartment." He turned to Caine. "Next time I won't be as accommodating."

Roger spit a mouthful of blood onto the marble floor tiles. "Next time will be your last time, Caldwell."

Trent stared after Roger and the guards until they had exited the building. Then he turned to Angel. "Did he hurt you?"

"No."

"What did he whisper in your ear?"

"He thinks I'm Sarah. He accused me of helping you trick him."

"That man's got t'be stopped," muttered Mrs. Kearn.

"He'll be locked away soon enough, Moira."

"Humph! Probably get himself a fancy lawyer and be out in no time. Just like that other one."

Trent didn't respond. He lifted Sunshine from Angel's arms into his. "Weren't we going shopping?" he asked her.

She wrapped her arms around his neck and buried her face in his chest. "Dat man very mean, Daddy! He call you bad names. Sister Mags gots to punish him for having potty mouf."

THIRTY-FIVE

"There comes a time, Devon, when one must take the bull by the horns and face the situation squarely," said Seamus.

"And 'tain't no problem can't be solved when good Irish heads get together over a few pints," added Liam, raising his glass. He took a long swig, then smacked his lips. "Don't you worry. We'll keep an eye out. When the time's right, we'll strike. Just like in the old days."

Devon rose from the table. "I knew I could count on my friends."

"Always." Seamus raised a glass in toast:

> *Here's to you and yours*
> *And to mine and ours.*
> *And if mine and ours*
> *Ever come across to you and yours,*

I hope you and yours will do
As much for mine and ours
As mine and ours have done
For you and yours!

"Leave it to Seamus to go on so long we all die o' thirst!" said Liam. He raised his glass to Devon. "Health to your enemy's enemies!"

"And to yours! *Sláinte!*"

"*Sláinte!*"

THIRTY-SIX

Monday morning Roger entered the lobby of Montgomery Aeronautics headquarters and marched past the guard's desk. No one stopped him.

Several company employees entered the elevator with him, but none of them spoke during their ascent to the thirty-seventh floor. Still, he sensed their furtive sideways glances. *Screw 'em!* Low level bean counters and pencil pushers. He knew their names, and when the dust settled, they'd pay for their insolence with their jobs. He straightened his silk tie, shot his cuffs, and stared straight ahead.

When the elevator doors opened, he headed for his secretary's desk. Dispensing with any ritual morning pleasantries, he fired off a list of files he wanted retrieved. Immediately. Then, taking note of the look of consternation on her face, he strode into his office and slammed the door behind him.

At the credenza he noticed his ice bucket was not filled and made a mental note to find a suitable punishment for the bitch. If she thought he was going to roll over and play dead for Trent Caldwell, she was in for a big surprise. Loyal to Abel for years, she, too, had always disliked him, but he'd kept her around because he wanted everything that had belonged to Abel. Including Helen, his overweight, gray-haired stupid cow of a secretary. It was past time for her to go.

He poured himself a glass of Scotch, neat, and sauntered over to the windows behind his desk. Sipping the only nourishment his body craved lately, he gazed out over the city. Years of sucking up to Abel Montgomery and that pussy-whipping bitch Whitney had earned him this view, and no one was going to rob him of it. No one.

He settled down in front of his computer, typed in his password, and hit the Enter key. ACCESS DENIED. *What the hell!* Roger stared at the flashing red words. He retyped his five-digit code and pounded the Enter key. ACCESS DENIED. Again. ACCESS DENIED. Again. ACCESS DENIED.

"Nooooo!" With a violent thrust of his arm he swept the monitor and keyboard from his desk.

The crash brought Helen racing into the room. When she saw the remains of the equipment scattered in pieces across the carpet, she stopped short and brought the tips of her fingers to her lips. "Oh, my."

"*Oh, my?*" Roger sneered at her. She knew they'd locked him out! The stupid cunt must have been snickering behind his back from the moment he entered the office. He polished off the remainder of his drink, slamming the empty glass on the desk. "Is that all you can say? *Oh, my?* Where are those files I asked for?"

"I'm sorry, sir. They're all classified."

"Classified! On whose authority?" He held up his hand. "No, wait. Don't tell me. Let me guess. Trent Caldwell, right?"

She hesitated, then took a step backwards, reaching for the doorknob. "Maybe I should call someone for you, sir."

Roger picked up the empty tumbler and hurled it across the room, missing the woman's head by at least three feet. It struck the wall and shattered, raining jagged daggers of glass onto the carpet. "Call yourself a fucking cab. You're fired!"

She glanced at the broken crystal before spearing him with a disdainful glare. "I don't think so, sir. You no longer have that authority."

She closed the door behind her, leaving him with his bottle of Scotch, his empty ice bucket, his smashed computer. And his thirty-seven story view.

* * *

Trent leaned against the doorframe and watched Angel's fingers fly as she deftly wove Sunshine's unruly curls into two tamed braids on either side of her head.

"Sit still," she warned the squirming child. "We don't trim the tree until your hair is combed."

Sunshine cast pleading eyes, designed to melt the heart of the Abominable Snowman, in his direction. He held up his hands, palms outward, and shook his head. "Don't look to me for a stay of execution. This is Angel's bailiwick."

Sunshine scrunched up her nose and giggled. "You talks funny, Daddy."

"He talks truth," said Angel. "Now sit still, you squirmy worm!" She reached down and tickled Sunshine in the ribs, producing a peal of laughter and more fidgeting.

"Well, that should get the desired results," said Trent. "I think

I'll leave you two ladies to your task." He chuckled all the way back to the kitchen.

Moira sat at the table, a selection of cookbooks spread out before her. He glanced over her shoulder and pointed to one of the cookie recipes. "These look good."

"Maybe," she said, inserting a bookmark before flipping the page, "I'll consider it."

"Well, thank you, ma'am. It's refreshing to see how much weight my opinion carries in my own home." He pulled out a chair opposite her and sat.

"'Tis been a long time since we had so much laughter within these walls," she said, ignoring his sarcasm.

"Hmm." *Too long,* he thought. Too long since he'd felt like laughing. Too long since he'd felt like living. The change had crept over him gradually, but he'd sensed it from the very beginning. And fought it with a vengeance. A tormented soul was the cross he condemned himself to bear for the rest of his life. Before Angel. Now everything had changed, and he felt guilty for not feeling guilty.

He studied his housekeeper, his constant companion through the black years since his loss. He was not the only member of the household affected by Angel. Her healing spirit had softened the crusty old woman's bitterness over her own tragedy.

She might always carry in her heart an unyielding hatred for the Montgomery family, but that malice no longer consumed her days. She, too, now welcomed each new morning, viewing it as more than simply another twenty-four hours to endure.

"She's changed us, Moira. You and I. We're different people. She came into our lives and brought life with her."

She earmarked another recipe, closed the book, and set it aside.

Raising her chin, she trapped him with a piercing emerald green gaze. "So when're you goin' to tell the lass how you feel about her?"

The question caught him off guard. He wasn't certain he was ready to admit his feelings to himself, much less Angel. He made a pathetic stab at sidestepping the query with some ill-placed humor. "Who? Sunshine?"

She slammed her hands on the table. "Aren't you one pitiful excuse of a man! Angel, you dimwit!"

Even as a child, he could never pull anything over on her. She'd always caught him and Brendan just as their hands entered the cookie jar, never after the contraband was safely shoved into their mouths. Long ago he'd come to the conclusion that Irish women were born with radar. "Nothing like being ambushed in your own home. How the hell do you know how I feel?"

"'Tis written all over that stubborn puss of yours, case you never look in a mirror." She pushed herself away from the table and stood. "The lass is your one hope of salvation, lad. We both know it for sure. An' you're in love with her, whether you're willin' to admit it or not. 'Tis high time you did something about it before 'tis too late."

"For God's sake, Moira, she still doesn't even know who she is!"

"She knows what's in her heart. 'Tis enough."

Trent's jaw dropped. "She told you that?"

His housekeeper offered him a knowing smile. "She didn't have to."

"I don't know," he said, shaking his head. He rose and left the kitchen. "I just don't know."

"She'd want you to move on," she called after him. "She'd be horrified to see what you've become."

He didn't have to ask whom she meant. He knew.

And he knew she was right about something else. He had fallen in love with Angel.

From the entrance of his study he could see her, smiling at him from her perch on the desk. He crossed the room, picked up the picture frame, and studied Caitlin, her beauty frozen for all time. This was the way he liked to remember her, not his last memory when he held her mangled body in his arms and helplessly watched the life seep from her.

Yet Caitlin's physical beauty had paled in comparison to her inner beauty. Hers had been a selfless love. The gentlest of souls, she had dedicated her life to helping others. Was she doing so even now, from beyond the grave?

Perhaps, there was something to Moira's superstitious beliefs. Angel had entered his life at the lowest of points, an ebb tide of grief that had given birth to a bitter, empty shell of a man. Was Angel's accident merely a cruel twist of fate, or was it part of a larger cosmic plan? And after he thought her lost, was it coincidence or divine intervention that had guided her to Haven?

"Daddy!" Sunshine's sweet warble raced down the hallway ahead of the pitter-patter of tiny feet slapping against the terra cotta tiles. "We ready," she said, dashing into the study. Dancing from foot to foot, she tugged on his sleeve. Then she noticed the photograph in his hands. "Who dat?" she asked.

Trent hesitated for a moment, unsure how to explain a dead wife to a child who still didn't accept the death of her own mother. "Someone very special."

"Where she at?"

"She lives in Heaven."

Sunshine stopped hopping. A thoughtful frown clouded her

face. She chewed on her lower lip and worried her braid in much the same manner as Angel often worried her curls. "My mama wents to visit God in Heaven." She pointed to Caitlin. "Will she come back with my mama?"

"No, she has to stay in Heaven."

Sunshine's lip began to tremble. "Does my mama gots to stay, too?"

Trent nodded. He placed the photo on his desk and lifted her onto his lap.

Wrapping her pudgy arms around his neck, she buried her face in his chest and cried softly. "First I gots a mama and no daddy. Now I gots a daddy and no mama." She lifted her head and looked him in the eye, her features a study in determination. "Angel be my new mama," she said resolutely.

Trent glanced once more at Caitlin's shining eyes. *Is this also your doing?*

No blinding white light, no heavenly chorus of angels answered him, but Trent suddenly felt infused with an inner peace and the strength to resume living. He opened the bottom drawer of his desk and gently placed the picture frame inside, convinced Caitlin would want it that way.

THIRTY-SEVEN

In the five days since he'd trashed his office Roger had not set foot outside the upper West Side apartment. With a bottle of liquid fortification always within easy reach, he fantasized Trent Caldwell's downfall and his own resurrection, visualizing in blinding detail each groveling peon as they came begging for their jobs. But first he had to strip the emperor of his clothes in full view of all the turncoats.

He lifted the emerald and burgundy engraved invitation, now dog-eared and splattered with Scotch, from his desk and leered at it. Caldwell's first mistake, forgetting to pull his name from the guest list, gave Roger the perfect venue. Not only would all of Montgomery Aeronautics' chief executives be privy to Caldwell's humiliation and destruction, so would the top management at every other Trentwell holding.

Caldwell's annual Christmas party, always the talk of the

town, would have tongues wagging for years to come, but this year they wouldn't be clucking about the table decorations or desserts. They'd remember this as the year Roger Caine exposed the corrupt persona Caldwell had labored to conceal from the corporate world.

Roger brought the nearly empty bottle of Scotch to his lips and took a long swig. Amber liquid dribbled down the corners of his mouth and around his chin. He wiped his face with the back of his hand, raking it across several days' growth of beard, then twisted his wrist to consult his watch. Time to get ready, he decided, staring at the blurred hands of the fifty thousand dollar Patek Philippe he'd recently purchased for himself. He hoisted his body out of the chair and staggered off to the bathroom.

The phone rang an hour later. Roger took one final stroke of the razor against his jaw before answering. "Yes?"

"Your car is here, sir."

Stupid fool doorman! "I told you I wanted a limo for seven, Hughes. Can't you get anything right?"

"It's ten past, Mr. Caine."

Roger slammed the phone down and yanked open his closet. One by one he tossed suits, shirts, and trousers onto the floor in search of his tuxedo. Twenty minutes later he emptied his bureau drawers onto the bed in pursuit of a cummerbund and matching bow tie.

Forty minutes after the doorman's call, he stepped from the elevator.

"Enjoy your evening, sir," said Hughes.

Roger grinned. "Oh, I intend to."

The limo driver tipped his hat and opened the door for him. "Evenin', sir."

He offered the chauffeur a condescending nod. "Trentwell Arms Hotel."

"Yes, sir." The driver closed Roger's door. With a tip of his hat to the doorman, he slipped behind the wheel, released the brake, and pulled into traffic.

After driving for several blocks he lifted his chin, scrutinizing Roger from the rearview mirror. "We'll be needin' to take a slight detour, sir. Bad fire over on Sixty-third off Park. Traffic's all backed up."

"Fine. Just get me there." Roger settled back against the seat, reached into his topcoat for his flask, and began nursing the mellow spirits down his throat. Closing his eyes, he allowed his mind to drift into pleasant speculation over his upcoming triumph. He didn't concern himself with how he'd approach Caldwell or what he'd say. At some point during the evening, the perfect opportunity would present itself, and Roger would strike. Swiftly. Ruthlessly. And he wouldn't let up until the bastard broke.

The limo came to a jerky stop, throwing Roger off balance and causing him to spill several drops of Scotch on his cashmere topcoat. Muttering an ethnic slur, he brushed at the stain with his bare hands, causing the liquid to spread farther and absorb into the wool.

When he looked up, he discovered the driver had pulled the car down a dark alley. He twisted his head around and stared out the back window. The street behind him was lined with abandoned warehouses. In the distance he heard the sound of water lapping against a dock. "Where are we? This isn't the hotel."

"End o' the road, *sir*."

The back door opened, and a rush of cold air swept through

the vehicle, sending a shiver up his spine. A large, gloved hand reached in, yanking him from the car and forcing him facedown against the hood. The business end of a gun dug into the back of his neck.

"Please, don't hurt me," he whimpered. "My wallet's in my back pocket. Just take it, and leave me alone."

The gunman growled. "Not another word."

The driver stepped from the limousine. Juggling a roll of duct tape between his hands, he grinned, exposing a mouth of nicotine-stained teeth and gold caps. "Like I said, *sir*, 'tis the end o' the road." He ripped off a length of tape and slapped it over Roger's mouth.

* * *

"Bootiful!" Standing at the ballroom entrance, Sunshine clapped her hands together, her eyes bright with excitement. "I matches!"

Trent had insisted on taking both Sunshine and Angel shopping for dresses for his annual Christmas party, even though Angel maintained she could wear the black cocktail dress she'd worn to the gallery opening.

"Black for a Christmas party?" he asked. "You need something more festive."

"Not according to Coco Chanel. Besides, you're wearing a black tuxedo, aren't you? Or have you ordered a red one trimmed with white fur for yourself?"

"Do you always have to be so stubborn?"

In the end they compromised when he pointed out that the women always wore long gowns to the yearly event. So Angel chose a floor length deep burgundy velvet Vera Wang with a cowl neck and long sleeves, the least expensive of all the gowns she'd been shown at Bergdorf's.

"It's still equivalent to the gross national product of Zimbabwe," she said.

"Stubborn and prone to exaggeration," he muttered.

She didn't even bother to challenge him when he picked out a five-hundred-dollar fairy princess dress for Sunshine. She was his ward now, and he could spend whatever he wanted on her, even if the dress would wind up spattered with chocolate sauce by the end of the evening. Besides, it matched perfectly the décor the decorators had chosen for the ballroom.

The main ballroom of the Trentwell Arms Hotel sparkled like a fairy tale setting. Trent had granted the hotel decorators free reign and an unlimited budget. In return they'd given him the kingdom of the Sugar Plum Fairy, transforming the ballroom with pink, silver, and white gossamer and tulle. Shimmering crystal snowflakes hung suspended from the ceiling. Centerpieces of creamy roses, silver French-wired ribbon, and mirrored star wands decorated each table. A crystal trough with floating translucent confetti and silver snowflake candles encircled each floral arrangement. The scent of bayberry wafted through the air.

Although Trent had insisted that she and Sunshine attend the annual holiday dinner he gave each year for his top-level employees and their families, Angel had expected to be seated at an inconspicuous table off in a corner with Mrs. Kearn and Mr. O'Hara. To her surprise, they were led to the main table, joining Mrs. Kearn, Trent, his secretary, her husband, and their six-year-old son. One empty place remained.

"Daddy!" Sunshine jumped into his lap.

"Sunshine, what did you promise?" asked Angel.

"I be's big girl." She scooted off Trent's lap and onto the empty chair beside him.

"How's she doing?" he whispered to Angel. The toddler hadn't let either of them out of her sight after her encounter with Trent earlier in the day. They both understood why. Angel had kept Sunshine upstairs during the cocktail hour, insisting the child needed a nap before dinner, but her real reason was to ensure Trent some time with his guests.

"Confused. When she woke from her nap, and you weren't there, she panicked."

Trent scowled. "Is she still calling you mama?"

Angel nodded. "Let's discuss this later." She glanced at the empty chair. Is that for Mr. O'Hara?"

"Yes." Frowning, Trent turned to Mrs. Kearn. "He is coming, isn't he?"

"He had some family business to attend to. I guess he's runnin' a might late." She twisted around in her chair and scanned the entrance of the ballroom. "Here he comes now," she said.

O'Hara took his place at the table. "Sorry," he said to Trent. "Couldn't be helped."

"Everything all right?"

"'Tis now." He nodded a greeting to the rest of the members of the table, then leaned over and planted a peck on Mrs. Kearn's cheek. "Merry Christmas, m'love."

A deep crimson blush spread up the housekeeper's neck and quickly covered her face. She swatted his shoulder. "Sure an' you're nothin' but an old Irish fool."

* * *

Angel stood beside Trent as he accepted the thanks of his departing guests. An hour earlier Mrs. Kearn had offered Mr. O'Hara's services to carry Sunshine upstairs. The toddler had fallen asleep in her arms somewhere between the fifth and sixth courses.

"But you'll miss the rest of the party," said Angel. "I'll take her."

Mrs. Kearn thumped her fist against her breastbone. "This old body's all partied out, lass." She nodded in Mr. O'Hara's direction. "An' if that old fool helps himself to another bottle o' Mr. Trent's champagne, we'll be needin' a flatbed truck to cart him home. You stay. Enjoy yourself."

She stood and nudged Mr. O'Hara. "Move your bones, and watch your step. You're to be carryin' precious cargo."

"Yes, mum!" He rose, lifted Sunshine into his arms, and tossed Angel a wink. "Dance one for me, lassie."

Now, alone in the ballroom except for the busboys and musicians, Trent escorted her to the parquet dance floor and signaled the conductor. Music filled the near-empty room, an old Cole Porter standard extolling the wonders of love, drowning out the clatter of cleanup.

He took her into his arms, sweeping her across the dance floor, but her feet never touched the ground. Or so it seemed. Instead, she floated on a cloud of magic, her body an extension of his.

The song at an end, the music stopped. Behind her, she heard the musicians packing up their instruments, but in her head their melody played on. Trent released her right hand but kept his arm circled around her waist. Only a whisper of air separated their bodies. With his index finger he raised her chin, then slowly outlined her jaw with his thumb. He held her gaze with green and brown flecked eyes that spoke of love and need and yearning. For her.

All rational thought fled, erotic dizziness taking its place. Her nerve endings tingled. Her pulse thrummed. Her insides turned to crème brûlée. As Trent lowered his head to meet her lips, he drew her nearer, eliminating the infinitesimal space that had separated them. Angel felt their hearts meld and the love flow between them. Their bodies now linked, Trent captured her lips in a kiss of promise, a kiss of...forever.

No! The air fled from her lungs. Gasping for breath, her head spinning, she pulled away from him, turned, and ran. Needing air, she raced across the ballroom to the French doors that led out onto the ice-covered balcony.

A bitter wind slammed against her chest, needles of sleet and icy rain stung her face and quickly seeped through her dress, but the late December weather paled in comparison to the freezing whirlpool trapping her heart. She leaned against the ice-covered concrete railing and offered her body to the punishing elements.

"I'm not worth a case of pneumonia," he said, coming up behind her. He slipped off his tuxedo jacket and draped it over her drenched and frigid shoulders.

The tightness in his voice did nothing to mask the pain she knew she'd inflicted on him. A shudder racked her body, but it had nothing to do with the wind and snow and stinging rain. She tightened her grip on the slippery balustrade, afraid to turn to face him.

"I'm sorry if I offended you," he continued. "I misread your feelings."

"No," she whispered, shaking her head. "You didn't."

"Then, why—" Trent grabbed her by the shoulders and spun her around. She twisted her head, attempting to hide her tear-stained face from him, but he grabbed her chin with one hand and forced her to look at him. "Are you saying you love me?"

"Yes."

"Then what's wrong? Why did you run?"

"It's me," she cried. "The real me. What if she comes back, and you don't like her? What if *I* don't like her? How can there be anything between us when neither of us knows who I am?"

Her teeth began to chatter. Her body trembled.

Trent wrapped his arms around her. "Please. We can't stay out here. You're turning blue." He led her back into the ballroom.

Guiding her to the nearest table, he sat her down in one of the chairs and signaled a passing busboy. "Get me some brandy. And a pot of coffee."

The busboy stopped and stared dumbly at Angel. Bedraggled and trembling, she huddled on the chair, hugging her knees to her chest.

"Now!" yelled Trent.

While he waited for the beverages, he swung a chair around to face her, sat down in front of her, and began massaging warmth back into her arms. "That was a pretty damn stupid stunt."

"But—"

"Shut up, damn it. *You* are the person seated before me, whether your name is Angel or Agatha or Annabelle. *You* are the woman I love, and that won't change, no matter what happened in your past."

The busboy returned with the brandy and coffee. Trent poured an equal amount of both into a cup, leaned forward, and held it to her lips. "Drink this."

She wrapped her hands around his and sipped at the liquid. The stinging warmth spread through her.

"But what if I can't remember because I didn't want to be that person any longer?" she asked, as he refilled the cup. "What if she...I was a horrible person? Maybe that's why no one has ever claimed me. Maybe when I disappeared, they shrugged and said, good riddance. You could wake up one morning and find yourself living with a shrew. Or worse."

"Drink." He held the refilled cup to her lips. "I seriously doubt that. I refuse to believe a knock to the head could cause such a drastic change in personality. Whoever you were, you had to have been the same sweet, loving person you are today—the woman I want to spend the rest of my life with."

He placed the cup on the table and knelt on one knee in front of her. Taking her hands in his, he raised them to his lips. "If you'll have me."

Angel slipped a hand from his grasp and placed her icy fingertips alongside his face. Even without knowing anything of her past, she knew she had never loved anyone the way she loved Trent Caldwell. The past no longer mattered. He was her present and her future. Her life began today. Here. With him.

She leaned forward, offering herself to him. "You are my life," she said a moment before their lips met.

THIRTY-EIGHT

There is no cure for grief but to put it under your foot.

"A long time in comin'," said Liam.

"Aye, but as any Irishman knows, 'the one who waits the fine day, will get the fine day.'"

"And all else is goin' accordin' to plan?"

"Better than expected."

Liam poured them both a drink. "Sure then, 'tis time to move on to other concerns." He lifted his glass in a toast. "To the ol' sod! *Sláinte!*"

Devon nodded. "*Sláinte! They shall seek peace, and there shall be none.*"

Liam raised an eyebrow in question.

"Ezekiel seven twenty-five."

THIRTY-NINE

Quiet greeted them inside the apartment. Mrs. Kearn had retired to her room, leaving only a small lamp lit in the foyer and the white icicle lights that decorated the perimeter of the ceilings in the main living areas.

They tiptoed down the hall to check on Sunshine. The child lay snuggled beneath a Winnie-the-Pooh quilt, Bun-bun nestled under her arm, a thumb securely tucked in her mouth. Angel bent down and gently kissed her cheek.

"She's a feisty little thing," said Trent. "She's going to be fine." He wrapped his arm around her and led her from the room.

Angel shuddered. "But you're not," he added, "if you don't get out of those wet clothes and into a hot shower." He gently pushed her into her room and shut the door behind her.

Angel scowled at the closed door. Yes, she needed a hot shower, but she needed him more. She closed her eyes and conjured up a vision of a steaming bubble bath for two, complete with soft music, candlelight, and champagne. Had she missed something? She had no memories of prior experiences in this area. She was treading on virgin territory.

A shiver coursed up her spine, but not from the cold. *Virgin territory!* Good Lord! For all she knew, she might *be* a virgin. The thought had never occurred to her. Had it occurred to Trent?

Angel groaned. Would her life ever be more than unanswered questions?

* * *

A shower later she stood in front of the full-length mirror and studied her reflection. Wrapped in her chenille robe, her hair freshly washed and dried, her face free of makeup, she found a naive child, filled with uncertainty, staring back at her. Instinctively, she reached for a lock of hair and twisted it around her finger.

I don't know what to do. Is he waiting for me to come to him?

She paced back and forth across the bedroom several times before curling up on the windowsill. The sleet and rain had turned to snow, the free-fall ballet of the flakes captured stories below in the spotlights of the streetlamps and car headlights. Like miniature snow fairies they danced across the night sky to...to a soulful tune?

When had the music begun?

Angel listened to the rich, yearning notes of the saxophone. *Night and Day.* The same Cole Porter melody they'd danced to earlier in the evening. Softly, she sang along as he played, the words springing to her lips as naturally as water bubbled from a brook, although she had no idea how she knew the lyrics.

No more questions. No more uncertainty. Angel rose from her

window seat and followed the music to its source.

* * *

Trent lowered the instrument from his mouth and stared in awe at the woman standing in the doorway. So unsure of herself. So beautiful, yet so innocent. An angel. *His* Angel. He placed the saxophone on his desk and went to her.

"I wasn't sure you wanted me to come," she said.

Trent offered her a smile of reassurance. "How could I not want you?" With feather-like strokes he ran his fingertips along the fine curves of her face and down her neck to the delicate V of flesh partially hidden beneath her tightly cinched robe. His fingers explored where his lips yearned to travel, loosening the robe slightly to expose the uppermost edges of her firmly rounded breasts.

It was then that he realized she wore no other garments beneath the robe. Trent removed his hand and stepped back from the temptation. Sixteen hours ago, he'd fought a battle with himself, finally admitting his feelings for her. Now she stood before him offering him the most precious of gifts. "I didn't plan for this to happen," he said. "I'm not prepared."

Angel lowered her gaze. A blush of sweet innocence spread across her cheeks. "Have you checked your nightstand drawer lately?"

"My nightstand drawer?" Trent raised an eyebrow, intrigued by the combination of bold query and shy response. He crossed the room and opened the door that led directly from the study into his bedroom. Angel followed as far as the doorway, waiting between the two rooms.

Standing next to the bed, Trent pulled open the drawer in question. "*I* didn't buy these," he said, turning back to her, a small box in his hand. "How did you know?"

Angel reached into the pocket of her robe and removed an identical packet. "I suppose you weren't responsible for these, either?"

Trent shook his head. "Where did you find them?"

"In *my* nightstand drawer."

Trent chuckled. He knew of only one person audacious enough to pull such an act. Someone who had pushed for this moment from the beginning. "When?"

"A day or two after you found me at Haven."

Trent joined her in the doorway, drawing her body against his. He lifted her chin and gazed into her eyes. "An Irish elf?" he asked, skimming his lips across the rim of her ear.

"Must be."

He kissed his way down the side of her neck. "Wouldn't be right to disregard such thoughtfulness."

A sigh of pleasure escaped from deep inside her. "An insulting lack of manners on our part. I doubt she'd ever forgive us."

He lifted her into his arms, kicking the door closed before carrying her to the bed. "I want to spend the rest of my life making love to you," he said, placing her on the quilt and parting her robe. His mouth went dry. The air fled from his lungs as he gazed at pure perfection.

She crossed her arms over her breasts and offered him a bashful smile, but in the dim glow of the table lamp he detected slight lines of tension at the corners of her mouth and eyes.

"Day and night?" Her voice held a scant tremble.

"Night and day." He gently unfolded her arms. "Let me look at you."

"I...I'm—"

"You're beautiful."

"No, it's not that. It's just I...I don't..." She averted her eyes.

Then it dawned on him. If she had no memory of her past life, she had no way of knowing whether she...Trent lifted her into his arms. "Of course," he said. "I understand. This may be your first time."

She nodded.

"Then I'll have the pleasure of guiding you through a magical discovery." He kissed the tip of her nose. "Or rediscovery." He felt the tension ease from her body.

"I'd like that."

He needed to taste her. All of her. He captured her mouth with his and savored as he explored, relishing in the explosive assault to his senses. Gently lowering her back onto the bed, he once again began his journey, this time aware that she had embarked on one of her own. With her fingers. And then her hands. And finally, her lips.

"Don't be shy," he said, encouraging her.

He parted her thighs and cruised along the inner passage to the heart of where he knew she burned for him. Angel gasped. Then moaned. Her body rocked beneath him, opening wider, encouraging him forward. When he sensed she could stand the sweet torture no longer, he reached for the package he had placed on the nightstand.

She was tight but yielding. Pausing, he lifted his head and studied the surprised expression on her face. "That solves one mystery," he said.

"Part of me hoped otherwise."

"It doesn't matter. Only the future counts."

Nature and instinct took over where memory failed. Angel

wrapped her legs around his waist and responded to each thrust with wanton enjoyment, soaring along with him and climaxing simultaneously.

He had nearly drifted off to sleep, her body tucked neatly against his, when she whispered, "Trent?"

"Hmm?"

"How many in the box?"

FORTY

Sarah woke with a start. Disoriented, she sat up and scanned the room, her gaze landing on the man who slept beside her. "Oh, my God!"

Tossing the quilt aside, she jumped from the bed. She grabbed her robe, ran to the window, and stared out across the city. It had all come back to her. Somewhere in the night the millions of locked memories had finally escaped.

She remembered. She remembered everything. Including the fact that she was married to another man—a man she despised. A man who had betrayed her and her grandfather. A whimper of despair forced its way to the surface. *What do I do now?*

"Angel?"

She turned and faced the man she loved.

"What's wrong?"

"Everything." The despair in her voice filled the room, closing in on her from all sides. Although his face was bathed in darkness, she could sense his alarm. "Everything," she repeated, crumbling to the floor.

He leaped from the bed and scooped her into his arms. "Don't shut me out. Whatever it is, we'll deal with it together."

He rose and carried her back to the bed. Propping her against the headboard, he climbed in beside her and pulled the quilt up around them. "Talk to me."

"I remember," she began, clasping her hands tightly in front of her. "All of it. Roger was right. I *am* Sarah Montgomery. That's why the photos in the bedroom spoke to me. It all makes sense now."

Trent wrapped his arm around her shoulders and drew her closer. "That's not possible. Sarah died."

She shook her head. "No. She...I didn't. Whoever was in that car, it wasn't me. I was in John Ferguson's office. Roger went ballistic when he learned Granddad left me in control of the company. That's when I first learned of the embezzlement and coverup."

She paused for a moment, taking a deep shuddering breath. "That's when I realized Roger had married me only to get his hands on the company."

"According to the police report, Sarah's body was identified by her wedding band."

"Yes." She recounted how she had taken the ring off and placed it on John's desk, asking the attorney to begin divorce proceedings. "As I started to leave, John picked up the ring and handed it back to me, but I couldn't bring myself to slip it back on my finger. It was a token of deceit, not love. I tossed it into my purse.

"I was on my way back to the parking garage when the cab

struck me."

"What about the nightmares? The fire?"

Sarah closed her eyes. Tears streamed down her cheeks. She saw herself stepping from her car. The explosion rang in her ears. Flames consumed the house. Once again, she heard the screams. Felt the helplessness. Her mother. Her father. Trapped. "A gas explosion." She gulped back a cry. "My parents never made it out."

He held her in his arms, stroking and comforting her while she sobbed. "They're all gone. My parents. My grandparents. Even Whitney. There's no one left except Roger." A wracking sob shook her body. "My God, Trent, I'm still married to Roger."

"Shh." He ran his fingers through her hair and planted a series of kisses along her brow. "Roger is a minor problem. Something for the lawyers to handle."

"And Mrs. Kearn?"

"Moira? What's she got to do with this?"

"She hates my family. I've heard the comments she's made. Why?"

He explained about the plane crash and how Mrs. Kearn had refused to accept the FAA ruling of pilot error, railing about government cover-ups and big business conspiracies.

"I remember that crash," she said. "My father and grandfather were beside themselves with grief over the loss of life. It was a charter flight taking several families on vacation to Hilton Head. But my father and grandfather were good men, Trent. They never would have allowed a defective plane to leave the factory. They even hired their own investigators to double-check the FAA findings."

"I know, darling. I knew your grandfather. I never once believed he was responsible for the accident, but grief produces anger, and anger creates irrational thought."

"What do I do? How do I tell her?"

"You have to remember that Moira loves you. From the moment she saw you, she was convinced you were my destiny, an angel sent to save me from my own grief." He reached over and picked up the box sitting on the nightstand and waved it under her nose. "And don't forget, she's done everything in her power to make it happen."

"But she didn't know I'm a Montgomery."

"And once she finds out, you'll become her salvation as well. She'll realize how misplaced her hatred has been and finally set it aside."

Sarah tugged on a curl. "I hope you're right."

"Trust me. I know I am."

* * *

The next morning, while Sunshine watched cartoons in the den, Sarah and Trent spoke to the housekeeper. Sarah wasn't certain what she expected, but she found Mrs. Kearn's quiet acceptance of the news disconcerting. Beneath the surface smile, she saw a glazed sadness settle across the older woman's features, and although she went about her tasks as though nothing had changed, she spoke little and refused to make eye contact with Sarah. More than once she referred to her as Angel.

By lunchtime Sarah's uneasiness over Mrs. Kearn's odd behavior had escalated to alarm. She confronted Trent. "I'm worried. She's not acting like herself."

"Nonsense," he assured her. "She just needs some time to get used to the idea. She's carried that grudge around for a long time. The two of you need to talk. I'll take Sunshine out for a little while."

At the time Sarah had thought his suggestion a good idea, but once Trent and Sunshine left the apartment, her attempts at opening a dialogue with Mrs. Kearn met with stony silence.

"Please, talk to me," she begged.

The housekeeper stared past her as she left the kitchen.

In frustration Sarah sank into one of the kitchen chairs and buried her head in her arms. When she heard Mrs. Kearn return a short time later, she raised her head and stared in horror at the gun pointed at her. Her gaze traveled to Mrs. Kearn's face. The housekeeper's features were set in steely determination, but her eyes held regret.

"Why?"

"I have no choice, lass."

"We always have choices."

Mrs. Kearn shook her head. "'Twould've been best for everyone had you not regained your memory. I'm truly sorry, but you're one o' them. You should've died with your parents, but you didn't."

An eerie dread crept through Sarah, one that had nothing to do with the gun aimed at her heart. "What are you saying? My parents died in a gas explosion in their home. An accident."

The corners of Mrs. Kearn's mouth twisted upward in a self-satisfied smile. "'Twas only meant to look that way."

Her head reeling, her lungs fighting for air, Sarah clutched the edge of the table. *This was all some horrible nightmare. This couldn't be happening.* She forced herself to ask the question, then steeled herself for the answer she hoped not to hear. "You killed my parents?"

"And your grandparents. Among others."

"No. Granddad died from a heart attack. In the hospital."

"I know. I was there."

My God! The woman was a monster! "Why? What did they ever do to you?"

Anger contorted the housekeeper's face. Her body tensed. Deep purple blotches spread across her cheeks and down her neck. "What did they do?" she screamed. "They killed my Danny! They took him and his family from me. Even my innocent little grandbaby! And they won't be at peace until you all pay. An eye for an eye according to the Bible!"

The woman was beyond rational thought, but Sarah realized her only chance was to keep her talking. She had to reason with her, had to make her understand. Her very life depended on it. "The plane crash was an accident, Mrs. Kearn. Please. You have to believe me. You know I wouldn't lie to you."

"'Twas murder!"

Sarah shook her head. The hate had festered inside the elderly woman for too long. How could she, a Montgomery, possibly hope to get through to her? "Murder is what *you've* committed. What you're about to commit again."

"'Tis the Lord's work. I don't expect the likes of you to understand."

"The Lord's work?" Sarah's voice grew hysterical. "You expect me to believe God wants you to murder me? Wanted you to murder my family? You've broken His laws! *Thou shalt not kill.* Ever hear of it? It's one of the Commandments. And what about forgiveness? Doesn't the Bible speak of that?"

"Don't you go throwin' Scripture at me! I've had enough of this. Move." With her free hand she yanked Sarah out of the chair, waving the gun in the direction of Trent's bedroom.

A sinking feeling in the pit of her stomach, Sarah realized she had gone too far. Instead of making Mrs. Kearn see reason, she'd only succeeded in angering the woman further. She was running out of options. "You'd do this to Trent?"

"No, lass, you will. You're going to jump from the balcony in Mr. Trent's bedroom."

"Why would I do that?"

"Because when you regained your memory, you were overcome with grief at the loss o' you're one remaining relative, your husband."

"Roger? You killed Roger, too? He wasn't even part of the family five years ago!"

"He was a thorn in Mr. Trent's side. Some friends took care of him last night."

Last night? Sarah's mind raced. "Mr. O'Hara?" Mrs. Kearn had told Trent he was taking care of some family business. That's why he arrived late for the party. "*He* killed Roger?"

"We Irish have a saying—'pity the man in a country where there is none to take his part.' Good friends are always there for one another. We've helped each other out on many an occasion."

"He's killed for you before?"

"When necessary. As have others. And I for them."

Sarah thought of the other murders that had occurred over the past few months. Whitney. Felicia. Charmaine. Did Mrs. Kearn have a hand in those as well? One by one she whispered their names, and one by one her fears were confirmed. "You had them all killed? Even Charmaine? Why?"

"My good friend Seamus took care of Felicia. I never could stand that woman. She was all wrong for Mr. Trent. Then, after what she tried to do to you..." Mrs. Kearn shrugged. "Well, someone had to do something."

347

Sarah couldn't believe what she was hearing. "You had Felicia killed for trying to kill me, and now you're going to kill me yourself? You don't see something twisted in that logic?"

The woman shrugged her shoulders a second time. "I told you, 'twould have been best had your memory not come back. Anyway, as for Whitney, I took care of her myself. Like your parents. Bombs have always been my specialty."

Sarah noted the pride in her voice. *Bombs have always been my specialty.* How many other bombs had she constructed in her lifetime? How many other victims? "And Charmaine? What did she ever do to you?"

"Nothin' but when I saw the way Mr. Trent reacted to Sunshine at Thanksgivin', I knew he needed her. Besides, I was doing the little one a favor. What kind o' life did she have to look forward to with a whore for a mother?"

"So you had Charmaine killed, and somehow knew I'd insist Trent adopt Sunshine?"

"If you hadn't, I would've. But you couldn't have played your role better had I handed you a script, lass."

"How lucky for you!"

The front door opened. Laughter danced down the hallway, followed by the sounds of scampering feet and a heavier tread. *Sunshine! Trent!* Sarah saw the panic in Mrs. Kearn's face. "It's over, Mrs. Kearn. Put down the gun. Please."

"No!" She released the safety.

"Trent!"

* * *

Sarah's blood-curdling scream sent Trent racing the last few feet down the hall to the kitchen. He stopped short at the entrance, stunned by the sight before him. "Moira? What are you doing?"

"She's crazy, Trent. She killed my parents and grandparents. And Whitney. And Roger. And Felicia. And—" She stopped short, her gaze flying to Sunshine. The child had come up behind him and grabbed hold of one of his legs. He reached for her arm and forced her to remain behind him.

Trent stared at Moira in disbelief. He'd grown up loving her like a second mother. The sight of her holding a gun was obscene, unreal. Moira Kearn was a nurturer, not a murderer. "Tell me this isn't true," he pleaded with her.

"'Tis."

Trent felt his world crumbling around him. "Moira, please! Don't do this."

"I'm sorry, lad. I love you like a son, but I have to do this for Danny."

"Danny?" She was making no sense. *Who the hell was Danny?*

"You knew him as Brendan."

In the small corner of his brain that still functioned, Trent recalled the curiosity of his youth. He remembered the day he had made the connection between the ongoing unrest and killings in Belfast and Mrs. Kearn and her son coming to live with them. The reality he had once refused to consider, now bubbled to the surface. "Who are you?"

FORTY-ONE

Brady switched off the ignition and set the hand brake, activating the bomb. Ten minutes, Devon had said. Ten minutes to saunter over to the Pig and Whistle and get lost within the raucous Friday night pub crowd. Ten minutes until the skies rained British scum. Brady locked the car door and strode across the street.

"Hey, you! Stop right there, Mick!"

Brady wasn't about to stop, wasn't about to take the time to see who was shouting or even if the words had been directed at him. Instinct told him to get the hell out of there. He sped through the labyrinth of familiar dark alleys. The rhythmic beat of his feet against the cobblestones kept time with the hammering inside his chest. A resounding echo of footfalls followed fast on his heels.

"Halt or I'll shoot!"

Take your best shot, you Limey bastard.

The first bullet whizzed past his head. The second grazed his shoulder. Brady grabbed his arm and hurled a string of curses behind him, never slowing his pace. He needed a diversion, needed that bomb to detonate. As he darted through the next alley, the deafening explosion shook the ground and lit up the sky.

You're a bloody fine bomb maker, Devon, he thought, a split second before the next bullet pierced his heart.

* * *

She knew something had gone wrong before she opened the door. The expressions on their faces confirmed her worst fear. All day a premonition had nagged at her. Then he had held her too long before he left, stared too deeply into her green eyes, as though he were trying to imprint her very being on his soul for all eternity, and she had known. She had wanted to plead with him to call it off, but he would have scoffed, teasing her for believing in superstitious nonsense. So, she had smiled stoically and watched him stride from their home.

There was no time to mourn. She had to get the boys to a safe house. The British soldiers would be coming for them. She gathered up the few valuables she owned—her mother's silver candlesticks, the family Bible, the meager savings hidden under the loose kitchen floorboard—and scurried off into the riotous bedlam which had enveloped the city.

The escape plan, financed by Irish comrades living overseas, had been in place for months, should anything go wrong. Soon she would be in America, just her and her youngest child. She would never pray over Brady's body, never see her two older sons again. They would stay and avenge their father's death. They would gun down a hundred Protestants each. They would make the British pay for taking Brady from her, from them all.

FORTY-TWO

Mrs. Kearn raised her chin, pride sounding in her voice as she spoke. "The name's Curry. Devon Curry."

Curry. The name triggered another memory. Michael Quinn. Sean Timmons. Brady Curry. Leaders of an IRA splinter group, the three men were responsible for scores of deaths in the early seventies. Their lack of regard for human life had filled Trent with such revulsion that even after all these years he still remembered their names and deeds.

Quinn and Timmons were serving life sentences. Curry had been gunned down on the streets of Belfast. After reading about the three men, Trent had curtailed his research, fearful that he might discover something he didn't want to know.

Until now. "What's your connection to Brady Curry?" he asked.

Her hand shook at the mention of the name. "That was a long

time ago. It doesn't matter."

"Tell me!"

"He was my husband." She steadied the gun with both hands and aimed it at Sarah.

"Don't you hurt my mama!"

"Sunshine! No!"

The toddler broke free from Trent's grasp and darted towards the housekeeper, hurling her body into the woman. Tiny fists pummeled Devon's legs with little effect. Releasing one hand from its grip on the gun, Devon ripped Sunshine from her side and flung her across the room and into Sarah.

Dropping to the floor, Sarah covered the screaming toddler with her body while Trent lunged for Devon, knocking her off-balance and the gun from her hand. They both reached for the gun at the same time.

The first shot hit Trent.

The second hit Sarah.

* * *

Sprawled across the floor, Sarah stared in lightheaded confusion at the red tributaries spreading along the grout lines between the tiles. Beneath her, close to her ear, she heard muted whimpering, nearly drowned out by the primordial Banshee wail coming from above.

"*Go dtachta an diabhal thú!*"

The strange sounds made no sense to her, but she felt their wrath rip into her body like barbs. She struggled to lift her head. Blinding pain tore through her shoulder, down her arm and into her chest, stealing the air from her lungs. Fighting to keep from passing out, she focused on the blurry image in front of her. Mrs. Kearn. No, not Mrs. Kearn. A crazed woman. Devon. She knelt over an inert mass and continued to rail until she realized Sarah was watching her.

"You! You did this!" she screamed, pointing to the lifeless figure in front of her. "This is your doin'!"

This? Disoriented from a combination of pain and loss of blood, Sarah stared dumbly at the mound lying between her and the woman. Slowly, her eyes focused, and the amorphous form took shape. *Trent!*

"Please..." It took all her remaining strength to force the words out. "Get help..."

"Help?" Devon's hysterical cackle sent an ominous chill through her. Tears spilled down her cheeks, splashing onto Trent's lifeless body. "'Tis far too late for that." She rose to her feet, her entire body shaking with grief. "For both o' you."

Unable to move for fear of exposing Sunshine, Sarah watched in horror as Devon lifted a trembling arm and pointed the gun at her. "*D'anam don diabhal!* Your soul to the devil!"

Sarah squeezed her eyelids shut.

Devon squeezed the trigger.

FORTY-THREE

Blood trickled down her forehead. She felt it settle in the corners of her eyes and dribble along the side of her nose. In the distance she heard a pounding noise that continued to grow fainter. Then one loud bang and...silence.

She forced open one eyelid and stared at the shattered remains of a floor tile. Every few seconds a drop of blood slid off the tip of her nose and splattered onto the floor in front of her.

The crackle of the gunshot still reverberated in her ears, but gradually she began to realize the bullet had missed its intended target. She wasn't dead. The bullet must only have grazed her head. Still, she felt the life seeping out of her. The pool of blood on the floor kept growing, fed by the first bullet.

She shifted her weight, attempting to free the trapped child beneath her. A shock wave of fresh pain ripped through her body. "Sunshine?"

"Mama!" She hiccupped a sob but stayed huddled against Sarah's body. "I's scared!"

"I know...but...you...you were very...brave." Sarah felt blackness closing in on her and fought to maintain consciousness. Her life depended on it. Gasping for breath, she forced herself to continue speaking as calmly as possible to the child. "It's...all over...now...but...I need...I need you to be...a...a big girl and...and help me. C...can you...s...stand up?"

"Don't wants to. I's scared."

The edges of reality blurred, the sharp lines of the kitchen coalescing to form an oppressive gray whirlpool. From its center, long fingers emerged, reaching for her. Grabbing hold, they began sucking her under.

In a strangled voice she forced out one final word before the dark mire engulfed her. "Phone..."

* * *

The moment she opened her eyes and found Sister Mags standing over her, Sarah realized the nightmare that had wakened her was, in fact, reality. The worried expression on the nun's face quickly scattered any remaining cobwebs lingering inside her brain, triggering vivid images of the violent scene that had unfolded in Trent's kitchen. A closer inspection of the sister's ashen complexion revealed the answer to the question Sarah dreaded asking. Trent was dead.

The corners of Sister Mags' mouth turned up in a slight smile. She reached for Sarah's hand and clasped it between both of hers. "You're going to be fine, my dear."

Hardly. She would never again be *fine*. Trent was dead, and what about Sunshine? The sister made no mention of her. Panic seized Sarah. She searched her mind trying to remember everything that had happened before she lost consciousness. Had Mrs. Kearn taken the toddler? Would she harm her? Once she would have trusted the faithful housekeeper with her life, but she'd been wrong. Dead wrong.

Sarah struggled to sit up. "Sunshine. Where's Sunshine?"

Sister Mags gently forced her back against the pillow. "Lie down. You'll tear open your stitches."

"Did Mrs. Kearn take her?"

"Sunshine's at Haven. No one's going to harm her. The police are combing the city for Moira. They'll find her."

"She had help. Mr. O'Hara. And others."

Startled, the nun withdrew her hand and grasped the bedrail. "What do you mean? Sunshine said nothing about anyone else in the apartment."

"She called the police?" All Sarah could remember was a frightened body quivering beneath her as she lay, unable to move, on the kitchen floor.

Sister Mags nodded. "She wasn't very coherent, but the 9-1-1 dispatcher understood enough, and they had the address from their caller ID system."

Squeezing her eyelids shut, Sarah offered up a silent prayer. "What will happen to her?" she asked.

"Let's not worry about that for now, my dear. Everything's in God's hands. You must have faith."

Sarah shook her head. How could she not worry? Poor Sunshine. The little girl had witnessed more violence in a few minutes than most people do in a lifetime. And now with Trent gone, Children's Services would insist on taking her.

Depression closed in on Sarah from all sides. A feeling of hopelessness, greater than any she had sustained during her bleakest days of amnesia, consumed her. She drew in a calming breath, but her body shuddered in response. A tear escaped the corner of her eye and slid down her cheek, dropping onto the pillow beneath her head.

Sister Mags plucked a tissue from a box on the nightstand and gently wiped away the moisture. She continued her pep talk. "The doctors assured me your injuries were minor, and they wouldn't dare lie to a nun. The bullet passed through your shoulder, but you lost a lot of blood. The surgeon pumped in a few fresh pints and stitched up some torn muscle and skin. Luckily, Moira's a lousy shot. The second bullet only grazed the side of your head."

For the first time since waking, Sarah scanned her bandaged torso. Her left shoulder and arm were swaddled in gauze and strapped against her chest. A tube snaked from the back of her right hand up to a glass jar of clear fluid suspended from an IV pole. She felt additional gauze wrapped around her head.

"Antibiotics," said the nun, following Sarah's gaze. "Just precautionary. The doctors plan on kicking you out of here in a few days."

And then what? Pick up the pieces of a shattered life?

I'm truly alone now. Everyone she had ever loved was dead, thanks to a sick, vengeful woman. Except Sunshine. And Sarah held out little hope of the ACS bureaucrats allowing the toddler to stay with her, even though she no longer had amnesia and had plenty of money. She didn't have the connections that had enabled Trent to override ACS and take custody of the child.

Sister Mags dragged over a chair and sat at her bedside. "What happened, Angel?"

Angel. Sister Mags didn't know. How could she? "I'm not Angel," she said. "I'm Sarah Montgomery." With a faltering voice she recounted the events of the past twenty-four hours, leaving out only the intimate details of the previous night.

Sister Mags listened in shocked silence.

Then, her heart broken, Sarah succumbed to the tears welling up inside her.

Sister Mags stroked Sarah's cheek, offering soft consoling words, but she wanted no part of them. "Please," she said. "I want to be alone."

"All right, my dear. I understand." She stood. "I'll check on Trent and stop back to see you before I leave."

Trent!?! Sarah gulped back a large sob. "What did you say?"

"That I'd be back to see you after I looked in on Trent."

Could it be? Was it possible? "He...he's not dead?"

"Is that why you're crying?"

Sarah nodded. Fresh tears streamed down her face, but these were tears of relief, not despair. "I thought she killed him."

"She almost did."

He's alive! Trent's alive! "I want to see him."

"Maybe after you've gotten some strength back," said the nun. Her eyes clouded over with hesitation.

Apprehension built inside Sarah. "No! Now!"

"I don't think that's such a good idea—"

"I don't care what you think!" She threw back the flannel blanket and struggled with the bed's side rails, rattling them like a caged animal. "I have to see him!"

* * *

Fifteen minutes later she sat in a wheelchair beside his bed in the intensive care unit. Once more, Sister Mags consoled her as she wept.

Trent was alive. Barely. His body hidden under countless

snaking tubes. All around him various machines bleeped and whirred as they performed and recorded each bodily function. Sarah slipped her free hand through the bedrails, entwining her fingers with his. She refused to leave his side.

"Visiting hours are over," insisted one of the nurses after entering the room a short time later. "You need your rest, too." She checked the digital readings of the various machines, then jotted several notations on Trent's chart. When Sarah ignored the order, the nurse cast a pleading glance toward Sister Mags.

"I'm not leaving," said Sarah. "Don't look to her for help."

"I'm going to have to insist, miss."

Sarah gazed down at Trent's body and concentrated on the steady rise and fall of his chest. The scene was eerily familiar. Only months before, she'd sat beside a similar bed surrounded by similar equipment in this same hospital. And well-meaning personnel had convinced her to go home and get some rest. The woman she now knew as Devon Curry, the woman who had killed her grandfather that September night, was still at large. "No. I'm not making the same mistake twice."

* * *

Once Sister Mags notified the authorities of Devon Curry's murder confessions to Sarah, the police doubled their round-the-clock protection of both Trent and Sarah. Only then did Sarah agree to return to her room. She spent the next several hours ensconced with two detectives, answering endless questions and wracking her brain for anything that might help them track down the self-proclaimed executioner and her accomplices.

* * *

By the third day Devon was still at large, but Sarah was well enough to be discharged. Sister Mags came to escort her to Haven.

"You'll stay with me until you're fully recovered," she ordered.

Sarah didn't argue. She had no desire to return to the empty house she'd shared with Roger or either of her grandfather's residences. The memories were still too fresh. Too painful. Besides, she missed Sunshine.

She allowed Sister Mags to help her dress. With Sister Mags and two police officers following alongside, an elderly volunteer orderly wheeled her down to the ICU for one last visit with Trent before leaving the hospital.

Listed as critical, Trent's condition had improved only minimally in the three days since the shooting, but Sarah clutched onto any signs of slight progress. Her entourage waited outside the room while she sat beside his bed. Holding his hand, she spoke to him in a voice filled with forced confidence—a confidence her own heart lacked.

"He's too heavily sedated to hear you," said a nurse who had entered the room to check Trent's fluids and adjust the multitude of computerized machinery surrounding his bed.

Sarah ignored her. She knew otherwise. Trent understood, and he responded to her. She could feel the minute change in pressure from his fingertips, see the weak twitch of a muscle around his eyes or the corners of his mouth.

"I have to leave now," she told him after Sister Mags reentered the room. She lifted his hand to her cheek and whispered, "I love you."

Trent replied with a nearly indiscernible stroke of his finger against her parted lips.

Sarah was wheeled from the intensive care unit toward the elevator leading to the main lobby. She closed her eyes to the hustle and bustle of the hospital routine, but the sights and sounds and smells intruded anyway, the bright lights, persistent announcements, and antiseptic odors filling her with an overwhelming sense of emptiness and grief.

"I feel like I'm deserting him," she said, reaching over to grab Sister Mags' sleeve. "He needs me to stay."

The nun patted her hand. "He needs his rest, my dear. We'll come back for a bit tomorrow."

Sarah sighed, the void within her growing more cavernous as the distance between her and Trent's room increased.

"Besides," the nun continued. "Sunshine needs you more right now."

And I need her, thought Sarah. She yearned for the sound of the toddler's childish giggles filling the air, assuring her the world had not gone mad. But the world had gone mad—insanely mad—and Sarah wondered if Sunshine would ever again laugh the laugh of the innocent.

A *ping* sounded, and the elevator doors opened in front of them.

"Trent's color was better today, don't you think?" asked Sister Mags, as the elevator carried them down to the ground floor.

Sarah responded to the nun's question with little more than a nod and a shrug.

"Sarah?" She rested her hand on Sarah's good shoulder.

"I suppose."

"He's going to pull through. You must have faith in the Lord."

The elevator came to a stop. The doors opened, and the orderly wheeled Sarah down the hallway. Beyond the glass-doored entrance, a police cruiser waited for them. Sarah gasped in dismay at the throng of reporters and curious onlookers milling under the porte-cochere, blocking the path from the doors to the police car.

"Stay here until we disperse them," ordered one of the policemen.

The two officers stepped outside and cleared a path, holding the crowd to either side of the walkway. With arms held akimbo, they blocked the aggressive press from converging on Sarah as the orderly wheeled her to the car.

After setting the brake and pushing aside the footrests, the man grasped her uninjured arm, helping her to her feet. "Easy does it, lass," he said. "Mind your head gettin' in the car."

Sarah's heart jumped into her throat at the sound of *lass*. The woman she'd known as Mrs. Kearn had admitted to having accomplices. Lots of accomplices. Sarah turned to one of the officers, but before she could say anything, someone shouted out her name.

"Sarah Montgomery!"

She froze. She knew that voice.

Behind her someone screamed. "She's got a gun!"

The hand on her arm tightened. The orderly spun her around, then shoved her directly in front of Devon.

In rapid succession three bullets slammed into her chest.

EPILOGUE

Giggling with delight, the little girl bounced up and down on her father's lap. "Dis my Daddy" she informed the man wheeling them down the hall to the elevator. "We's going home today."

"Yes, I know."

"Dis my mama," Sunshine continued, reaching for Sarah's hand.

The orderly smiled at the child, then at Sarah before pushing the button to summon the elevator.

"Sit still, or you'll have to walk," admonished Sarah.

"She's fine," Trent assured her. "I won't break."

Sarah winced. *You almost did.* Twice, during his long recovery, Trent had taken a turn for the worse, once developing an infection, then pneumonia. She shuddered to think how close she'd come to losing him. The doctors offered little hope, and for the past three months she'd held her breath each time the phone rang, expecting the worst whenever the hospital called.

But they didn't know Trent.

"Nothing could keep me from you," he'd told her. "Not even bullets."

But every time Sarah heard a loud noise, she froze in terror, remembering that fateful day and how one woman's twisted sense of justice had nearly destroyed their lives.

Devon Curry's bullet had taken its toll on Trent's soul as well as his body. Still reeling from Felicia's treachery, he found the betrayal of the woman he'd known for decades as Moira Kearn to be unbearable. Decades of love and trust had evaporated in a split second. Wracked with guilt over his blindness, he began to question his judgment in all areas of his life.

As his body healed, he spent more and more time ruminating on his own inadequacies, and his spirits plummeted. Frightened by his constant self-flagellation, Sarah enlisted the aid of both Dr. Pierce and Sister Mags. The healing of his spirit took nearly as long as the healing of his body, but Trent wanted closure and worked as hard at understanding his own psyche as he did at his physical therapy sessions. Slowly, he began to mend. Inside and out.

As the car descended towards the lobby, Trent reached up and laced his fingers through hers. "Are you all right?" he asked.

Sarah nodded. For the past three months she had made this same trip every day—down the elevator to the hospital vestibule and out the main doors. Each time she relived the horror of that December afternoon. Each time she paused to whisper a silent prayer of thanks to the policeman who had insisted on the bullet-proof vest that saved her life.

Still, Trent was not the only one who had benefited from the expert counseling of Dr. Pierce and Sister Mags. The doors opened. Silently she repeated the clichéd mantra that had sustained her through her daily journeys. *When you fall off a horse, you get right back on.*

Taking a deep breath, she peered down the corridor and out the entrance to the waiting car. No hovering crowds. No hidden danger. Devon Curry was dead, felled by a policeman's bullet. Her accomplices now resided in the state penitentiary where they would live out the remainder of their days. *When you fall off a horse, you get right back on.*

"Dat our new driving man." Sunshine tugged on the orderly's sleeve and pointed to the chauffeur standing beside the car. "Mr. O'Hara gots to go bye-bye."

Devon Curry's smallest victim had proved to be the most resilient of all of them, but even Sunshine had not gone unscathed. Weekly sessions with a child therapist who specialized in trauma were helping, but Sarah fretted about long-term repercussions.

She felt Trent's fingers tighten around hers in a reassuring squeeze. "She's doing fine," he said. "We're all doing fine."

They had survived the horror. Their love for each other had sustained them through the blackest of nights and would see them through whatever the future held. Of that she was certain. She turned her gaze toward the man she loved, and returned the gesture. "Yes, we are."

ABOUT THE AUTHOR

USA Today and Amazon bestselling and award-winning author Lois Winston writes mystery, romance, romantic suspense, chick lit, women's fiction, children's chapter books, and nonfiction. *Kirkus Reviews* dubbed her critically acclaimed Anastasia Pollack Crafting Mystery series, "North Jersey's more mature answer to Stephanie Plum." In addition, Lois is an award-winning craft and needlework designer who often draws much of her source material for both her characters and plots from her experiences in the crafts industry.

Connect with Lois at her website, www.loiswinston.com, where you can learn more about her and her books, sign up for her newsletter, and find links to follow her on social media.

www.ingramcontent.com/pod-product-compliance
Lightning Source LLC
Chambersburg PA
CBHW021131260626
47169CB00005B/1558